CW01163487

Modern Czech Literature
Writing in Times of Political Trauma

Edited by

Andrew M. Drozd
University of Alabama

Series in Literary Studies

Copyright © 2025 by the Authors.

All rights reserved. No part of this publication may be reproduced, stored in a retrieval system, or transmitted in any form or by any means, electronic, mechanical, photocopying, recording, or otherwise, without the prior permission of Vernon Art and Science Inc.

www.vernonpress.com

In the Americas:	In the rest of the world:
Vernon Press	Vernon Press
1000 N West Street, Suite 1200	C/Sancti Espiritu 17,
Wilmington, Delaware, 19801	Malaga, 29006
United States	Spain

Series in Literary Studies

Library of Congress Control Number: 2024946673

ISBN: 979-8-8819-0059-5

Product and company names mentioned in this work are the trademarks of their respective owners. While every care has been taken in preparing this work, neither the authors nor Vernon Art and Science Inc. may be held responsible for any loss or damage caused or alleged to be caused directly or indirectly by the information contained in it.

Cover design by Vernon Press with elements from Freepik.

Every effort has been made to trace all copyright holders, but if any have been inadvertently overlooked the publisher will be pleased to include any necessary credits in any subsequent reprint or edition.

Table of contents

	Editor's acknowledgements	v
	Introduction Andrew M. Drozd *University of Alabama*	vii
Chapter 1	**Responsibility vs. greed for power: Karel Čapek's *The White Plague* in a cultural context** Karen von Kunes *Yale University*	1
Chapter 2	**Kundera, Tolstoy, and the lightness of being** Mary Orsak *University of Oxford*	15
Chapter 3	**Injurious attachments and dangerous culs-de-sac: gendered reading and deconstructing "deconstructive" logic of selected early Czech novels by Milan Kundera** Jan Matonoha *Institute of Czech Literature of the Czech Academy of Sciences, Czech Rep.*	37
Chapter 4	**Reluctant dissidents, writer-philosophers, Kundera and Hrabal** Jonathan Lahey Dronsfield *Institute of Philosophy of the Czech Academy of Sciences, Czech Rep.*	73
Chapter 5	**Normalization in contemporary Czech prose: between nostalgia, ironizing, payback, and problematizing** Marek Lollok *Masaryk University, Czech Rep.*	103

Chapter 6   **Against everything: the brothers Topol and
the second generation of the underground**   147
Daniel Webster Pratt
McGill University

Chapter 7   **Eda Kriseová: Writing human ecology.
Serving poetic justice to truth and love**   169
Hana Waisserová
University of Nebraska

About the contributors   209

Index   213

Editor's acknowledgements

I would like to thank all the contributors for their participation, suggestions, and feedback, but I want to highlight the special contribution of Karen von Kunes to this volume. As the chair of the original conference panel, I was the one contacted by Vernon Press and asked to edit the volume. However, von Kunes was the organizer of the panel. In addition, I have consulted with her extensively throughout the entire process. She read the initial call for papers I produced, she helped to recruit contributors, I consulted with her on possible names for the volume, she has read the introduction more than once, and so forth. I also thank Jan Čulík for providing the requested bibliographic material. In an attempt to prepare for all possible contingencies, I ordered an *extremely* large number of materials via the Inter-library Loan Service at the University of Alabama. I am grateful to the staff at ILL for getting me these materials in a timely manner. Finally, the contributors and I would like to thank the three peer-reviewers for their efforts and their suggestions.

Introduction

Andrew M. Drozd
University of Alabama

With the proclamation of an independent Czechoslovakia in 1918, as the First World War was winding down, the Czech nation experienced much euphoria and hope. Despite some problems and disappointments, the first fifteen years of the First Republic were relatively stable.[1] This period saw the productive unleashing of many previously restrained cultural forces and it would later be perceived nostalgically by many Czechs. However, with the rise of the Nazis in neighboring Germany in the 1930s, dark clouds began to appear on the Czech horizon, setting off a long series of traumatic events. Because of the numerous traumas experienced by the Czechs, Derek Sayer has characterized Prague as the capital of the dark twentieth century.[2]

The current collection of articles, which originated in a panel ("Betrayal, Anxiety, and Rebellion in Milan Kundera and in Contemporary Czech Literature") at the 52nd Annual ASEEES Convention in 2020, seeks to provide treatments of some of the responses to these traumas in Czech literature.[3] The

---

[1] For those unfamiliar with the vicissitudes of Czech history, see Hugh LeCaine Agnew, *The Czechs and the Lands of the Bohemian Crown* (Stanford: Hoover Institution Press, 2004). For a treatment of Czechoslovakia from its inception until the Communist takeover, see Victor S. Mamatey and Radomír Luža, eds., *A History of the Czechoslovak Republic, 1918–1948* (Princeton: Princeton University Press, 1973).

[2] Derek Sayer, *Prague, Capital of the Twentieth Century. A Surrealist History* (Princeton: Princeton University Press, 2013), 8-12. In recent decades Czech scholarship has been devoting more attention to the theme of trauma. Jan Matonoha, one of the contributors to this volume, would like to draw the reader's attention to the following: Alexander Kratochvil, ed., *Paměť a trauma pohledem humanitních věd. Komentovaná antologie teoretických textů* (Prague: Akropolis, 2015); Alexander Kratochvil, *Posttraumatické vyprávění. Trauma – Literatura – Vzpomínka* (Brno: Host, 2023).

[3] While no comprehensive survey of Czech literary history is available in English, the combination of Novák's survey with Holý's will provide the necessary coverage for those readers in need of more background. Arne Novák, *Czech Literature*, trans. Peter Kussi, ed. William E. Harkins (Ann Arbor: Michigan Slavic Publications, 1976); Jiří Holý, *Writers*

chapters in this volume help shed further light on the various responses by Czech writers when confronted with often very trying circumstances. One of the earliest responses to the time of trauma was the work of Karel Čapek, who was one of the leading Czech prose writers in the first half of the twentieth century. Čapek's novel *The War with the Newts* (*Válka s mloky*) was very much concerned with the growing Nazi menace and has been much discussed by scholars. In her chapter, Karen von Kunes focuses on Čapek's play *The White Plague* (*Bílá nemoc*), which was also a response to the Nazi pressure. While von Kunes recognizes the importance of the immediate context of the play, she focuses on the larger theme of the issue of personal responsibility which remained central to Czech (and Slovak) intellectuals and artists in subsequent eras. Her analysis connects the pre-1948 period of Czech literature with developments after the Communist takeover. In particular, von Kunes connects this theme as it appeared in Čapek's play with its presence in the Slovak-language film *The Shop on Main Street* (1965). Not only is there a connection in theme, but there are direct parallels between characters in Čapek's play and characters in the film, which is set in a Slovak village. Von Kunes also ties the theme of responsibility to Václav Havel's call for a better future by awakening a sense of responsibility as well as its appearance in other works by Čapek. In short, von Kunes demonstrates a consistency in response to totalitarianism that transcended the particular traumas of one regime.

The current collection contains three essays that are concerned with the recently deceased Milan Kundera. This is quite justified since he was one of the major Czech prose writers of the twentieth century, the only one to have acquired a sizable international audience. Above and beyond this fact, Kundera is a good example of an individual response to the traumas of Czech history. As Jan Čulík has stated, "His story is that of many Czech intellectuals of his generation: it is the story of freeing oneself of Marxist dogma and of gaining and communicating important insights based on the traumatic experience of life under totalitarianism in Eastern and Central Europe."[4] In response to the Nazis, Kundera started out as a Communist true believer who came to be very

---

under Siege. Czech Literature since 1945, trans. Jan Čulík and Elizabeth S. Morrison (Brighton and Portland: Sussex Academic Press, 2008). For readers seeking a very concise summary of Czech literary history but which also provides extended coverage of many of the most significant writers of the last century, see Chapter Six in Craig Cravens, *Culture and Customs of the Czech Republic and Slovakia* (Westport, CT: Greenwood Press, 2006).
[4] Jan Čulík, "Milan Kundera," in *Twentieth-Century Eastern European Writers. Third Series*, ed. Stefan Serafin, Dictionary of Literary Biography (Detroit: The Gale Group, 2001), 210.

much disappointed with the reality of Communist-controlled Czechoslovakia. His disillusionment was so profound that he emigrated from the country in 1975, settled in France, began to publish his work in French translation before the Czech original appeared, and even began to write in French. There was a distinct sense of wounded pride on Kundera's part after he left the country. Whereas the pop singer Karel Gott, who went abroad in 1971, was invited by the Communist regime to return without penalty, Kundera was not.[5] Instead, the regime deprived him of his citizenship in 1978. Kundera's alienation from his homeland was so profound that not only did he not return after 1989, but he was reluctant to allow publication of his works there.

The theme of responsibility also appears in the work of Milan Kundera, demonstrating further continuity between the different eras in which Czech authors operated. In Kundera's work, responsibility is unbearable for most human beings. In her chapter, Mary Orsak explores the theme of the "lightness of being" as found in Kundera and Leo Tolstoy, but within the context of the ideas of Nietzsche and Parmenides. Kundera's relationship with Russian literature was not necessarily a harmonious one: despite his obvious familiarity with it, he tried to distance himself from it.[6] Nevertheless, the relationship between Kundera's novel *The Unbearable Lightness of Being* and Tolstoy's *Anna Karenina* is impossible to miss. Not only is Tereza identified by her heavy copy of Tolstoy's novel, but Tomáš and Tereza name their dog Karenin. Michael Heim apparently viewed Kundera's novel as a playful response to *Anna Karenina*.[7] Orsak argues, however, that the tie with Tolstoy goes much

---

[5] In *The Book of Laughter and Forgetting*, Kundera purports to quote a letter from Gustáv Husák to Karel Gott, in which Husák begs Gott to return. Milan Kundera, *The Book of Laughter and Forgetting*, trans. Michael Henry Heim (New York: Knopf, 1981), 181. Such a letter seems to be a mystification on Kundera's part, although an oral invitation to return was given to Gott. See Jan Čulík, "Mystification as an Artistic Strategy in Milan Kundera's Work," *Slavonica* 23, no. 2 (2018): 121–22.

[6] Arguably, he owed much to Tolstoy for his novel *The Joke*. The idea that life is a cruel joke played on mankind is found in Tolstoy's "Confession": "My mental condition presented itself to me in this way: my life is a stupid and spiteful joke someone has played on me." Leo Tolstoy, "Confession," in *The Portable Tolstoy*, ed. John Bayley (New York: Penguin, 1978), 679.

[7] In her study Banerjee refers to a paper given by Heim on the topic. As far as I have been able to determine, Heim never published this paper. Maria Němcová Banerjee, *Terminal Paradox. The Novels of Milan Kundera* (New York: Grove Weidenfeld, 1990), 285. Throughout her study, Banerjee makes repeated comparisons between the classics of Russian literature and Kundera's works although she does not necessarily argue for direct influence.

deeper than just *Anna Karenina*. She demonstrates that there are extremely close correspondences between Kundera's phrase "unbearable lightness of being" used in two of his novels (*The Unbearable Lightness of Being* and *Immortality*) and passages involving Andrei Bolkonsky in Tolstoy's *War and Peace*. Orsak also examines further ties between Kundera's fiction and Tolstoy's *Anna Karenina*, specifically, the theme of suicide. However much he might protest otherwise, Kundera's work reveals a deep connection to Russia and its literature.

In the Western world, Kundera has become infamous for the misogyny and sexual violence contained in his novels. Much discussion of these themes has been produced by critics and literary scholars. For his part, Kundera was rather unapologetic on this point and in his works written with a Western audience in mind, he threw down the gauntlet. For example, in *The Book of Laughter and Forgetting*, one of his characters declares that "only the best of men are misogynists" and that "a woman can be happy only with a misogynist."[8] In his chapter, Jan Matonoha argues for a reassessment, focusing particularly on Kundera's *Life is Elsewhere* and *The Farewell Party*. Matonoha accepts much of the results of prior scholarship, particularly the work of John O'Brien (*Milan Kundera & Feminism: Dangerous Intersections*), but argues for the need to expand the scope. Matonoha concludes, contra O'Brien, that there is a more complex, triadic structure to Kundera's sexism. Matonoha agrees with O'Brien that there is an overt level of misogyny in Kundera's novels, which is then deconstructed on a less overt level. Where Matonoha disagrees with O'Brien, however, is that there is yet a third level to Kundera's fiction, which ultimately reaffirms the misogyny.

In response to the traumas of the twentieth century, some dissident Czech intellectuals developed the concept of an inner metaphysical freedom. In his chapter, Jonathan Lahey Dronsfield examines both Milan Kundera's and Bohumil Hrabal's engagement with this concept. Dronsfield's chapter is much more philosophical in nature. That is, he examines Kundera's and Hrabal's use of philosophy in their fiction. While both writers introduced material from philosophy into their respective works, they resisted the notion that works of literature are philosophical tracts. Kundera, in particular, was insistent that literature, especially the novel, has its own form and that approaching a fictional work as a philosophical treatise impoverishes it. Rather, both writers subscribed to the notion of polyphony, the multitude of voices within a literary work, and the philosophical content is merely one of those voices without any

---

[8] Kundera, *The Book of Laughter and Forgetting*, 132.

Introduction

claim to the ultimate truth. Finally, Dronsfield considers both Kundera and Hrabal to be dissidents, despite the fact that they were not comfortable with that label. Indeed, Kundera explicitly rejected it as yet another ideologization and politicization of art. Nevertheless, because they rejected the concept of an inner metaphysical freedom under totalitarianism, Dronsfield concludes they were still dissidents. In effect, the Communist insistence on the intimate tie between the personal and the political forced them to be "reluctant dissidents."

Daniel Webster Pratt's chapter is transitional in two senses. First, in chronological terms, it transcends the divide of 1989, focusing on the work of the Topol brothers, Filip and Jáchym, before and after that date. The essay also transcends fields in that it is concerned not only with literature but also with the rock music scene. Pratt challenges the conventional narrative regarding the music scene, both the exaggerated role assigned to it in bringing down Communism as well as the typical view that the musicians involved faded into obscurity after the Velvet Revolution. Pratt stresses that the Topol brothers, like others in the so-called second generation of dissent, never knew the freedom of the Prague Spring, and their experience was, therefore, fundamentally different. The period of Normalization and its associated traumas, however, were very much a part of this generation's experience. Their response was an almost total nihilism, a rebellion against existence itself. In contrast to the usual names of Havel, Kundera, Hrabal, and Škvorecký, this group is less well-known in the West. Pratt's chapter will serve as a valuable introduction to them for many readers. Pratt stresses that there were significant differences between the music underground and the dissidents. This became clear whenever the dissidents, or even the music underground itself, came to be seen as a new "establishment." Pratt's essay also points to the issue of moral responsibility, a theme that continued to engage Czech artists and intellectuals across the decades.

In Marek Lollok's chapter, the fictional treatment of the period of the Normalization is the primary concern. Whereas Pratt examines how these themes were handled by authors writing during that period, Lollok is focused on post-Communist treatments. Indeed, Lollok insists that fiction written after the Velvet Revolution was created in a very changed set of conditions and, therefore, is fundamentally different. Not only was the censorship no longer a factor, but the Normalization was now history, not the lived present. Lollok divides the material into five different narrative modes. Since he focuses on more recent authors, the chapter covers writers who are lesser known in the English-language world; some of their works not yet translated. As a result, this chapter will be a valuable first introduction to these authors for some readers.

Lollok's chapter effectively demonstrates that the trauma of the Normalization is an integral part of the Czech collective memory and has strongly influenced the society. Finally, as the earlier essays have indicated, Czech prose of the post-Communist period continues to be engaged with moral issues.

In the last chapter, Hana Waisserová focuses on Eda Kriseová, who published much of her work in the post-Communist era. Her career is a good example of what has been referred to as writing for one's own desk drawer. That is, some of her texts were written well before the Velvet Revolution but were published only in its aftermath. Kriseová was closely tied to Václav Havel, and her work reflected his, as well as the general Czech intellectual, focus on moral issues like truth, love, and responsibility. Kriseová is not a figure well-known to the English-language world and Waisserová's chapter provides a good introduction to her fiction. Many of Kriseová's works deal directly with the traumas of Central Europe and the multigenerational pain arising from them. In the middle part of the chapter, Waisserová argues for a new framework in which to approach women's fiction. While Kriseová is acknowledged as a dissident, she and other women dissident writers have been marginalized within this narrative. In the later part of the chapter Waisserová chronicles Kriseová's transition in the post-Communist era into being a writer concerned with and treating global issues.

Bibliography

Agnew, Hugh LeCaine. *The Czechs and the Lands of the Bohemian Crown.* Stanford, CA: Hoover Institution Press, 2004.

Banerjee, Maria Němcová. *Terminal Paradox. The Novels of Milan Kundera.* New York: Grove Weidenfeld, 1990.

Cravens, Craig. *Culture and Customs of the Czech Republic and Slovakia.* Westport, CT: Greenwood Press, 2006.

Čulík, Jan. "Milan Kundera." In *Twentieth-Century Eastern European Writers. Third Series,* edited by Stefan Serafin. Dictionary of Literary Biography, 208–26. Detroit: The Gale Group, 2001.

———. "Mystification as an Artistic Strategy in Milan Kundera's Work." *Slavonica* 23, no. 2 (2018): 113–134.

Holý, Jiří. *Writers under Siege. Czech Literature since 1945.* Translated by Jan Čulík and Elizabeth S. Morrison. Brighton and Portland: Sussex Academic Press, 2008.

Kratochvil, Alexander, ed. *Paměť a trauma pohledem humanitních věd. Komentovaná antologie teoretických textů.* Prague: Akropolis, 2015.

Kundera, Milan. *The Book of Laughter and Forgetting.* Translated by Michael Henry Heim. New York: Knopf, 1981.

Mamatey, Victor S., and Radomír Luža, eds. *A History of the Czechoslovak Republic, 1918–1948.* Princeton: Princeton University Press, 1973.

Novák, Arne. *Czech Literature.* Translated by Peter Kussi. Edited by William E. Harkins. Ann Arbor: Michigan Slavic Publications, 1976.

Sayer, Derek. *Prague, Capital of the Twentieth Century. A Surrealist History.* Princeton: Princeton University Press, 2013.

Tolstoy, Leo. "Confession." Translated by Aylmer and Louise Maude. In *The Portable Tolstoy*, edited by John Bayley, 666–731. New York: Penguin, 1978.

Chapter 1

Responsibility vs. greed for power: Karel Čapek's *The White Plague* in a cultural context[1]

Karen von Kunes
Yale University

Abstract

Within a larger cultural context, this contribution focuses on Karel Čapek's anti-military utopian play *The White Plague*, which centers around a worldwide deadly pandemic and simultaneously serves as a satire of rising Nazism. The themes of responsibility, opportunism, and power–bouncing against one another–are personified by major figures of the play: Dr. Galén (a humanist who has discovered a cure for the terrible pandemic but treats only poor folks), Baron Krüg (the owner of a weapons factory) and the Marshal (a personification of the war-time leader, whose ideological language is aimed convincing the masses to favor the war). The issue of Galén's ethical dilemma– as to whether he has a responsibility to release the secret of his cure to *all* humanity as his medical profession requires–is analyzed against the basic theories of the moral accountability of fairness as introduced in psychology by R. Jay Wallace in his *Responsibility and the Moral Sentiments*. Additionally, it is presented within other Karel Čapek's works, and Václav Havel's philosophy of social responsibility and historical references to Masaryk, and more recently, Milan Kundera.

Keywords: Duty, Fanaticism, Hippocratic Oath, Ideology, Intolerance, Nazism, Opportunism, Pandemic, Plague, Responsibility, Rashomon Effect, Selective Attention, Utopian.

* * *

---

[1] A shorter version of this paper–with a different focus–was presented at the ASEEES conference in 2021 and was supported by the Yale Council on European Studies.

The proverbial lore that "history repeats itself" is attributed to a variety of sources. The Irish playwright George Bernard Shaw saw how unprepared man was for unexpected repetitions, only proving how little human beings had learned from past experiences. In one of its recent series "The Czech Books You Must Read," Radio Prague International has introduced a book about a pandemic, stating: "A disease that infects the whole world, takes it by storm. China provides us with an interesting new strain of something almost annually. A good five million have died of it to date, 20 million have it now, and at least three times as many are going about their business lively, unaware."[2]

On the surface, the above statistics appear to be released during the twenty-first-century coronavirus pandemic; however, as stated above, "history repeats itself"–this time originating from Karel Čapek's *The White Plague*, an anti-military utopian play and a satire of the rising Nazism in the 1930s, portrayed against the background of the deadly global pandemic, affecting people over the age of forty-five. At its premiere on January 29, 1937, in the Prague Stavovské divadlo (The Estates Theater), the play received long, standing ovations because the Czech audience interpreted it as an attack on Nazism and its leader, Hitler, in the character of a dictator, the Marshal. The play was equally successfully staged in Prague's National Theater, in Brno, and in additional cities around Europe.

For Czech audiences, the most poignant aspect of the play was the Marshal's self-aggrandizing propaganda as a victorious war leader. To brainwash the masses, he uses ideological slogans: "If the Nation can't govern, let it perish… All that matters is the Nation, the Nation and victory! … [I'll] head the parade when the troops come home victorious… war's a beautiful thing. Nothing can give a man more satisfaction."[3] With the involvement of the Minister of Information, the pro-war crowd becomes larger and more intoxicated, singing, shouting, waving flags and cheering: "Long live the Marshal! We want war!"[4]

Karel Čapek claimed this play to be about a "decline and decay" at the political and social levels. The ideas of responsibility, humanity, democracy, and civilization seemed to him as being gradually replaced by chaos and disintegration during the not-so-far-away period of WWI and the Spanish Flu, both that had ravaged the world, and put down the seeds for a fascist climate:

---

[2] Radio Prague International: https://english.radio.cz/czech-books-you-must-read-8506310/20.
[3] Karel Čapek, "The White Plague," trans. Michael Henry Heim, *Cross Currents, A Yearbook of Central European Culture* 7 (1988): 495–500.
[4] Ibid., 503.

hunger for territory, power, and money. Choosing a malady that attacks human beings without discrimination, young and old, wealthy or poor, would be a kind of uniform, if not a pacific approach. But Čapek's "white plague," also called Cheng's disease–a devastating and highly contagious infection that resembles leprosy–serves him as a tool to show the fanaticism of a dictator, whose propaganda devoid of responsibility caters to the younger generations and, at the same time, serves his own means while opportunists profit around him, in particular Baron Krüg whose factory provides military arms.

The dynamics of a middle-class family, that appears in the play twice, is evocative of the society at large. Before Dr. Galén's cure for the disease is announced publicly, the Father laments how unfair it is for people in his age group to be dying. The Daughter has a simple and straightforward response: "To give young people a chance, make room for the younger generation..."[5] The Son joins in, hinting at the unemployment of young people in the hope that it will now change. "If it weren't for the disease, how would we end up?"[6] he asks.

In this scene, the Father blames China for its backwardness, disorder, poverty, hunger, and lack of hygiene, seeing a possible remedy and the restoration of the order via the annexation of China to Europe as its colony. A perfect example of a metaphorical chameleon, the Father shows his true face in the second act: thirty of his colleagues have passed away from Cheng's disease, which has allowed him to be promoted to the position of the Accounting Department Director at the Baron Krüg ammunition factory. Now, no longer scolding China for spreading of the fateful malady, he praises the disease, accusing Dr. Galén of selfishness, for the doctor treats only poor patients. The Father disapproves of Galén's utopian ideas about world peace. "Does the honor of a country mean nothing?"[7] he explains to his wife, the Mother, attempting to convince her that their country needs a bigger territory and that war is an inevitable solution. "Would anyone give land to another nation as a good gesture? Anyone who says it's wrong to kill is opposed to our most vital interest, do you understand?"[8] he insists. The Mother, a pacifist, whose role is subservient, shows confusion about what is going on. Her humanism, as expressed in small gestures, such as her suggestion to take food

---

[5] Ibid., 447.
[6] My free translation of the play passage in the Czech original. *Karel Čapek, Loupežník, R.U.R., Bílá nemoc* (Praha: Československý spisovatel, 1983), 247.
[7] Ibid., 272.
[8] Čapek, "The White Plague," 469.

to the neighbor who had contracted the disease and is left to die alone, is not brought to fruition. On the contrary, Mother's fate is obvious from a white spot on her neck, the first signs of Cheng's disease, which later manifests itself by a repugnant odor of dying flesh falling off the bodies of affected people. Patients die within three to six months.

Čapek skillfully interweaves hints of the Nazis' ideology of concentration camps into the everyday communication. When the Mother asks what should be done to prevent the disease, the Father comes up with the ultimate solution: "to lock them up, away with them." While Čapek does not mention the name of the country in the play, inevitably, Czechoslovakia comes to mind, not only because the author was Czech but, above all, because he hints at territorial annexation, war preparation, and deportation of one kind of population.

In the introduction to his translation of the play, the late Michael Heim referred to the signing of the Munich Agreement in 1938 by England and France.[9] British Prime Minister Neville Chamberlain pursued a policy of appeasement as the solution to the Sudetenland dispute in order to avoid war. This involved ceding to Hitler the regions of Czechoslovakia bordering Germany. In his broadcast on "National Programme" on September 27, 1938, Chamberlain referred to Czechoslovakia as "a faraway country we know nothing about."[10] However, in no time, England was to learn about the existence of the "faraway country" through Čapek's *The White Plague*. In the year of signing the Munich Pact, it was adapted to the English stage under the title of *Power and Glory* and the play was used as propaganda. Čapek's idea of portraying Dr. Galén as a humanist, who intends to save the world from war, was distorted, if not entirely lost in the English adaptation. Čapek's Dr. Galén cures poor folks from the horrific worldwide pandemic, refusing to release the secret of his successful cure until all nations' leaders stop producing military weapons and declare peace. As some critics suggested, the English adaptation placed both, Dr. Galén and the Marshal–the personification of Hitler–on equal footing; the two opposing protagonists are portrayed as "equally dangerous fanatics."[11] Heim, on the contrary, argued against the idea of the unintended distortion of the characters' ideas represented in the English version. He

---

[9] Michael Henry Heim, "The Plague Years," *Cross Currents: A Yearbook of Central European Culture* 7 (1988): 429.
[10] This adapted quote is a reference from https://www.bbc.co.uk/archive/chamberlain-addresses-the-nation-on-his-negotiations-for-peace/zjrjgwx.
[11] Heim, 429–30.

asserted that it was he, Čapek himself, who had "laid the groundwork for their interpretation."[12]

Karel Čapek was representative of the democratic tradition along with other intellectuals, such as his brother Josef–a painter, writer, and coauthor with Karel Čapek–as well as the writers and journalists Eduard Bass, Karel Poláček and Ferdinand Peroutka. They all contributed to the prestigious *Lidové noviny* (*The People's Newspaper*) along with other prominent personalities of the time: the composer Leoš Janáček, presidents Tomáš Garrigue Masaryk and Edvard Beneš. Karel Čapek sympathized with American pragmatism and relativism, the prevalent philosophical trends in the 1920s. He viewed knowledge, truth, and morality not necessarily as an absolute entity but as a reflection of the cultural history of a society that incorporates many viewpoints. He favored multiple interpretations and truths that he believed could coexist in a single work. For instance, in *Povětroň*, the second work of his trilogy *Hordubal*, *Povětroň* (*Meteor*) and *Obyčejný život* (*An Ordinary Life*), Čapek saw space for different interpretations through a plurality of voices by various characters to create an understanding of how complex and spacious reality could be. He perceived the plurality of voices as a structure of polyphony, rather than as chaos and uncertainty. The so-called "Rashomon effect," the retelling of one and the same event by several witnesses but which gives rise to contradictory opinions, applies to additional Čapek's works, including *An Ordinary Life*, the last novel of his trilogy. If the attitude of "neither the Marshal nor Galen was all right or all wrong"[13] is considered, it brings out the issues of responsibility, opportunism, and power, bouncing against one another in the play.

While the author addresses the issue of Galén's ethical dilemma through the interaction of fictional characters–as to whether he has a responsibility to release the secret of his cure to all humanity as his medical profession requires–Čapek and his play have been attacked by medical experts for unethical behavior. These critics took his play literally as the subject of medical practice rather than as an investigation of human vices. They overlooked the purpose of art–an artful representation of complex reality–aimed at an idea or topic to provoke a reaction and evoke feelings. Referring to medical protocol, they suggested that Dr. Galén violated the Hippocratic Oath–an oath of ethics historically taken by medical students upon their graduation: "I will remember that I remain a member of society, with special obligations to *all* my fellow

---

[12] Ibid.
[13] Ibid.

human beings, those sound of mind and body as well as the infirm."[14] Medical professionals called Dr. Galén's disgraceful behavior an insult to their profession, claiming that no doctor would act like Dr. Galén. Čapek defended himself in a letter, explaining that his allegorical play was not about a physical malady but rather about curing the societal ills of approaching war and totalitarianism, none of which, in Čapek's view, could be remediated by the passivity of citizens.

Čapek named Dr. Galén after the Greek figure Claudius Galenus, the Roman Empire's greatest physician and surgeon and a personal physician to Rome's Emperor Marcus Aurelius. Galenus was an innovator of experimental medicine, dissecting animals to understand how living organs function in the human body. As a writer and philosopher, he compiled medical discoveries into several volumes, which are still in existence. Likewise, Čapek's Dr. Galén is of Greek origin and a unique innovator, being the only physician who found the cure for the assumed pandemic. Nicknamed "Dětina" (naïve as a child), Dr. Galén is humble, often humiliated, at times evoking pity, but stubborn and unusually determined. The chief physician of the Lilienthal Clinic, Dr. Sigelius, lets him take care of the poorest and most desolated patients located in the Ward No. 13, hoping to obtain glory from Galén's medical successes. The vicious circle of greed for money, power, and glory spreads within the Clinic to the medical assistants, and the hope for a cure connects Dr. Galén with the powerful players of the country: the dictator–Marshal, and the manufacturer of war weapons–Baron Krüg, whose name Čapek concocted from *Krieg*, the German word for *war* and *Krupp*, the name of the German dynasty, that has been producing artillery and ammunition for centuries.

In addition to greed for power, the examination of the major characters in the play leads to the question of social responsibility and moral accountability of fairness. The system of ethics proposes that everyone's decisions and actions should benefit the whole society and contribute to the welfare of everyone. This is where Dr. Galén errs in his decision to assist only a disadvantaged population. His act leads to the destruction of the societal fabric. Middle-class patients, as well as those of means and in power, pretend to be at the bottom of society, using a variety of ruses, hoping to receive Dr. Galén's treatment. The Father, who brings the Mother for treatment, is uncovered as working at the weapons plant and is requested by Dr. Galén to tell his boss, Baron Krüg, to stop producing ammunition for the upcoming war. While Dr. Galén's demand

---

[14] Quoted in its modernized 1964 version by Dr. Louis Lasagna at Tufts Medical School: https://www.pbs.org/wgbh/nova/doctors/oath_modern.html.

may be sound within social responsibility, his approach is disputable within moral accountability of fairness. In his volume, *Responsibility and the Moral Sentiments*, R. Jay Wallace asserts the general belief "to hold people morally responsible is to be prepared to blame or sanction them for their moral offenses."[15] These sanctions, as R. Jay Wallace claims, lead toward punishment. He further explains that "holding people responsible cannot be reduced to a behavioral disposition, because moral blame has an essential attitudinal dimension."[16] In Wallace's concept, Dr. Galén's blaming the Marshal and Baron Krüg for their "moral offense"–the preparation of war–would be Galén's "attitudinal dimension" that punishes the whole world: the deadly pandemic could easily destroy every nation, the entire world, just as much as the war could.

Arne Novák, whose translated works into English contributed to the understanding of Czech literature by American scholars and readers, sees Čapek's writings "cleansed of its negativist tendencies through infusions of Pragmatism as well as a highly sober form of humanism."[17] As an adherent of relativism, Čapek subjected himself to a skepticism, that Arne Novák labels "down-to-earth." However, Galén's stubbornness reaches absurdity in the blind rhetoric of his demand. During a crucial meeting with Galén, the Marshal pleads with the doctor to save Baron Krüg, his only friend, who has contracted the disease. But Galén replies: "You are the only one who can save him. Him and all the lepers. Just say you're willing to make a lasting peace, sign a multilateral treaty, and that's it."[18] One can detect the plurality of voices even within these two opposing characters. Galén pleads with the Marshal to sign the peace treaty if not for anyone else, so at least for Baron Krüg. The Marshal, on the other hand, defends his act of preparing war not as his own will but as God's call in the name of all people: "If the Nation feels that a war is in its best interest, it is my duty to prepare it for that war."[19]

In psychology, Dr. Galén would be a subject of study for *selective attention*: in his process of thinking and acting, Galén focuses on one object–the Marshal– choosing to ignore, at the same time, a variety of interplaying factors. In Dr.

---

[15] R. Jay Wallace, *Responsibility and the Moral Sentiments* (Cambridge: Harvard University Press, 1998): Chapter 3.
[16] Ibid.
[17] Arne Novák, *Czech Literature*, trans. Peter Kussi (Ann Arbor: The University of Michigan, 1986), 97.
[18] Čapek, "The White Plague," 488.
[19] Ibid.

Galén's view, if the Marshal would say he wanted peace, "the whole world would disarm at once."[20] Galén's *selective attention* acts as a filter, depriving him from seeing the whole picture: the human race could become extinct if his cure is not extended to *all*. Thus, Dr. Galén can be viewed as no less dangerous, selfish, or fanatical than the Marshal. The two-sided dialogue reveals each defending his actions within his own spectrum. The Marshal supports his claim: "I think war is better than peace–if it ends in victory" as "a higher power called upon by God,"[21] and Dr. Galén perceives his agenda as a civic duty, a mission of "an ordinary citizen." To some extent, they both demonstrate indifference to humanity and are blind to the responsibility they should have instilled in themselves. The vehicle behind the Marshal's indifference is his opportunism at the expense of human oppression and death. As a result of *selective attention*, Dr. Galén, too, avoids responsibility to humanity, denying the opportunity to all people to be saved, as the medical Hippocratic Oath requires: to treat *all* the patients.

The issue of responsibility, or a lack of thereof, has been embedded in the history of the Czechs and Slovaks due to many upheavals during their existence. For instance, in the postwar period, Ján Kadár and Elmar Klos masterfully incorporated indifference, opportunism, and oppression as the usual antipode of responsibility, portrayed in the ordinary citizens of a Slovak village in the Oscar-winning film *Obchod na korze* (*The Shop on Main Street*). The message was explicit: everyone shared responsibility for the installation of the Nazis' regime and the deportation of the Jewish population because no one opposed it openly. The main character, Tono, exhibits passive resistance, and while at times confused, he understands too well what potential atrocities could be caused by the newly installed Nazi regime that is led in his village by his own brother-in-law, Markus. Seen in the reduced scale of a small village, Markus would be aligned with Čapek's Marshal. Using an ideological approach, Markus–like the Marshall–is a fanatical opportunist, willing to sacrifice the lives of villagers and even of his own brother-in-law to achieve power and wealth. *Obchod na korze* was produced in 1965, two decades after the end of WWII, and while the film's plot focuses on the year 1942 during the Aryanization program, its film directors attack indifference, opportunism, and lack of responsibility not only during the war period but also metaphorically in the post-war Communist regime in Czechoslovakia.

---

[20] Ibid.
[21] Ibid., 489.

Responsibility vs. greed for power

Tono, a simple guy, a carpenter, is tossed between good and evil, often making wrong decisions based on his intuition or poor moral judgment rather than on rational thinking. He is a reminder of the three characters who open Čapek's play. Each contracted the white disease, trying to understand what they are punished for. One of them suggests: "You know what they really ought to call it? Retribution. Something as dangerous as that–it doesn't just ... happen; it's divine retribution."[22] Another one argues: "Retribution! Retribution! For what? Tell me! All I got to show for my life is poverty. What kind of God takes His anger out on the poor?"[23] Eventually, he finds the reason, concluding: "There's too many people. Half of us got to lay down and die to make room for the other half."[24]

As a propaganda tool, the idea of God's intervention of retribution is used in the Slovak village, too. The tower that is being built during the course of the film, advertises "Life for God, Freedom for Nation" in huge and glowing letters. Interpolated with one of the opening scenes of prisoners walking in a circle in a jail's courtyard, the audience interprets the tower's slogan as a hint at exterminating one segment of the population. A similar idea of isolating the diseased population is hinted at by several characters in *The White Plague*. That territory is intended to be protected by the barbed wire fence to be produced in Baron Krüg's factory. Once he has contracted the white plague, Baron Krüg realizes the life irony: his factory production would contribute to his own imprisonment and death.

Tono wrestles with greed and guilt, ironically manipulated by his wife and brother-in-law, especially when Markus appointed him an Aryan comptroller of a Jewish widow's button store. Instead of confiscating her store, he gradually befriends her, and she treats him as a close relative, on occasion alluding to, if not taking him for, her deceased husband. Their untraditional romantic relationship climaxes in dream scenes, which, according to the view of the film directors, indicates that the harmony of people, religions, races, and ages can exist only in the other world. When the authorities order all Jews in town to be deported in cattle wagons, frenetic Tono faces a moral dilemma of either saving the Jewish widow's life or his own. Only then he begins to understand the heavy burden of personal responsibility that was put on his shoulders by the people and the system: his wife, his brother-in-law, and the Nazis' politics. Finding no solution out of the vicious circle, he hangs himself. Similarly, once contracting

---

[22] Ibid., 432.
[23] Ibid.
[24] Ibid.

the white plague, the Marshal and Baron Krüg feel the iron hand of responsibility for their own lives. Just like Tono and the Jewish widow, they both perish–Baron Krüg taking his own life. Just before their death, a sense of responsibility is stirred in the Marshal and Baron Krüg: in the moment of the dilemma between life and death, they comply with Dr. Galén's demand to stop the approaching war. When Čapek passed away in 1938, there was still hope that a disastrous war might be averted; but in Kadár's and Klos's time, WWII had become a *fait accompli*.

The idea of responsibility has been weighty throughout Czech history. For instance, in most recent times, after taking over the Presidential office in 1990, Václav Havel's motto for a better future was "awakening a universal sense of responsibility in each citizen." Havel's idea was in line with other Czech and Slovak pacifists, pointing out the clash of power and responsibility, each drawing from the regime of his time. Tomáš Garrigue Masaryk, the first President of newly established Czechoslovakia in 1918, was a moralist and philosopher like Václav Havel. "They were deeply concerned with the moral basis of politics, and in particular, the moral bases of their own participation in politics."[25] Havel, for instance, understood the "universal sense" as a moral and individual responsibility to oneself, to his fellow neighbor, to the society, as well as to the global world. According to him, and according to Milan Kundera (the best-known contemporary Czech/French novelist), the twentieth century was marked by the departure from God, creating "the first atheistic civilization" that manifests itself by bloodshed, confusion, loss of roots, and loss of one's identity. Focusing on individuality, moral and personal responsibility, Václav Havel opposed the centralization of power, and like Čapek, he pointed out the dehumanizing elements of wars, bureaucratic institutions, and fast-paced technology. Both Havel and Čapek saw the current civilization as endangered by the irresponsibility embedded in human nature.

In another play, *R.U.R. (Rossum's Universal Robots)*, Čapek not only enriched the world languages with the word *robot*, but in this utopian play, he above all emphasized the destructive forces of technological advances, showing how dangerous technological instruments could be. While Helena, who was visiting Rossum's secret factory for the production of robots, believed that the best worker was the one who is honest and dedicated to contributing to the society's welfare, the factory director Domin attempts to convince her that the best workers are the cheapest ones who have the least needs and who have no

---

[25] Ernest Gellner, "The Price of Velvet: Thomas Masaryk and Václav Havel," *Czech Sociological Review* 3, no. 1 (1995): 45.

knowledge or sensation of feelings and death. Mechanically and intelligence-wise, these robots are more perfect than humans because, as Domin explains to Helena, they are more rarified than nature would be able to create them. The consequences of robots taking over man result in the destruction of humanity and the human race. Here Čapek is a precursor of Havel and Kundera in their beliefs in the values of "the old world" in which the goodness of the human heart was guided by the sense of moral and personal responsibility of each individual. Personal and national satisfaction was valued above greediness because people believed in the higher realm of God and powers of nature, hovering above them and guiding their actions.

The issue of the ethics of responsibility lies in Karel Čapek's additional works. It suffices to mention one of the twentieth century's greatest satirical science fiction novels, *Válka s mloky* (known in the English translation under the title *War with the Newts*, or *Salamander Wars*), which became an inspiration to a number of writers, including George Orwell and Kurt Vonnegut. Like his *R.U.R.*, Čapek's novel *War with the Newts* attacks man's thirst for control, domination, and exploitation of a species of the animal kingdom that man considers *weaker* than himself. He trains and exploits the newts for his own purposes of rising to power and control, forgetting that the species of newts is highly intelligent. Ultimately, the newts revolt, calling to arms to challenge man's position of superiority and domination. Like many of Čapek's works, this novel pinpoints the disintegration caused by the presence of moral and societal decay. The innocent species is enslaved by a technocratic syndicate of men, whose interests are economic wealth at the expense of the life of weaker creatures.

It is not only greediness and lack of responsibility that are detected in Čapek's works. Hope is lingering everywhere but it might remain unnoticed or misinterpreted in the complexity of the thoughts and actions of the individual characters. Female characters are endowed with a soft side of compassion and understanding. For instance, it is the Marshal's daughter who convinces her father–who has been himself stricken with the white plague–to accept Dr. Galén's condition to give up on war to save himself and humanity from the devastating disease via Galén's miraculous medication: "Daddy, please. What about the people who are deathly ill? Think of them,"[26] she insists in the crucial moment of fear and anxiety. He agrees reluctantly, saying, "You're right, Annette," perceiving himself as a defeated leader: "No longer leading victorious troops. No. Leading an army of foul, rotting flesh... Let me have it, Annette."[27]

---

[26] Čapek, "The White Plague," 501.
[27] Ibid., 502.

He grabs the phone and calls Dr. Galén, asking him to come over and agreeing with Galén's request to stop wars. However, in the final scene, the crowd's fanaticism that was created by the Marshal and his friend the Baron Krüg overcomes the individual responsibility of each member of the mob. In front of the Marshal's balcony, pro-war admirers fueled by horde psychosis trample Dr. Galén to death because he refuses to join in shouting, "Long live the War." The doctor's suitcase with curing ampules is destroyed by the angry mob, which includes the son from the first act, who now behaves in the most brutal way towards the doctor, kicking him and crushing him to death. The Marshal's willingness to make concessions to Dr. Galén came too late, leaving the audience in gloom over the play.

If the play has a pessimistic ending, the film version of the same title *The White Plague*, released at the end of 1937 and directed by Hugo Haas–who also starred as Dr. Galén–retains hope. The director took some liberties in one of the final scenes by letting Dr. Galén share his serum formula with another doctor from a small and disease-stricken country. Likewise, after human beings are destroyed in *R.U.R.*, two robots develop feelings for one another, giving hope for a new species of beings to be born or created, and that humanity will be renewed.

In a variety of ways, the ethical concerns of our present century's post-pandemic climate are a reminder of the issues that Karel Čapek treated in his play *The White Plague*. They also prove that George Bernard Shaw's idea of human unpreparedness for repetitive disasters remains alive and of serious concern. As plays, novels, films, and other media of the literary and creative arts have attempted to warn us, we ought to be aware of problems and put individual responsibility and hope in humanity on the highest level of our moral values to supersede intolerance, fanaticism, and economic interests of the world dominated by technology and human greediness. However, it is not easy in our present world of divided politics and animosity between various segments of the global population.

Fortunately, the most recent pandemic has been curtailed with medical advances of the twenty-first century and without "Dr. Galén's" intervention. As a result of several years of confusion and deprivation, however, our pandemic culminated in what Čapek was afraid of and why he created his play: in a time of war. Human despair has overlooked the essence of individual responsibility to one another and did not cure greediness, thirst for money, power, and territory. On the contrary, the issues that Čapek was concerned with some ninety years ago, have again led to "repetitive disasters," today dominated by two wars, one in Russia-Ukraine and the other in the Israeli-Gaza strip. As

Milan Kundera remarked in his *The Art of the Novel*, Descartes' famous formulation of man being "master and proprietor of nature," has remained a subject of controversy. Man is realizing and proving again and again that he is "master neither of nature (it is vanishing, little by little, from the planet), nor of History (it has escaped him), nor of himself (he is led by the irrational forces of his soul)."[28]

Bibliography

Čapek, Karel. "The White Plague." Translated by Michael Henry Heim. *Cross Currents: A Yearbook of Central European Culture* 7 (1988): 431–504.

Čapek, Karel. *Loupežník, R.U.R., Bílá nemoc*. Praha: Československý spisovatel, 1983.

Chamberlain, Neville. "Chamberlain addresses the nation on peace negotiations," https://www.bbc.co.uk/archive/chamberlain-addresses-the-nation-on-his-negotiations-for-peace/zjrjgwx.

Gellner, Ernest. "The Price of Velvet: Thomas Masaryk and Václav Havel." *Czech Sociological Review* 3, no. 1 (1995): 45.

Heim, Michael Henry. "The Plague Years." *Cross Currents: A Yearbook of Central European Culture* 7 (1988): 429–30.

Kundera, Milan. *The Art of the Novel*, trans. from the French by Linda Asher. New York: Harper & Row, 1986.

Lasagna, Louis. Tuft Medical School https://www.pbs.org/wgbh/nova/doctors/oath_modern.html.

Novák, Arne. *Czech Literature*. Translated from the Czech by Peter Kussi. Ann Arbor: The University of Michigan, 1986.

Radio Prague International. "The Czech Books You Must Read". https://english.radio.cz/czech-books-you-must-read-8506310/20.

Wallace, R. Jay. *Responsibility and the Moral Sentiments*. Cambridge: Harvard University Press, 1998.

---

[28] Milan Kundera, *The Art of the Novel*, trans. Linda Asher (New York: Harper & Row, 1986), 41.

Chapter 2

Kundera, Tolstoy, and the lightness of being

Mary Orsak
University of Oxford

Abstract

This chapter reevaluates Leo Tolstoy's influence on the Czech émigré writer Milan Kundera. Although Kundera often attempted to distance himself from the Russian literary tradition, Kundera engaged with Tolstoy far more than scholars have previously noted. This chapter identifies two striking connections between the works of Tolstoy and Kundera: the relationship between Tolstoy's concept of the "joyful and strange lightness of being" (*radostnoi i strannoi legkosti bytiia*) and Kundera's "unbearable lightness of being" (*nesnesitelná lehkost bytí*), and the fascination with female suicide.

Keywords: Kundera, Tolstoy, *Unbearable Lightness of Being*, *War and Peace*, Nietzsche, eternal return, *Anna Karenina*, suicide.

* * *

In 1985, the Czech émigré Milan Kundera published an article in *The New York Times* ahead of the English-language premiere of his play "Jacques and His Master."[1] In this essay, Kundera linked the Warsaw Pact Invasion in 1968 to the nineteenth-century Russian novelist Fyodor Dostoevsky: "When in 1968 the Russians occupied my small country, all my books were banned, and I suddenly lost all legal means of earning a living. A number of people tried to help me; one day, a director came and proposed that I write a stage adaptation, under his name, of Dostoevsky's *The Idiot*. So I reread *The Idiot* and realized that even if I were starving, I could not do the job."[2] Anticipating that some

---

[1] The play, "Jacques and His Master," premiered at the American Repertory Theory in Boston, MA, under the direction of Susan Sontag.
[2] Milan Kundera, "An Introduction to a Variation," *The New York Times*, January 6, 1985, sec. Book Review. Reprinted in Milan Kundera, "An Introduction to a Variation: Diderot

readers might attribute his criticism of Dostoevsky to contemporary geopolitics, Kundera continued: "Was it the anti-Russian reflex of a Czech traumatized by the occupation of his country? No, because I never stopped loving Chekhov."[3] Kundera conceded that his distaste for *The Idiot* arose from the *climate* of Dostoevsky's oeuvre: "a universe where everything turns into feeling; in other words, where feelings are promoted to the rank of value and of truth."[4]

A month later, the Russian émigré Joseph Brodsky responded with unmistakable vitriol in his own essay, "Why Milan Kundera Is Wrong About Dostoevsky." Vexed by Kundera's sweeping generalizations about Russian sentimentality, Brodsky challenges Kundera's latent Orientalism: "The sad truth about him (and many of his East European brethren) is that this extraordinary writer has fallen an unwitting victim to the geopolitical certitude of his fate–the concept of an East-West divide."[5] While Brodsky's diatribe against Kundera contains its own generalizations, Brodsky aptly diagnoses the deceptive allure of the East-West divide: "Yet tragic as the notion of a world apportioned in this fashion may be, it is not without mental coziness. It offers the handy dichotomies of feeling-reason, Dostoyevsky-Diderot, them-us and so forth."[6]

Throughout much of his mature non-fiction and literary criticism, Kundera has located himself unmistakably on the side of Diderot. Identifying as a "European" writer–and later, as a "Central European" writer–Kundera rejected the Western urge to identify him with any sort of "Slavic" canon. In his 2005 work of literary criticism, *The Curtain*, Kundera characterized this tendency as reminiscent of "deportation":

> in the late 1970s, I was sent the manuscript of a foreword written for one of my novels by an eminent Slavist, who placed me in permanent comparison (flattering, of course; at the time, no one meant me harm)

---

or Dostoevsky," *Cross Currents, A Yearbook of Central European Culture* 5 (1985): 469. This version used for citation. An amended translation was published in Milan Kundera, *Jacques and His Master*, trans. Simon Callow (London: Faber & Faber, 1986).
[3] Ibid., 469.
[4] Ibid.
[5] Joseph Brodsky, "Why Milan Kundera Is Wrong About Dostoevsky," *The New York Times*, February 17, 1985, sec. Book Review. Reprinted in Joseph Brodsky, "Why Milan Kundera Is Wrong about Dostoevsky," *Cross Currents, A Yearbook of Central European Culture* 5 (1985): 481. This version used for citation.
[6] Ibid., 481.

with Dostoyevsky, Gogol, Bunin, Pasternak, Mandelstam, and the Russian dissidents. In alarm, I stopped its publication. Not that I felt any antipathy for those great Russians; on the contrary, I admired them all, but in their company I became a different person. I still recall the strange anguish the piece stirred in me: that displacement into a context that was not mine felt like a deportation.[7]

Kundera's 1985 *The New York Times* article and his 2005 work of literary criticism demonstrate his persistent discomfort in his relationship with the Russian literary canon.

However, Kundera's extensive corpus of literary criticism includes countless favorable references to another member of the Russian literary pantheon: Leo Tolstoy. Even in the 1985 article that disparages Dostoevsky, Kundera praises Tolstoy for how his 1878 novel *Anna Karenina* "posed the issue of human action in a manner radically new in the history of the novel; [Tolstoy] discovered the fatal importance of rationally elusive causes in decision making."[8] Despite these numerous allusions to Tolstoy, few scholars have noted Tolstoy's influence on Kundera's oeuvre.[9] Amidst this limited corpus of scholarship, no scholars to date have identified two striking connections between the works of Tolstoy and Kundera: the relationship between Tolstoy's concept of the "joyful and strange lightness of being" (*radostnoi i strannoi legkosti bytiia*) and Kundera's "unbearable lightness of being" (*nesnesitelná lehkost bytí*), and the fascination with female suicide.[10] Ultimately, this reevaluation of Tolstoy's influence on Kundera will further complicate the question of Kundera's relationship to the Russian literary tradition. While Kundera's diatribe against Dostoevsky and Russian sentimentalism presents the Czech émigré as an antagonist to the Russian literary tradition, his literary oeuvre muddles the "Dostoevsky-Diderot" divide that Brodsky observes.

---

[7] Milan Kundera, *The Curtain: An Essay in Seven Parts*, trans. Linda Asher (New York: HarperCollins, 2007), 44–45.
[8] Kundera, "An Introduction to a Variation," 474.
[9] For example, Miglena Dikova-Milanova's paper, "The Responsibility of the Spectator: Milan Kundera's Reading of Tolstoy," presented at the AATSEEL Conference, Vancouver, Canada, 2015.
[10] The BBC Russian-language obituary for Milan Kundera briefly mentions that both Tolstoy and Kundera employ the phrase "lightness of being." "Nevynosimaia legkost' zhizni ne zdes'. Umer Milan Kundera," *BBC News Russkaia sluzhba*, accessed January 19, 2024, https://www.bbc.com/russian/features-55552154.

The lightnesses of being

Milan Kundera's most commercially successful novel, *The Unbearable Lightness of Being*, introduced the eponymous philosophical conception to explain both the ephemerality of an individual life as well as the weightlessness of a life free of "burdens." However, Kundera may have found inspiration for this coinage in Leo Tolstoy's nineteenth-century novel *War and Peace*. On his death bed, Prince Andrei Bolkonsky muses about the "joyful and strange lightness of being" and dreams that death merely represents an awakening, a notion that echoes Friedrich Nietzsche's "eternal return." While Kundera does not attribute this phrase to Tolstoy, the etymological similarity between the two phrases, as well as Kundera's numerous allusions to Tolstoy, demand further study.

Kundera first introduces the titular phrase nearly halfway through the novel. While describing the artist Sabina after she abandons her lover Franz and flees to Paris, Kundera writes that "What fell to her lot was not the burden but the unbearable lightness of being."[11] This oxymoron draws upon the early chapters of the novel, which explore the philosophies of Friedrich Nietzsche and Parmenides. Nietzsche's conception of eternal recurrence and Parmenides' essential opposites provide a framework to categorize and comprehend the main characters of the novel as well as those in Kundera's later novel *Immortality*, which the author acknowledged should have been titled *The Unbearable Lightness of Being*. While Kundera explicitly borrows from the fifth-century Greek philosopher Parmenides and the nineteenth-century German philosopher Nietzsche–albeit with some unorthodox interpretations–he only subtly alludes to the Russian novelist Leo Tolstoy in his novel *The Unbearable Lightness of Being*. For example, Tereza materializes in the novel armed with the "thick" (*tlustý*) novel *Anna Karenina* and a "large and enormously heavy" (*veliký a nesmírně těžký*) suitcase. The etymological similarity between the Czech adjective "*tlustý*" and Tolstoy's surname, which derives from the Russian adjective for "thick" (*tolstyi*), amplifies this allusion and further affixes Tolstoy to the trope of heaviness and its fictional embodiment, Tereza. These adjectives–thick, large, and heavy–align Tereza with heaviness, the descriptor that defines her character throughout the novel and juxtaposes her with the "light" Sabina. Moreover, Tomáš gifts a puppy to Tereza, and to stress that the

---

[11] Milan Kundera, *The Unbearable Lightness of Being*, trans. Michael Henry Heim (New York: Harper & Row, 1987), 121. (*Na Sabinu dopadlo nikoli břemeno, ale nesnesitelná lehkost bytí.*) Milan Kundera, *Nesnesitelná lehkost bytí* (Toronto: Sixty-Eight Publishers, 1985), 113.

dog belongs to Tereza, Tomáš names the mutt Karenin in honor of Tereza's arrival in Prague with the weighty novel. While Kundera's knowledge of Tolstoy's canon does not definitively prove that he intentionally borrowed the phrase from *War and Peace*, Tolstoy's "joyful and strange lightness of being" offers a productive comparison for understanding Kundera's famous phrase.

Nietzsche's eternal return and Parmenides' opposites

Kundera begins *The Unbearable Lightness of Being* by discussing Nietzsche's "mad myth" of eternal recurrence. Although Nietzsche offered several formulations of this concept throughout his canon, the notion of eternal return frequently appears in the form of a question: "Do you desire this once more and innumerable times more?"[12] Interpretations of this concept abound, but the scholarship on Nietzsche's eternal return generally consolidates his many "communications" of this thought, a phrase coined by follower Martin Heidegger, into two main interpretations: the cosmological and the practical. The cosmological communication suggests that a finite amount of energy in a finite amount of space and time would only produce a finite number of configurations. Therefore, the same configurations must recur infinitely. Interestingly, Kundera's novel *Immortality* includes a pared-down version of this argument: "If our planet has seen some eighty billion people, it is difficult to suppose that every individual has had his or her own repertory of gestures...Without the slightest doubt, there are far fewer gestures in the world than there are individuals."[13] While Kundera employs this logical principle to question the inimitability of the individual, Nietzsche fervently believed in the cosmological scope of his argument. According to the scholar Walter Kaufmann, Nietzsche trusted that modern science would vindicate this thesis.[14] Despite Nietzsche's failure to establish a credible cosmological communication of eternal return, this concept remains essential to Nietzsche's philosophy.

---

[12] Friedrich Nietzsche, *The Gay Science*, trans. Walter Kaufmann (New York: Random House, 1974), 341.
[13] Kundera, *Immortality*, trans. Peter Kussi (New York: HarperCollins, 1999), 7. (*Jestli od chvíle, co se objevil na zeměkouli první člověk, přešlo po zemi asi osmdesát miliard lidí, lze těžko předpokládat, že by každý jedinec měl svůj vlastní repertoár gest...Bez nejmenších pochyb je na světě mnohem méně gest než individuí.*) Milan Kundera, *Nesmrtelnost* (Toronto: Sixty-Eight Publishers, 1993), 15.
[14] Walter Kaufmann, *Nietzsche: Philosopher, Psychologist, Antichrist*, 4. ed., 20th pr. (Princeton: Princeton University Press, 2011), 326.

On the other hand, the practical communication of eternal return is often understood as an existentialist thought experiment. In *The Gay Science*, Nietzsche describes the concept of eternal recurrence in the following way:

> The greatest weight.–What if, some day or night a demon were to steal after you into your loneliest loneliness and say to you: "This life as you now live it and have lived it, you will have to live once more and innumerable times more; and there will be nothing new in it, but every pain and every joy and every thought and sigh and everything unutterably small or great in your life will have to return to you, all in the same succession and sequence– even this spider and this moonlight between the trees, and even this moment and I myself. The eternal hourglass of existence is turned upside down again and again, and you with it, speck of dust!" Would you not throw yourself down and gnash your teeth and curse the demon who spoke thus? Or have you once experienced a tremendous moment when you would have answered him: "You are a god and never have I heard anything more divine."[15]

The absurdity of this situation, epitomized by the appearance of a demon, lends itself well to the interpretation of eternal recurrence as merely a thought experiment. This hypothetical situation, therefore, would simply test one's willingness to acquiesce to fate–or rather, one's *amor fati*. In his "formula for greatness in a human being," Nietzsche prizes this *amor fati* as one of the chief virtues of the Übermensch.[16] Upon hearing the divine revelation of the demon, the Übermensch would rejoice: she would exult her own fullness of being for eternity. Only a weak individual, whose life lacked complete joy and purpose, would "throw [oneself] down and gnash [one's] teeth and curse the demon who spoke thus."[17]

Although Kaufmann believed that eternal recurrence only evaluated the totality of a person, as opposed to individual decisions, some readers, such as Kundera himself, emphasize the gravity of choice in a world of eternal return. Explaining the "unbearable responsibility" that humans experience in a world that recurs infinitely, Kundera writes: "we are nailed to eternity as Jesus Christ

---

[15] Nietzsche, *The Gay Science*, 341.
[16] Friedrich Nietzsche, *On the Genealogy of Morals & Ecce Homo*, trans. Walter Arnold Kaufmann (New York: Vintage Books, 1989), 258.
[17] Nietzsche, *The Gay Science*, 273.

was nailed to the cross."[18] Despite the suffering caused by eternal recurrence, Kundera expresses his preference for recurrence over ephemerality: "the myth of eternal return states that a life which disappears once and for all, which does not return, is like a shadow, without weight, dead in advance."[19] Consequently, without eternal return, historical figures like Robespierre and Hitler receive pardons, because "in the sunset of dissolution, everything is illuminated by the aura of nostalgia, even the guillotine."[20] Kundera's ethical dilemma–that "everything is pardoned in advance" in a transient world–diverges from Nietzsche's formulation of the question in *Gay Science*. The interjection of the moral element of the existential problem, however, does not necessarily represent a misreading of Nietzsche, but rather poses a different question: how would societies change if they were plagued by eternal recurrence?

This conflict between the heavy burden of eternal recurrence and the weightlessness of an ephemeral world connects the philosophy of Nietzsche with that of Parmenides. According to Kundera, Parmenides categorized the world into pairs of opposites–"light/darkness, fineness/coarseness, warmth/cold, being/non-being"–which each corresponded to either a positive or negative pole.[21] Parmenides, thus, prized weightlessness over heaviness. However, Kundera's reading of Parmenides errs several times. In Kundera's defense, Parmenides does write in one of the fragments of his poem that "they chose opposites in body and assigned them marks separate from one another, on the one hand aethereal fire of flame, being mild, immensely light, the same with itself in every direction but not the same as the other; that, on the other hand, being likewise in itself the opposites, unintelligent night, a dense and heavy body."[22] However, the passage explains the inaccurate belief of mortals, who divide the world into two Forms. As a monist, Parmenides argued for the essential unity of all matter; therefore, such a division would contradict his

---

[18] Kundera, *The Unbearable*, 5. (*jsme přikováni k věčnosti jak Ježíš Kristus ke kříži.*) Kundera, *Nesnesitelná*, 10.
[19] Kundera, *The Unbearable*, 3. (*Mýtus věčného návratu říká per negationem, že život, který zmizí jednou provždy, který se nenavrátí, je podoben stínu, je bez váhy, je předem mrtvý.*) Kundera, *Nesnesitelná*, 9.
[20] Kundera, *The Unbearable*, 4. (*Červánky zániku ozařují všechno kouzlem nostalgie; i guillotinu.*) Kundera, *Nesnesitelná*, 10.
[21] Kundera, *The Unbearable*, 5. (*světlo – tma; jemnost – hrubost; teplo – chlad; bytí – nebytí*) Kundera, *Nesnesitelná*, 11.
[22] A. H. Coxon, *Fragments of Parmenides: A Critical Text with Introduction and Translation, the Ancient Testimonia and a Commentary*, trans. Richard McKirahan (Las Vegas: Parmenides Publishing, 2009), 80–82.

entire philosophical system.[23] Despite Kundera's misreading of Parmenides, the value judgment of "weightlessness" and "heaviness" constitutes a crucial element of Kundera's concept of the unbearable lightness of being. In a typical Kunderian fashion, the author attempts to destabilize the reader's preconceived notions about the two poles. Typically, lightness connotes ease and the absence of concerns, whereas heaviness implies "dramatic situations."[24] However, Kundera appears to redefine lightness as meaningless and untethered, and heaviness as committed and fulfilled.

Ultimately, Kundera explicitly relates his own coinage to the philosophical frameworks of both Nietzsche and Parmenides and thus identifies himself as a descendant of both the Classical Greek and the German intellectual traditions. However, this essay will additionally argue that Kundera's most famous phrase may have roots in the Russian literary canon, a tradition with which Kundera actively tried to disassociate himself.[25]

Prince Andrei Bolkonsky and the "joyful and strange lightness of being"

Tolstoy, although writing a few decades before Nietzsche, directly engages with these questions of eternal return, *amor fati*, and the lightness of being. In one of Tolstoy's only uses of nonlinear narrative, which further heightens the conception of eternal recurrence, the Russian novelist explores Andrei's intellectual voyage toward his acceptance of fate and eternality. The scholar Edward Wasiolek in *Tolstoy's Major Fiction* conceives of Andrei's quest for truth as a cyclical disappointment with life: "Whenever faith has filled his heart, life has poisoned it."[26] Emerging in the novel with a "grimace that spoiled his handsome face" and a "weary, bored gaze," Prince Andrei embodies aristocratic ennui.[27] However, despite his avowed estrangement from life, Andrei resists succumbing to complete nihilism and strives to find meaning throughout the novel by means of various forms of engagement with the world. He seeks his

---

[23] Leonardo Tarán, *Parmenides: A Text with Translation, Commentary, and Critical Essays* (Princeton: Princeton University Press, 1965), 226.
[24] Kundera, *The Unbearable*, 121. (*Životní drama*) Kundera, *Nesnesitelná*, 113.
[25] Kundera, *The Curtain*, 43–45.
[26] Edward Wasiolek, *Tolstoy's Major Fiction* (Chicago: University of Chicago Press, 1981), 71.
[27] Leo Tolstoy, *War and Peace*, trans. Richard Pevear and Larissa Volokhonsky (London: Vintage Classic, 2011), 14. (*усталого, скучающего взгляда…С гримасой, портившею его красивое лицо*) Lev Tolstoi, *Voina i mir*, 4 vols. (Moskva: Molodaia gvardiia, 1978), 1: 23.

own "Toulon" and fights in the Battle of Austerlitz; he completes the reforms on his estate, such as freeing his serfs; he aids Mikhail Speransky in his liberal agenda; he falls in love for a second time with the vivacious Natasha. On the night before the Battle of Borodino, Andrei scoffs at these former pursuits: "Glory, the general good, the love of a woman, the fatherland itself–how grand those pictures seemed to me, how filled with deep meaning! And it's all so simple, pale, and crude in the cold, white light of the morning that I feel is dawning for me."[28] In the face of imminent death, Andrei once again experiences the familiar "cynical disillusionment in life," to borrow from the scholar R. F. Christian.[29] Although Tolstoy endows Andrei with "character, keen insight, intelligence, independence, high birth, wealth, courage," all of which should assist Andrei in his spiritual voyage, Andrei's circular path toward enlightenment recurs five times throughout the novel.[30] However, the Battle of Borodino provides Andrei with the final catalyst in his "moral quest."[31]

After suffering a fatal wound at the Battle of Borodino, Andrei experiences a revelatory "rebirth." In the grips of debilitating pain, Andrei once again reflects upon his life and his impending death:

He experienced an awareness of estrangement from everything earthly and a joyful and strange lightness of being (*On ispytyval soznanie otchuzhdennosti ot vsego zemnogo i radostnoi i strannoi legkosti bytiia*). Without haste or worry, he waited for what lay ahead of him. The dread, the eternal, the unknown and far off, of which he had never ceased to feel the presence throughout his life, was now close to him and–by that

---

[28] Tolstoy, *War and Peace*, 833. (Слава, общественное благо, любовь к женщине, самое отечество – как велики казались мне эти картины, какого глубокого смысла казались они исполненными! И все это так просто, бледно и грубо при холодном белом свете того утра, которое, я чувствую, поднимается для меня.) Lev Tolstoi, *Voina i mir*, 3: 209.
[29] Reginald Frank Christian, *Tolstoy's "War and Peace": A Study* (Oxford: Clarendon Press, 1962), 171.
[30] Wasiolek, *Tolstoy's Major Fiction*, 71.
[31] John Hagan, "A Pattern of Character Development in *War and Peace*: Prince Andrej," *The Slavic and East European Journal* 13, no. 2 (1969): 166, https://doi.org/10.2307/306784.

strange lightness of being he experienced–almost comprehensible and palpable.[32]

This lightness of being appears to offer Andrei not only solace but also joy in his final few days. In this euphoria of revelation, Andrei forgives his former rival Anatole Kuragin and accepts God as the true source of all love. One scholar, John Hagan, conceives of this enlightenment, in which Andrei "learns to accept death itself, not only without fear, but with positive joy," as a fulfillment of Marya's prophecy: "Against your will He will save and have mercy on you and bring you to Himself, for in Him alone is truth and peace."[33] Ultimately, whereas Sabina cannot bear her lightness of being, Andrei seems to rejoice in this new awareness that dispels his former fear of death.

However, Tolstoy immediately undermines Andrei's revelation by describing Andrei's mental state as "suffering solitude and half delirium."[34] These musings, according to Tolstoy, emerge from the disoriented mind of a dying man: Tolstoy explicitly states that "Something was lacking in them [Andrei's thoughts], there was something one-sidedly personal, cerebral."[35] Wasiolek admits that although Andrei's compassion toward Anatole and his acceptance of God align Andrei with Tolstoy's later values, "they do not fit in with the "truths" that Tolstoy dramatizes in the novel itself: there is little talk of God in the novel, and the sacramental scenes–those in which we know that something true and real have been touched–have more to do with an immersion in the sensuous life of this world than with Christian beliefs."[36] Thus, even if these thoughts provide the dying Andrei solace, his complete rejection of life does not communicate the essential truths of the novel. Instead, one might argue that Tolstoy's *War and Peace* offers a polemic against "an estrangement from everything earthly" (*otchuzhdennosti ot vsego zemnogo*).

---

[32] Tolstoy, *War and Peace*, 982. (Он испытывал сознание отчужденности от всего земного и радостной и странной легкости бытия. Он, не торопясь и не тревожась, ожидал того, что предстояло ему. То грозное, вечное, неведомое и далекое, присутствие которого он не переставал ощущать в продолжение всей своей жизни, теперь для него было близкое и — по той странной легкости бытия, которую он испытывал, — почти понятное и ощущаемое.) Lev Tolstoi, *Voina i mir*, 4: 65.
[33] Hagan, "A Pattern," 186.
[34] Ibid.
[35] Tolstoy, *War and Peace*, 984. (Чего-то недоставало в них, что-то было односторонне-личное, умственное) Tolstoi, *Voina i mir*, 4: 68.
[36] Wasiolek, *Tolstoy's Major Fiction*, 82.

Similarly, Andrei's conclusion to spurn earthly love deeply hurts his family. Like Sabina, Andrei betrays those closest to him, including his former fiancé Natasha, his sister Marya, and his son Nikolai, out of fear. Admitting that "Love hinders death," Andrei coldly recoils from his loved ones in preparation for his imminent passing.[37] Andrei even refuses to offer a heartfelt goodbye to his son Nikolai, and he only provides his son with the necessary blessing at Marya's urging. Ultimately, Natasha and Marya recognize that Andrei "sank deeper and deeper, slowly and peacefully, somewhere away from them."[38] Although Tolstoy employs the language of heaviness here, Andrei's withdrawal from life resembles Kundera's description of a weightless existence: Andrei seems to "be lighter than air, to soar into the heights, take leave of the earth and his earthly being, and become only half real, his movements as free as they are insignificant."[39]

Tempted by love for Natasha, Andrei wobbles on his commitment to a complete renunciation of life, once again undermining the sincerity of this "enlightenment." However, through the Dionysiac medium of the dream, Andrei succumbs entirely to this "strange lightness," as he contemplates the potential for eternal return. In this dream, which offers an abstract version of Andrei's own life, Prince Andrei struggles to lock a door, on the other side of which stands his fear of death and death itself. Yet, despite his herculean efforts, Andrei cannot lock the door. Thus, fear of death surpasses Andrei's "weak, clumsy" attempts, and Andrei dies.[40] Remembering that this is simply a dream, Andrei wakes himself up and concludes that "Yes, that was death. I died–I woke up. Yes, death is an awakening."[41] Andrei tries to employ his intelligence and keen insight throughout the novel to understand his life, but only the irrational dream of the unconscious mind offers him the truth that he seeks.

The imagery of Andrei's dream evokes Nietzsche's eternal return. Andrei perceives this dream death as his true passing, which results in his

---

[37] Tolstoy, *War and Peace*, 984. (*Любовь мешает смерти.*) Tolstoi, *Voina i mir*, 4: 68.
[38] Tolstoy, *War and Peace*, 985-86. (*он глубже и глубже, медленно и спокойно, опускался от них куда-то туда*) Tolstoi, *Voina i mir*, 4: 70.
[39] Kundera, *Unbearable*, 5. (*stává lehčí než vzduch, vzlétá do výše, vzdaluje se zemi, pozemskému bytí, stává se jen napůl skutečný a jeho pohyby jsou stejně svobodné jako bezvýznamné.*) Kundera, *Nesnesitelná*, 11.
[40] Tolstoy, *War and Peace*, 985. (*слабы, неловки*) Tolstoi, *Voina i mir*, 4: 69.
[41] Tolstoy, *War and Peace*, 985. («*Да, это было смерть. Я умер — я проснулся. Да, смерть — пробуждение!*») Tolstoi, *Voina i mir*, 4: 69.

reawakening, and this cycle of life and death suggests Andrei's belief in a cosmological return. Of course, Andrei does not concern himself with the practical and existentialist concerns of eternal return but rather believes in the potential for life after death. This possibility of return after death does not invoke in Andrei the same dread as in Nietzsche; instead, this return promises Andrei lightness. Interestingly, Tolstoy anticipates Nietzsche's conception of the curtain from *Birth of Tragedy,* which hides the abyss, as Tolstoy writes: "the curtain that until then had concealed the unknown was raised before his inner gaze."[42] This curtain, which had separated Andrei from his imminent death, now reveals the truth of eternal return to the prince in his final days.

While Andrei describes his final moments as a "strange and joyful lightness of being," the titular character of *Smert' Ivana Il'icha* (translated as *The Death of Ivan Ilyich*) reevaluates his life of "lightness" and ultimately renounces a life absent of weight. Throughout the novella, Tolstoy repeatedly characterizes Ivan Ilyich's life as "light": the statesman enjoys an "easy and pleasant situation for himself" in the provinces (*legkoe i priiatnoe polozhenie*), has a "inclination for light merriment" (*sklonnost' k legkomu vesel'iu*), and maintains "light and playful relations with [his wife] Praskovya Fyodorovna" (*igrivie, legkie otnosheniia s Praskov'ei Fedorovnoi*).[43] Juxtaposed with Ivan Ilyich's "light" life, his fatal abdominal pain is described as "heavy": "the consciousness of a constant heaviness in his side" (*v soznanie tiazhesti postoiannoi v boku*).[44] At this point in the novella, this dichotomy of light versus heavy corresponds to the consensus of "light" as pleasant and "heavy" as painful. However, while wrestling with an unidentifiable and incurable affliction, Ivan Ilyich reassesses his life's central aim: to live "easily, pleasantly, and decently" (*legko, priiatno i prilichno*).[45] Instead, Ilyich realizes that "All that you've lived and live by is a lie, a deception, concealing life and death from you."[46] By preserving his life of ease, Ilyich has eschewed the rewarding depth of meaningful relationships and

---

[42] Tolstoy, *War and Peace*, 985. (*завеса, скрывавшая до сих пор неведомое, была приподнята перед его душевным взором.*) Tolstoi, *Voina i mir*, 4: 69.

[43] Leo Tolstoy, *The Death of Ivan Ilyich and Other Stories*, trans. Richard Pevear and Larissa Volokhonsky (Vintage Classics, 2010), 48, 50. Lev Tolstoi, *Smert' Ivana Il'icha*, in L. N. Tolstoi: *Sobranie sochinenii*, 20 vols., vol. 12 (Moskva: Khudozhestvennaia literatura, 1964), 67, 70. As the translated quotations demonstrate, the Russian word "легкий" can mean "light-hearted" and "easy" as well as "light."

[44] Tolstoy, *The Death*, 60. Tolstoi, *Smert'*, 81.

[45] Tolstoy, *The Death*, 58. Tolstoi, *Smert'*, 78.

[46] Tolstoy, *The Death*, 89. Tolstoi, *Smert'*, 113. (*Все то, чем ты жил и живешь, — есть ложь, обман, скрывающий от тебя жизнь и смерть.*)

a sense of purpose. Like Andrei, Ilyich only reaches this epiphany in the liminal space between life and death, and after attaining this enlightenment, Ilyich finally resigns himself to his fate and accepts his impending death.

Ultimately, both *War and Peace* and *The Death of Ivan Ilyich* anticipate Kundera's novel *The Unbearable Lightness of Being*. Although it is nearly impossible to prove that Kundera borrowed this phrase from the Russian novelist, the deaths of both Andrei and Ivan Ilyich offer fruitful comparisons to Kundera's famous phrase.

Kundera's *Unbearable Lightness of Being* and *Immortality*

The characters Sabina from *The Unbearable Lightness of Being* and Agnès from *Immortality* offer Kundera vehicles through which to explore the motif of lightness. As mentioned previously, Kundera introduces the eponymous phrase through the perspective of Sabina, a talented artist. Essentially rebellious, Sabina betrays everything and everyone. As a child, Sabina first rejects her father's Catholicism and then his Communist ideals. These betrayals, which Kundera defines as "breaking ranks and going off into the unknown," at first offer Sabina a sense of exhilarating freedom.[47] When Sabina's kind and intelligent lover Franz professes his desire to abandon his wife for a life with her, she resists the weighty burden of a public relationship for "the expanse of freedom before her, and the boundlessness of it excited her."[48] However, Sabina soon recognizes the unbearableness of her constant betrayals, and she experiences an overwhelming sense of "melancholy."[49] Like Andrei, Sabina has spurned all earthly connections. While this negation of the self appears to offer Andrei solace and peace in the face of his imminent death, Sabina struggles with its "unbearable lightness," an oxymoron that suggests her inability to tolerate her "half real" state. Sabina finds this lightness intolerable because, in contrast with her Tolstoyan counterpart, she must continue to live while half-dead.

Despite Sabina's recognition of the insufferable nature of her lightness, she never attempts to change the trajectory of her life. Kundera notes that "in the mind of a woman for whom no place is home, the thought of an end to all flight

---

[47] Kundera, *The Unbearable*, 91. (*Zrada znamená opustit řadu a jít do neznáma.*) Milan Kundera, *Nesnesitelná*, 86.
[48] Kundera, *The Unbearable*, 116. (*Zdálo se jí, že je před ní ještě nesmírný prostor svobody a dálka té prostory ji vzrušovala.*) Kundera, *Nesnesitelná*, 108.
[49] Kundera, *The Unbearable*,121. (*z melancholie*) Kundera, *Nesnesitelná*, 113.

is unbearable."⁵⁰ Thus, Sabina faces an unsolvable dilemma: to continue spurning her connections to others would prove unbearable, as would an end to her constant flight. Hence, Sabina continues to betray those she loves and moves farther and farther from her home. Eventually, she dies in California, thousands of miles from Prague. She even chooses to die "lightly":

> one day she composed a will in which she requested that her dead body be cremated and its ashes thrown to the winds. Tereza and Tomas had died under the sign of weight. She wanted to die under the sign of lightness. She would be lighter than air. As Parmenides would put it, the negative would change into the positive.⁵¹

Even in death, Sabina refuses to remain close to the earth. Cremation allows Sabina to symbolically spurn the earth and embody lightness.

In his subsequent novel *Immortality*, which Kundera acknowledged should have been titled *The Unbearable Lightness of Being*, Kundera further explores the themes of lightness and eternal return through the voice of his protagonist, Agnès. Unlike Sabina, Agnès sustains her earthly connections to her husband and daughter despite a desire for lightness. Still, Agnès yearns for "one deep and systematic act of betrayal": to abandon her family and seek refuge in Switzerland.⁵² Agnès's father similarly seeks a burden-free life after the death of her mother: he moves into a bachelor apartment and destroys family photos. Agnès eventually decides to abandon the world and move to Switzerland, where she may resuscitate the fabled lifestyle of the cloister. Distancing herself from reality, she imagines the ending of Stendhal's novel *The Charter House of Parma*, in which Fabrice retires to a charterhouse. Agnès laments that "our century refuses to acknowledge anyone's right to disagree with the world, and therefore, there are no longer cloisters to which a Fabrice might escape."⁵³

---

⁵⁰ Kundera, *The Unbearable*, 125. (*a pro ženu, která nikde nemá stání, je nesnesitelná představa, že by se její útěk navždy zastavil*) Kundera, *Nesnesitelná*, 116.

⁵¹ Kundera, *The Unbearable*, 273. (*Napsala proto jednoho dne závěť, v níž stanovila, že její mrtvé tělo má být spáleno a popel rozprášen. Tereza a Tomáš zemřeli ve znamení tíže. Ona chce zemřít ve znamení lehkosti. Bude lehčí než vzduch. Podle Parmenida je to proměna negativního v pozitivní.*) Kundera, *Nesnesitelná*, 247.

⁵² Kundera, *Immortality*, 30. (*jediná hluboká a systematická nevěra*) Milan Kundera, *Nesmrtelnost* (Toronto: Sixty-Eight Publishers, 1993), 36.

⁵³ Kundera, *Immortality*, 265. (*Naše století odmítá přiznat lidem právo nesouhlasit se světem, a proto kláštery, do nichž by se mohl utéci Fabricius, se už nevyskytují.*) Kundera, *Nesmrtelnost*, 264–65.

Echoing the sentiments of Andrei, Sabina, and even Tolstoy at the end of his life, Agnès articulates an abandonment of life, the complete negation of the Übermensch's will to live.

Agnès, unable to follow Fabrice and retire to a cloister, engages with Nietzsche's existential question of eternal recurrence, but she adds new conditions: "You would be asked whether after death you wished to be reawakened to life. If you truly loved someone, you would agree to come back to life only on the condition that you'd be reunited with your beloved."[54] This is, of course, radically different than Nietzsche's formulation. Instead of returning *ad infinitum* to repeat one's own life exactly as it has occurred, Agnès' scenario would simply offer someone a second chance at life. In Agnès' scenario, the Übermensch would only choose to return under the condition of repeating life exactly as she has already lived it. However, Agnès would only return under either of two conditions: 1) that she would not have to return to her family, or 2) that she would return without her own face, or rather her own identity. For Agnès, "what is unbearable in life is not *being* but *being one's self*," and thus, to return to the system as an individual with a face, the symbol Agnès repeats to represent identity, would prove unbearable.[55] She would prefer, however, to simply "be," which she conceives as "becoming a fountain, a fountain on which the universe falls like warm rain."[56] In the words of Andrei's revelation, Agnès imagines herself returning to "the common and eternal source [of love]."[57] Within the framework of Nietzsche's philosophy, Agnès epitomizes the negation of the Übermensch and *ressentiment*. She cannot assent to life and love her fate without parameters, and unlike both the young girl whose suicide causes Agnès's death and Tolstoy's Andrei, she lacks the resolve to intentionally choose death either. She floats through her life half-dead, half-alive.

---

[54] Kundera, *Immortality*, 264. (*zeptají se vás, zda byste se po smrti chtěli znovu probudit k životu. Milujete-li skutečně, budete souhlasit jen pod tou podmínkou, že se znovu shledáte se svým milovaným*) Kundera, *Nesmrtelnost*, 264.
[55] Kundera, *Immortality*, 265. (*To, co je na životě nesnesitelné, není být, ale být svým já.*) Kundera, *Nesmrtelnost*, 265.
[56] Kundera, *Immortality*, 266. (*Proměnit se v kašnu, kamennou nádrž, do které padá vesmír jako vlahý déšť.*) Kundera, *Nesmrtelnost*, 265
[57] Tolstoy, *War and Peace*, 984. (*к общему и вечному источнику*) Tolstoi, *Voina i mir*, 4: 68.

Kundera's many restagings of *Anna Karenina*

Suicide–and in particular, suicide by female characters–constitutes one of the recurring "variations" that appear throughout Kundera's oeuvre and further illustrates Tolstoy's influence on the Czech émigré writer. While only two male characters either contemplate or attempt suicide throughout Kundera's eleven novels, Kundera discusses suicide in relation to over half a dozen female characters, nearly all of whom threaten to commit suicide over the romantic rejection of a man.[58] The scholar John O'Brien has suggested that the prevalence of female suicides in Kundera's oeuvre reflects his belief in the inherent weakness of women: "the boiled down moral is a tired one: women, when they are weak (as they generally are) must find a way to turn their weakness into a weapon."[59] O'Brien aptly critiques the hackneyed trope of the spurned woman who commits suicide to seek revenge, but Kundera's enduring fascination with Tolstoy's 1878 novel, *Anna Karenina*, might offer an alternate– if not, contradictory–explanation for the repetition of female suicide in Kundera's oeuvre.

As previously mentioned, Kundera's 1985 article published in *The New York Times* on Dostoevsky and sentimentalism alludes to his interest in Tolstoy's representation of suicide. Criticizing the numerous contemporary adaptations of Tolstoy's novel as mere digests, Kundera writes that "Every adaptation of this novel must, by the very nature of the digest approach, attempt to make the causes of Anna's behavior clear and logical, to rationalize them; the adaptation thus becomes the negation, pure and simple, of the novel's originality."[60] In the following year, Kundera revisits Anna's suicide in *L'art du roman* (published in English as *The Art of the Novel*), a rewriting of his 1960 work of socialist literary criticism by the same name. In *The Art of the Novel*, Kundera argues that Tolstoy employs "(for the first time in the history of the novel) an almost Joycean interior monologue to reconstruct the subtle fabric of fleeting impulses, transient feelings, fragmentary thoughts, to show us the suicidal journey of

---

[58] The two male characters that either contemplate or attempt suicide in Kundera's oeuvre are Josef Stalin's son, who throws himself into an electric fence after a disagreement over defecation with British soldiers in a Nazi work camp in *The Joke*, and Jakub, who acquires a poisonous pill from a friend while a serving as political prisoner in the Soviet Union in *Farewell Waltz*.

[59] John O'Brien, *Milan Kundera & Feminism: Dangerous Intersections* (Basingstoke: MacMillan, 1995), 42.

[60] Kundera, "An Introduction to a Variation," 474.

Anna's soul."[61] Finally, almost two decades later, Kundera offers his longest meditation on Anna Karenina's suicide in *The Curtain*. With meticulous attention to detail, Kundera plots Anna's final day to demonstrate the absence of premeditation. As Kundera notes, Anna does not contemplate suicide to escape her tragic separation from her son or her anxieties about her relationship with Vronsky; rather, two memories–the memory of her near-death experience during childbirth and of the train that crushed a bystander the day that Anna first met Vronsky–"subtly whisper...it to her."[62] Denying Anna the gravity of Oedipus' fated suicide, Tolstoy concludes the titular character's narrative with a banal and even pleasant final thought: "A sensation gripped her like one she used to feel long ago when, off for a swim, she prepared to plunge into the water."[63] In *The Curtain*, Kundera characterizes this conclusion as "a miraculous sentence!" The enigma of Anna's final day and the irrationality that Tolstoy captures earned three separate mentions in Kundera's non-fictional work over two decades and informed the numerous representations of suicide that appear throughout Kundera's eleven novels.

The variations on the theme most obviously indebted to Tolstoy appear in Kundera's novels *Žert* (published as *The Joke*), *La Lenteur* (published as *Slowness*), and *L'ignorance* (published as *Ignorance*). In each of these novels, Kundera attempts to capture the rash and illogical thought process that precedes the unsuccessful suicide attempts by his female characters. In the 1967 novel, *The Joke*, Helena, seduced and then abandoned by Ludvík in his revenge fantasy against his former classmate, fantasizes about committing suicide to punish Ludvík for his cruelty. After swiping a bottle of pain relievers from her young colleague, Helena first swallows two pills while contemplating that "Two, that's enough, that should help, of course Algena can't help me with the illness of my soul, unless I swallow all the tablets in the bottle, because it's poisonous in massive doses, and Jindra's bottle is nearly full, maybe it would be enough."[64] This "idea, a sudden flash" (*jen nápad, pouhá představa*)

---

[61] Kundera borrows the exact phrase, "an almost Joycean interior monologue," from his 1985 NYT article, which includes the line: "Tolstoy goes so far as to use an almost Joycean interior monologue to delineate the network of irrational motivations which drives his heroine to it." Milan Kundera, *The Art of the Novel*, trans. Linda Asher (London: Faber and Faber, 1990), 59.
[62] Kundera, *The Curtain*, 21.
[63] Ibid., 25.
[64] Milan Kundera, *The Joke*, trans. Aaron Asher (HarperPerennial, 2001), 286. (*Dvě, to je dost, to mi snad pomůže, ovšem od bolesti duše mi algena nepomůže, leda že bych snědla*

repeatedly returns to Helena, and the once desperate and transient thought transforms into a "source of bliss" (*divně sladce*). While the following sentence begins with the thought "I had no intention of poisoning myself," Helena's stream of consciousness rapidly transforms: "I merely squeezed the bottle in my palm and said to myself *I'm holding my death in my hand*, and I was enthralled by so much opportunity, it was like going step by step to an abyss, not to jump into it, just to look down."[65]

Here, Kundera attempts to replicate Tolstoy's depiction of Anna's irrational thought process in her final moments. Helena's thoughts transform imperceptibly over several minutes: the once ludicrous intrusive thought becomes more and more entrancing to Helena as it recurs in her mind. However, Kundera does not afford Helena the dignity of death: instead, Ludvík and Jindra find Helena in an outhouse, deathly pale from diarrhea with her underwear around her ankles, as Jindra has disguised his laxatives in an Algena pill bottle. This *deus ex machina* moment–at once, fortuitous and cruel– perhaps confirms O'Brien's contention that Kundera considers women too weak, capricious, and incompetent to orchestrate their own suicides.

The other two suicide attempts in Kundera's oeuvre unfold similarly. In *Slowness*, Immaculata, rejected by Berck and trailed by a rapacious cameraman, "suddenly sees with utter clarity the snare closing around her: her pursuer behind, the water ahead. She understands clearly that this encirclement affords no way out; that the only way out available to her is a crazy way out; that the only reasonable action left for her is an insane action; so with the full power of her will she chooses madness: she takes two steps forward and leaps into the water."[66] Kundera's diction, such as the words "crazy," "insane," and "madness," demonstrate the irrationality of human action that he prized so highly in Tolstoy's *Anna Karenina*. Moreover, this particular method of suicide–drowning–evokes Anna's final memory of the pleasant sensation of plunging into the water before a swim. As in *The Joke*, Kundera mocks Immaculata's desperate gesture: the lovesick young woman has thrown herself into a pool too shallow to allow herself to drown. Instead, Kundera remarks

---

celou tubu, protože algena ve velkém množství je jed a Jindrova tuba je skoro plná, to by možná stačilo.) Milan Kundera, *Žert* (Toronto: Sixty-Eight Publishers, 1989), 248.

[65] Kundera, *The Joke*, 248. (*Položila jsem si na jazyk ještě jednu tabletku, vůbec jsem nebyla rozhodnuta, že se otrávím, jenom jsem tiskla tu tubu v ruce a říkala jsem si "držím v ruce svoji smrt" a byla jsem okouzlena tou jednoduchostí, bylo mi, jako bych se krůček po krůčku přibližovala k hluboké propasti, ne snad abych do ní skočila, nýbrž jen abych se do ní podívala.*) Kundera, *Žert*, 248.

[66] Milan Kundera, *Slowness*, trans. Linda Asher (London: Faber & Faber, 1996), 107.

"Thus she proceeds, like some aquatic animal, a mythological duck letting its head vanish beneath the surface and then raising it, tipping it upwards."[67] This absurd characterization once again stresses the irrationality that seizes Immaculata at this moment.

Several years later, Kundera describes a similar suicide attempt in *Ignorance*. The failure of a teenage romance drives Julie to plot her suicide on a school field trip. After careful consideration of various plans, Julie schemes to wander off from the group, swallow a handful of sleeping pills, and freeze to death in the snow. Once again, Kundera stresses the irrationality of this plan:

> It was grotesque, heartbreakingly grotesque: here she was prepared to give him everything, her virginity of course, but also, if he wanted it, her health and any sacrifice he could think up, and still she couldn't bring herself to disobey a miserable school principal. Should she let herself be defeated by such pettiness? Her self-disgust was unbearable, and she wanted to get free of it at any cost; she wanted to reach some greatness in which her pettiness would disappear; a greatness before which he would ultimately have to bow down; she wanted to die.[68]

Unlike Helena and Immaculata, Julie "laid plans for her death with her usual practicality." However, despite this practicality, Julie recognizes the absurdity of this gesture: "Could she not see a blatant disproportion between the triviality of the cause and the hugeness of the act? Did she not know that her project was excessive? Of course, she did, but the excess was precisely what appealed to her. She did not want to be reasonable. She did not want to behave in a measured way. She did not want to measure, she did not want to reason. She admired her passion, knowing that passion is by definition excessive."[69] This rejection of reason in favor of excessive performativity diverges from Tolstoy's muted description of Anna's suicide. Although Tolstoy denies the reader the spectacle and the chaos that follows Anna's final moments at the train station, both Tolstoy and Kundera demonstrate a fascination with the irrational and the unpredictable in the decision-making process.

---

[67] Ibid., 108.
[68] Milan Kundera, *Ignorance*, trans. Linda Asher (London: Faber & Faber, 2003), 104.
[69] Ibid., 106.

Conclusion

As Kundera acknowledges in *Immortality*, "Many people, few ideas: we all think more or less the same, and we exchange, borrow, steal thoughts from one another."[70] Fascinated by intertextuality, Kundera frequently inserts allusions to writers, philosophers, artists, and musicians whom he admires, and his 1985 adaptation of Denis Diderot's "Jacques le Fataliste" confirms his interest in revisiting the canon. In the *New York Times* article "An Introduction to a Variation," Kundera offers the following defense of his "variation on Diderot": "No one contests the originality of a Rousseau, a Laclos or a Goethe on the grounds that they owe a great deal (they and the evolution of the novel in general) to naive old Richardson. If the similarity between Sterne and Diderot is so striking, it is only because their common enterprise has remained isolated in the history of the novel."[71]

Kundera's eagerness to attribute ideas and themes to other artists raises the question of why the Czech author does not readily credit Tolstoy. Perhaps, wary of exile within the "Slavic" canon by Western intellectuals preoccupied with the Cold War binaries, Kundera eschews any links between his work and the Russian literary tradition in favor of residing alongside Diderot over Dostoevsky. However, a closer examination of Kundera's oeuvre reveals that his novels complicate "the handy dichotomies of feeling-reason, Dostoyevsky-Diderot."

Bibliography

BBC News Russkaia sluzhba. "Nevynosimaia legkost' zhizni ne zdes'. Umer Milan Kundera." Accessed January 19, 2024, https://www.bbc.com/russian/features-55552154.

Brodsky, Joseph. "Why Milan Kundera Is Wrong about Dostoevsky." *Cross Currents, A Yearbook of Central European Culture* 5 (1985): 477-83.

——. "Why Milan Kundera Is Wrong About Dostoevsky." *The New York Times*, February 17, 1985, sec. Book Review.

Christian, Reginald Frank. *Tolstoy's "War and Peace": A Study.* Oxford: Clarendon Press, 1962.

Coxon, A. H. *Fragments of Parmenides: A Critical Text with Introduction and Translation, the Ancient Testimonia and a Commentary.* Translated by Richard McKirahan. Las Vegas: Parmenides Publishing, 2009.

---

[70] Milan Kundera, *Immortality*, 205.
[71] Kundera, "An Introduction to a Variation."

Hagan, John. "A Pattern of Character Development in *War and Peace*: Prince Andrej." *The Slavic and East European Journal* 13, no. 2 (1969): 164-90, https://doi.org/10.2307/306784.

Kaufmann, Walter Arnold. *Nietzsche: Philosopher, Psychologist, Antichrist.* 4. ed., 20th pr. Princeton: Princeton University Press, 2011.

Kundera, Milan. "An Introduction to a Variation." *The New York Times*, January 6, 1985, sec. Book Review.

——. "An Introduction to a Variation: Diderot or Dostoevsky." *Cross Currents, A Yearbook of Central European Culture* 5 (1985): 469-76.

——. *Ignorance.* Translated by Linda Asher. London: Faber & Faber, 2003.

——. *Immortality.* Translated by Peter Kussi. New York: HarperCollins, 1999.

——. *Jacques and His Master.* Translated by Simon Callow. London: Faber & Faber, 1986.

——. *Nesmrtelnost.* Toronto: Sixty-Eight Publishers, 1993.

——. *Nesnesitelná lehkost bytí.* Toronto: Sixty-Eight Publishers, 1985.

——. *Slowness.* Translated by Linda Asher. London: Faber & Faber, 1996.

——. *The Art of the Novel.* Translated by Linda Asher. London: Faber and Faber, 1990.

——. *The Curtain: An Essay in Seven Parts.* Translated by Linda Asher. New York: HarperCollins, 2007.

——. *The Joke.* Translated by Aaron Asher. HarperPerennial, 2001.

——. *Žert.* Toronto: Sixty-Eight Publishers, 1989.

Nietzsche, Friedrich. *On the Genealogy of Morals & Ecce Homo.* Translated by Walter Arnold Kaufmann. New York: Vintage Books, 1989.

——. *The Gay Science.* Translated by Walter Kaufmann. New York: Random House, 1974.

O'Brien, John. *Milan Kundera & Feminism: Dangerous Intersections.* Basingstoke: MacMillan, 1995.

Tarán, Leonardo. *Parmenides: A Text with Translation, Commentary, and Critical Essays.* 3. Pr. Princeton: Princeton University Press, 1965.

Tolstoi, Lev. "Smert' Ivana Il'icha." In L. N. Tolstoi, *Sobranie sochinenii*, 57-115. 20 vols. Vol. 12, Moskva: Khudozhestvennaia literatura, 1964.

——. *Voina i mir.* 4 vols. Moskva: Molodaia gvardiia, 1978.

Tolstoy, Leo. *The Death of Ivan Ilyich and Other Stories.* Translated by Richard Pevear and Larissa Volokhonsky. Vintage Classics, 2010.

——. *War and Peace.* Translated by Richard Pevear and Larissa Volokhonsky. London: Vintage Classic, 2011.

Wasiolek, Edward. *Tolstoy's Major Fiction.* Chicago: University of Chicago Press, 1981.

Chapter 3
Injurious attachments and dangerous culs-de-sac: Gendered reading and deconstructing "deconstructive" logic of selected early Czech novels by Milan Kundera[1]

Jan Matonoha
Institute of Czech Literature of the Czech Academy of Sciences, Czech Rep.

Abstract

Focusing on two early novels by Milan Kundera and drawing on the book penned by John O'Brien, *Milan Kundera and Feminism: Dangerous Intersections*, the author–while agreeing and admiring the logic and the argument put forward in the given book–aims at taking the analysis a step further. He postulates not a binary or dual-logic feminist reading of Milan Kundera's (in this particular case, early, but by extension all his) novels, but a triple one. Thus, instead of apparent sexism and machismo to be overdrawn or overwritten by underlying feminist leanings in Kundera's prose, as argued in O'Brien's treatise, the author argues for the need to take a further step, pointing out Kundera's sexism, misogyny and phallocentrism on the third, less obvious and palpable, but no less (if not even more) dangerous level. The author designates this insidious logic–having been inspired by the concepts of Wendy Brown and Judith Butler–by the term *injurious attachments*.

Keywords: Milan Kundera, the novels *Life Is Elsewhere* and *Farewell Waltz*, gender critique, triple, not a dual criticism of the gender logic of Kundera's

---

[1] This text was proofread within the project Development of Research and Popularisation Resources of the Institute of Czech Literature of the CAS, CZ.02.2.69/0.0/0.0/ 18_054/0014701, co-funded by the EU's European Structural and Investment Funds within the operational programme Research, Development and Education.

novels, literary text, interpretation of literary text and interpellation of readers, discursive emergence of silence, injurious attachments.

* * *

Dangerous intersections or injurious attachments? Introduction and conceptual approach

"Upon close scrutiny, Kundera's self-conscious use of binary oppositions in the representation of women actually maximizes the possibility of breaking down or transcending simplistic representations," says a crucial thinker on the issue of the difficult relationship between Kundera and feminism, John O'Brien.[2] He follows this by saying that Milan Kundera's[3] work "*exposes not espouses* [emphasis mine, JM] misogynistic representations and perspectives of women."[4] I completely agree with John O'Brien's point that one must not rush to draw conclusions regarding MK's fiction, as its characters, more often than not, are turned into their opposites.[5] However, while I consider O'Brien's account of MK's misogynistic tropes as thoroughly convincing, as well as his deconstruction of this sexism, I find it–in certain regards–worth re-thinking. What I am after is a somewhat more complex nature of sexism.[6] Here, I am aiming to address what I see as a difficult, thorny, and profoundly troublesome issue of MK and his relationship to the gendering of characters in his early Czech stories and novels (although by no means do the issues discussed below

---

[2] John O'Brien, *Milan Kundera & Feminism: Dangerous Intersections* (New York: St. Martin's Press, 1995), 64.
[3] From now on as MK only (unless otherwise stated).
[4] O'Brien, 70.
[5] Examples abound; for the sake of argument, let's mention almost all of the characters in *The Joke*; the ginger-haired girl in *Life Is Elsewhere* shown (eventually) not as the naive and simple character she initially appears to be but as a sexually experienced and unfaithful one that deceives Jaromil (although in love with him); the American spa resident Bertleff in the *Farewell Waltz* changes from a generous and almost god-like man to a naïve (or alternatively consenting) cuckold, etc.
[6] Also, John O'Brien reads MK's novels as a case of unseen "deconstruction," of which I am rather skeptical, for the reasons I aim to show below. Quotation marks are due here not because of a quotation but due to MK's dislike of post-structuralism and preference for either lucid French Enlightenment authors or Central European Austrian authors such as Hermann Broch or Robert Musil. MK, as just mentioned, claims to be a great fan of the Enlightenment, but his view of this period is very different from, let's say, Theodor Adorno, Max Horkheimer or Michel Foucault. Cf. among others Theodor W. Adorno and Max Horkheimer, *Dialectic of Enlightenment* (Stanford: Stanford University Press, 1947).

pertain to just these). Somewhat differently from O'Brien, I postulate not a dichotomic structure of male chauvinism to be later deconstructed in Kundera's "deconstructive" logic, as John O'Brien does, but rather a triadic one. The sequence I posit is the following: a) an overt sexism, b) deconstructive tropes of such sexism, c) less obvious (and hidden within the deconstructive tropes) and all the more dangerous and injurious sexism (i.e., based on injurious attachments that obscure a clear view, see below). In other words, it is precisely these alibis of (sometimes more, sometimes less) complex ambiguities and paradoxes that make MK's fiction very appealing, yet also at the same time–gender-wise–injuring.[7] I choose to label this more complicated triadic structure–of overt and obvious sexism, deconstruction of sexism, and eventually sexism occurring upon a less obvious and perceptible, and therefore more profound level–as *injurious attachments*, i.e., such attachments which invite identifications, yet are paradoxically detrimental to a reader.

---

[7] Feminism, of course, covers a large area of (often mutually contradictory) approaches, ranging–roughly speaking–from the paradigm of (radical) difference, as can be best exemplified by names such as Luce Irigaray or Hélène Cixous, over to the arguably most prominent paradigm of equality of genders to deconstructive (Monique Wittig, Judith Butler, etc.) approach arguing that it is not only gender that is culturally constructed, but the very notion of seemingly *a priori* given and fixed as essentially discursively constructed (yet strategically forgotten as such). Feminist literary theory views literary texts as a means of interpellations of the reader and his/her vision of the world (Fetterley, Felman), as a site in which subjectivity is negotiated (Belsey), and as such it needs to be critically analyzed with respect to the unseen patriarchal presuppositions and preferences implicit in it, preferences with which the reader may unconsciously identify within the reception of the text and its narrative strategies. In addition to the need for a critical reading of the canonical work of male authors (Gilbert and Gubar), feminist literary scholarship has also emphasized a focus on the autonomous, embedded tradition of women's literary production (Showalter). Overall, feminism is a broadly diverse field of movements, be it Marxist oriented approaches (Rowbotham, Eagelton, Barrett, Mouffe, Kaplan, etc.), psychoanalytical ones (Mitchell, Kristeva, Grosz etc.), postmodern, poststructuralist, and deconstructive ones (Flax, Jardine, Meese, Johnson, Elam, Waugh, Kirby etc.), Deleuzian, and posthumanist ones (Braidotti, Haraway, Colebrook etc.), engaged in postcolonial studies (bell hooks, Spivak etc.), narratological approaches (Lanser, R. R. Warhol, Bal), especially in connection with critical readings of the literary canon (the aforementioned S. Gilber and S. Gubar, Kolodny), the logic of the gaze (Mulvey, T. de Lauretis, Silverman), the critical examination of popular culture (Radway), etc. Out of this broad field of approaches, I have chosen one particular feminist (or broadly philosophical) approach, that of *wounded attachments* and *injuring (or injurious) identities*, coined by Wendy Brown and Judith Butler, respectively (see below).

In discussing the early works by MK, I rely generally upon a structure I followed in my earlier works.[8] This structure–of a paradoxical and contradictory logic (as far as the literature is concerned[9])–stands as follows: while the alternative literary scene (if we choose to label MK as such, although this is by no means true, for instance, regarding his early poetry,) stood in opposition to the then official regime, it remained complicit with it in terms of the issues of gender emancipation. To grasp this issue conceptually, I set out from the concepts coined by Wendy Brown and Judith Butler[10] and choose to call this complex mechanism (as noted above) *injurious attachments* and *the discursive emergence of silence*.[11] In a nutshell, I propose to discuss the ways gender was excluded or silenced by interpellating[12] readers, in the first step, through positive, dignified values (e.g., sophisticated deconstructive games in MK's novels); these, however, are at the same time, on the second and much

---

[8] Cf. among others Jan Matonoha, "Dispositives of silence: gender, feminism and Czech literature between 1948 and 1989," in *The Politics of Gender Culture under State Socialism: An Expropriated Voice*, ed. Hana Havelková and Libora Oates-Indruchová (London: Routledge, 2014), 162–87.

[9] But Hana Havelková reaches an identical conclusion regarding general gender dynamics on the social level as well. Compare Hana Havelková and Libora Oates-Indruchová, *The Politics of Gender Culture under State Socialism: An Expropriated Voice* (London: Routledge, 2014).

[10] Wendy Brown, *States of Injury: Power and Freedom in Late Modernity* (Princeton: Princeton University Press, 1995); Judith Butler, *The Psychic Life of Power: Theories in Subjection* (Stanford: Stanford University Press, 1997).

[11] Although it does not relate directly to my take on the topic, one of the important books on the currency of silence as a discursive trope is Maria-Luisa Achino-Loeb, ed., *Silence: The Currency of Power* (New York: Berghahn Books, 2006). For a more comprehensive overview on the secondary literature focusing on the issue of "silence," see Jan Matonoha, "Dispositives of silence."

[12] By the expression "interpellating," I refer to the (post)Marxist concept of interpellation coined by Althusser, meaning that in the modern industrial era, a person has internalized the sense of being docile and ready to make him-/herself available to official power without ever questioning the source of authority to which he/she subjects him-/herself. The example Althusser provides is that of a person who readily produces his/her ID when approached by a policeman without ever questioning the authority with which the policeman is endowed by a state. But in general, Althusser argues, modern subjects (sic!) have made themselves docile and available to the power of the modern state in a very broad sense, internalizing such a stance and ceasing to be aware of it. See Louis Althusser, "Ideology and Ideological State Apparatus," in his *Essays on Ideology* (London: Verso, 1970).

more difficult level to notice and grasp, wounding and dis-empowering.[13] Building upon Althusser's notion of *interpellation* (here, to address an implied and invoked reader's response), I am trying to capture this by concepts of *injurious attachments* and *discursive emergence of silencing*, which leads to what (echoing Foucault's term *dispositive*) I choose to refer to as *dispositives of silence*.

There has been a significant body of literature written on the relationship between gender and independent Czech literature prior to 1989[14] and the topic

---

[13] As far as MK's own position towards feminism goes, I want to situate it in the context of the following that could be mentioned, when asked specifically about his attitude towards women (and a reproach which could be levelled against him from feminist positions), he replied, symptomatically enough, in the way that seemed to satisfy a respondent (or at least did not provoke further questions), yet is typically and traditionally essentialist (and what I find rather frustrating, in a manner of satisfied confidence which, to my mind, is far from granted here). MK stated there that–copping out of the responsibility to tackle the question to some degree–women are a mysterious enigma that cannot be easily solved and seen through. Cf. Jordan Elgrably, "Conversations with Milan Kundera," in *Critical Essays on Milan Kundera*, ed. Peter Petro (New York: G. K. Hall & Co, 1999), 67-68. Kundera thus, to my mind, simplified the complexity of female identity to a one-dimensional conventional impenetrable otherness that at last cannot speak and requires a male narrator to provide her with his own voice. Compare, for example, the issue of the hairdresser Lucy from the novel *The Joke* who is the only one who does not fall prey to sophisticated yet ultimately mistaken interpretations as all the other characters do, yet paying the price for such a privileged position, by being deprived of her own voice, remaining silent. See Matonoha, "Dispositives of silence."

[14] Paulina Bren, *The Greengrocer and His TV. The Culture of Communism after the 1968 Prague Spring* (Ithaca: Cornell University Press, 2010); Peggy Watson, "The Rise of Masculinism in Eastern Europe," *New Left Review*, no. 198 (1993): 71-82; Alena Wagnerová, "České ženy na cestě od reálného socialismu k reálnému kapitalismu," in Marie Chřibková, Josef Chuchma, and Eva Klimentová, eds., *Feminismus devadesátých let českýma očima* (Praha: One Woman Press, 1999), 80-90; Jiřina Šiklová, "Feminism and the Roots of Apathy in the Czech Republic," *Social Research* 64, no. 2, (1997): 258-80; Gerlinda Šmausová, "Emancipace, socialismus a feminismus," in *Tvrdošíjnost myšlenky, od feministické kriminologie k teorii genderu*, ed. Libora Oates-Indruchová (Praha: Sociologické nakladatelství – SLON, 2011 [2006]); Hana Havelková, "Women in and after a 'classless' society," in *Women and Social Class. International Feminist Perspectives*, ed. Christine Zmroczek and Pat Mahony (London: Taylor and Francis/UCL, 1999), 69-84; Hana Havelková and Libora Oates-Indruchová, *The Politics of Gender Culture under State Socialism: An Expropriated Voice* (London: Routledge, 2014); Madelaine Hron, "'Word Made Flesh': Czech Women's Fiction from Communism to Post-Communism," *Journal of International Women's Studies* 4, no. 3 (2003): 81-98; Tiina A. Kirss, "Přítelkyně z domu

of gender in literature involves a number of critical issues and pertains to a number of literary texts by significant authors of Czech (independent) literature–among others–Ludvík Vaculík, Václav Havel, Josef Škvorecký, Pavel Kohout, Ivan Klíma, Arnošt Lustig, Alexandr Kliment (as well as Bohumil Hrabal, to some extent), etc., as well as female authors such as Eda Kriseová, Eva Kantůrková, Tereza Boučková, Iva Pekárková, and others. MK, being the most visible case as one of the most important "Czech" authors (or at least he is perceived so), deserves special attention in this context though.[15] In the text

---

smutku Evy Kantůrkové, Genderová mapa vězení," *Jedním okem/One Eye Open*, special issue, *Gender and Historical Memory* 1 (1998): 109-21; Zsófia Lóránd, *The Feminist Challenge to the Socialist State in Yugoslavia* (London: Palgrave Macmillan, 2018); Agnieszka Mrózik, "Crossing Boundaries: The Case of Wanda Wasilewska and Polish Communism," *Aspasia. The International Yearbook of Central, Eastern, and Southeastern European Women's and Gender History* 11 (2017): 19-53; Nicola Nixon, "Cinderella's Suspicions: Feminism in the Shadow of the Cold War," *Australian Feminist Studies* 14, no. 35 (2001): 209-23; Libora Oates-Indruchová, "The Beauty and the Loser: Cultural Representations of Gender in Late State Socialism," *Signs. Journal of Women in Culture and Society* 37, no. 2 (2012): 357-83; Libora Oates-Indruchová, "Unraveling a Tradition, or Spinning a Myth? Gender Critique in Czech Society and Culture," *Slavic Review* 75, no. 4 (2016): 919-43; Laure Occhipinti, "Two Steps Back? Anti-Feminism in Eastern Europe," *Anthropology Today* 12, no. 6 (1996): 13-18; Marci Shore, "Narrative / Archive / Trace: The Trial of Milada Horákové," *Jedním okem/One Eye Open* 1 (1998): 27-41; Elena Sokol, "Vaculík a Procházková: Czech Sexual Poetics or Polemics?" *Slovo a smysl* 2, no. 3 (2005): 197-210; Jiřina Šmejkalová, "Co je feminismus? Kam s ní/m? Na okraj ženské otázky a současného feminismu," *Tvar* 2, nos. 37-41, parts 1-5 (1991): 16; Jiřina Šmejkalová, "Do Czech Women Need Feminism? Perspectives of Feminist Theories and Practices in Czechoslovakia," *Women's Studies International Forum* 17, no. 3 (1994): 277-82; Eva Věšínová, "Feminismus ... ano?" *Iniciály* 2, no. 25 (1992): 1-6; Eva Věšínová, "Backlash a osudy feminismu (interview by Naďa Macurová)," *Tvar* 6, no. 1 (1995): 12; Eva Věšínová-Kalivodová, "Czech Society in-between the Waves," *European Journal of Women's Studies* 22, no. 4 (2005): 421-35; Mirek Vodrážka, "Před velkým exodem. Kořen českého antifeminismu," *Tvar* 4, nos. 49-50 (1993): 1, 8-9; Mirek Vodrážka, *Rozumí české ženy vlastní historii?* (Praha: Academia, 2017); Peggy Watson, "The Rise of Masculinism in Eastern Europe," *New Left Review*, no. 198 (1993): 71-82; etc.

[15] As to the work of MK specifically, a truly vast body of literature exists (of which I name just a few). However, regarding links (or arguably, their absence) between MK and feminism, three works must be named here on which I rely (and debate), namely the book by John O'Brien and articles by Bronislava Volková and Anželina Penčeva (see note #32 below). See also these books by Czech authors: K. Chvatík, *Svět románů Milana Kundery* (Brno: Atlantis, 1994); Tomáš Kubíček, *Vyprávět příběh: naratologické kapitoly k románům Milana Kundery* (Brno: Host, 2001); Tomáš Kubíček, *Středoevropan Milan Kundera* (Olomouc: Periplum, 2013); Jakub Češka, *Království motivů. Motivická analýza*

románů Milana Kundery (Praha: Togga, 2005); Jakub Češka, *Za poetikou Milana Kundery* (Brno: Host, 2022); Jiří Dientsbier and Jiřina Dientsbierová, eds., *Evropan Milan Kundera* (Praha: Rada pro mezinárodní vztahy, 2010); Aleš Haman, *Tři stálice moderní české prózy: Neruda, Čapek, Kundera* (Praha: Karolinum, 2014); Jan Novák, *Kundera: Český život a doba* (Praha: Argo, Paseka, 2020); and others. Or within the international sphere (with some of them by Czechs living abroad), e.g., R. C. Porter, *Milan Kundera: A Voice from Central Europe* (Aarhus: Arkona, 1981); Ch. Buchwald, *Der Kitsch, der Liebesakt und die Fallen der Welt* (Munich: Hanser, 1984); M. Němcová-Banerjee, *Terminal Paradox: The Novels of Milan Kundera* (New York: Grove Weidenfeld, 1990); A. Aji, ed., *Milan Kundera and the Art of Fiction: Critical Essays* (New York: Garland, 1992); F. Misurella, *Understanding Milan Kundera. Public Events, Private Affairs* (Columbia: University of South Carolina Press, 1993); M. Řízek, *Comment devient-on Kundera, images de l'écrivain, écrivain de l'image* (Paris: L'Harmattan, 2001); H. Píchová, *The Art of Memory in Exile. Vladimír Nabokov and Milan Kundera* (Carbondale: Southern Illinois University Press, 2002); T. C. Merrill, *The Book of Imitation and Desire, Reading Milan Kundera with René Girard* (New York: Continuum, 2013); N. Porta, *Auf der Suche nach eine reigenen Identität zwischen Osten und Westen, die Mitteleuropa-Konzeption: bei Czesław Miłosz, Jan Patočka und Milan Kundera* (Herne: Schäfer, 2014); K. von Kunes, *Milan Kundera's Fiction, A Critical Approach to Existential Betrayals* (Lanham, Maryland: Lexington Books, 2019); E. Le Grand, *Kundera aneb paměť touhy* (Olomouc: Votobia, 1998). As to articles in the international sphere, I would–truly selectively only–name the following: J. Čulík, "Milan Kundera," in *Twentieth-Century Eastern European Writers*, ed. S. Serafin (Gale Group: Detroit, 2001), 208-26; M. Goetz-Stankiewicz, "Life in a Group," in M. Goetz-Stankiewicz, *The Silenced Theatre* (Toronto: De Gruyter, 1979), 190-223; D. Lodge, "Milan Kundera, and the Idea of the Author in Modern Criticism," *Critical Quarterly* 26, no. 1-2 (1984): 105-21; T. Eagleton, "Estrangement and Irony," *Salmagundi*, no. 73 (1987): 25-32 (Seven articles about MK in this issue); R. Rorty, "Philosophers, Novelists and Inter-Cultural Comparisons, Heidegger, Kundera and Dickens," in *Culture and Modernity: East-West Philosophic Perspectives*, ed. Eliot Deutsch (Honolulu: University of Hawaii Press, 1991), 3-20; A. Thomas, "Fiction and Non-Fiction in Milan Kundera's *Book of Laughter and Forgetting*," in A. Thomas, *The Labyrinth of the Word: Truth and Representation in Czech Literature* (Munich: R. Oldenbourg Verlag, 1995); T. Parnell, "Sterne and Kundera: The Novel of Variations and the 'noisy Foolishness of Human Certainty'," in *Laurence Sterne in Modernism and Postmodernism*, ed. David Pierce and Peter de Voogd (Amsterdam-Atlanta: Rodopi, 1995), 147-56; P. Steiner, "*The Joke* by Milan Kundera," in P. Steiner, *The Deserts of Bohemia* (Ithaca: Cornell University Press, 2000), 196-217; X. Galmiche, "Le Rire jaune dans l´oeuvre de Milan Kundera," *Esprit*, no. 281 (2002): 52-61; H. Píchová, "Milan Kundera and the Identity of Central Europe," in *Comparative Central European Culture*, ed. Steven Tötösy de Zepetnek (Purdue: Purdue University Press, 2002), 103-14; P. Bugge, "Clementis's Hat; or, Is Kundera a Palimpsest?" *Kosmas* 16, no. 2 (2003); P. Hrubý, "Milan Kundera's Czech Problem," *Kosmas* 17, no. 1 (2003); S. Höhne, "Exil-Kulturen, Zur Problematik des Interkulturellen bei Milan Kundera," *Brücken. Neue Folge* 11 (2003): 285-96; V. Papoušek, "Kundera's Paradise

below, I proceed in quite a traditional manner in subchapters ordered by individual significant characters featuring in the given two novels (with a particular "preface" of the given issue present by no means in MK's fiction only).

Novels by MK as injuring gender blind-spots not as an exception but a rule in the Czech literature after 1948 (A handful of examples)

Libuše Heczková maintained that there was virtually no feminism present in Czech literature after 1948, and this is (arguably with few–implicit–exceptions such as Alena Vostrá or Zdena Salivarová) undoubtedly true, and the work of MK is a good case here. However, the situation is by no means so simple and straightforward, as I will try to demonstrate by the critical reading of an undoubtedly interesting book by John O'Brien. I will begin, however, with a somewhat broader topic, that of the scholarly literature that focuses on Czech literature and gender. Thus, in order to emphasize that the texts by MK examined below do not stand as a solitary exception at all, I would like to summarize (albeit only partially) some examples from my earlier paper.[16] At the outset, I have to emphasize that I deeply value both the artistic quality and personal bravery of the authors mentioned below. Out of the several examples I discussed here, I shall mention just a few of them, some connected by the aspect of a voice, or rather a symptomatic absence of it, as well as further

---

Lost," in *The Exile and Return of Writers from East-Central Europe*, ed. John Neubauer and Borbála Zsuzsanna Török (Berlin–New York: De Gruyter, 2009), 384-95; A. Catalano, "Metamorfosi di un mito, Julius Fučík e Milan Kundera tra stalinismo e normalizzazione," *eSamizdat* 7, nos. 2/3 (2009): 15-27; M. Havelka, "Der Prager Frühling in einer Perspektive generationenspezifischer Erwartungen. Zur Diskussion zwischen Milan Kundera und Václav Havel im Winter 1968/69," in *Die Kunst des Überwinterns, Musik und Literatur um 1968*, ed. Jörn Peter Hiekel (Köln: Böhlau Verlag, 2011), 103-16; Ch. Sabatos, "Shifting contexts: The boundaries of Milan Kundera's Central Europe," in *Contexts, Subtexts and Pretexts. Literary translation in Eastern Europe and Russia*, ed. Brian James Baer (Amsterdam: John Benjamins, 2011), 19-32; J. Rubeš, "Translation as condition and theme in Milan Kundera's novels," in ibid., 317-22; Kh. Maier, "Prevrashaia Albaniiu v Siriiu – ideologiia i «operativnosť» poeticheskoi kartografii v perevodakh Milana Kundery kontsa 1940-kh – nach. 1950-kh godov," *Acta slavica Estonica* 10 (2018): 375-95; Jessie Labov, "Divergent definitions of Central Europe, Miłosz and Kundera," and "Flight from Byzantium, Kundera vs. Brodsky on Dostoyevski," both in Labov, *Transatlantic Central Europe: Contesting Geography and Redefining Culture beyond the Nation* (Budapest–New York: Central European University Press, 2019); and Elgrably, "Conversations with Milan Kundera."

[16] Matonoha, "Dispositives of silence."

aspects. I shall also include very brief remarks on other authors I focus more extensively elsewhere.[17]

I shall start with one paradigmatic case, that of a silent–and supposedly sublime, yet in fact, leading to silence–female voice. In an influential *shoa* text by Arnošt Lustig (himself a Holocaust survivor) in the 1964 novel *A Prayer for Katerina Horovitzova*, the eponymous female character decides to bring about her own dignified, self-chosen annihilation by grabbing a gun from a Nazi official enchanted by the look of her young, beautiful, naked body and shooting him, being "rewarded" by a number of gunshots from a group of Nazi soldiers in response. In short, the character of Katerina Horovitzova has a beautiful, seductive body (and even the crucial feature of agency–shooting a Nazi official dead), yet an absent voice. The other example is the novel *Too Loud a Solitude* (1977), penned by Bohumil Hrabal, that features the crucial character of a Roma girl whose name keeps escaping the narrator's (the character Haňťa) mind (re-appearing only at the moment–in one of the versions of the text at least–of his suicide, thus underlining her importance for him). Yet, as in both cases just mentioned, the female character does not have a voice of her own, she is silent.

Another example that could be quoted are plays by Václav Havel, among others, his *Ztížená možnost soustředění* (*The Increased Difficulty of Concentration*, 1969, or *Largo desolato*, 1984) where female characters appear mostly not as autonomous beings but (to put it mildly) as the mere marginalized, reductive functions of lovers, objects of desire or manipulation, at times helpers or witnesses or projections of male (super)ego and his endless narcissistic, moral self-scrutinizing. The structure it offers is a very traditional one: on the one hand, there is (by his oppression) a morally privileged, (self)doubting, thinking, and talking male. On the other, a merely passively participating and on-looking female. What is different about this position from the traditional standing of women as "other" described by Simone de Beauvoir or Luce Irigaray, is its affective seductiveness, guaranteed by a specific symbolic capital of the haunted and marginalized–and thus paradoxically (in the eyes of both today's readers of canonical works and the then readers of *samizdat* texts) privileged voice of a dissent writer inviting the reader to make identifications which are however profoundly injurious ones. What disappears

---

[17] I have published several articles on these issues in a more extensive way (see the footnote below and the list of secondary literature below).

from view is that the female figures consistently feature here as mere helpers, or downright sexualized objects of male desire, not as autonomous figures.

Yet the most symptomatic, for the present case, is Václav Havel's essay (or rather a particular part of it) from April 1985 entitled *Anatomy of a Reticence* (*Anatomie jedné zdrženlivosti*). There, he claims that both dissent and feminism are *dada*, yet–I would argue–he uses the term *dada* in two completely different ways. I believe that Havel's argument of the type "dissent as dada" and "feminism as dada" has two very different meanings: a) the first: a playful, irreverent, and quirky one that stresses the undermining, subversive nature of the dissent movement; b) the second: a negative, derogative, bizarre, and laughable one–in feminism.

A paramount text of Czech *samizdat*, *The Czech Dream Book* (*Český snář*, 1981) by Ludvík Vaculík could also be listed here in this context. This work can be, rightly, I think, considered a fascinating key literary text of (not only) the dissent movement. It features–and is thus intriguing to read through such a broad scope of figures–major names from the dissent culture.[18] Seen from a gender perspective, though, it can be considered as highly sexist and–in my words–injurious. These fascinating and, at the same time, injurious features cannot be easily separated. *The Czech Dream Book* thus represents yet another example of many other dissents, exile, and *samizdat* works of fiction that suffer from an identical problem: they are great and very appealing. From a gender perspective, though, they can be seen as profoundly troublesome.[19]

In *The Czech Dream Book*, the narrative reveals that, given his unfortunate political circumstances (of having been thrown out of work at a prestigious Czech weekly), the authorial subject does not spend his time at home on domestic chores but compensates for his forced passivity with other activities:

---

[18] For instance, Jan Patočka, Václav Černý, Dominik Tatarka, Jan Trefulka, Jiří Dienstbier, Sr., Eva Kantůrková, Eda Kriseová, Ivan Binar, Jiří Gruša, Karol Sidon, Radim Vašinka, Sergej Machonin, Ladislav Hejdánek, Zdeněk Rotrekl, Andrej Stankovič, Jiří Pechar, and many others.

[19] While it is undoubtedly true that there are strong moments of auto-subversion of referentiality, lapses in a time continuum, tongue-in-cheek games, and discrepancies between time narrated and narrative time, or in short, strong post-structuralist moments in what appears–at first glance–as a piece of an autonomous autobiographical document from dissent environment (and Irina Wutsdorff clearly points all this out in her paper), in terms of its gender articulation, this text is far away from being anything but post-structuralist, I would argue. See Irina Wutsdorff, "Post-Structuralism under Communist Conditions? The Construction of Identity in Czech Dissident Literature," *Slovo a smysl* 7, no. 14 (2010): 103–14.

writing and publishing the *samizdat Petlice* (Padlock edition, which is symbolically titled, referring to the officially published series called "The Key"). Although at home, his entire attention is focused on the public sphere, his *samizdat* publishing activities, and their consequences.

The existing social set-up (cast upon and subsequently internalized) of double burden and more or less compulsory emancipation (expropriated from feminism by a ruling regime)[20] generated a (sub-conscious, unaware) fascination (as a sort of counter-model) with the conventional bourgeois household model that was, in the given moment and period (and hopefully forever), unavailable. Almost thirty years after *The Feminine Mystique* and *The Female Eunuch*, the situation is missed (in the text "Exercise in Carelessness" summarized by the narrator) when "men cease to be men and women cease to be women."[21]

Regarding Drahomíra Pithartová, the wife of the lawyer and post-1989 senator Petr Pithart, the narrator comments approvingly that she had welcomed him at home "in the role of a completely happy and satisfied woman with children at school and a husband at work, an apartment all tided-up, dinner ready, spending her day reading."[22] From a feminist standpoint, a commentary would be redundant here.

Finally, what I find quite eye-catching is the division between (creative) writing as opposed to (granted) crucial, yet still simply reproductive copying. The narrator says that should he find a free and available pair of women's hands, he would have a particular paper (by evangelical theologian, writer, and dissident Jan Šimsa on [Karel] Havlíček) copied.[23] Women are presented in Vaculík's "documentary" novel as surely risk-taking and courageous but mostly dealing in common day-to-day issues as *samizdat* "editors," transcribers, etc. By no means do I mean to say this work is not praiseworthy.[24]

---

[20] Cf. Havelková and Oates-Indruchová, *The Politics of Gender*.
[21] Ludvík Vaculík, *Český snář* (Brno: Atlantis, 1981) 41.
[22] Ibid., 42.
[23] Ibid., 54.
[24] Cf. here crucial names such as Kamila Bendová, Eva Kantůrková, Ruth Klímová, Eda Kriseová, Kamila Ruth Křížková, Anna Marvanová, Dana Němcová, Anna Šabatová, Eva Šimečková, Petruška Šustrová, Zdena Tominová. For more on this see Mary Hrabik-Samal "Ženy a neoficiální kultura a literatura v Československu v letech 1969–1989," in *Přítomnosť minulosti, minulosť přítomnosti*, ed. Jolana Kusá and Peter Zajac (Bratislava: Nadácia Milana Šimečku, 1996), 81–95; Jiřina Šiklová, "Women and the Charta 77 Movement in Czechoslovakia," in *Conscious Acts and the Politics of Social Change*.

However, it is a work that is strictly *reproductive, not a productive one*. That is, men write and create; women do not, they only transcribe. They are praised for their work in Vaculík's novel (the praise having unmissable sexist undertones here), but they have no agency either.

Another example that could be cited is a novel by Pavel Kohout titled *The Hangwoman* (*Katyně*).[25] It is a story–conceived purposefully and in a challenging and provocative cold-blooded manner–of the career of a withdrawn, inert, cold girl. From a gender perspective and within the context of Czech fiction of the 70s and 80s, it is quite noteworthy that the protagonist is female. In most other cases in works by Ludvík Vaculík, Václav Havel, Ivan Klíma, Milan Kundera, Josef Škvorecký, Jiří Gruša, Jan Novák, Jan Pelc, and others, female characters are cast–at best–mostly in a secondary role assisting male figures, at worst in roles that are downright scopophilic and sexist. The job of the female protagonist is, however–in a purposefully bizarre slapstick manner–a truly shocking one: she works (in a dark parody of violent practices of official "Communist" power) as a professional executioner (in Czech, *katyně*, a female form derived from *kat*). The ironic observation that could be drawn here is rather obvious: in a rare instance when a female protagonist occupies a central character, the job and identity of the character is a *hangwoman*.[26]

Although a number of other examples could be quoted as instances of male chauvinism prevailing in the post-WWII Czech high culture, the male

---

Feminist Approaches to Social Movements, ed. Robin Teske and Marry Ann Tétrault (Columbia, S.C.: University of South Carolina Press, 2000), 265–72; Jiřina Šiklová, "O ženách v disentu," in *Rod ženský: Kdo jsme, odkud jsme přišly, kam jdeme?*, ed. Alena Vodáková and Olga Vodáková (Praha: Sociologické nakladatelství – SLON, 2003), 204–07; Jiřina Šiklová, "Podíl českých žen na samizdatu a opoziční činnosti v Československu období tzv. normalizace v letech 1969-1989," *Gender, rovné příležitosti, výzkum* 9, no. 2 (2008): 39–44; Kamila Bendová, "Ženy v Chartě 77," in *Opozice a odpor proti komunistickému režimu 1968–1989*, ed. Petr Blažek (Praha: Dokořán, 2005), 54–66. Cf. here also among others a recent book of interviews with dissent women: Naďa Straková and Marcela Linková, eds., *Bytová revolta: Jak ženy dělaly disent* (Praha: Academia, 2017). And there are surely exceptions as to literary work, e.g. Eva Kantůrková, Věra Jirousová or Eda Kriseová (cf. also Šiklová "Podíl českých žen").

[25] Originally published in German as *Die Henkerin* in Switzerland in 1978, in Czech in exile in Cologne, 1980, in English translation (New York: Putnam, 1981) by Káča Poláčková-Henley.

[26] See more closely, Jan Matonoha, "A Preliminary Survey of the Near Past: Periodizing Works of Czech Literary Authors Published from 1948 to 1989 from a Gender Perspective, with Special Regard to Dissent and Exile Literature of the 1970s and 1980s," *Kontradikce/Contradictions* 4, no. 2 (2020), 87–111.

chauvinism being obscured by a beneficial and thus, at the same time, invisible gloriole of fiction that opposes the rhetoric of the official regime, constituting what I refer to–following Wendy Brown and Judith Butler–*injurious attachments*, I choose to conclude this preface or introductory passage with a short overview of the seminal docu-fiction penned by the female author, Eva Kantůrková. Kantůrková (now more than ninety years of age) is a well-known figure of Czech dissent movement. While keeping the reasons for her politically motivated imprisonment rather mute in a very modest manner, she painted a colorful image of the predicaments of her female prison-mates in Prague's Ruzyně prison house in her "documentary" novel *My Companions in the Bleak House* (*Přítelkyně z domu smutku*).[27] Thus, apart from recording her own ways of experiencing her imprisonment, the ways these female figures have been portrayed are the crux of my discussion here. As the very title of the "docu-novel" suggests, Kantůrková herself might consider those prison-mates as her "friends." However, the text itself does not shy away from showing them in a not-very-likable perspective. Unlike in most other cases of dissent fiction of the period in question, it is populated with female heroines only, yet all of them (with the notable exception of the major dissent actor or agent, Jiřina Šiklová) –and that is the heart of the issue here–are (petty) criminals.

This critique of the feminist voice having been expropriated (as Hana Havelková puts it)[28] by the official sphere of the time could also be leveled regarding the seemingly more positive feminist dimension of leftist, "official" authors of the 1950s and beyond. Their "gender trouble" is that their feminist agenda, which is–unlike in the case of dissent authors, clearly present–does not stand on its own but, having been expropriated by official so-called Communist discourse as a mere prop or a building block of the egalitarian project, disappeared as an autonomous voice.[29] This issue could be seen by authors (who are both looked down upon as traditional apparatchiks yet are, in fact, rather intriguing) such as Jan Otčenášek, Marie Majerová, Marie Pujmanová, Valja Stýblová, Jarmila Loukotková, and a number of others.

To conclude this subchapter, I also aim to touch upon the non-fictional, yet culturally defining, text from the dissent sphere, the paradigmatic essay by Václav Benda titled "Parallel polis" from 1978. Here, he called for independent information, education, economic structures and–at least for the beginning of–

---

[27] Published in exile in 1984 in Cologne by Index publishers.
[28] See Havelková and Oates-Indruchová, *The Politics of Gender Culture*.
[29] Ibid.

parallel political life, and even for independent foreign policy.[30] From an intellectual of strongly conservative and Catholic leaning, one can hardly expect a significant reflection of the feminist agenda. At the same time, however, one can say that this independent parallel polis, which strove for "normality" within so-called "normalization" did indeed suffer from one blind spot, and that was a complete ignorance of possible gender reflection.[31]

Culs-de-sac and triadic structure of gender interpellations in MK's early(ier) fiction

As to the works by MK, there is, of course, an extensive list of secondary resources available there but only a few items concern the issue at hand. I find four of them truly relevant, the aforementioned book by John O'Brien, a book by Bronislava Volková, a paper by Iva Popovičová which, however, discusses a novel that is not in the focus of the present work, and a paper by Anželina Penčeva.[32] Thus, in their essays on the matter, Volková, Popovičová and Penčeva all remarked that female characters have, in general, primarily instrumental roles only in MK's fiction, being mere functions of the main male characters (mostly as lovers, partners, etc.). Also, female characters are often nameless and, more often than not, they are beautiful and, as such, serve as anonymous props in MK's multiple narrative strands. These observations, however, require additional attention and further critical feminist and "deconstructive" reading (against the backdrop of John O'Brien's book), I believe, hence my treatment of the subject.

I have commented upon the novels *The Joke* and *The Unbearable Lightness of Being* as well as on the short-story collection *Laughable Loves* (*Směšné lásky*,

---

[30] Jonathan Bolton, *Worlds of Dissent* (Cambridge: Harvard University Press, 2012), 30.
[31] For more on this, cf. Matonoha (forthcoming 2024). Cf. also Bolton; Vodrážka, *Rozumí*; Barbara J. Falk, "Reappraising Civil Society, Feminist Critiques," in her *The Dilemmas of Dissidence in East-Central Europe* (Budapest-New York: CEU Press, 2003), 325-27, as well as many of his earlier texts.
[32] Bronislava Volková, "Image of Women in Contemporary Czech Prose," in her *A Feminist's Semiotic Odyssey Through Czech Literature* (New York, Edwin Mellen Press, 1997), 69-88; Iva Popovičová, "Gender and the Kundera Paradigm: 'Truth-telling' in *The Book of Laughter and Forgetting*," *Jedním okem / One Eye Open* 1 (1998): 132-51 (not in my focus but a very good paper); Anželina Penčeva, "Znásilněný archetyp. Ženy v románech Milana Kundery," in *Česká literatura v perspektivách genderu. Jiná česká literatura...*, ed. J. Matonoha (Praha: Akropolis, 2011), 181-91.

1967) in my earlier papers.[33] Here, for the sake of brevity, I focus on two novels written in between the two aforementioned, namely *Life Is Elsewhere* and *Farewell Waltz*.[34] As partly hinted above, both Volková and Penčeva point out what pertains to the two novels in question here: the female characters (unlike their male protagonists) are primarily linked to nursing, caring, or serving roles such as a waitress, a hairdresser, a nurse, a shop assistant (although there are exceptions as well, such as for instance a medical doctor in the story "Symposion" in *Laughable Loves* or the character of the university student in *Life Is Elsewhere*. Both of them are, however, young or in the beginning stage of their career). If a female character is more artistic, then it is in the sphere of mimesis (painter, photographer–in *The Unbearable Lightness of Being*, although the situation is not that straightforward, but space does not allow for discussion here).[35] But to get to the discussion of the tricky culs-de-sac nature of MK's early novels (which are the focus here, although the issue is not too limited to them, I think) paradoxically operating through a triadic structure, let us take a closer look at the two aforementioned early Czech novels by MK (written in Czech and while still in Czechoslovakia).

---

[33] Jan Matonoha, "Dispositives of silence"; "A Preliminary Survey"; "Dispozitivy mlčení, zraňující identity a diskurzivní konstituce mlčení. Gender, feminismus a česká literatura v období 1948-1989," in *Vyvlastněný hlas. Proměny genderové kultury v české společnosti 1948-1989*, ed. Hana Havelková and Libora Oates-Indruchová (Praha: Sociologické nakladatelství SLON, 2015), 351-91.

[34] I will not therefore comment here any further on them, but let me just provide one brief example here of the story "The Hitchhiking Game" ("Falešný autostop") in the collection *Laughable Loves*: a couple plays a game of fake hitchhiking that turns ugly and becomes a violent sexual act. The scene of reification and violation of the female body is, however, as if muted by a "higher" deconstructive level of constant mutual misrepresentations and instability of meaning. On the third level though, this misogynistic theme (which serves simply as a carrier and is hidden in its supposed higher deconstructive game) works in an even more mute, indirect, less obvious, and hence more injurious manner and, thus, has, I think, an even more significant impact. Cf. a similar observation already in Barbara Einhorn's book *Cinderella Goes to Market. Citizenship, Gender and Women's Movements in East Central Europe* (London: Verso, 1993), 236.

[35] See Penčeva, "Znásilněný archetyp."

Life Is Elsewhere

The novel *Life Is Elsewhere*[36] is both very entertaining[37] and interspersed with intriguing biographical references to canonical authors.[38] The plot of the novel, in its focus on an immature central character, could be likened to Josef Škvorecký's *The Cowards* or Bohumil Hrabal's *Closely Watched Trains* (although major differences are clear here). Arguably, as a counterpoint to Goethe's *Wilhelm Meister*, it is deliberately not straightforward (as is the rule in Kundera's novels, and the novel pays homage to musical composition by its sonata-like set-up).[39] A summary could be given as follows: Jaromil, the spoiled only child of his overprotective mother, aspires to be a great writer, while in reality, as we gradually learn, is (having started as a surrealist poet) at best a mediocre, politically loyal (i.e., loyal to a dictatorial régime) author of poetry of the day, faithfully responding to the call of the so-called Socialist Realism.[40] (One might think that Milan Kundera pokes fun at his youthful, although slightly avant-garde, adherence to the Communist official artistic style of the 1950s, but he does not seem to hint at this at all). As Martin Pilař observes, the lyrical, emotional, naive, and immature character of Jaromil could be likened to that of the nineteenth-century novelist turned informant Karel Sabina, who arguably worked for the Austrian government.[41] However, I would argue that a more complex, yet also ironic portrait of the given historical figure is provided later in the novels–in terms of literary history, very well-versed works–by the literary historian and semiotician Vladimír Macura.) To fully enjoy the projective, dreamy image of the imaginary character Xaver he has created and

---

[36] It was published first in French translation in 1973 and then in the original Czech at Škvorecký's exile publishing house 68 Publishers in Toronto in 1979. Here, I refer to the Czech edition of the novel published in 2016 by Czech publishing house Atlantis in Brno.
[37] And together with Pavel Kohout's *Katyně*–which, alas, is equally gender troublesome (cf. above Matonoha, "A Preliminary Survey")–could be seen as written with cold rage and profound irony.
[38] Such as Georg Trakl, Rainer Maria Rilke, Sergei Yesenin, Vladimir Mayakovsky, Alexander Blok, Mikhail Lermontov, Alexander Pushkin, Oscar Wilde, Charles Baudelaire, Arthur Rimbaud, Jiří Orten, etc.
[39] Cf. Martin Pilař, "KUNDERA, Milan: *Život je jinde,*" in *Slovník české prózy*, ed. Miroslav Dokoupil and Blahoslav Zelinksý (Ostrava: Sfinga, 1994). Available online at https://slovnikceskeliteratury.cz/showContent.jsp?docId=1489.
[40] The parody of Marxism, to my mind, completely misses the point of more sophisticated Marxist theories, such as the inversion of the base and superstructure, etc. Cf. e.g., L. Althusser, "Ideology and Ideological State Apparatus," in L. Althusser, *Essays on Ideology* (London: Verso, 1970) or the works by Antonio Gramsci, etc.
[41] Pilař, "KUNDERA, Milan: *Život je jinde.*"

imagines, Jaromil dives into frequent daydreaming. Yet instead of perishing by a tragic and heroic event like Xaver does in Jaromil's dreams, he dies a trivial death of pneumonia caused by his failed attempt to impress his audience (being thrown to the house balcony out of an apartment and catching cold, unwilling to humiliate himself by pleading to be let back in). The imaginary character of Xaver could be read, on the one hand, as a critique of the male ideal, yet on the other hand, it means implicitly that such–in Kundera's vision– is a heroic male identity one could and should strive for.

An important role is played by Jaromil's overprotective mother, whom Kundera belittles, thus being another case in a long line of Kundera's negative and ironic portrayals of women. Jaromil, while seemingly rebelling against her ideals and her very identity, remains in her life sphere for virtually all of his life. Another misogynistic moment of the novel is that the father (see below), who has perished during WWII, remains a distant yet, longed-for, lost ideal (and is shown as very likable character, not least in that his infidelity towards Jaromil's mother is shown to be as justified). Further still, another misogynistic moment is the narrator's portrait of the ginger-haired girl whom Jaromil seduces and, ultimately, throws (as well as her brother) into jail by informing the police on her brother's intentions (see more detailed comments further).

There are moments in the novel that can be read as witty and amusing jokes (which often resurface in MK's earlier fiction), such as, for instance, when Jaromil stares at his image in a mirror and detects features in his face that appear to oscillate between an ape and Rilke.[42] And there are indeed, although barely, moments that could be labeled as–mildly–pro-feminist.[43] For example, Jaromil's important (though nameless) love partner (not the ginger-haired one, however; see below) studies natural sciences. The downside of this image is, however, that her intelligence is not a relevant topic there, and this character functions more than anything as a mere prop for Jaromil's (non)appearing

---

[42] Certainly, in 1978, when animal studies were then in their infancy and surely were neither in MK's nor in any other Czech writer's focus, it would be arguably a slightly strict critique. However, what is meant to be an amusingly tight juxtaposition of two very remote subjects, is rather troublesome seen from a different vantage point, what is lost in this amusing witticism is that Rilke himself wrote several poems that could be read (although surely critically at times) within the context of animal studies (leaving aside that a text by another "Prague" author, Franz Kafka, *Report to an Academy*, is a paramount literary piece of the animal studies approach featuring an ape as its narrator).
[43] See for instance Milan Kundera, *Life Is Elsewhere*, trans. by Peter Kussi (London-Boston: Faber and Faber, 1987), 117-18; Milan Kundera, *Život je jinde* (Brno: Atlantis, 2016), 139.

erections.[44] Another example is when the housemaid, Magda, is secretly watched through a keyhole when taking a bath (in a typical to-be-looked-at manner): she is most likely aware of that and (partly in an embarrassed, partly kind way) returns the gaze. However, the overall nature of Jaromil and Magda's relationship is not of two equals but of a servant (although wise in both her life choices and losses) and her superior.[45] Or, when the surrealist painter wonders whether we live in a world where men without heads desire pieces of headless women's bodies.[46]

At the same time, however, the surrealist painter (another crucial character of the novel) himself is shown not to encounter his female lover, Jaromil's mother, during their love-making but runs his own artistic and erotic image of her in his head.[47] Moreover, what matters here is not his egocentric vision of Jaromil's mother's sexualized body but rather her inability to live up to his avant-garde expectations in general.[48]

The majority of the novel in question, anyway, I would argue, is troublesome, seen from a gender perspective, presenting us (as outlined above) with the triple layer structure of 1) overt sexism; 2) overwriting and reassessing of sexism (as O'Brien puts it); 3) less apparent yet still blatant and profoundly injurious sexism indeed. Here, as well as in the following subchapters, let us take a closer look at the individual characters of the novel.

---

[44] Kundera, *Life*, 144; *Život*, 169.
[45] Kundera, *Life*, 56; *Život*, 66. This scene is one among the stereotypes O'Brien points out that are deconstructed further down the narrative. O'Brien, *Milan Kundera & Feminism*, 40. Apart from my other doubt described above, what remains as a question though, I suspect, is whether these deconstructive steps do not leave behind a bitter taste of– nevertheless–the figure of naked female body in a bathtub being watched by a male spectator.
[46] Kundera, *Life*, 38; *Život*, 48.
[47] Kundera, *Life*, 50; *Život*, 59.
[48] Without wanting to go into a complicated debate over the pornography and feminism issue and well-known names such as Andrea Dworkin or Catharine MacKinnon on one side and Linda Williams or Wendy Brown on the other, and many others (and using these simplistic binaries), this is by no means to say my feminist critique would want to be anti-pornographic, as the examples of Jean Genet or Georges Bataille show (although partly troublesome as they might be), even very explicit representations of sexuality do not have to necessarily be sexist. My view is that the imagery of a given literary text should not run alongside popular gender stereotypes, what matters is not *what* but *how*, and *in what manner*.

An improbable (anti-)hero, Jaromil

A central topic of the novel (written in 1969, thus in the heyday for such topics, not in the early 1950s when MK was a prolific regime poet himself) is an implicit critique of the so-called totalitarian regime born in the early 1950s. This critique is carried out via the portrayal of the central character of Jaromil, who is implicitly shown in an unsettling manner as a truly disgusting character. Jaromil, the protagonist of the narrative, is (counter-intuitively and deliberately) portrayed as an immature, self-centered egocentric who prevails only through a series of mistakes and misunderstandings, a portrait that is clearly understandable in the protagonist's narrow focus, his immaturity, and egocentric "lyricism" (to put it in Kundera's terms). In short, what the narrator views as the demise of–we might say–conventional, traditional masculinity.

I see two troublesome issues here, however. First, the portrait of failing masculinity, so much present in the image of Jaromil as a factor to be taken into account when thinking about Czechoslovakia in 1948, is, arguably, fairly reductive and simplistic in terms of the complex relationship to the harsh reality of the fifties that need to be read and understood in the context of WWII, alongside, arguably, Walter Benjamin, Theodor W. Adorno, Hannah Arendt, and others. In many regards, it hinders rather than helps to grasp the nature of the so-called totalitarian situation and its motivation. Second, when speaking of an image of "true" masculinity–of Jaromil's father as a soldier, soccer player, and prisoner[49] or the role of the ex-RAF pilot and ginger-haired girl's lover (from the penultimate chapter)–a whole slew of issues could and would need to be raised as to what is meant by Jaromil's failing masculinity in the first place, when seen in the context of more recent gender and masculinity studies where, to put it crudely, a right to fragility, openness, and frankness has been reclaimed.[50]

At the very end of the novel, Jaromil, terminally ill with pneumonic fever (having got pneumonia in his spectacular humiliation when he hesitated to re-enter a balcony door through which he had been thrown out by his opponent as well-deserved payback for all his choices and steps taken) hallucinates about seeing Xavier and protests to him by insisting that he is not a *woman*. This

---

[49] Cf. Kundera, *Life*, 168; *Život*, 196.
[50] One (seemingly) gender positive point being that the unlikeable character of Jaromil is shown as violent towards his ginger-haired lover, thus implicitly yet clearly casting a negative light on violence against women. Kundera, *Life*, 282. This, however, could come down arguably to something very remote from feminism, a rather conventional image of men as knights of female "fragility."

ultimate scene where Jaromil's humiliation is completed thus tightly links him with the female element. In other words, this scene could be interpreted as follows: being a male equals being cold, rational, successful, brave, daring, adventurous, inquisitive, etc., (such as the dreamed-up figure of Xavier or the real figure of a forty-year-old ex-RAF pilot), while being a female is just the opposite. No further feminist comment, I assume, is required here.

Jaromil's alter ego, Xavier

As mentioned, Jaromil can be seen as a portrait of the profound failure of a supposedly true, real, mature, adult masculinity whose ironic counter-portrait (as is clear and as O'Brien points out)[51] is given through a dream-like narrative of Jaromil's fanciful alter ego Xaver. However, the irony of this profound failure of Jaromil's masculinity (as portrayed by the omniscient narrator), of course, presupposes or silently implies, in its negative form, that true masculinity should be hard, heroic, self-dependent, or independent (not dependent on a mother), etc., a portrait that is, seen from a feminist or masculinity studies (if not any) perspective deeply troublesome.

Maman, Jaromil's (Oedipal) mother

No less ironic (as told from the narrator's perspective)–and all the more painfully uncomfortable from a feminist perspective–is the portrait of Jaromil's domineering, Oedipal, self- and status-obsessed (while lost to her own self) mother (*maman* in the English translation). Here, I very much share O'Brien's feminist objections to the representation or construction of this character.[52] The picture of this character as a woman and a mother is off-putting (though not in the way intended by the authorial subject and narrator of the novel). On the level of the author's intention, we are disgusted by the given character (interchangeably by her pathological and obsessive "love," self-obsession, and hatred). On the feminist level, it is rather dubious that if a female character happens to occupy the center stage as one of the central characters, this character must be such a monster. Symptomatically, while the mother is portrayed (no matter that it is completely, deliberately intended to provoke the reader) as a thoroughly pathetic, sentimental, and kitsch-prone person, her husband is likeable, rational, nicely sarcastic, resisting the Nazi occupiers. As it later turns out, he is sent to an extermination camp where he perishes not for

---

[51] O'Brien, 88.
[52] Cf. O'Brien, 60-61.

his brave resistance but for having a half-Jewish lover whom he refused to leave behind when she had been sent to an extermination camp herself. In short, while the mother is a monster here, the father is a hero (and ironically cheating on the mother as well). Also symptomatically, Jaromil's mother–which is the case with almost no exception for all female characters in Kundera's novels–is presented in a typical to-be-looked-at and reifying manner.[53]

Jaromil's tutor, as well as a ("class") enemy, the Surrealist painter

There are significant counter-heroes to the ironic portrait of the protagonist, namely the ginger-haired lover of Jaromil's life (whom, as we learn at the end of the novel, is sent to prison, see below) or the Surrealist painter. The fact that this character of the Surrealist painter (in contrast to Jaromil, who occupies the center stage and, at the same time, counter-intuitively horrifies the reader) functions as an undisputedly positive one is yet another example of injurious attachments at work. The reader is led to sympathize and to side with this character, who is firm in his artistic and political convictions, a position driving him to the fringes of contemporary society. What is overlooked in this portrait is that part of his avant-garde, non-conformist status is also being a notorious womanizer. (And to be noted here, importantly, is that it would be perfectly fine if this setting took place, prophetically, within the paradigm of polyamory of the 1990s or even free love for both genders of the 60s, but in this case, what we encounter is a case of a conventionally one-sided and masculine paradigm.)

The love of Jaromil's life, the ginger-haired girl

The character of the ginger-haired girl (tellingly, she is not given a name in the novel) plays a crucial role in the narrative. She is emancipated but only to a certain extent (she works behind the counter at a cashier's desk, yet her boss is, unsurprisingly, male). She falls victim to her own lies, inadvertently throwing her brother into prison for an attempted escape from Communist

---

[53] Leaving aside that motherhood is, as it is often the case in Kundera's fiction, portrayed as rather obtrusive, obnoxious in an often ironically condescending manner, it is arguably understandable within the context of the official "cult of motherhood" of Husák's era which was in stark contrast to the 50s and 60s in Czechoslovakia. Cf. Havelková and Oates-Indruchová, *The Politics of Gender Culture*. While in feminism this could be put into sharp contrast (e.g., pointing to works by Luce Irigaray, Sara Ruddick, Melanie Klein, etc.), it is seen as a truly important topic–for instance, in Julia Kristeva's sense as a space of crucially and radically ambivalent *jouissance* standing as an abject outside of both object and subject.

Czechoslovakia. She herself is imprisoned for three years because of the false accusation which she unknowingly initiated herself, trying-out of good intentions–to keep her infidelities hidden and salvage her relationship with the protagonist Jaromil. She turns out (truly not for selfish reasons, it seems) to choose Jaromil eventually over a now working-class, former RAF pilot (who lost his wife during the Blitz in London, now–for political reasons–demoted and sacked from the army). However, she is a cheater and a liar: an experienced sexual gesture of her hand that looks improbable for a virginal girl (learned from her occasional experienced lover and womanizer, the ex-RAF pilot mentioned above) eventually betrays her to Jaromil. Thus, the ginger-haired girl, against initial expectations (or rather against the expectation with which an almost entire novel is imbued), is very experienced sexually, to the point that she pursues a playful lesbian relationship. However, it seems more than likely from the context of the narrative that the reason for doing so is not to fulfil her own sexual identity and desire but to entertain her occasional male lover (whom she keeps seeing while dating Jaromil).[54] Also, tellingly, being an occasional lover of the forty-year-old ex-RAF fighter is *his*, not *her* choice.

Further characters and the motif of an old body

As in many other instances (and as pointed out by both Volková and Penčeva, see above), female characters (crucial in the protagonists' love life), such as the second-grade female classmate, do not have a name and are referred to only by general names (e.g., simply as a classmate, *spolužákyně*)[55] and their purpose is not to portray a female character but–in a rather instrumental manner–to illustrate the male protagonist.

Also, there is, at the first sight, an interesting amount of attention given to an aging or old body,[56] though the reason why Jaromil pays attention to it is, in reality, his avoidance of a young female body he both desires and is horrified by at the same time. However, when rendering this topic, the old body is characterized as poor, worn down, and pitiful. Of course, here one might wonder why an appraisal of the old body had to be characterized necessarily by the above-mentioned attributes and not in any other, less condescending manner.[57]

---

[54] Kundera, *Life*, 312; *Život*, 274–75.
[55] Kundera, *Life*, 107; *Život*, 126.
[56] Kundera, *Life*, 138; *Život*, 161.
[57] While indirectly trying to cop out of his juvenile career choices (as hinted at partly in the novel *The Book of Laughter and Forgetting*), one needs to be aware of the fact that an

Farewell Waltz

Let us move to the other novel in question now. Later, in 1972 (as MK states at the end of the text) he wrote the novel *Farewell Waltz* with the thrilling motif of a misused suicidal pill as well as the equally thrilling choice of the father of the baby carried by the pregnant spa nurse named Růžena (the motif to be touched upon later). First, however, let us start with the issue of the plot of this satirical novel, which in itself is rather ambiguous in terms of its genre, ranging from the sordid farce, bitter comedy, discourse on morals and politics, or philosophical criminal fiction.[58] It takes place in a smallish spa town in roughly the mid-60s (surely prior to the 1968 invasion of the Warsaw Pact Armies). Its pivotal figure is the young nurse Růžena, portrayed in a rather slightly condescending manner, who is pregnant–most likely–by her mundane boyfriend František, but raises the claim that the child is that of the famous Prague jazz trumpet player and notorious womanizer, Klíma. He had a one-night stand with Růžena, exploiting her naivety and his image of a worldly playboy (which, one could add, sounds rather grotesque given the parochial nature of Prague itself). Here, one might add, that Kundera is again indulging in his misogyny and preference for moral conundrums as displayed by Klíma, who is both irresistibly drawn to the infidelities he commits, yet deeply in love with his wife at the same time. Apart from the fact that Růžena is drawn to Klíma by his fame, she is also desperate by being placed amidst a series of women treating their infertility in the spas. Klíma is, however, despondent by having learned that Růžena is expecting their child and does his utmost to persuade her (through various sophisticated means) to have an abortion.

The character of Dr. Škréta, the spa gynecologist, pokes fun at the official state rhetoric of population growth, when Dr. Škréta tries to unite all people as mutual sisters and brothers–by inseminating infertile spa patients with his own sperm surreptitiously (or–one might argue–covers up his own libido with his

---

ironic portrayal of poetry as a form of ideology would be more acceptable, I suspect, if it did not come from an author who–up to the mid-50s, produced poetry mostly in accordance with the official Communist line of the early 50s (or challenged it just to such an extent as to be acceptable for official publishing houses), such as the poetry collection *Člověk zahrada širá* from 1953 or the long, allusive poem *Poslední máj* from 1955. Cf. in detail, e.g., Jan Novák, *Kundera*. Additionally, what might be further considered is the role of MK's beloved and celebrated father, Ludvík Kundera, a topic treated critically by Holt Meyer.

[58] Cf. Martin Pilař, "KUNDERA, Milan: *Valčík na rozloučenou,*" in *Slovník české prózy*, ed. Miroslav Dokoupil and Blahoslav Zelinský (Ostrava: Sfinga, 1994). Available online at https://slovnikceskeliteratury.cz/showContent.jsp?docId=1490.

seemingly beneficial grand narrative). Another important character, besides Dr. Škréta, the gynecologist, is an American of Czech origin called (in Czech, the name sounds rather pretentious) Bertleff, endowed with almost supernatural wisdom and serenity, and who, in his overarching and manipulative nature, resembles Shakespeare's Oberon from *A Midsummer Night's Dream*.[59]

One would-be, near-feminist character is that of the young Olga, if only her independence were not achieved–again and unsurprisingly in Kundera's novel–by seducing her older protector Jakub, a man who is about to emigrate from Czechoslovakia. Jakub visits Dr. Škréta and returns him the poisonous pill he acquired from Škréta in the 50s in case he should be accused and tried as a victim of one of the spectacular political show trials. By a twist of circumstances, this very pill mistakenly ends up in the hands of Růžena, who, having spent the night with Bertleff (the obnoxiously super-wise and super-human man endowed with equally obnoxious sexual healing powers), readily agrees with the termination of her pregnancy. Unfortunately, she swallows the poisonous pill by mistake and–a motif often present in Kundera's novels, truly unexpectedly–dies. One almost fully feminist character would be that of Klíma's wife, a well-known actress from Prague, if it were not for the fact that she is casually cheated upon by her husband, who supposedly loves her but cannot–supposedly–stop cheating on her.

The novel, full of parodic pretensions reminding us of the oeuvre of Moliere or Diderot (Kundera's beloved author), in sum, does not result in some sort of catharsis, and the life of the novel's characters goes on with all its cold and impenetrable cruelty.[60] It namely pokes fun at the institution of fatherhood (which appears in various forms, from the unwilling–character of Klíma, spiritual–Bertleff, or pandemic–Dr. Škréta)[61] and testifies, I believe, indirectly to the tacitly phallocentric priority of fatherhood (over motherhood, namely in radical Julia Kristeva fashion), yet as well as Kundera's profound skepticism towards having progeny and becoming a parent. I shall start this subchapter with the character of nurse Růžena.[62]

---

[59] Ibid.
[60] See Ibid.
[61] Cf. Ibid.
[62] The novel was first published in French translation in 1973, and then in the original Czech at the Škvorecký' exile publishing house Sixty-Eight Publishers in Toronto in 1979. Here, I refer to the Czech edition of the novel published in 2008 by Czech publishing house Atlantis in Brno.

Nurse Růžena

This female protagonist, who appears to have no will of her own,[63] is, granted, not shown as simple-minded per se. However, the way she chooses to achieve her goals is not through her working career but through marriage choices. She is given no chance to make use of the stability and self-esteem she finally achieved because she accidentally poisons herself. This very fact is again underlined by her being within the sphere of male influence, having been enchanted by the male figure of an idealized, patriarchal, old, wise, and womanizing Czech-American with the (what I find irritatingly) seductive and strange or uncommon sounding name of Bertleff (who himself, however, is later stripped down from his mysterious charm and revealed as a cuckold, see below).

When Olga, Růžena's flatmate, antipode, and (what could be said to be her) enemy (see below), protests against being filmed in the spa swimming pool by a film crew (as an act of infringement of her privacy),[64] a sharp contrast is being drawn here between, on the one hand, her and, on the other, Růžena and the crowd of "*fat*" (not my word but the narrator's) women delivering merry welcoming cheers upon this occasion. The narrator does not hesitate to add an explanation of where their enthusiasm for being filmed (in spite of their supposed *ugly* bodies, again, not my word) comes from on the part of older women. The narrator "explains" (and this is not "deconstructed" any further in the novel's text, as far as I am aware) that their motivation stems from their jealous hatred towards sexually attractive young women whose beauty, youth, and slimness they are trying to tear down and ridicule by their obvious and explicit showing off of their old and–again, to use the narrator's word–"*fat*" bodies. In MK's view, thus, women should be young, slim, and beautiful, while those who do not fit these criteria should keep themselves well hidden (not to disturb the male gaze). No further comment is needed here, I assume.[65]

The successful jazz musician Klíma

The following motif runs across the whole novel, from its very beginning almost to the very end, it is not clear–mostly since she cannot make up her own mind–

---

[63] Gendered comment on this might ensue, but this is counterweighted by the character of Klíma's wife Kamila, who, although she is strung along and controlled by passions of jealousy throughout the novel, at the end of it she finds a way of her own (see below).
[64] Milan Kundera, *Farewell Waltz*, trans. Aaron Asher (London-Boston: Faber and Faber, 1998), 147; *Valčík na rozloučnou* (Brno: Atlantis, 2008), 126.
[65] Perhaps except that now, unlike in the 1970s, there is a term for such a hateful attitude.

whether the character of Růžena fell pregnant by her steady (but dull) boyfriend or by the famous Klíma, during a one-night stand they had together. In all cases, Růžena does (up until the last few hours of her life) look to Klíma as a savior of what she otherwise sees as a trivial life in a parochial town. Some motives belong to the narrative strand of characters, not the omniscient narrator, so he could not be blamed for them, but at no point is Klíma shown as a completely negative person, only as a pathological and chronic womanizer (a portrait that is not disputed or deconstructed at any later point of the novel). At the same time, Klíma fears the breakdown of his marriage or the departure of his wife–who, at the end of the novel, seems indeed ready to overcome her fears and dares to embrace a newly found freedom.

In this context, one might wonder over the following two motifs. The first one might illustrate Klíma's nonchalant, if not careless, attitude to women when he is shown to be relieved that his random lover's bleak tone of voice comes down not to her impregnation by him but to her mother's demise.[66] Therefore, what matters is the womanizer's state of mind, while the emotional fate of this marginal female character is completely secondary. In the second instance, Klíma is portrayed as completely satisfied by the "generous" offer made by his fellow musician, although he rejects it: he has offered to account for Růžena's possible impregnation by Klíma as impossible to prove because all the band members engaged in group sex with her. One might wonder here, does this offer stand on the level of the character's narrative strand, or should it be taken aboard as if it is speech delivered by the omniscient narrator? In all cases, the general setup is not disputed in the novel at any point, and that is the status of central figures, on the one hand, Klíma, a famous womanizing musician (who cheats on his wife for which he eventually pays a price, although in the prospect of a future not portrayed in the novel) and his one-night-stand lover Růžena whom Klíma is trying to convince to have an abortion. Thus, while both are shown as troublesome figures for their own sakes indeed, Klíma is a worldly womanizer, Růžena, a simple and indecisive, petite woman from a local spa town with her opinions and speculations swung by momentary moods (and on the top of that is shown as a cheating woman herself). Male-centered and conventional motifs abound here.

---

[66] Kundera, *Farewell*, 9; *Valčík*, 16.

The spa patient Olga

In spite of the initial denigration of Olga's physical appearance (as O'Brien points out),[67] Olga can be said to be the rare, truly feminist example of a female figure[68] not (so much) defined by her body and physicality but by her intellectual capacities. Although initially portrayed as being rather plain or even ugly looking, she questions the male gaze as a supposed defining feature when looking into a mirror herself. Rather, she is portrayed as being defined by her intelligence and a sharp mind. At the end of the novel, she is not defined by her body and instead matures for being curious about her existential life horizons.

However, the emphasis lies, again, not on her own intellectual development and relationships (as it is the case with male characters) but on her sexual life and personal affinities and animosities: she dislikes Růžena (which is mutual) and is shown as wishing to seduce her patron Jakub, although–granted–this fulfilled dream of hers is not an ultimate goal for her and only opens further perspectives for her. These (just like in the case of Růžena or Klíma's wife Kamila), alas, are not developed any further (see more on this in the context of Kamila below). However, it is often the case in MK's fiction that it is not sufficient if female characters are good at their job and display a sharp intellect. Rather, their physical appearance is what matters and is explicitly judged, irrespective of whether they are supposedly ugly, as is the case with Jaromil's ginger-haired girlfriend (see above), "average" looking like Olga, or beautiful like the female film director at the end of the novel. In short, what matters is their sexual (not other, e.g., intellectual) life.

The patron and émigré-to-be Jakub

Jakub (Olga's patron, a crucial figure in the novel), having been ex-communicated from his professional posts, is about to leave his country (legally). As to his gender politics, the usual undertones that a feminism-conscious reader finds truly troublesome can be heard. For example, in Chapter 10, Day 3, Olga (or the voice of a narrator, rather) says that she knows

---

[67] O'Brien, 19.
[68] Inversions of gender stereotypes can clearly occur, as the case of Sabina from *The Unbearable Lightness of Being* shows, with Sabina being an independent, self-confident, "light" character. But her "journey" or rather escape both from Czechoslovakia after 1968 and then from Switzerland, but also, arguably from her very self, ultimately ends in the middle of nowhere, finding herself forlorn and detached from all her previous surroundings as well as people she knew in a social, psychological, and affective vacuum.

he has had many female sexual partners. In so speaking, a reader has to be aware that Jakub is a very experienced lover. Here again, as so often in Kundera's fiction, we find an older male character who is sexually experienced, having sex with a younger female character (although this young woman, Olga, turns out to be rather implicitly feminist in considering this brief affair with her patron as any other act of experience in her expanding mental and epistemological universe).

The old, wealthy American Bertleff

At the end of the novel, this character by the name of Bertleff is shown to be a trusting cuckold–or, alternatively, a man whose Christian magnanimity or simply erotic generosity reaches so far as to getting his wife pregnant, no matter who the father of the baby is (himself or Dr. Škréta). In any case, for the entire novel, Bertleff is portrayed as an overwhelmingly generous and wise old man almost up to the point of being saintly (and the character Růžena, just before her untimely death, becomes spellbound by him). However, gender stereotypes of an old, rich, womanizing American (he is portrayed as having plenty of sexual experiences)[69] abound here (and stand out, namely when compared to his female counterpart, the plain, simple, parochial young woman Růžena).

Another example of Bertleff's womanizing, rich (yet or, on top of that, almost saintly) man[70] is when he boasts about a mature man's capability that, according to him, is not to know how to seduce a woman smoothly but to forsake her without causing her harm. The story Bertleff tells further on is a nice and sensitive one, but the bitter taste remains, in two respects. First, a breakup here, in his rendition, is not a dramatic event (which, in most cases, I assume, it is) but an orchestrated elegant affair that a man smoothly executes to get rid of the parental bonds to a woman. And second, it is a man forsaking a woman (and not vice versa) in which (in spite of the following rather moving story told) I still find and sense condescending undertones.

As always with novels by MK, the narrative is dotted with witticisms and wisecracks abound. Feminist doubts remain here, however. For instance, at the concluding part of one chapter,[71] Bertleff chides and chastens Klíma (like Bertleff, himself a chronic womanizer and adulterer) for loving his wife too

---

[69] Kundera, *Farewell*, 66; *Valčík*, 61.
[70] Kundera, *Farewell*, 29; *Valčík*, 32.
[71] Kundera, *Farewell*, 32; *Valčík*, 34.

much, which paradoxically–by elevating one single woman against all others–smells of heresy and lack of reverence to all creatures. Bertleff thus argues that all women are worthy of veneration, irrespective of their (marital) position. But, here, one might wonder, is this a stance of Christian acceptance, or the notion of–important to note, sharply different from feminist polyamory–a rather macho polygamy?

Granted, the context immediately following wittily undermines the initial sentence blaming Bertleff's open and self-professed misogyny on homosexuality or impotence ("You don't seem to be impotent or homosexual"),[72] saying that he, Bertleff, is guilty of something even worse than this, and it is that he loves his wife too much.[73] The implication of which being that homosexuality and sexual impotence are not *that bad*, after all. The bitter taste of a statement that homosexuality or impotence equals misogyny–which is, of course, far from true–remains though, of course.

At one point, Bertleff says that he has been blessed by having had many (female) lovers who had fallen in love with him.[74] A feminist commentary would be superfluous here I assume, let us just add that here the troublesome motif is "expiated" by the fact (in general terms, a strategy often to be found in Kundera's novels too) that this happens to a man who had faced prosecution and death by Nazis. Following the logic of injurious attachments, sexism thus abounds yet is not so palpable and obvious since it is hidden within the narrative of a heroic and venerated figure.

Doctor Škréta

The portrait of Doctor Škréta is (I presume) supposed to be an ironic portrayal of this god-like figure of an inseminator fathering a lot of children by using his own sperm in the surreptitious artificial-insemination treatment he organizes. Yet this irony is very gentle, and most of the time, it is almost unperceivable. Let me give one example. One might say that both the characters of the jazz musician Klíma, and Doctor Škréta are, in fact, negative, but this is not that obvious, and one might suspect that still early in a novel,[75] the narrator of the novel did not mean to reveal both characters as disgusting (yet). In the passage described below–unless the novel aims to prove both characters, at this stage

---

[72] Kundera, *Farewell*, 30; *Valčík*, 33.
[73] Kundera, *Farewell*, 31.
[74] Kundera, *Farewell*, 130; *Valčík*, 112.
[75] Kundera, *Farewell*, 71-75; *Valčík*, 67-69.

at least, as self-centered misogynists and sexists, which I doubt[76]–Doctor Škréta is portrayed as a complete misogynistic "monster" who reifies female bodies. Here, in a supposedly entertaining scene, Doctor Škréta's close friend, the aforementioned Klíma, poses as a doctor as well, first treating a female patient in a condescending manner and, by exploiting her private parts, he reifies and objectifies her body. This scene of a medical gynecological examination is clearly an unbalanced situation imbued with power and gender in the utmost negative form (and a Kunderaesque ironic critique of human physicality is not– I suspect–of much help here).

Klíma's wife Kamila

Klíma's wife Kamila–whom I find to be a rather unique case of a woman in this novel–finds, after what must have been a frustrating marriage with the notorious womanizer, her own perspective and wider horizon in life. This, however, takes place again against the backdrop of his sexual affairs and constant infidelities, as well as her constant suspicions about her cheating husband. And, equally, alas, her newly discovered freedom finally arrives only at the very end of the novel, and there is no chance for it to be developed any further–unlike her previous existence defined by traditional jealousy–in any palpable details as it all falls out of the novel's narrative.

Conclusion: Injurious Attachments and Discursive Emergence of Silence

MK's treatment of female characters, I think, is threefold, not only twofold, as O'Brien suggests. First, it consists of intentionally downgrading (such as in the case of the figure of a domineering, self-centered, and overwhelming mother in *Life Is Elsewhere*). Second, and contrary to the first, after several inversions and going beyond the layer of initial paradoxical negative treatment, the reader gradually learns that what initially appeared to be off-putting characters are very generous, sublime figures that could be read along feminist lines as well. While the second category looks very promising from the feminist perspective, in reality, to put it harshly, these figures (granted, not always beautiful) who are–seen at the third, ultimate level–troublesome in other regards from a feminist point of view (see below), namely being treated as *victims*. For example, of a gang rape, in the case of Lucie in *The Joke*, or in the case of a ginger-haired cashier, Jaromil's love (who is to be betrayed and dispatched to

---

[76] Cf. equally critical remarks on this passage by O'Brien, 30–31, plus the scene occurring at roughly only one-third of the way into the novel.

a prison by his own choice). Few of Kundera's female characters stand higher than other (male and female) characters, yet they are shown to be rather simple personalities (as Penčeva pointed out, e.g., Lucie–a hairdresser, the ginger-haired lover without a name, etc.) and their (timidly) extolled existence in fact replicates the usual gender stereotypes–being mostly reduced to sex and mystery. Such is the case of Lucie (in the novel *The Joke*), when she turns out to be a victim of a violent gang-rape, hence her silence due to her inability to verbalize her experience which is impossible to put into words, or the ginger-haired, experienced lover falsely pretending to Jaromil (whom she loves) that she is completely inexperienced (so as not to hurt his obsessive and possessive ego), etc. In both cases (Lucy and the ginger-haired girl), the narrative (through their initial degradation) elevates them to an almost martyr-like state, but at a clear feminist cost by being primarily defined by their bodies and sexuality.

Thus, I believe there is clearly room within which the concept of injurious attachments could be used in Kundera's work, as they help to capture the troublesome nature of his portrayal of women, which lies not only on a dual level as John O'Brien–insightfully–observed, but on a triadic, triple-level: a) clear misogyny b) followed by sophisticated deconstructive tropes (both skillfully demonstrated in John O'Brien's book) c) yet resulting in–all the more injurious–misogyny, which is easy to miss, thus representing what I (following Wendy Brown and Judith Butler) choose to call *injurious attachments*. One tends to disregard this ultimate "gender trouble" in Kundera's fiction, giving preference to other sophisticated topics of his novels, but this clearly amounts to what I choose to refer to as *discursive emergence of silence*, and as combined with *injurious attachments*, these twofold elements together comprise *dispositives of silence*.

Bibliography

Achino-Loeb, Maria-Luisa, ed. *Silence: The Currency of Power.* New York: Berghahn Books, 2006.

Adorno, Theodor W. and Max Horkheimer. *Dialectic of Enlightenment.* Stanford: Stanford University Press, 2009 / 1972 / 1947.

Althusser, L. "Ideology and Ideological State Apparatus." In L. Althusser, *Essays on Ideology*, 141-51. London: Verso, 1984 / 1970.

Bendová, Kamila. "Ženy v Chartě 77." In *Opozice a odpor proti komunistickému režimu 1968–1989*, edited by Petr Blažek, 54–66. Praha: Dokořán, 2005.

Blažek, Petr. "Svědectví neokázalé emancipace." In *Bytová revolta. Jak ženy dělaly disent*, edited by Naďa Straková and Marcela Linková, 19–25. Praha: Academia, 2017.

Bolton, Jonathan. *Worlds of Dissent*. Cambridge: Harvard University Press, 2012.

Bren, Paulina. *The Greengrocer and His TV. The Culture of Communism after the 1968 Prague Spring*. Ithaca–London: Cornell University Press, 2010.

Brown, Wendy. *States of Injury: Power and Freedom in Late Modernity*. Princeton: Princeton University Press, 1995.

Butler, Judith. *The Psychic Life of Power: Theories in Subjection*. Stanford: Stanford University Press, 1997.

Češka, Jakub. *Království motivů. Motivická analýza románů Milana Kundery*. Praha: Togga, 2005.

——. *Za poetikou Milana Kundery*. Brno: Host, 2022.

Dientsbier, Jiří and Jiřina Dientsbierová, eds. *Evropan Milan Kundera*. Praha: Rada pro mezinárodní vztahy, 2010.

Einhorn, Barbara. *Cinderella Goes to Market. Citizenship, Gender and Women's Movements in East Central Europe*. London–New York: Verso, 1993.

Elgrably, Jordan. "Conversations with Milan Kundera." In *Critical Essays on Milan Kundera*, edited by Peter Petro, 53–68. New York: G. K. Hall & Co, 1999.

Falk, Barbara J. "Reappraising Civil Society. Feminist Critiques." In Barbara J. Falk, *The Dilemmas of Dissidence in East-Central Europe*, 325–27. Budapest–New York: CEU Press, 2003.

Foucault, Michel. *Discipline and Punish: The Birth of the Prison*. New York: Vintage Books, 1995 / 1975.

Haman, Aleš. *Tři stálice moderní české prózy: Neruda, Čapek, Kundera*. Praha: Karolinum, 2014.

Havelková, Hana. "A Few Prefeminist Thoughts." In *Gender Politics and Post Communism*, edited by Nanette Funk and Magda Müller, 62–73. New York: Routledge, 1993.

——. "Ignored but Assumed. Family and Gender Between Public and Private Realms." *Czech Sociological Review* 4, no. 1 (1996): 63–79.

——. "Women in and after a 'classless' society." In *Women and Social Class, International Feminist Perspectives*, edited by Christine Zmroczek and Pat Mahony, 69–84. London: Taylor and Francis/UCL, 1999.

——. "Náměty k diskusi o českém genderovém kontextu." In *Ročenka katedry genderových studií FHS UK 2005–2006*, edited by Blanka Knotková-Čapková, 108–24. Praha: FHS UK, 2007.

Havelková, Hana and Libora Oates-Indruchová. "Expropriated voice, transformation of gender culture under state socialism. Czech society 1948–89." In *The Politics of Gender Culture under State Socialism. An expropriated voice*, edited by Hana Havelková and Libora Oates-Indruchová, 3–27. London: Routledge, 2014.

Havelková, Hana and Libora Oates-Indruchová, eds. *Vyvlastněný hlas. Proměny genderové kultury v české společnosti 1948–1989*. Praha: Sociologické nakladatelství SLON, 2015.

Heczková, Libuše. *Píšící Minervy, vybrané kapitoly z dějin české literární kritiky.* Praha: Filozofická fakulta Univerzity Karlovy, 2009.

Hrabik-Samal, Mary. "Ženy a neoficiální kultura a literatura v Československu v letech 1969-1989." In *Přítomnosť minulosti, minulosť přítomnosti,* edited by Jolana Kusá and Peter Zajac, 81-95. Bratislava: Nadácia Milana Šimečku, 1996.

Hron, Madelaine. "'Word Made Flesh,' Czech Women's Fiction from Communism to Post-Communism." *Journal of International Women's Studies* 4, no. 3 (2003): 81-98.

Kirss, Tiina A. "Přítelkyně z domu smutku Evy Kantůrkové. Genderová mapa vězení." *Jedním okem/One Eye Open,* special issue, *Gender and Historical Memory* 1 (1998): 109-21.

Kantůrková, Eva. *Přítelkyně z domu smutku.* Cologne: Index, 1984.

Kristeva, Julia. *Powers of Horror. An Essay on Abjection.* New York: Columbia University Press, 1982.

Kubíček, Tomáš. *Vyprávět příběh: naratologické kapitoly k románům Milana Kundery.* Brno: Host, 2001.

———. *Středoevropan Milan Kundera.* Olomouc: Periplum, 2013.

Kundera, Milan. *Farewell Waltz.* Translated by Aaron Asher. London-Boston: Faber and Faber, 1998. (First published in 1976 as *The Farewell Party,* translated by Peter Kussi.)

———. *Life Is Elsewhere.* Translated by Peter Kussi. London-Boston: Faber and Faber, 1987. (First published in 1974.)

———. *Valčík na rozloučenou.* Brno: Atlantis, 2008. (First published in French in 1976.)

———. *Život je jinde.* Brno: Atlantis, 2016. (First published in 1973 in French; in 1979 in Czech by Sixty-Eight Publishers in Toronto.)

Le Grand, Eva. *Kundera aneb paměť touhy.* Olomouc: Votobia, 1998.

Linková, Marcela. "Disidentská herstory. Ženy a jejich činnost v prostředí Charty77." In *Bytová revolta. Jak ženy dělaly disent,* edited by Naďa Straková and Marcela Linková, 373-89. Praha: Academia, 2017.

Lóránd, Zsófia. *The Feminist Challenge to the Socialist State in Yugoslavia.* London: Palgrave Macmillan, 2018.

Matonoha, Jan. "Dispositives of silence, gender, feminism and Czech literature between 1948 and 1989." Translated by Dagmar Pegues. In *The Politics of Gender Culture under State Socialism: An Expropriated Voice,* edited by Hana Havelková and Libora Oates-Indruchová, 162-87. London: Routledge, 2014.

———. "Dispozitivy mlčení, zraňující identity a diskurzivní konstituce mlčení. Gender, feminismus a česká literatura v období 1948-1989." In *Vyvlastněný hlas. Proměny genderové kultury v české společnosti 1948-1989,* edited by Hana Havelková and Libora Oates-Indruchová, 351-91. Praha: Sociologické nakladatelství SLON, 2015.

———. "A Preliminary Survey of the Near Past: Periodizing Works of Czech Literary Authors Published from 1948 to 1989 from a Gender Perspective, with Special Regard to Dissent and Exile Literature of the 1970s and 1980s." *Kontradikce/Contradictions* 4, no. 2 (2020): 87–111.

———. "Přítomný ženský hlas, zmizelý ženský subjekt. Hrabalova trilogie *Svatby v domě*." In *Obrazy, ze kterých žiji. Dílo Bohumila Hrabala v proměnách. Ke 100. výročí autorova narození*, edited by Roman Kanda, 141–45. Praha: Ústav pro českou literaturu AV ČR, 2016.

Mrózik, Agnieszka. "Crossing Boundaries. The Case of Wanda Wasilewska and Polish Communism." *Aspasia. The International Yearbook of Central, Eastern, and Southeastern European Women's and Gender History* 11 (2017): 19–53.

Nixon, Nicola. "Cinderella's Suspicions. Feminism in the Shadow of the Cold War." *Australian Feminist Studies* 14, no. 35 (2001): 209–23.

Novák, Jan. *Kundera: Český život a doba*. Prague: Argo–Paseka, 2020.

Oates-Indruchová, Libora. *Discourses of Gender in Pre- and Post-1989 Czech Culture*. Pardubice: Fakulta humanitních studií Univerzity Pardubice, 2002.

———. "The Beauty and the Loser, cultural representations of gender in late state socialism." *Signs. Journal of Women in Culture and Society* 37, no. 2 (2012): 357–83.

———. "Unraveling a Tradition, or Spinning a Myth? Gender Critique in Czech Society and Culture." *Slavic Review* 75, no. 4, (2016): 919–43.

O'Brien, John. *Milan Kundera & Feminism: Dangerous Intersections*. New York: St. Martin's Press, 1995.

Occhipinti, Laure. "Two Steps Back? Anti-Feminism in Eastern Europe." *Anthropology Today* 12, no. 6 (1996): 13–18.

Penčeva, Anželina. "Znásilněný archetyp. Ženy v románech Milana Kundery." In *Česká literatura v perspektivách genderu. Jiná česká literatura...*, edited by J. Matonoha, 181–91. Praha: Akropolis, 2011.

Penn, Shana. *Solidarity's Secret. The Women Who Defeated Communism in Poland*. Ann Arbor: University of Michigan Press, 2006.

Pilař, Martin. "KUNDERA, Milan: *Život je jinde*." In *Slovník české prózy*, edited by Miroslav Dokoupil and Blahoslav Zelinský. Ostrava: Sfinga, 1994. Available online at https://slovnikceskeliteratury.cz/showContent.jsp?docId=1489.

———. "KUNDERA, Milan: *Valčík na rozloučenou*." In *Slovník české prózy*, edited by Miroslav Dokoupil and Blahoslav Zelinský. Ostrava: Sfinga, 1994. Available online at https://slovnikceskeliteratury.cz/showContent.jsp?docId=1490.

Popovičová, Iva. "Gender and the Kundera Paradigm. 'Truth-telling' in *The Book of Laughter and Forgetting*." *Jedním okem / One Eye Open* 1 (1998): 132–51.

Shore, Marci. "Narrative / Archive / Trace. The Trial of Milada Horáková." *Jedním okem / One Eye Open* 1 (1998): 27–41.

Sokol, Elena. "Vaculík a Procházková. Czech Sexual Poetics or Polemics?" *Slovo a smysl* 2, no. 3 (2005): 197–210.

Straková, Naďa and Marcela Linková, eds. *Bytová revolta. Jak ženy dělaly disent*. Praha: Academia, 2017.

Šiklová, Jiřina. "Feminism and the Roots of Apathy in the Czech Republic." *Social Research* 64, no. 2 (1997): 258–80.

———. "O ženách v disentu." In *Rod ženský: Kdo jsme, odkud jsme přišly, kam jdeme?*, edited by Alena Vodáková and Olga Vodáková, 204–07. Praha: Sociologické nakladatelství – SLON, 2003.

———. "Podíl českých žen na samizdatu a opoziční činnosti v Československu období tzv. normalizace v letech 1969-1989." *Gender, rovné příležitosti, výzkum* 9, no. 2 (2008): 39–44.

———. "Women and the Charta 77 Movement in Czechoslovakia." In *Conscious Acts and the Politics of Social Change. Feminist Approaches to Social Movements*, edited by Robin Teske and Marry Ann Tétrault, 265–72. Columbia, S.C.: University of South Carolina Press, 2000.

Šmausová, Gerlinda. "Emancipace, socialismus a feminismus." In *Tvrdošíjnost myšlenky, od feministické kriminologie k teorii genderu*, edited by Libora Oates-Indruchová. Praha: Sociologické nakladatelství – SLON, 2011 [2006].

Šmejkalová, Jiřina. "Co je feminismus? Kam s ní/m? Na okraj ženské otázky a současného feminismu." *Tvar* 2, přílohy, parts 1-5, nos. 37–41 (1991): 16.

———. "Do Czech Women Need Feminism? Perspectives of Feminist Theories and Practices in Czechoslovakia." *Women's Studies International Forum* 17, no. 3 (1994): 277–82.

Vaculík, Ludvík. *Český snář*. Brno: Atlantis, 1981.

Věšínová, Eva. "Backlash a osudy feminismu (interview vedla Naďa Macurová)." *Tvar* 6, no. 1 (1995): 12.

———. "Czech Society in-between the Waves." *European Journal of Women's Studies* 22, no. 4 (2005): 421–35.

———. "Feminismus... ano?" *Iniciály* 2, no. 25 (1992): 1–6.

———. "Ženy v literatuře. Komparativní téma." In *Žena – Jazyk – Literatura*, edited by Dobrava Moldanová, 208–11. Ústí nad Labem: PF UJEP, 1996.

Vodrážka, Mirek. "Před velkým exodem. Kořen českého antifeminismu." *Tvar* 4, nos. 49–50 (1993), 1, 8–9.

———. *Rozumí české ženy vlastní h_storii?* Praha: Academia, 2017.

Volková, Bronislava. "Images of Women in Contemporary Czech Prose." In Bronislava Volková, *A Feminist's Semiotic Odyssey Through Czech Literature*, 69–88. New York: Edwin Mellen Press, 1997.

Wagnerová, Alena. *Žena za socialismu. Československo 1945–1974 a reflexe vývoje před rokem 1989 a po něm*. Praha: Sociologické nakladatelství, 2017.

Watson, Peggy. "(Anti)feminism after communism." In *Who's Afraid of Feminism? Seeing Through the Backlash*, edited by Ann Oakley and Judith Mitchell, 144–61. New York, New Press, 1997.

———. "The Rise of Masculinism in Eastern Europe." *New Left Review*, no. 198 (1993): 71–82.

Wutsdorff, Irina. "Post-Structuralism under Communist Conditions? The Construction of Identity in Czech Dissident Literature." *Slovo a smysl* 7, no. 14 (2010): 103–14.

Chapter 4
Reluctant dissidents, writer-philosophers, Kundera and Hrabal

Jonathan Lahey Dronsfield

Institute of Philosophy of the Czech Academy of Sciences, Czech Rep.

Abstract

What makes both Bohumil Hrabal and Milan Kundera reluctant dissidents is that whilst they refused to take a political stand against totalitarianism, they nonetheless proposed worlds at odds with it and individuals with views independent of it. The characters in their novels become who they are through interactions with others and arrive at descriptions of themselves relationally through others. They are not models of the metaphysical subject, which could be said to have inner freedom. On the contrary, both authors put inner freedom into question, in my view. Metaphysics is a matter of play for Hrabal, irony for Kundera, by means of which the two of them unground it. By shaking up binary opposites and disordering basic distinctions, these writers produce literature resistant to the impositions of an oppressive totalitarianism. My particular focus is how both writers undo the distinction between philosophy and literature, Hrabal by using philosophical texts as literary material, Kundera by synthesizing philosophy with literature. Above all, what makes Hrabal and Kundera dissidents is that they show how necessary freedom of expression is if human beings are to become the free selves they are.

Keywords: Bohumil Hrabal, Milan Kundera, Dissent, Inner freedom, Totalitarianism, Freedom of expression, Freedom of assembly, Freedom of thought, Richard Rorty, Immanuel Kant, Friedrich Nietzsche, Philosophy, Metaphysics, Irony, Play.

* * *

The metaphysics of man is the same in the private sphere as in the public one. (Milan Kundera)

I.

Metaphysics is no different in the private sphere than it is in the public in that the human being's freedom does not happen or exist in an inner private mental space. It is something public, given in and by language, in being with others. If there is such a thing as inner freedom, if there is, then it is responsive and after the fact, not metaphysical and *a priori*. The novels of Milan Kundera and Bohumil Hrabal make overt the derivativeness of inner freedom. Kundera and Hrabal are in the minority, writers who, during the period of Communist totalitarianism, rejected the concept of metaphysical inner freedom. For the majority of dissidents during this time, inner freedom was a central premise of resistance. Both Kundera and Hrabal explicitly rejected any identity with the term *"dissident."* But in my view, both were dissidents in their rejection of metaphysical inner freedom. Because if you believe that freedom of thought follows from freedom of expression and freedom of assembly, then you will defend these freedoms above all, and these freedoms are precisely what totalitarian regimes seek to repress. The novels of Kundera and Hrabal defend freedom of expression through play (Hrabal) and irony (Kundera). Neither writer falls back on distinctions such as good and evil, terror and utopia, but instead, both show how such distinctions are more a question of play between them in the ways people live their lives under conditions of repression, to the extent that characters oscillate between and within them.

Speaking at the Czechoslovak Writers' Congress in 1967, Milan Kundera had this to say about freedom of expression:

> Any interference with freedom of thought and word, however discreet the mechanics and terminology of such censorship, is a scandal in this century.[1]

To undo the link between speech and thought is perhaps the main way totalitarianism tries to control the people. But Kundera's resistance to such interference, his non-conformity with the totalitarian regime, consists in taking action not in the sense of speaking out according to a political aim or an ideological objection, but in presenting a different, independent view of the world. For Kundera, writing cannot be determined in advance by any idea, and this includes dissent.[2] He has no time for the word "dissident": "I must confess

---

[1] Milan Kundera, "Comedy is everywhere," *Index on Censorship* 6, no. 6 (1977): 4.
[2] Milan Kundera, *The Art of the Novel*, revised edition, trans. Linda Asher (London: Faber and Faber, 1999), 119.

I don't like the word 'dissident.'"³ Kundera is not a dissident in the sense we give that term when we refer to those who speak out and protest, but in how his work dramatizes a crucial premise of freedom: that freedom of thought follows from freedom of expression. He may not give us dissident characters who protest the right to speak out, but he does give us characters whose selves are experimental, becoming who they are through what they do and say and do not do and do not say, showing us that there is no freedom of thought without the freedom to express and the freedom to associate with whomsoever we wish to associate.[4] Moreover, if characters are going to experiment through expression and association and diversity, then the space in which they can best do so will need to be tolerant. Kundera's dissidence consists in establishing such space for characters to experiment with their selves, or in showing how experimentation reveals the extent to which society is tolerant.

I am sympathetic to Kundera's view that the term "dissident" is overdetermined and ideological:

> I must confess I don't like the word 'dissident', particularly when applied to art. It is part and parcel of that same politicising, ideological distortion which cripples a work of art.[5]

Yet, I would not want to say that ideology ruins all works of art, even if it has a tendency to do so. I want to suggest that the term "dissident" is an open predicate; or at least, there is no consensus as to whom or to what it refers. If we think that it implies "speaking out," then there can be no silent dissidence—no dissent of the inner freedom—or a dissent which does not express itself or make itself explicit or identify itself as such. If we think that it is possible to dissent inwardly, in the sense that "no one can stop me from thinking what I want to think," then freedom of expression is, perhaps, not something worth dying for.

Why does Kundera say "The novel is incompatible with the totalitarian universe. This incompatibility is deeper than the one between dissident and apparatchik?"[6] Because the incompatibility between the novel and totalitarianism is for Kundera ontological. The novel is never one single truth. On the contrary, the spirit of the novel is comprised of relativity, doubt, and

---

[3] Kundera, "Comedy," 6.
[4] Kundera, *The Art of the Novel*, 31, 34, 144.
[5] Kundera, "Comedy," 6.
[6] Kundera, *The Art of the Novel*, 13.

questioning.[7] Kundera tends to distinguish between philosophy and the novel along ontological lines, as if philosophy cannot accommodate multiple perspectives on an idea, uncertainty over truth claims, or a questioning which does not presuppose an answer. In my view, he is mistaken to do so: the deconstruction of Jacques Derrida and the relativist pragmatism of Richard Rorty, to name just two, are philosophies contemporary with Kundera which do precisely this, and I will discuss a certain solidarity Rorty feels for Kundera's novels. In an interview given in the summer of 1989, Kundera distinguishes between the meditative novel, or "novelistic meditation," and the "philosophical novel." What differentiates them is the respective order of dependence between philosophy and literature. The philosophical novel is subordinated to philosophy, it merely serves philosophy and illustrates ideas; whereas the meditative novel takes hold of ideas and problems that philosophy has sought to preserve as its domain, metaphysical problems and problems of human existence, and does what philosophy has always failed to do and grasps these problems in their concreteness. Rorty appreciates this distinction. Kundera says that the novel is the "paradise of individuals."[8] For Rorty a paradise is a world in which the relation between what individuals say and the reality of the world is not a matter of truth.[9] Kundera's novels are, for Rorty, a paradise in precisely this non-correspondence.

II.

The novels of Bohumil Hrabal, too, are concerned with problems of existence and metaphysics, and whilst not being philosophical novels in Kundera's sense, neither are they meditative. Instead, they are dynamic, they put into motion encounters with philosophical texts and philosophical ideas, particularly those of Immanuel Kant and Friedrich Nietzsche, without being reducible to or illustrative of the ideas they contain. The forms Hrabal gives these encounters are playful, irreverent, less stable than Kundera's. "I feel sure," says Hrabal, that "the language of action... has always been present at the very origin of all our thinking and therefore of art too."[10] If what we think originates in what Hrabal calls the language of action, then thinking originates

---

[7] Ibid., 14.
[8] Ibid., 161.
[9] Richard Rorty, *Objectivity, Relativism, and Truth: Philosophical Papers* (Cambridge: Cambridge University Press, 1990), 41-42.
[10] Jiří Menzel and Bohumil Hrabal, *Closely Observed Trains* (film script), trans. Josef Holzbecher (London: Lorimer Publishing, 1971), 8.

in what we do in the world with others. Hrabal translates everything about this reality of being with others into the language of action, "even its transcendent and slightly metaphysical elements." It would be wrong to think that he seeks a metaphysical explanation for how things are. No sooner is there a suggestion of a metaphysical explanation, than things flip over into their opposite—especially if that explanation is sought in the so-called inner world.

Hrabal, too, is a dissident writer, albeit reluctantly. It is not that he spoke out on the basis of a political position or idea, or at least not after he had begun to be read widely, or not until after the suppression of the Prague Spring.[11] Rather, Hrabal is a dissident writer because he too is a writer for whom inner freedom, if there is such a thing, is derivative of the freedom of expression—and it is the experience of freedom of expression as prior which I think one gains from his novels. Who or what one is, is not given in advance, it is a discovery; who or what one is, is a play between conflicts and contradictions. Hrabal is right to say that "people only find things out by talking and living; they don't know everything at once, a priori, but only *ex post.*"[12] We must include freedom in those things we do not know until after the fact, after the fact of expression, after the fact of assembly, after the fact of being with others. One correlative of this is that there is no such thing as "inner freedom," or at least, metaphysical inner freedom. If there is an inner space, it is not an *a priori* one, it is constructed in language, it is a rhetorical *topos.*

Hrabal is one of the minority of writers under Communism who do not presuppose an *a priori* inner freedom. His autobiographical utterances articulate the experience of writing in terms of how it gives the writer a sense of self, of how one does not gain a sense of self any other way than through being with others in language: "Writing is an enquiry into who one is... writing is raising questions via others, invocation."[13] For Hrabal, this can appear to go all the way down, to the extent that one feels that the ownness of one's words can only come through having been authored by someone else: "I could have a sense, gazing at those pages of text, that they'd been written by someone

---

[11] See Alexander Kaczorowski, "Was Bohumil Hrabal a Politically Engaged Writer?" *Aspen Review* (March 15, 2017), https://aspen.review/article/2017/was-bohumil-hrabal-a-politically-engaged-writer%3F.
[12] Bohumil Hrabal, *Pirouettes on a Postage-stamp, An Interview-Novel with Questions Asked and Answers Recorded by László Szigeti,* trans. David Short (Prague: Karolinum Press, 2014). (ebook)
[13] Ibid.

else."[14] "I am much given to quoting what others have said. When I share their identity that way, I agree with them, but I keep on asking about myself."[15] One's thoughts do not originate in some "inner" space inside one's head, but come to one via expression, "through the typewriter."[16] What is inner is given to one and made to appear by what one writes: "my long text actually becoming an image of my inner self."[17] Such self-formation is achieved the more one writes: "as there is less of me, the more I write, so there is more of me."[18] One becomes a self and comes to know oneself through others, or through writing, through writing others. The movement of questioning self through others is in *Pirouettes on a Postage Stamp* given particular form by its construction, as indicated by the subtitle: *An Interview-Novel with Questions Asked and Answers*. It moves towards summations of becoming self such as this:

> it was really only when I got down to writing that I began to discover what my actual essence was… only when the text is written down do I learn, or discover *a posteriori* from it, all the things I've revealed about myself.[19]

Selves are after-the-fact, and once this is grasped, one can play with their construction. As a writer-down, a transcriber, as Hrabal so often describes himself, one must be not just receptive to what is given, but responsive to it. In responding, one makes oneself. To do this in literature implies a receptivity to the given, which is neither mimesis nor repetition, it is a productive responsiveness, it re-works the given into one's voice. We have been speaking of self, but we do not imply something personal. Rather, the self given by being with other persons, other texts, is a depersonalized self, an impersonal self. The selves in novels are this impersonal self; the novels fictionalize possible ways in which human beings may write and re-write themselves. Kundera calls the wisdom of the novel suprapersonal wisdom, which explains, he says, "why great novels are always a little more intelligent than their authors."[20] We become wiser when accepting our impersonality.

---

[14] Bohumil Hrabal, *Why I Write? And Other Early Prose Pieces*, trans. David Short (Prague: Karolinum Press, 2019), 11.
[15] Hrabal, *Pirouettes*.
[16] Hrabal, *Why I Write?*, 15.
[17] Ibid., 16.
[18] Ibid.
[19] Hrabal, *Pirouettes*.
[20] Kundera, *The Art of the Novel*, 160.

III.

What Kundera writes in *The Unbearable Lightness of Being* about Nietzsche's eternal return has "nothing to do with a philosophic discourse," he says.[21] Then should we not read these words as philosophy? When challenged on the passage by his interviewer—"What's that but a philosophical idea developed abstractly, without characters, without situations?"—Kundera retorts:

> Not at all! That reflection introduces directly, from the very first line of the novel, the fundamental situation of a character–Tomas; it sets out his problem: the lightness of existence in a world where there is no eternal return.[22]

Tomas' words on Nietzsche are a reflection. Philosophy in the mind of a situated character is reflection. Of course, this does not mean that the character is not doing philosophy, but if he is, then it must be read not as philosophy but as the character Tomas' encounter with it in his reflections, which means it lacks what Kundera calls affirmation, the surety of the character regarding his own thoughts. Part of Kundera's humor is how he shows what happens when a character tries to use philosophy socially, by foregrounding it *as* philosophy, as pure idea, the user fails to get along in that world:

> an effective quotation from a philosopher might charm the butcher's wife's soul, but it stood as an obstacle between the butcher's wife's body and his own.[23]

It might seem that Kundera is indifferent to philosophy. But it's not that, it's that he displaces the distinction between the proper and the improper in philosophy, between who has the right or the authority to speak it, and who does not. Hrabal does this still more intensely, as we will see. The novel, for Kundera, is question and hypothesis, "essentially inquiring, hypothetical."[24] It would make no sense to argue with still less to refute Tomas' reflections on Nietzsche's eternal return on the level of whether you think his interpretation

---

[21] Milan Kundera, "Clarifications, Elucidations: An Interview with Lois Oppenheim," *Dalkey Archive Press*, https://www.dalkeyarchive.com/2013/08/02/a-conversation-with-milan-kundera-by-lois-oppenheim/.
[22] Kundera, *The Art of the Novel*, 29.
[23] Milan Kundera, *The Book of Laughter and Forgetting*, trans. Aaron Asher (London: Faber and Faber, 1996), 164.
[24] Kundera, *The Art of the Novel*, 80.

or understanding of Nietzsche is sound.[25] Instead you must read them as a point of departure for Tomas' way through life. If becoming a self involves Tomas in trying to think through the paradox of Nietzsche's eternal return, then how he lives his life and interacts with others will reveal his thoughts about Nietzsche's eternal return.

Part of what Kundera wants to insist on, I think, is that the order of dependency between philosophy and literature is not one way. The narration of a philosophical problem does not begin with that problem's abstraction by philosophers. Take the example of existentialism. The novel was already evolving away from the psychology of characters to existential analyses of their situations as a way of understanding their actions and thoughts long before existential philosophy.[26] What Kundera terms "novelistic thinking," even if it explicitly invokes philosophical ideas and texts or the proper names of philosophers, is independent of the ideas exposited to the extent that it can be said to be "purposely a-philosophic, even anti-philosophic, that is to say fiercely independent of any system of preconceived ideas."[27] In my view, this is what makes Kundera a writer-philosopher. His writings are spaces of thought in which a problem can be approached from diverse perspectives, including philosophy, and the value of these perspectives, including philosophy, is not decided in advance of their situatedness in the novel.

Kundera gives as examples of the philosophical novelist Sartre and Camus. The latter's *La Peste*, a "moralizing novel," is "almost the model" of what Kundera rejects. The novelists Musil and Broch, on the other hand, have made of the novel "a supreme poetic and intellectual synthesis and accorded it a preeminent place in the cultural totality."[28] Theirs are syntheses which "marshal around the story all the means–rational and irrational, narrative and contemplative–that could illuminate man's being."[29] To make "intellectually rigorous thinking" an inseparable part of the novel's composition is "one of the boldest innovations any novelist has dared in the era of modern art."[30] What Musil and Broch are doing with philosophy is synthesizing its rationality with

---

[25] Nietzsche, *The Gay Science*, trans. Josefine Nauckhoff (Cambridge: Cambridge University Press, 2001), 194-95.
[26] Milan Kundera, *The Curtain: An Essay in Seven Parts*, trans. Linda Asher (New York: Harper Perennial, 2008). (ebook)
[27] Ibid.
[28] Kundera, "Clarifications."
[29] Kundera, *The Art of the Novel*, 16.
[30] Kundera, *The Curtain*.

the irrationality of how existence happens. It is an "appeal of thought" to which Kundera, too, is responsive in his own work.[31] Kundera too, is after this synthesis. By the term synthesis he means grasping the subject

> from all sides and in the fullest possible completeness. Ironic essay, novelistic narrative, autobiographical fragment, historic fact, flight of fantasy: The synthetic power of the novel is capable of combining everything into a unified whole like the voices of polyphonic music.[32]

One sees in Kundera's novels sections as movements arranged in counterpoint and rhythmed by repetition and variation, ideas joining and disjoining through the alternation of the voices of the characters separated out under the headings of proper names. About the discussion of Nietzsche's eternal return, which opens *The Unbearable Lightness of Being*, Kundera states that it

> has nothing to do with a philosophic discourse; it is a continuity of paradoxes that are no less novelistic (that is to say, they *answer* no less to the essence of what the novel is) than a description of the action or a dialogue.[33]

Kundera thus makes of philosophy, its rationality and its contemplativeness, material for the novel no more or less part of what is synthesized by the novel than the more conventional elements of action, dialogue, and narrative. The task, for Kundera, is to find new forms with which to unify them.

IV.

Novels, for Kundera, are born of "the spirit of humor,"[34] something discovered by the great experimenters, for instance, Rabelais, Diderot, and Sterne. These experimenters understood the novel as a "great *game.*"[35] And their novels' "play essence" is what Kundera thinks the literature of the twentieth century has been deprived of due to its "betrayal" by the novel of the nineteenth.[36]

---

[31] Kundera, *The Art of the Novel*, 16.
[32] Philip Roth and Milan Kundera, "The Most Original Book of the Season," trans. Peter Kussi, *The New York Times Book Review* (November 30, 1980). https://archive.nytimes.com/www.nytimes.com/books/98/05/17/specials/kundera-roth.html.
[33] Kundera, "Clarifications."
[34] Kundera, *The Art of the Novel*, 162.
[35] Roth and Kundera.
[36] Kundera, "Clarifications."

Hrabal's novels are far more excessive in their humorous play than Kundera's, far more overloaded with laughter. If Kundera's play is ironic, Hrabal's is delirium. For Kundera, the entire period of Stalinist terror was "collective lyrical delirium,"[37] but it is Hrabal who sets forth the delirium itself, lets his writing be carried off by it, and incorporates his characters into it, whereas Kundera's characters meditate as a response to it, stilling it. Hrabal elevates playful enjoyment to the status of metaphysics. It is difficult to exaggerate the extent to which Hrabal's writings play: play-acting, playfulness, foreplay, the play of rhythms, playing with ideas. One of the three epigrams for the short story collection *Rambling On* goes: "Essential to playing is freedom. Immanuel Kant, philosopher of the Enlightenment."[38] Hrabal's term for play is "ludibrionism"—a neologism derived from ludibrious: apt for scorn, mockery, or scoffing at (from the Latin *ludibrium*: sport, jest, and *ludere*: play)—which we might more colloquially render as ludicrousness. It is a term he develops from the work of another writer-philosopher, Ladislav Klíma. Play, too, is necessary for becoming a self; such was Klíma's playfulness that, for Hrabal, it was like a god playing, thus play in the metaphysical sense, because "you want to discover what you are and what the others are."[39] In this Klíma was Nietzsche's successor, he staked his whole existence on play, not least the play between philosophy and literature. And Hrabal, in turn, takes his point of departure from Klíma's ludibrionism.

Of the textual material Hrabal works with in becoming self, it is the works of philosophers which play the leading role. What Hrabal does with philosophy is different from Kundera, but what he does with it makes him no less a writer-philosopher. When he says "essential to playing is freedom," what he is paraphrasing is the play at work in judgements. For Kant, what stimulates the harmonious "free play" of our cognitive faculties, understanding and imagination, are beautiful objects, and we take aesthetic pleasure in this. For Hrabal, the shit and terror and incoherence of life are what do with this, the common and the everyday. Hrabal is beholden to the beauty in the prosaic, this is what makes his pleasure "metaphysical."[40] Time and again, Hrabal invokes the same phrase, or variations on it, by Kant:

---

[37] Roth and Kundera.
[38] Bohumil Hrabal, *Rambling On: An Apprentice's Guide to the Gift of the Gab*, trans. David Short (Prague: Karolinum Press, 2014). (ebook)
[39] Hrabal, *Pirouettes*.
[40] Bohumil Hrabal, *I Served the King of England*, trans. Paul Wilson (London: Vintage Books, 2009), 230.

Two things fill the mind with ever new and increasing admiration and reverence, the more often and more steadily one reflects on them: *the starry heavens above me and the moral law within me.*[41]

These are the opening lines of the conclusion to Kant's Second Critique, the *Critique of Practical Reason*. (They also happen to be what is inscribed on Kant's tombstone in Kaliningrad, not just in German but in Russian.) But in Hrabal's hands, these lines do not become over-determining in their authority, nowhere do we find the novel reduced to an illustration of the idea. When, in "Mr. Kafka," the first story of the 1965 collection *Want-ad for a House I No Longer Wish to Live In*, the "practical philosopher" is asked to "kindly explain Kant's *Critique of Practical Reason*" we never get to read the philosophical explanation:

> he invites me for a grilled sausage, and on the way, on Rybnička Street, he gives me an explanation. Then he makes the sign of the cross over his fly and slaps himself so hard on the forehead that he sets the streetlamps trembling.[42]

Then, when an old lady inquires about the time, the practical philosopher "lifts a finger to the sky":

> The night is full of black slag, silver pinwheels, nuts and bolts. It is redolent of ammonia, sour milk, the intimate toiletry of women, essential oils, lipstick. The clock on Štěpánská Street begins to sound the stroke of midnight; other Prague clocks chime in, then those that are running behind. The practical philosopher eats his grilled sausage with gusto, then walks away without a word of farewell.[43]

This is Hrabal's practical explanation of those lines from Kant's *Second Critique*. Not just one side of it, "the starry heavens above," for it is in the way the practical philosopher shows the explanation wherein lies the second part, the moral law. The moral law as it exists for you or for me, "within" you,

---

[41] Immanuel Kant, *Practical Philosophy*, trans. Mary Gregor (Cambridge: Cambridge University Press), 269.
[42] Bohumil Hrabal, *Mr. Kafka and Other Tales*, trans. Paul Wilson (London: Vintage, 2016), 12-13. Wilson suggests *Want-ad for a House I No Longer Wish to Live In* as a translation of the original Czech title of this collection of short stories. Ibid., 140
[43] Ibid., 13

"within" me, cannot be seen outside of our actions. In Jiří Menzel's film *Larks on a String*, based on "Mr. Kafka" and a screenplay on which Hrabal collaborated, a film not released until after the fall of Communism, the practical philosopher declaiming Kant on "making me independent of the senses" disappears falling down a hole: "this is man's glory, his head full of ideals, his feet stuck in shit."[44] The "metaphysical" elements of reality become abyssally and comically ungrounded in Hrabal's language of action. The movement between these two poles, "the starry heavens above" and "the moral law within," becomes the very motion of one novel, *Too Loud a Solitude*, where the author's life is rhythmed by the constant looking upward at night through the five stories of an air shaft, and the constant looking inward, where lie the thoughts composed of what unwittingly he has read from the books he spends his days compacting.[45]

V.

Hrabal sets into motion a maxim taken from Klíma: that "everything arises from its opposite."[46] Hrabal quotes it as the epigraph to *Dancing Lessons for the Advanced in Age:*

> Not only may one imagine that what is higher derives always and only from what is lower; one may imagine that—given the polarity and, more important, the ludicrousness of the world—everything derives from its opposite: day from night, frailty from strength, deformity from beauty, fortune from misfortune.[47]

And, we might add, beauty from shit. For Hrabal, "where everything arises from its opposite; it is the laughter of the gods of antiquity at how opposites stand juxtaposed"; "that is... ludibrionism, those contrasting opposites, those contradictions that say that all opposites are true."[48] Kundera, too, appeals to a similar premise:

---

[44] Jiří Menzel, *Larks on a String* (Prague: Filmové Studio Barrandov, 1969).
[45] Bohumil Hrabal, *Too Loud a Solitude*, trans. Michael Henry Heim (London: Abacus, 1993), 51.
[46] Hrabal, *Pirouettes*.
[47] Ladislav Klíma in Bohumil Hrabal, *Dancing Lessons for the Advanced in Age*, trans. Michael Henry Heim (New York: Harcourt Brace and Company, 1995), unpaginated.
[48] Hrabal, *Pirouettes*.

The evil is already present in the beautiful, hell is already contained in the dream of paradise and if we wish to understand the essence of hell we must examine the essence of the paradise from which it originated.[49]

Both Hrabal and Kundera are, in their different ways, freeing literature from the order of pre-given dualisms. Hrabal makes of Klíma's maxim an organizing principle of his work. It is a plea for tolerance. He describes situations in terms of opposites, where both descriptions are equally plausible, both are apt, and neither have a claim over the other regarding truth. There is no concern for truth in Hrabal, or at least no elevation of it into something unconditioned; instead, there are intensities of words and re-orderings of words that put into question the conditions of truth. What Hrabal does is show how thinking oscillates between the rational and the irrational, his characters are moved in both directions, and actions are set into playful motion by the tension between them. It is a technique of reversal, oscillation and vibration: "everything I see in this world, it all moves backward and forward at the same time, like a blacksmith's bellows."[50] A "continuum of reversible intensities," as Gilles Deleuze and Félix Guattari might put it, in which dualisms break open.[51] Such literature is what Deleuze and Guattari call minor, in a world governed by dualisms it makes other ways of writing possible. In my view, Hrabal's and Kundera's different ways of shaking up and disordering binary opposites, distinctions between inner and outer, rational and irrational, true and false, make possible a literature resistant to the impositions of an oppressive totalitarianism.

In his Introduction to Hrabal's *I Served the King of England*, Adam Thirlwell asserts "Everything in Hrabal's style depends on this reversal of perspective."[52] Thirlwell is only partially right, he does not go far enough. It would be insufficient simply to reverse the perspective, for that would retain the opposition and leave it static. What Hrabal does is set the opposition of perspectives into motion, and lets it vibrate, to the extent that the intensities utilize each other to become what they are.[53] Something happens between the polarities, in the between, in a movement iterated throughout between inhalation and exhalation. Here, we must disagree with Jiří Pelán, for whom

---

[49] Roth and Kundera.
[50] Hrabal, *Too Loud a Solitude*, 48.
[51] Gilles Deleuze and Félix Guattari, *Kafka: Toward a Minor Literature*, trans. Dana Polan (Minneapolis: University of Minnesota Press, 1986), 22.
[52] Adam Thirlwell, "The Death of Mr Hrabal," in Hrabal, *I Served the King of England*, xi.
[53] Deleuze and Guattari, 22.

Hrabal's works are "underpinned by a clear metaphysical perspective."[54] It is the reversibility of perspective which matters, its elasticity, as the last words of *"Beautiful Poldi"* the final story in *Want-ad for a House I No Longer Wish to Live In*, have it: "Everything exists in the elasticity of perspective."[55]

It is an elasticity put into play in the hilariously funny *"*Breaking Through the Drum" of the same collection. The ticket-taker in the Waldstein Gardens understands why Waldstein had to build a wall to separate "the Prague Municipal Symphony Orchestra, under the baton of Doctor Smetáček" from "Mr. Polata's Šumava Regional Brass Band," as if Waldstein had "known all along that the Czech nation would be divided."[56] There was nothing but conflict between them, and the ticket-taker had always been on the side of symphonic music. Until one day the course of his thinking was reversed. As the symphony orchestra "takes on" the brass band, he begins to hear the latter differently, as an ally rather than an enemy. More than that, "as though they'd been written by the same composer."[57] The more the ticket-taker "learns to listen to everything at once" the more he feels the urge to see what was happening over on the other side of the wall, and when he finally looks down, he sees that other side "*through* the Symphonie Pathétique" (my emphasis). It was, he says, as if he were looking down "at the other half of my new self."[58] But the ladder the ticket-taker had used is taken over by members of the symphony orchestra, and players from the brass band fetch their own ladders, and before he knows it, a fight ensues between them. And because, as the ticket-taker puts it, he could "no longer acknowledge the truth of either side with my fists," he began conducting instead, and the brass band began to play again. Such was the resultant frenzy that a fan of the music pulled on the ticket-taker's jacket, causing him to fly through the air and crash into the brass band. The ticket-taker had "kicked [his] way through a drum and come out somewhere on the other side."[59]

It is an invented scene of a democratic dance floor. It is the becoming of music. It is the coming to self through art. First, the opposition of intensities, then the reversal of perspective, then the elasticity between perspectives, then

---

[54] Jiří Pelán, *Bohumil Hrabal: A Full-Length Portrait*, trans. David Short (Prague: Karolinum Press, 2019), 32.
[55] Hrabal, *Mr. Kafka*, 135, 136.
[56] Ibid., 111.
[57] Ibid., 112–13.
[58] Ibid., 113.
[59] Ibid., 118.

the fluxing together and the conflict and play between them, all at the same time, and all in the end as movement towards toleration. The making audible to both sides of the wall a comradeship and commonality across all musics. The egalitarian power of music. A reversal pivoting either side over a wall, over a threshold of toleration, overcoming the wall, making irregular the beat of the drum, which is at the same time giving the scene entirely new tempi, improvised and fluid, taking to its limit the delirium of polyphony, then unifying it by the renunciation of order, allowing another order to be perceived.

VI.

With his very first novel, *The Joke* published in 1967, Kundera began to grasp the problematic of inner freedom. In a system in which he believes, the character Ludwig makes a joke about that system, and, as a result, is sent to a labor camp. There are two fellow inmates there who appear to be free. Honza, who has no attachments and whose freedom is insolent. And Bedrich, the most eccentric one, whose "rare feeling of inner freedom" was given him because he had spoken out, and after which, in the camp, was expressed by staying silent.[60] Part of the irony of Ludwig's situation is that the authoritarian regime could only perceive his joke as the consequence of inner freedom; about his joke, the regime says to him:

> How you wrote it is immaterial. Whether you wrote it quickly or slowly, in your lap or at a desk, *you could only have written what was inside you.* That and nothing else. Perhaps if you'd thought things through, you might not have written it. As it is, you wrote what you really felt. As it is, we know who you are. We know you have two faces—one for the Party, another for everyone else.[61] (My emphasis)

This passage is crucial for an understanding of totalitarian repression. It is a world in which there is no materiality of writing, in which how something is written, or the context in which it is said, makes no difference to its meaning. The *what* is understood merely in terms of its propositional content, and thus has an objective meaning. In such a world, it is impossible to express something which is not the truth, the knowable reality, of a pre-existing inner. It is a rigid, causally expressivist understanding of thought, that whatever is said outwardly is an expression of what is first thought inwardly, a determinate

---

[60] Milan Kundera, *The Joke*, revised edition (London: Faber and Faber, 1992), 54–55.
[61] Ibid., 38.

link that totalitarian regimes both insist on and seek to determine. Totalitarianism cannot accept that there is no such "inner," and its determination of the objectively true extends into that inner. Such is the way that even those closest to him, his friends in the Communist Party, fall in with this determination, including Marketta, the one to whom he had addressed his joke on a postcard, that he begins to feel as his own the guilt that had been foisted upon him by the Party. He begins to believe that he might not be a true proletarian revolutionary after all and that it is no accident that he had expressed such words and that this must make him individualistic. And because he still sought to cling to being a member of the Party, he internalizes the conception of the inner that had been forcibly imposed upon him and accepts his punishment.

In my view, there is, throughout Kundera's novels, a resistance to the idea that one is innerly free. Take, for instance, *Immortality*, the novel he plays with synthesizing discrete sections in the way Broch does in *The Sleepwalkers:*

> Philosophers can tell us that it doesn't matter what the world thinks of us, that nothing matters but what we really are. But philosophers don't understand anything. As long as we live with other people, we are only what other people consider us to be.[62]

Here, the character Paul is wanting to say that there is no self-perception but through the eyes of another. The appearance-reality distinction is giving way. He wants to say that there is nothing wrong or superficial about being concerned with one's image, because it is through the mediation of the eyes that selves have direct contact. It is not that the image is the appearance of the self, shrouding its reality, it is the reality, and he believes he sees his own image in Agnes his wife's eyes.

When Kundera speaks of the inner it tends to be in the form of the "inner world," and he does so, placing it as an early stage in the development of persons and the cultural development of humankind:

> I have long seen youth as the lyrical age, that is, the age when the individual, focused almost exclusively on himself, is unable to see, to comprehend, to judge clearly the world around him.[63]

---

[62] Milan Kundera, *Immortality*, trans. Peter Kussi (London: Faber and Faber, 1991), 142.
[63] Kundera, *The Curtain*.

In *Life is Elsewhere*, Jaromil's celebrated talent for depicting the inner world does not last beyond primary school.[64] So Kundera does not show what happens in Jaromil's head, he shows what happens in his own. But he can only do that by going via Jaromil and writing through Jaromil.[65] In *The Curtain*, Kundera sees Hegel's elevation of the lyrical, in the form of lyric poetry and lyricism in music, as but a stage of immaturity.[66] Erotic passages by Georges Bataille are memorable because they go beyond the lyrical, to meditate on the philosophical.[67] Above all other forms it is the novel which reaches maturity by going beyond the lyrical to the meditative. What is the "inner" as it is expressed by the history of the novel? For Kundera it is equated with all that is obscure, hidden, unknown, irrational, elusive. Ambiguity, uncertainty. The forgetting of being.[68] The novel is that out of which the freedom of the individual emerges when trying to find words to express these states. If the soul is infinite—"the great illusion of the irreplaceable uniqueness of the individual"[69]—it is because this process of becoming a self is an unending one.

VII.

Hrabal did not speak out after the Prague Spring. Instead, he "emigrated inwardly" as he puts it.[70] There was a time in the 1960s when he, together with the likes of Kundera, did speak out, when there was a debate as to how far and how fast to push for changes.[71] Certainly, one could not tie the name Hrabal to an ideological objection. What he did instead was to form a way of life, which was itself writing, which captured the living of a life in opposition to the strictures of a totalitarian regime, a life which, if it was lived, was lived because it was written. As Miroslav Holub says of Hrabal:

---

[64] Milan Kundera, *Life is Elsewhere*, trans. Aaron Asher (New York: Alfred A Knopf, 2000). (ebook)
[65] Kundera, *The Art of the Novel*, 31.
[66] Kundera, *The Curtain*.
[67] Roth and Kundera.
[68] Kundera, *The Art of the Novel*, 5.
[69] Ibid., 8.
[70] Bohumil Hrabal, *Total Fears: Selected Letters to Dubenka*, trans. James Naughton (Prague: Twisted Spoon Press, 1998), 161.
[71] See Kaczorowski.

[He] creates somehow all the time, at every step, sitting, walking, standing. Hrabal is the contents of his works and their episodes, and they in turn are the entire life-contents of Hrabal.[72]

Such a life is unpredictable. By itself, this would be resistance. Writing under Communism was to be a writing of Communism, a writing of lives either as they were lived under Communism because of Communism, or of lives as they ought to be lived under Communism. Hrabal's writing is of a life as it was lived despite Communism, and if it was because of Communism, it was not because of what Communism offered as an idea, but because of what Communism produced by way of chance and unintended consequence and the elevation of the common to the status of a funny metaphysics. Of course, the common is a field for Hrabal, insofar as much of his dialogue is generated by the talk of men in pubs. But what makes it the common is its way of working a space for actions which disprove Communism in their unpredictability. You do not need Communism as a support to live the kind of life Hrabal's characters do. Hrabal's novels are indifferent to Communism. This is their blindspot as well, in that one does not find shown there the overt repression and the suppression carried out by the authoritarian regime.

For Josef Škvorecký, Hrabal was the first to break with the social-realist convention of three social categories of human types: positive, negative, and wavering hero.[73] If we agree with Škvorecký it is because in Hrabal's work, the latter—"the figure of a beer drinker who thinks like an intellectual but speaks the language of the palavering populace"—traverses all three categories, becoming a hero through the intensive vibration of the opposition between positive and negative. Hrabal did not protest, he chose the pub, the pub was where he emigrated to inwardly.[74] The common in the form of the pub became the inner to which Hrabal retreated. Being in the pub all the time meant that Hrabal often missed opportunities to speak out or protest, either because he was drinking in his favorite pub *U Zlatého tygra* [The Golden Tiger] or because he was waylaid to this or that other pub.[75] It was because he was out drinking with a friend in some other pub that Hrabal missed a meeting with Václav

---

[72] Miroslav Holub, "Hrabal happenings," *The Times Literary Supplement* (May 15, 1992): 9.
[73] Josef Škvorecký, *Talkin' Moscow Blues* (London: Faber and Faber, 1989), 181–82.
[74] Hrabal, *Total Fears*, 161.
[75] Ibid., 88–89.

Havel,[76] who had come to Hrabal's favorite pub to get him to sign the manifesto *Několik vět* [A Few Sentences].[77]

Hrabal remarks that he was called a collaborator for not signing *Několik vět*, yet even though he says shortly afterward that he most likely would have signed it at the time (just as he would have signed Ludvík Vaculík's manifesto *Dva tisíce slov* [Two Thousand Words] in 1968, had not Vaculík changed his mind and got him to author a public text instead), Hrabal insists he did the right thing in not signing it. Why? "Because I wouldn't swap that signature on 'A Few Sentences' for eighty thousand copies of my *Too Loud a Solitude*."[78] He is speaking in October 1989, a month before the Velvet Revolution. He appears to think it was either/or. He describes *Několik vět* as "the acid test for those in favour of rigid dogma and those in favour of creative dogma."[79] He chose to live his life in such a way as best enabled him to create, because writing was the "only salvation from that gentle police terror."[80]

The problem with inner emigration is that you cannot know when you are self-censoring. This is something Hrabal would come to admit in the months leading up to the Velvet Revolution in letters to his one-time lover Dubenka in 1989: "I had never known that what I had experienced, this was also totalitarian... everything that had happened to me without my being conscious of it... I had let myself be drawn into this game, for which I had no desire."[81] Hrabal was prevented from publishing anything during the period of "normalization" following the Prague Spring. It was then that he "broke, or rather bent somewhat," as Škvorecký puts it,[82] and allowed his work to be censored for publication.[83] After the Velvet Revolution Hrabal confesses his fear. He succumbed to it, yet at the same time it impelled him to write: "I like to be afraid, it makes me write better."[84] The Interior Ministry, he says, forced

---

[76] Ibid., 73.
[77] Václav Havel, Alexandr Vondra, and Jiří Křižan. *Několik vět* [A Few Sentences]. Originally broadcast by Radio Free Europe on June 29, 1989, then published abroad the next day, before being published in Prague in samizdat *Lidové noviny* in July.
[78] Hrabal, *Total Fears*, 73.
[79] Ibid.
[80] Ibid., 176.
[81] Ibid., 165–71.
[82] Škvorecký in Bohumil Hrabal, *Closely Watched Trains*, trans. Edith Pargeter (Evanston: Northwestern University Press, 1998), xvii.
[83] An example is provided by Škvorecký in Bohumil Hrabal, *The Little Town Where Time Stood Still* and *Cutting it Short*, trans. James Naughton (London: Abacus, 1994), xiv.
[84] Hrabal, *Total Fears*, 176.

him to make use of his fear: "the only defence against fear in the end was this literature, this typewriter of mine."[85] Hrabal wrote with his fear. The fear was part of the process of writing. Mixed with the unstoppable alcohol and the unceasing playfulness, the ever-present fear was an essential part of the delirium of writing.

VIII.

Too Loud a Solitude is Hrabal's great work. Part of its greatness consists in what it does with philosophical texts. In order of appearance: Hegel, Nietzsche, Schiller, Schelling, Kant, Schopenhauer, Sartre, Camus, Aristotle, Plato... amongst others. Haňťa, the lead character, is a paper-compactor, his job is to compact wastepaper. He receives thousands of books which, like Hrabal's own when he set out as a writer, were consigned by the authorities to be pulped, either because, like Hrabal's, they are banned (*Too Loud a Solitude*, published in samizdat form in 1976, was not given an official print run until after the fall of Communism), or because they have become neglected and forgotten. Hrabal gives these books a new ordering, new configurations of them, impenetrable to the eyes of the censors, which they always were and always will be for those whose reading is blinded by ideology, for those who can espouse only a blind ideology, seeking to produce, as do all totalitarianisms, a culturally illiterate people. For thirty-five years, deep underground, Haňťa compacts these books along with all the other wastepaper into bales, glued together with the blood and guts of mice and flies, all crushed together by a gigantic hydraulic press. And in the heart of these bales, he lays open a book of philosophy—"that the word might be made bloody flesh, an *Ecce Homo* by Friedrich Nietzsche,"[86] Nietzsche's treatise on "How to Become What You Are"[87]—then ties to each bale an image of a great master painting again ripped from books. He sends these bales back up and out of the underground bunker in which he carries on this work, great cubisms of dense individual compacts of heterogeneous elements, destined to become innocent paper for books deemed permissible.

A paper compactor kept underground for thirty-five years turns his entire existence towards forming these assemblages, words pulsed by the compacting movement of the hydraulic paper press according to the rhythm of a red button and a green button, retreat and advance, "like everything in my press, turning

---

[85] Ibid., 187.
[86] Hrabal, *Too Loud a Solitude*, 32.
[87] Friedrich Nietzsche, *The Anti-Christ, Ecce Homo, Twilight of the Idols, and Other Writings*, trans. Judith Norman (Cambridge: Cambridge University Press, 2005), 69.

into its opposite at the command of red and green buttons, and that's what makes the world go round."[88] The red button and the green button are opposites in that green is on, red is off, green is to go, red is to stop. Yet, in another, more fundamental sense of the novel they are not opposites so much as the polarities of a constantly varying dynamic rhythm. Through the press and release of these buttons, Haňťa makes relations between image and text, which only he will see. Hrabal overloads his bale texts with the mashing of the terms of oppositions, between the beautiful and the sublime, the infinite and the sensuous, the eternal and the everyday. There is nothing transcendent in Hrabal. Hrabal's is the realization that time has no transcendental meaning. The significance of time is immanent. The present moment is to be lived, because only it can be lived, or not; and it can only be lived, or not, it cannot be transcended. If there is any transcendence, if there is, it is given by what we make of the world in the present. This is what makes the present moment matter. The present moment redeems time. Hrabal's delirium of the present and its possibilities is the grasping of this gift of the world with all its lived disappointments, contingent wonders, and contradictory movements. What the paper-compactor produces are works which make of this impossible present, a world whose culture is repressed and pulped, refutations of Communism, works of individuality which no one will ever read. For thirty-five years, he did this, "living with, living through, a daily Sisyphus complex."[89] Hrabal pushes language to a certain limit, a language that reveals the poverty of the world from which these texts have been repressed. It is Hrabal's final inquiry into what there is. And what there is is what he makes of it.

The books of Kant have pride of place in this paper-compactor's world. The "pre-critical" Kant of the sublime and the ineffable, not the later critical Kant of inner freedom and the moral law. The Kant of "casts of mind that possess a feeling for the sublime are gradually drawn into lofty sentiments, of friendship."[90] The early Kant of:

> In the universal stillness of nature and the calmness of the senses the immortal spirit's hidden faculty of cognition speaks an ineffable

---

[88] Hrabal, *Too Loud a Solitude*, 48.
[89] Ibid., 68.
[90] Immanuel Kant, *Observations on the Feeling of the Beautiful and Sublime and Other Writings*, trans. Paul Guyer. (Cambridge: Cambridge University Press, 2011), 16; Cf. Hrabal, *Too Loud a Solitude*, 50.

language and provides undeveloped concepts that can certainly be felt but not described.[91]

becomes in Hrabal:

[I]n the silence, the absolute silence of the night, when the senses lie dormant, an immortal spirit speaks in a nameless tongue of things that can be grasped but not described.[92]

There could not be anyone further than Hrabal from the Kant of *The Doctrine of Virtue*, the Kant of self-mastery, reason's control, and the rule of inner freedom. It may have broken Haňťa's heart to see Kant's *Metaphysics of Morals* left unretrieved from the morass and fused with the entrails of animals,[93] but his freedom is not the inner one of "ruling oneself, that is subduing one's affects and governing one's passions,"[94] it is the passional one of realizing one's freedom through the words and texts of others. Hrabal's characters may be motivationally independent to make selves of themselves out of and under the circumstances, but not to constrain themselves to an *a priori* inner beaten into them by the total outer that totalitarianism is. Hrabal's characters are not *a priori* selves, sufficient unto themselves; no, they become selves through others, through processes of listening and responding to others and appropriating others, processes which never stop.

IX.

Hrabal may have emigrated inwardly, but in my view, he did not make his mind its own place, as Richard Rorty puts it in a phrase criticizing Heidegger for doing just that.[95] (In my view, Heidegger's abstention from action in favor of the thinking of being was, in large part, the appeal of his work for many dissident figures in Eastern Europe under Communism.) Hrabal did not abstain from action, the actions of friendships or associations. He may have renounced action in the conventional sense of "speaking out" as political protest, but he did not abstain from action in his writing practice. His practice

---

[91] Immanuel Kant, *Natural Science*, trans. Olaf Reinhardt (Cambridge: Cambridge University Press, 2012), 307.
[92] Hrabal, *Too Loud a Solitude*, 51-52.
[93] Ibid., 72.
[94] Kant, *Practical Philosophy*, 535.
[95] Richard Rorty, *Essays on Heidegger and Others. Philosophical Papers, volume 2* (Cambridge: Cambridge University Press, 1991), 70.

was one of composing accounts of what freedom looks like. He writes protest, comedic protest, comedic-moral protest. The ideology of Soviet repression was the pretense of there being no contradiction in lives as they are lived, and it is these lives of contradiction, lives granted the right to contradiction, lives born of the intensive vibration of contradictions, that the literature of Hrabal, and Kundera, give form to.

Encountering the work of Kundera is one of the factors leading Rorty to become a philosopher-writer. He may not have known or accepted that he was a philosopher-writer, but once he embraced literature as the space in which the problems with which philosophy deals are set into motion in a way that philosophy needs must take account of, he became a philosopher-writer. His style changed, the narratives developed, the books became assemblages of texts on more diverse figures and from multiple perspectives. The philosophers for whom he had more time in the latter part of his career–Derrida, Nietzsche, Kierkegaard–are philosophers in whose work the distinction between philosophy and literature is put into question, philosophers who use multiple voices and different personae and ways of writing to explore the distinction, philosophers who were at ease with narrative as much as theory, philosophers free of the presupposition that philosophy can know in advance of its encounter with literature where the distinction falls.

Rorty came to realize that professional philosophers tend to have imaginations which exclude culture, the culture of art and literature. Through an encounter with culture, especially literature, and in particular the novel, his writing freed itself to allow for the deepening of its imagination. One of the writers who drew him was Kundera. Kundera, for Rorty, was a writer with a healthy skepticism towards philosophy and theorizing. For all that, I find Kundera a writer-philosopher. Not because he wrote philosophical novels, on the contrary. Kundera is a writer-philosopher because in using philosophy and synthesizing it with forms which philosophy eschews, and in broaching the very problems philosophy treats as its own, he welcomes philosophy responsive to literature, and accords it the same equality he does every other element. This is one of the things which distinguishes Kundera as a writer, and Hrabal too. Hrabal's works are democratic because of how they incorporate philosophical text into their assemblages, where the philosophical is equal to any other material and has no jurisdiction over the ideas or the actions the novel describes.

If there is one idea Rorty finds in Kundera's conception of the novel which lends itself to Rorty's broader politico-moral project of diversity and tolerance, it is the idea that the novel is "a paradise of individuals."[96] The novel is literature's way of overcoming philosophy's being beholden to the appearance-reality distinction. If, for Kundera, the novel is the place "where no one possesses the truth… but where everyone has the right to be understood,"[97] then for Rorty the novel is to be celebrated as the space where a plurality of descriptions of the same events are equally plausible, the space of a democratic utopia.[98] "I don't know which of my characters is right" says Kundera.[99] This is his "equality of voices."[100] If the reader yearns for judgement in the world of the novel, then the novelist sets things up in such a way that the reader must do the work of judgment herself, assisted not by moral theories, political ideologies, or general principles, but with the aid only of proper names of characters.[101]

What Rorty thinks Kundera is encouraging is the creation of new genres in reaction to or as alternatives to the theorization of what human beings are or, more especially, should be. To the extent that the theories in question are ideological or theological, I agree, literature will always react against these. But if we are talking about theories which themselves put into question the distinctions between literature and theory, and literature and philosophy, then literature is quite able to use such theories as material. New forms and genres of literature arise less as a reaction than as a response to theory. Literature often takes from theory what it can use, lines of thought it can reroute, aporia it can step through, models it can deform. It seems to me that literature and theory work well together in the liberal West. After all, if literature is to become the evermore tolerant space answering to the "desirability of diversity,"[102] then it is only natural that it will incorporate philosophy. And in my view, vice versa, philosophy too is becoming more diverse, more tolerant, in the sense that it is developing and promoting sensitivity towards the history of its own intolerance and blindness—to the slave trade, for example, or to colonialism, not just examples among others. In becoming, let's say, more self-conscious of its own lack of diversity philosophy becomes not perhaps more attractive to literature, but differently so.

---

[96] Kundera, *The Art of the Novel*, 161; Rorty, *Essays*, 74–75.
[97] Kundera, ibid.
[98] Rorty, *Essays*, 74–75.
[99] Roth and Kundera.
[100] Kundera, *The Art of the Novel*, 77.
[101] Rorty, *Essays*, 78.
[102] Ibid., 81.

X.

If we think that there is no dissent without freedom of expression, no freedom of thought without the freedoms of expression and assembly, if we believe that to think freely, that is to think at all, is something given in language through being with others, then we can see how writing is a way first of becoming self, of finding oneself, and second of putting oneself back together after the self-censorship, the splits and the schisms and the divisions brought about by repression and the denial of freedom. Resistance does not have to take the form of ideology. In Hrabal's and Kundera's novels dissent takes the form of acts of freely living a social life, and experiencing that life, and retaining a memory of the acts of a life, which produces consequences that stand as resistance to an ideology which would dictate how life should be lived. Both writers happen to use texts of philosophy as material with which to show what freedom looks like.

Hrabal uprooted philosophy, and he showed how anyone can work with it. In doing so he also reconfigured the place of the visual in writing. As he stresses in his Introduction to the translation into English of the film script for *Closely Observed Trains*, there is a great deal of the visual in his prose.[103] But it is more than that. *Too Loud a Solitude* makes visual art with philosophy, Haňťa the paper-compactor processes philosophical texts and re-makes them into image-text book sculptures. Hrabal composes such book works because these philosophers, as philosophers, have no place in that world. It was his way of reinstating the questioning nature of a philosophy politically denuded of its questioning power. Hrabal thought in images.[104] He used a montage method to achieve the impact of a film, the law of the cut: cut up with scissors and piece together in a different order.[105] He questions the assumptions and the dictates of what totalitarianism deems should count as what is seeable and what can be put into words. To do this, he intervenes in the very distinction between the visible and the invisible. He does so from the side of literature, creating a novel, *Too Loud a Solitude*, which is a *philosophical* intervention in this respect.

Kundera says, "The metaphysics of man is the same in the private sphere as in the public one." And he says, "Politics unmasks the metaphysics of private life, private life unmasks the metaphysics of politics."[106] Private life does indeed unmask the metaphysics of politics—if, that is, it is freely able to enter the

---

[103] Menzel and Hrabal, 8.
[104] See for instance Hrabal's "A Betrayal of Mirrors," in *Mr. Kafka*, 77.
[105] Hrabal, *Why I write?*, 15.
[106] Roth and Kundera.

public realm. There is no free private life without that public realm. There is no inner freedom without politics. He could have said, "The metaphysics of man is the same in the public sphere as in the private one." There is no private metaphysics that is not given publicly. How does politics unmask the metaphysics of private life? Kundera's novels show that if you deny people the political in the form of freedom of expression and freedom of assembly then you deny them a free private life.

Kundera's novels and Hrabal's novels are entries of private life into the public realm. What they unmask is why totalitarianism seeks to deny free expression in the public realm: when speech and action are free, it produces hitherto unheard and unseen ways of being together, and dissensual forms of speaking them out. Free expression multiplies the differences, it diversifies the world endlessly. There is no determinate link between inner and outer, from the direction of thought to speech. The relation goes both ways. If totalitarianism seeks to break the free link between speech and thought, it does so because it wants to control the questioning nature of humankind, which is an essential part of its creativity and becoming. To repress speech and expression and the opportunities for people to gather freely and to discourse freely is to seek to determine the relationship between speech and thought and have it go in one way only, from speech to thought, from purely objective speech to a necessarily innerly-implied thought. As if one can never joke. To determine what counts as acceptable and unacceptable speech, and proper and improper speech, and serious and unserious speech, is to try to determine what can be thought. Totalitarianism ideologizes the speaking body, determining how, where, and what it can say. It goes as far as to decide what bodies are thinking when they say certain things.

Inner freedom is an unwitting accomplice in this totalizing endeavor. When Kundera says that totalitarianism "deprives people of memory and thus retools them into a nation of children,"[107] what he means, I think, is that if you deprive people of memory, you deprive them of the ability to re-think. All thinking is re-thinking. You cannot re-think without what is given inwardly being questioned. Totalitarianism knows that a freedom which is denied the possibility of being put into question by others is the myth of freedom. It knows that people will struggle to find the words to articulate their needs and desires or even to accept those needs and desires in themselves without the help of others and having them made visible by others. Inner freedom without freedom of expression is a prison, ownness without self, body without

---

[107] Ibid.

language, voice without words. Hrabal's approaching "oneself through others" shows that anyone can take hold of words, even words of philosophy, and make something of them, something which would give meaning to their lives and show others the possibilities of world. But for that you need words, ideas, and texts of others out there of which to take hold. Kundera's "equality of voices" shows how a world of tolerance is one which permits the same word to have different meanings, the same event to have different descriptions, the same aim to have different outcomes, and the same criteria for differentiating between these to have different ways of application. It is an equality out of which politics arises, and dissent is made possible.

Bibliography

Broch, Hermann. *The Sleepwalkers*. Translated by Willa and Edwin Muir. New York: Vintage International, 1996.

Deleuze, Gilles, and Félix Guattari. *Kafka: Toward a Minor Literature*. Translated by Dana Polan. Minneapolis: University of Minnesota Press, 1986.

Havel, Václav, Alexandr Vondra, and Jiří Křižan. *Několik vět* [A Few Sentences]. Originally broadcast by Radio Free Europe on June 29, 1989, then published abroad the next day, before being published in Prague in samizdat *Lidové noviny* in July.

Holub, Miroslav. "Hrabal happenings." In *The Times Literary Supplement*, 9-10. May 15, 1992.

Hrabal, Bohumil. *Closely Watched Trains* [originally 1965]. Translated by Edith Pargeter. Evanston: Northwestern University Press, 1998.

———. *Dancing Lessons for the Advanced in Age* [originally 1964]. Translated by Michael Henry Heim. New York: Harcourt Brace and Company, 1995.

———. *I Served the King of England* [originally 1971]. Translated by Paul Wilson. London: Vintage Books, 2009.

———. *Mr. Kafka and Other Tales* [originally 1965]. Translated by Paul Wilson. London: Vintage, 2016.

———. *Pirouettes on a Postage-stamp, An Interview-Novel with Questions Asked and Answers Recorded by László Szigeti* [originally 1986]. Translated by David Short. Prague: Karolinum Press, 2014.

———. *Rambling On: An Apprentice's Guide to the Gift of the Gab* [originally 1975]. Translated by David Short. Prague: Karolinum Press, 2014.

———. *The Little Town Where Time Stood Still* and *Cutting it Short* [originally 1973 and 1976 respectively]. Translated by James Naughton. London: Abacus, 1994.

———. *Too Loud a Solitude* [originally 1976]. Translated by Michael Henry Heim. London: Abacus, 1993.

———. *Total Fears: Selected Letters to Dubenka* [originally 1989-91]. Translated by James Naughton. Prague: Twisted Spoon Press, 1998.

———. *Why I Write? And Other Early Prose Pieces.* Translated by David Short. Prague: Karolinum Press, 2019.

Kaczorowski, Alexander. "Was Bohumil Hrabal a Politically Engaged Writer?" *Aspen Review,* March 15, 2017. https://aspen.review/article/2017/was-bohumil-hrabal-a-politically-engaged-writer%3F.

Kant, Immanuel. *Natural Science.* Translated by Olaf Reinhardt. Cambridge: Cambridge University Press, 2012.

———. *Observations on the Feeling of the Beautiful and Sublime and Other Writings.* Translated by Paul Guyer. Cambridge: Cambridge University Press, 2011.

———. *Practical Philosophy.* Translated by Mary Gregor. Cambridge: Cambridge University Press, 1996.

Kundera, Milan. "Clarifications, Elucidations: An interview with Lois Oppenheim." [originally 1989]. *Dalkey Archive Press,* 2013. https://www.dalkeyarchive.com/2013/08/02/a-conversation-with-milan-kundera-by-lois-oppenheim/.

———. "Comedy is everywhere." *Index on Censorship* 6, no. 6 (1977): 3–7.

———. *Immortality.* Translated by Peter Kussi. London: Faber and Faber, 1991.

———. *Life is Elsewhere* [originally 1973]. Translated by Aaron Asher. New York: Alfred A. Knopf, 2000.

———. *The Art of the Novel,* revised edition [originally 1986]. Translated by Linda Asher. London: Faber and Faber, 1999.

———. *The Book of Laughter and Forgetting* [originally 1979]. Translated by Aaron Asher. London: Faber and Faber, 1996.

———. *The Curtain: An Essay in Seven Parts* [originally 2005]. Translated by Linda Asher. New York: Harper Perennial, 2008.

———. *The Joke,* revised edition [originally 1967]. London: Faber and Faber, 1992.

———. *The Unbearable Lightness of Being* [originally 1984]. Translated by Michael Henry Heim. London: Faber and Faber, 1985.

Menzel, Jiří. *Larks on a String.* Prague: Filmové Studio Barrandov, 1969.

Menzel, Jiří and Hrabal Bohumil. *Closely Observed Trains,* film script. Translated by Josef Holzbecher. London: Lorimer Publishing, 1971.

Nietzsche, Friedrich. *The Anti-Christ, Ecce Homo, Twilight of the Idols, and Other Writings.* Translated by Judith Norman. Cambridge: Cambridge University Press, 2005.

———. *The Gay Science.* Translated by Josefine Nauckhoff. Cambridge: Cambridge University Press, 2001.

Pelán, Jiří. *Bohumil Hrabal: A Full-Length Portrait.* Translated by David Short. Prague: Karolinum Press, 2019.

Rorty, Richard. *Essays on Heidegger and Others. Philosophical Papers, volume 2.* Cambridge: Cambridge University Press, 1991.

———. *Objectivity, Relativism, and Truth: Philosophical Papers.* Cambridge: Cambridge University Press, 1990.

Roth, Philip, and Milan Kundera. "The Most Original Book of the Season." Translated by Peter Kussi. *The New York Times Book Review*, November 30, 1980. https://archive.nytimes.com/www.nytimes.com/books/98/05/17/specials/kundera-roth.html.

Škvorecký, Josef. *Talkin' Moscow Blues*. London: Faber and Faber, 1989.

Thirlwell, Adam. "The Death of Mr Hrabal." In Bohumil Hrabal, *I Served the King of England*, ix–xxxi. London: Vintage Books, 2009.

Vaculík, Ludvík. *Dva tisíce slov, které patří dělníkům, zemědělcům, úředníkům, vědcům, umělcům a všem* [Two Thousand Words, to Workers, Farmers, Officials, Scientists, Artists, and Everyone]. Prague: *Literární Listy*, June 27, 1968.

Chapter 5
Normalization in contemporary Czech prose: between nostalgia, ironizing, payback, and problematizing

Marek Lollok
Masaryk University, Czech Rep.

Abstract

The text deals with various ways of depicting normalization in Czech post-Communist literature. In the introductory passages, it considers the specifics of the treatment of historical facts in fiction, including the specifics that arise in comparison with other discourses. For this purpose, it defines terms such as past, history, contemporary history, (collective) memory, literature and others, using secondary historiographical literature. The ambiguous concept of normalization is also explained. To make the situation in this hitherto largely productive current clearer, we propose five specific modes–types within which normalization is presented in literature. Specifically, these are Mode 1: humorous, nostalgic, ironic; Mode 2: imaginative; Mode 3: payback, resistance; Mode 4: existential and Mode 5: problematizing. These modes are introduced in more detail with the help of about two-three examples, which illustrate the authors' approaches, forms, and styles, as well as thematic diversity of Czech prose about normalization.

Keywords: Contemporary Czech prose, history, collective memory, normalization.

* * *

Czech literature has always had a fairly close relationship to history. Not only have historical events frequently served as the subject of works of art and real figures from the past often taken on the role of main protagonists, but many works, as well as writers and their activities, remain a striking part of the national history. In the nineteenth and twentieth centuries especially, literature and writers significantly affected non-literary life and assumed an important role in public events, no matter if that was their intention or a matter of circumstance. For example, it is well known that two centuries ago, literature played an essential role in the Czech nation's struggle for self-determination, similarly as in the significant times during World War II or the 1960s, when the role of literature as the co-creator of national identity re-emerged. Although in the 1990s, the impression prevailed that with the fall of the Communist regime, "history had ended" and literature may remain in its "autistic and solipsistic isolation," it must no longer "bear the fate of the nation" and "be its conscience,"[1] the following development showed that this idea was wishful thinking rather than a realistic description of the then state of affairs or a reliable prognosis.

Despite the continuing marginalization caused by multiple factors, Czech literature has not lost contact with reality, and for many actors–authors as well as recipients–this contact is still crucial. Stories about the past occupy a prominent position, that is, texts based on the state of affairs, situations, events and occurrences with a real (verifiable) basis, however, "embroidered" by one's own invention. Not only do they enjoy the interest of readers, but in the Czech context, they somehow *a priori* raise considerable expectations: for many years, there has been a lookout for a work that would, if possible, synthetically and suggestively capture the last decades in which Czechs live.

Interest in contemporary history and normalization

The so-called contemporary history proved to be extremely attractive in literature after the fall of the Communist regime. The history of the recent past, as historians say, is unique in many ways and requires a special approach, as it is a "constant dialogue between then and now," and "the exact borderline between memory or testimony and a distanced analysis and interpretation is hard to draw."[2]

The depiction of history in prose is, of course, specific–it is not a matter of historiography, let alone the past as such, but of the use of history for literary purposes. With some simplification, it can be viewed as the programmatic fictionalizing of history. Although we do not require empirical verification of literature or demand complete accordance with the sources, the artistically processed past shares a lot with historical (historiographical) images. Crucial is

---

[1] Jiří Kratochvil, "Obnovení chaosu v české literatuře," *Literární noviny* 3, no. 47 (1992), 5.
[2] Pavel Kolář and Michal Pullmann, *Co byla normalizace?: studie o pozdním socialismu* (Praha: Nakladatelství Lidové noviny, 2016), 15.

the fact that it is not about reality itself, but about its–unavoidably reductive–interpretation.[3]

Moreover, the recent past necessarily occupies a privileged place in the public debate. Every day, a number of texts on this topic are created, and multimedia and multiperspective approaches are applied. In contrast to other time periods, lay people often comment on contemporary history.[4] It is, naturally, a popular and almost commonplace topic for politicians, political scientists, journalists, sociologists, cultural anthropologists, and other intellectuals, including artists and writers.[5] At the intersection of these views, the so-called collective memory[6] is formed, i.e., a common idea of what was, and at the same time, of what relationship it has to the current present and what it can mean for the future.[7]

Since the 1990s, there has been an enormous interest in the historical era of the so-called normalization, and paradoxically, this interest has not ceased with the progress of time, but instead has grown. After 1990, and especially in recent years, many works of prose have been published in which Czechoslovak normalization (in the sense of the period from the violent suppression of the Prague Spring by Warsaw Pact troops in 1968 to the fall of Communism in 1989) becomes a striking, or literally decisive, element in the story. The outline of the

---

[3] The narrativity of historiography, or the narration of history, is described in more detail in this monograph: Kamil Činátl, *Dějiny a vyprávění: Palackého Dějiny jako zdroj historické obraznosti národa* (Praha: Argo, 2011).

[4] See Milan Otáhal, *Normalizace 1969-1989: příspěvek ke stavu bádání* (Praha: Ústav pro soudobé dějiny AV ČR, 2002), 42.

[5] See, for example, Kamil Činátl, Jan Mervart, and Jaroslav Najbrt, eds., *Podoby československé normalizace: dějiny v diskuzi* (Praha: Ústav pro studium totalitních režimů, 2017).

[6] "At the forefront of the group's memory are reminiscences of events and experience associated with the largest number of its members. They are based either on the group's own life or on relationships with the nearest groups. Memories associated with only a small number of members, or even with only one of them, recede into the background, although they remain part of group memory because they arose, at least to some extent, within the group." Maurice Halbwachs, *Kolektivní paměť* (Praha: Sociologické nakladatelství, 2009), 72-73.

[7] "Collective memory thus operates in both directions, backwards and forwards. Memory reconstructs the past, but also organizes how we experience the present and the future. It would therefore make no sense to set the 'principle of hope' against 'the principle of recollection': they both condition each other, one cannot be conceived of without the other." Jan Assmann, *Kultura a paměť: písmo, vzpomínka a politická identita v rozvinutých kulturách starověku* (Praha: Prostor, 2001), 42.

typology of these works, as well as the presentation of their main characteristics and tendencies, is the main focus of this chapter.

The situation in literature corresponds to the development of Czech historiography, where the topic of normalization has enjoyed considerable attention for several decades. In particular, young researchers present new interpretations, alternatives to previous descriptions and interpretations, based on various sources and methodological approaches.[8] We also see a similar interest in this area in many popularizing, especially biographical works, which, in addition to capturing the life and work of remarkable figures, often have the ambition to depict broader contexts of the period in question.[9] Nor can film, television, theater, and music production be overlooked, thematizing, but to a large extent also recycling schemes of contemporary popular culture, including the participation of some still active normalization stars.[10] Of course, discussions of normalization do not end in political and societal debates: even more than thirty years after the change of regime, they go back to some specific cases and more general problems, such as membership in the Communist Party, cooperation with the State Security, signing or refusal to sign the Charter 77, the Anticharter and the like.

The consequence of the described trend is a certain preconception, operating with certain emblems and symbols of normalization: it is through them that we look at the seventies and eighties of the last century today, with their help, we evoke this period. There are countless examples: pre-fab housing estates, Spartakiad, queues for bananas, addressing each other as comrade, Tuzex

---

[8] For an overview, see Jan Mervart, "Rozdílnost pohledů na československou normalizaci," in *Podoby československé normalizace: dějiny v diskuzi,* eds. Kamil Činátl, Jan Mervart, and Jaroslav Najbrt (Praha: Ústav pro studium totalitních režimů, 2017), 40–80 or Otáhal, *Normalizace 1969–1989.*

[9] See, for example, Pavel Klusák, *Gott: československý příběh* (Brno: Host, 2021) or Marek Švehla, *Magor a jeho doba: život Ivana M. Jirouse* (Praha: Torst, 2017).

[10] Cf. Petr A. Bílek and Blanka Činátlová, *Tesilová kavalérie: popkulturní obrazy normalizace* (Příbram: Pistorius & Olšanská, 2010). Especially on the topic of normalization and film, many valuable contributions have been made in recent years, for example: Petr Kopal, ed., *Film a dějiny 4. Normalizace* (Praha: Ústav pro studium totalitních režimů, 2014). Paulina Bren researched television production in her monograph, *Zelinář a jeho televize: kultura komunismu po pražském jaru 1968* (Praha: Academia, 2013). Among the many attempts to portray the normalizing reality on the theater stage, let us highlight the concentrated production *Šedá sedmdesátá aneb Husákovo ticho (The Gray Seventies or Husák's Silence)* by director Jan Mikulášek and playwright Dora Viceníková (Divadlo Na zábradlí, 2013).

stores, foreign exchange promises and exit permits, May Day parades, Gustáv Husák, and others. The inherent danger of these (and other) unquestionable normalization attributes is their literary (cultural) conventionality and at least the potential oversimplification: they can easily become cheap props and clichés that a writer simply borrows for their needs from an imaginary reservoir without reflecting their true content or relevance to the text.

Past, history, historiography, memory and literature

Before we get to the introduction and categorization of normalization's depiction in contemporary literature, it will be useful to briefly recapitulate the key concepts crucial to the discussion. How do such broad, often multi-meaning concepts as the past, history, historiography, memory relate to each other, what is their relationship to literature, and what is the distinction between them?

Together with Petr Čornej, referring to K. R. Popper, we can understand the past as the most general concept, "not relating exclusively to humanity, but also to the existence of the Earth or the universe"; history is then "the past of the human race." "It is always necessary to distinguish unique, single and one history (sum of all events and phenomena) from written history (operating only with a selected set of facts), or history-text, which is the result of the historian's research and literary work," writes Čornej.[11] Language and imagination thus belong to the constitutive elements in historiography as well as in literature; historical knowledge has a non-negligible literary character, after all, it is "available almost exclusively in verbal form."[12]

Let us emphasize that "the literary organization [of a historiographic text–*ML note*] of a text does not necessarily lead to epic forms."[13] It is also possible to argue against the idea that "frames" or "matrices" of experiencing and remembering, as well as frames of recalling from memory to consciousness and explicit reminiscing, are narrative in nature," i.e., that "one (or a group of people) lives 'in a story' and remembers their past 'in a story.'"[14] According to

---

[11] Petr Čornej, "Věčný problém: Jak psát dějiny," in *O psaní dějin: teoretické a metodologické problémy literární historiografie*, eds. Kateřina Piorecká and Ondřej Sládek (Praha: Academia, 2007), 15.
[12] Ibid., 16.
[13] Zdeněk Vašíček, Robert Krumphanzl, and Karel Palek, eds., *Jak se dělají filosofie* (Praha: Triáda, 2012), 204.
[14] Jan Horský, *Teorie a narace: k noetice historické vědy a teorii kulturního vývoje* (Praha: Argo, 2015), 44.

Vašíček, it is more appropriate "to look at the structure of memory contents as a summary of diverse entities (perceptions, feelings, and emotional experiences, information, cultural variants) and their (freely associative, logical, etc.) configurations, which have different degrees of strength, variability, compatibility, etc." This presumed nature of memory can then be combined with the idea of an "image."[15]

In both literature and historiography, the concept of an image is used as a means of dampening efforts to translate the issue of historical representation exclusively into its–often too contrived–"story nature." Such a presentation is not always adequate: "The narrative structure of orientation in the contents of memory approached this way (as "images") is only one of the possible ways of remembering. Not only will we be able to relate a newly constructed narration, often a new storyline, to the same topic with each new remembering, but many recollections simply will not have a narrative structure. One does not only live their world in an epical way, but at least also in a lyrical way."[16]

As we have already mentioned, literature, as a highly significant cultural phenomena and social institution, undoubtedly contributes to the formation of a "group memory" of a given community and has, or at least can have, a significant impact on its self-understanding. It is similar to historiography as an academic discipline of the humanities, which is also intrinsically linked to memory. Memory theories agree on the necessary distinction between memory and objectifying and neutralizing historical science. Both phenomena are constructivist in nature, but memory is one of the "living bearers characterized by the engagement of perspective," while history "belongs to everyone and no one"–it is objective and therefore neutral in terms of identity formation.[17]

Viewed in these terms, literature is undoubtedly closer to memory than to historiographical science, given its subjectivism. We could hardly characterize literature as "history by other means"; rather it could be likened to a specific

---

[15] Vašíček, Krumphanzl, and Palek, *Jak se dělají filosofie*, 102–06.
[16] Horský, *Teorie a narace*, 45–46.
[17] Aleida Assmann, *Prostory vzpomínání: podoby a proměny kulturní paměti* (Praha: Univerzita Karlova, Nakladatelství Karolinum, 2018), 150. Assmann adds: "History and memory are always defined in relation to each other: one is always everything that is not the other. Historiography emerged as an emancipation from the official memory, but at the same time memory in all circumstances, exercises its right to stand against the dominant historical science." Ibid., 147.

recollection,[18] albeit programmatically and with a certain degree of admittedly expected invention (i.e., the so-called authorial license). The subjectivization of memory should be understood in both its dimensions: not only as an individual memory tied to the life of an individual, but also as a subjectivized memory of a certain group. "While the collective memory looks at the group 'from within' and tries to show such an image of its past in which it can be known in all its stages and in which therefore all deeper changes are erased, 'history,' on the contrary, removes these immobile times as 'empty' intervals and attribute the validity of a historical fact only to what, as a process or event, shows change."[19] Memory practice, whether as personal testimony and pop culture representation or literary and artistic productions, is the subject of memory research and studies.

In contrast to history (historiography), whose domains are systematization and generalization, literature focuses more on specifics and concrete matters, including various atypicalities, coincidences and deviations. If, in recent years, we have seen trends in modern historiography that reflect the previously somewhat overlooked private spheres of human experience, behavior and action (the so-called history of everyday life), it can be stated that literature somehow deviates from these areas in its nature. In addition to the presentation of everyday life, literary discourse seems to be suitable for the exposure and investigation of value systems and attitudes, as well as the life strategies of selected social groups and their collective identity; that is something that modern historiography is also interested in within the relatively recently established subdiscipline, called the history of mentalities.[20]

Literature thematizing the recent past is thus a blend of the basic memory frames as defined by Assmann, i.e., communicative and cultural memory. In this sense, communicative memory is a memory based on reminiscences that relate to the recent past and that one shares with their contemporaries. It is a generational memory: "This memory develops historically in a certain group, it emerges in time and disappears with time, or more precisely, it disappears

---

[18] "Thinking may be abstract, but remembering is concrete." Jan Assmann, *Kultura a paměť*, 38.
[19] Ibid., 42.
[20] "Mentality can therefore only be examined within a social group, never as an 'individual mentality.' The origins of such research go back to the French sociologist Emil Durkheim, who was the first to use the term 'collective representation' (1898)." Tomáš Dvořák and Tomáš Borovský, *Úvod do studia dějepisu* (Brno: Masarykova univerzita, 2014), 125.

with its bearers." It is the communicative memory that has a strong connection to the so-called oral history captured from the bottom (the aforementioned "history of everyday life"), while cultural memory tends to focus on more prominent "fixed points in the past." According to Assmann, cultural memory is an objective, mythicized, and "more formal" memory and also much more tied to "specialized bearers of tradition."[21] In none of these cases, however, can the past be preserved as such: it is inevitably subject to selection and integration processes.

It can be assumed that literature dealing with the (recent) past has the potential to bridge the gap between the often greatly simplified and purposeful depictions that appear in journalistic and political communication, and the more complex, professionally based, and methodologically elaborated concepts of historiography, which are, however, generally rather abstract. It has the opportunity to offer a more nuanced description of society, its lifestyle, as well as its value frameworks (both internalized or rejected). It can also help explain some specific social practices. Last but not least, literature has the possibility to independently analyze–real and perceived–marginals or extremes, as well as to let the voices of minorities, which are normally marginalized in the public space, be heard.

However, it is still true that despite all the overlaps and intersections with historiography, memory studies, or other humanistic disciplines, literature is teleologically primarily literature, i.e., an autonomous discourse that has its meaning "in itself" and whose criteria should be primary for judging specific works.

Contours of normalization

The era of normalization, also labeled as the period of late (state) socialism, is associated with the years following the occupation of Czechoslovakia by Warsaw Pact troops in August 1968. Whether we understand it as a purely domestic phenomenon or a consequence of (Soviet) dictates from the outside, it is a quite clearly definable time period lasting about twenty years from 1969 until the fall of the regime in 1989.[22] From a political point of view, it begins

---

[21] Jan Assmann, *Kultura a paměť*, 45–53.
[22] Sometimes the beginning of normalization is somewhat shifted, for example to the end of 1970, when the document *Poučení z krizového vývoje ve straně a společnosti po XIII. sjezdu KSČ. Rezoluce k aktuálním otázkám jednoty a strany* (Lessons from the Crisis Development in the Party and Society after the XIII. Congress of the Communist Party. Resolution on Current Issues of Unity and Party) was issued, a binding material of the

with the suppression of the reform movement in favor of the conservative wing of the Communist Party, which retained power until the collapse of state socialism.

It is usually perceived very negatively as a "synonym for the moral decay of individuals and society and serves as a negative model of personality habit based on greed and opportunism. According to many, both then contaminate the post-November development and the present."[23] The character of a dark age is attributed to normalization also by other historiographical descriptions, especially those authored by the older generation of researchers–it is believed that this period represented an "extraordinarily deep permanent decline in social morality, manifested in a 'cult of things,' in almost omnipresent smaller or greater stealing of social property, in the gradual increase of alcoholism and drug use, in the hooliganism and bad behavior of the youth, in the coarsening of speech and language, in the spreading and persistent vandalism, in the growth of crime (again especially in the youth), in the constant tendency to emigrate to the West, in the idealization of the local way of life, in the cold and non-engaged relationship of the common citizen to the nation and the homeland, to its historical values."[24]

However, a younger generation of researchers has recently challenged the account of the period as the government of a generally repressive totalitarian regime, which prevailed in social and historiographical discourse, especially in the 1990s, or as a period of unwritten "social contract" between the regime and society, which exchanged its share of political life for consumer pleasures.[25]

Central Committee of the Communist Party, which officially interpreted the events of the Prague Spring and the subsequent intervention of the Warsaw Pact troops. Alternatively, normalization was discussed a little later, especially after the beginning of the so-called *prověrky* (checks)–systematic purges in the Communist Party starting in 1972. On the other hand, some researchers, with a greater degree of generalization, sometimes speak about the principles of normalization in a larger time frame, i.e., with the continuity before 1969 and after 1989: Jan Mervart, "Rozdílnost pohledů na československou normalizaci," in *Podoby československé normalizace: dějiny v diskuzi*, eds. Kamil Činátl, Jan Mervart, and Jaroslav Najbrt (Praha: Ústav pro studium totalitních režimů, 2017), 65. For possible periodizations of normalization, see Milan Otáhal, *Normalizace 1969-1989*.
[23] Mervart, "Rozdílnost," 40.
[24] Vojtěch Mencl, *Křižovatky 20. století: světlo na bílá místa v nejnovějších dějinách* (Praha: Naše vojsko, 1990), 330-31.
[25] For example, Otáhal states, "Normalization represents a separate stage in the development of the Communist system in Czechoslovakia. A characteristic feature of the normalization regime was the restoration of the leading role, i.e., the monopoly of power

These researchers examine normalization not as an imported totalitarian regime, but as a specific "social practice" based on the consensus of the majority of the population.[26] At the same time, they programmatically refrain from the generalizing use of suprapersonal concepts such as "regime," "society," "system," "social contract," and the like. Although it is indisputable that the new conceptualization generates professional discussion, it has not reversed the prevailing opinion much (see the common usage in which these concepts continue to occur).

Despite divergent interpretive models, we can trace certain constants in the work of researchers dealing with the period. For example, there is an agreement on one of the most significant consequences of normalization, namely the early division of society. It is certainly a paradox, given the official goal of ideal socialist, or rather communist egalitarianism. On the one hand, there was a "class of the privileged, where above all the leadership of the Communist Party which had all the power, and members of the nomenclature belonged; in principle, it was not subject to laws and enjoyed benefits that other citizens did not have."[27] At the opposite pole, there were citizens affected by the post-August purges for their contribution to the revival process (not only non-Communists, but also expelled Communists), including their family members. These people were restricted in their rights, either they were prevented from finding a job that matched their qualifications, were prohibited from traveling or had restricted possibilities to study (especially their children). As Otáhal notes, it was a potential opposition base from which opponents of the regime were recruited.[28] In fact, the majority of the population was between these strata, but this area was far from homogeneous.

---

of the Communist Party, and the orientation towards the so-called consumer socialism. The relationship between power and citizens was based on the so-called social contract, according to which the ruling party provided citizens with a certain standard of living and social security and demanded that they give up participation in public affairs and realize themselves in the private sphere." Otáhal, *Normalizace 1969–1989*, 5. This concept de facto corresponds to the founding interpretations of the period of late socialism from the period before November 1989 by Václav Havel and Milan Šimečka. See their essays *Moc bezmocných* (The Power of the Powerless) and *Obnovení pořádku* (The Restoration of Order) (both from 1978).

[26] See Michal Pullmann, *Konec experimentu: přestavba a pád komunismu v Československu* (Praha: Scriptorium, 2011); Kolář and Pullmann, *Co byla normalizace?*.
[27] Otáhal, *Normalizace 1969–1989*, 53.
[28] Ibid.

Sociologist Jiřina Šiklová[29] systematically dealt with the stratification of the Czechoslovak normalized society and, especially, the broadest stratum mentioned above. She used the term "gray zone" in her work to name the space between demarcated and clearly identifiable establishment representatives and dissidents in the role of opposition.[30] The members of the gray zone– according to Šiklová, not identical to the consumer-oriented and politically indifferent "silent majority"–were characterized by the fact that although they were incorporated into existing structures, they considered the dissident opposition to be their reference group. According to Šiklová, such people did not have their own program, religion, or specific goals, but because they did not engage in open resistance to the establishment as dissidents, they did not forfeit the opportunity to study or develop professionally. According to Šiklová, this group never had "completely clean hands." That is, a completely and morally clear reputation, in terms of collaboration with the regime because they "hesitantly and reluctantly, but still, cooperated with the establishment and accepted certain benefits as a reward for their relative conformity."[31] At the same time, however, it was true for these people that "they are not indifferent, they are not cynics, but rather they profess traditional and historically proven individual values [...]." Therefore, and for their large numbers and vocational training, they should be crucial in further changes in society.[32]

An important factor influencing the daily lives of people in socialism, including their social stratification, was the centrally planned economy. The monopolistic ownership of the means of production and state paternalism in the redistribution of resources and goods resulted in low competitiveness of products and often a lack of them. This situation enabled the functioning of an

---

[29] Jiřina Šiklová and Vilém Prečan, eds., *Kočka, která nikdy nespí II: Jiřině Šiklové k narozeninám* (Praha: James H. Ottaway, Jr, 2015), 138–52; Jiří Linhart, "Šedá zóna," in *Sociologická encyklopedie*, ed. Zdeněk Nešpor (Praha Sociologický ústav AV ČR, 2018). Available from: <https://encyklopedie.soc.cas.cz/w/%E2%80%9E%C5%A1ed%C3%A1 _z%C3%B3na%E2%80%9C> [Accessed April 1, 2022].
[30] Pavel Machonin uses an alternative and relatively more open term "second society": "The second society was thus not a part of a social whole, separate from the 'first society,' but a sum of those real elements, phases and functions of almost the whole society, which came into growing conflict with the officially recognized functioning of the state socialist society." Pavel Machonin, *Česká společnost a sociologické poznání* (Praha: ISV nakladatelství, 2005), 129.
[31] Šiklová, *Kočka, která nikdy nespí*, 141.
[32] Ibid., 143.

illegal black economy, essentially linked to the legal economy.[33] However, in comparison with Western capitalist countries, the socialist economy as a whole demonstrably lagged behind, which, according to some, was one of the main reasons for the fall of socialism in Eastern Europe.

Another significant feature of normalization was the forced inclination towards the private sphere in human life at the expense of the public sphere. According to most researchers, private relations and especially the family remained the only area of relative freedom and space for self-realization, while job and career spheres lost their prestigious value as a result of constant political pressure.[34] As a result, the importance of upbringing in the family increased: "education for citizenship and morality stood and fell with its quality. The family was a space where it was possible to develop work activities, and it also compensated for the economic deficits of the state economy."[35]

The strict separation of the private and public spheres led to the phenomenon of "double speech," i.e., differentiated, often contradictory expressing of opinions on political and social issues in a family or friend circle and in the public. From the ruling party's point of view, the population did not necessarily have to agree with the ideology of the Communist Party and its practices, but

---

[33] See Katherine Verderyová, "Co byl socialismus a proč padl?" in *Podoby československé normalizace: dějiny v diskuzi*, eds. Kamil Činátl, Jan Mervart, and Jaroslav Najbrt (Praha: Ústav pro studium totalitních režimů, 2017), 269. See also Tůma and Vilímek, who state: "The illegal black economy, i.e., the provision of services and products against payment, proved, among other things, that workers focused on satisfying their material needs and raising living standards regardless of the interests of the economy and the state and also without fear of crime. It was a source of large incomes that often exceeded legal salaries. Moonlighting jobs, which were often performed during working hours and with stolen material, in some cases grew into a veiled private business within a company. ... The state suffered from the black economy, as it often provided services that the state was unable to provide. ... The money obtained from the black economy led not only to further demoralization of the population, but also to property differentiation. In part, they served to meet crucial needs, but above all they led to a higher standard of living: people bought luxury items, jewellery, cars, built houses and recreational facilities." Oldřich Tůma & Tomáš Vilímek (eds.), *Česká společnost v 70. a 80. letech: sociální a ekonomické aspekty* (Praha: Ústav pro soudobé dějiny AV ČR, 2012), 274-275.
[34] See Otáhal, *Normalizace 1969-1989*, 224.
[35] Květa Jechová, "Postavení žen v Československu v období normalizace," in *Česká společnost v 70. a 80. letech: sociální a ekonomické aspekty*, eds. Oldřich Tůma and Tomáš Vilímek (Praha: Ústav pro soudobé dějiny AV ČR, 2012), 176-246.

they were not allowed to manifest it externally.[36] In addition to greater or lesser socialist rituals in life expressing the required loyalty to power (not necessarily unconditional agreement with its ideology), there was a certain depoliticization of life, especially in those areas and cases where excessive initiative and involvement of an individual could uncertain the prevailing Communist order.

These dimensions of life under normalization are often thematized in prose after November 1989. Associated with specific historical facts of the given period (events, personalities, and other realities), they can serve as a significant "backdrop," but they often become one of the main objects of interest and a decisive factor in the story. They also differ in the degree of explicitness with which they become part of the fictional world: sometimes they are presented, or for various reasons directly explained in a broader context, sometimes it is expected that the reader will supplement the encyclopedia of the fictional world with their knowledge (of the history) of the real world.

Forms of normalization in Czech prose after 1989

As we have already mentioned, a considerable amount of prose has been published after 1989 in which normalization features as a striking element.[37] In their texts, authors from diverse natures, styles, and poetics engaged with this period, naturally pursuing their own literary goals. Consequently, their relationship to and evaluation of the period was often fundamentally different. However, they shared a tendency to combine fractography with fiction.

Prose written since the 1990s must be considered in a fundamentally different way than prose written under normalization. One of the reasons is the earlier segmentation of Czech literature into three de facto separate branches, i.e., official (published with the regime's approval), unofficial, branching into

---

[36] See also Havel's concept of "life in truth" versus "life in the lie" in his essay *Moc bezmocných (The Power of the Powerless)*. Václav Havel, *Moc bezmocných* (Praha: Československý spisovatel, 1990) or in English translation Václav Havel, *The Power of the Powerless*, ed. J. Keane (Armonk, NY: M. E. Sharpe, 1985).

[37] In addition to the works discussed below, we note many other significant works of prose after November 1989, in which the story takes place at least in part during normalization–e.g., Jan Musil's *Let blanokřídlého hmyzu* (*The Flight of Hymenopterous Insects*) (1995), *Stopy za obzor* (*Footprints beyond the Horizon*) by Pavel Kolmačka (2006), *Žítkovské bohyně* (*The Žítková Goddesses*) by Kateřina Tučková (2012), *Rybí krev* (*Fish Blood*) by Jiří Hájíček (2012), *Jiříkovy starosti o minulost* (*Jiřík's Worries about the Past*) by Jan Faktor, *Tiché roky* (*Silent Years*) (2019) by Alena Mornštajnová, and others.

domestic samizdat production (publications without approval) and foreign (exile).[38] Yet regardless of the branch, every author had to contend with centralized censorship before 1989. After the fall of Communism, this eventually withered away. Another fundamental difference is that in the case of the literature of the 1970s and 1980s, normalization was understood as a lived present, while after the November Revolution, the twenty years were not only psychologically but also factually a part of history–all the more so with increasing time.

The productive and, at the same time, diverse segment of Czech prose after November 1989 may be understood from a number of perspectives. One example is periodization according to the time of composition (publication) and, at the same time, according to the generational affiliation of the authors. Four basic groups of prose on normalization consequently emerge: (1) literary reactions to the immediate past by those who experienced normalization; (2) literary reflections of participants from a distance; (3) reflections of the generation of so-called Husák's children, i.e., witnesses who experienced normalization in childhood or adolescence; and, finally, (4) literary images of normalization presented by the generation that did not experience it personally and based their work only on mediation of witnesses (older generations) or other sources.

In the following passages, the material is stratified slightly differently. The following five different types–modes–of treatment of normalization in the prose are offered:

An alternative conceptualization is to stratify the material according to modes:
Mode 1: humorous, nostalgic, ironizing;
Mode 2: imaginative;
Mode 3: payback, resistance;
Mode 4: existential;
Mode 5: problematizing.

---

[38] Alena Šidáková Fialová and Eva Klíčová systematically dealt with prose created and officially published during normalization: Alena Šidáková Fialová, *Poučeni z krizového vývoje: poválečná česká společnost v reflexi normalizační prózy* (Praha: Academia, 2014); Eva Klíčová, "Lopaty, inženýři, inkousti a ostatní. Transformace hodnot v normalizační pracovní próz*e.*" (Ph.D. thesis, Masarykova univerzita, 2018), https://is.muni.cz/th/rmjc4/.

With references to selected representative texts, we identify the constant and specific traits of this significant and constantly renewed stream. Two to three samples of prose have been selected because of their former or continued resonance among experts (literary critics and researchers) and general readers. It is obvious that in some cases, these may be "not pure" examples, and in some aspects, they represent borderline cases, as all the works we with which work cannot be indisputably ascribed to just one of the categories as a whole. However, the basic directions in the approach to normalization in contemporary Czech prose, as we believe, follow from this categorization and the interrelatedness of the individual modes; the main tendencies are then summarized in the conclusion.

Mode 1: Humorous, nostalgic, ironizing

The fact that authors of the younger and middle generation experienced the seventies and eighties mostly or completely as children or adolescents, accounts for the frequency of this mode. Their own experience as an important source of literary inspiration is usually marked by the circumstances of an immature person who is still forming their idea of the world, looking for their place in it, simply put, the person is still maturing. This corresponds to the frequent optics of a child in these works, i.e., a kind of "stranger," unaffected by any preconceptions, conventions, and prejudice. Although the main characters are in the center of the action, the socio-political effects of normalization and possible traumas are usually perceived indirectly, through their loved ones, especially parents.

The stylized view of a child hero may be decisive for the whole work (e.g., *Hrdý Budžes*–best translated as *B. Proudew*, 1998), but sometimes the dynamics of the transition from the child's naive point of view to the more critical opinion of an adult or teenager is shown. We also often work with a double perspective, i.e., with a description of a child's authentic experiences from a certain distance, with a certain perspective and life experience (for example, *Báječná léta pod psa* [*Bliss Was It in Bohemia*], 2002 and *Jiříkovy starosti o minulost* [*Jiřík's Worries about the Past*], 2015), which is a feature appearing to a certain extent also in other modes. If we look at the conditions of the era from this perspective, a considerable field opens up for the comic, whether slightly ironic or, on the contrary, satirical and bitter. Opportunities for humor are primarily provided by the tension (contrast) between the yet uninformed, "uncorrupted" hero and the expectations placed on them by those around them. The characters often come across normalization "rules of the game," whether they know them at the time or not.

The emblematic titles in this group include the novel *B. Proudew* by Irena Dousková (born 1964), a humorous prose work whose main heroine is an eight-year-old schoolgirl Helenka Součková. The indiscriminate childish perception and excitable nature of the main character/narrator coincidentally collide with the norms predominant at school or elsewhere. The official Communist propaganda she is experiencing every day is mixed in the girl's head with the skeptical and even oppositional attitudes of her mother-actress. In addition, Helenka is stigmatized by her origins: her biological father (with Jewish roots) emigrated, which she cannot understand at her age and she considers her current mother's partner as her father. The little girl explains the complicated questions with her own imaginativeness–distorting, imagining, and confused by the various interpretations of teachers, classmates, relatives, and other characters. The following example is characteristic, illustrating Helenka's orientation in an ambivalent reality:

> But Kačenka, that's what I call my mum, so Kačenka didn't know why the school assistant did it. She then told Dad in the kitchen that she had been worn out by the bastards. She probably meant the Russians or maybe the Communists, because Russians and Communists are bastards, but you can't say that. But Kačenka and Andrea Kroupová still say it anyway, they sing the anti-Russian song *Už troubějí, už troubějí na horách je Lenin* and Kačenka does not want to allow me to join the Sparks, because Sparks and Communists are little Communists. So I don't know, our whole class goes there, and I would like to go there too. I already go to German classes, to drawing and ballet classes, because I'm fat, so I have to do exercise. But I would still like to join the Sparks.[39]

The light prose, reminiscent of Poláček, set in a fictional small town called Ničín, is based on all-pervading situational comedy.[40] It is characterized by a certain degree of autobiography and a very incomplete view of history, which enters Helenka's world through the education system, including commemorating various anniversaries, and, to a large extent also, as can be seen from the excerpt, through eavesdropping on adult conversations. The contrast between the real conditions in the difficult times and the child's peculiar understanding is powerful–this is one of the reasons for the enormous

---

[39] Irena Dousková, *Hrdý Budžes* (Praha: Hynek, 1998), 7. Unless otherwise noted, translations of included citations are my own.

[40] See Aleš Haman, "Poláčkovské téma z jiné perspektivy," *Nové knihy* 39, no. 1 (1999): 4; Jiří Brabec, "Druhá původní novinka," *Literární noviny* 10, no. 7 (1999): 16.

popularity of the work, reflected in the successful dramatization of the book starring Bára Hrzánová in the Příbram Theatre since 2002 (director Jiří Schmiedt).

Dousková applies a similar technique in the sequel to *Budžes* called *Oněgin byl Rusák* (*Onegin Was a Russky*, 2006)–Helenka, about eight years older, is now a high school student and once again struggles with life under real socialism. In contrast to the first novel, she quite understands the social and political situation–the teenage intellectual is aware of the apathy of people and sometimes her own helplessness towards the regime, and sometimes she sharply–but rather privately–opposes it. As is characteristic of Dousková, a light nostalgia-tinged style explores not only the teenage years of adolescent Helenka, but also the more general life strategies of people of that time:

> Ťuík is a blockhead, but it was no big heroism, even if he complained, nothing would probably happen to anyone, and the fact is that we are all in the SSM. All in one–me too. We don't go anywhere, we don't do anything, nothing happens and nobody, except perhaps Ťuík, wants anything from us. All we have to do is just be there, and that's about it. Nobody cares that it's just a formality, it's enough that everyone is at least a little soaked. Anyone who wants to go to college, and everyone wants it, knows that he has to be there, and that's it. Even my parents take it for granted, even if it's not nice. Another thing is party membership, that's the limit that our family doesn't go beyond, and there's no need to talk about it at all. It's clear. But all other parents are in the party, always at least one of them–usually the father.[41]

In this book, Dousková again applies an "amiable" view of normalization. According to Jandourek, it is characteristic of both books that they offer a "pleasant reminder of an unpleasant time. It is well written. The reader will become immersed in the text if they are at least a little attuned to the author's style. It is neither a poignant existential drama about a time crushing people mentally and physically, nor a writing in the style of 'we have to help each other.'"[42]

---

[41] Dousková, 50.

[42] Jan, Jandourek, "Oněgin byl Rusák, komunisti byli..." in *Aktualne.cz* (2006). Available from: <https://magazin.aktualne.cz/kultura/umeni/onegin-byl-rusak-komunisti-byli/r ~i:article:162231/> [Accessed April 1, 2022]. In some subsequent books, however, Dousková sharpens her view of normalization: the dysfunctional, unpleasant, and often

The canonical titles also include one of the first novels of this type after 1989, *Bliss Was It in Bohemia* (1992) by Michal Viewegh (born 1962). The very title of the successful novel depicting the life of an "ordinary" family from the 1960s to the early 1990s reflects the ambivalent nature of the era and the ambiguity of its evaluation of individual human life. In this case, the child's perspective appears only partly–it is the view of the future writer Kvido, who, years later, presents the publisher with a manuscript of the novel with the same name. The retrospective third-person narration is largely of a scenic nature: it involves a number of dialogical exchanges, sometimes even presented as a script with scenic annotations. However, there are also subjectivized "authentic" passages, such as excerpts from the diary of six-year-old Kvido, which captures the turbulent events of the autumn of 1968.

The constant existential difficulties resulting from the suppression of the reform movement of the 1960s are, as with Dousková, imbued with nostalgia for childhood and youth; the child is unaware of the troubles and worries of the parents, and also the parents are aware that, despite all the disappointments and inconveniences of the era, it is necessary to continue living. The normalization regime touched Kvido's father the most, a former co-actor of Šik's economic reforms, who is professionally and socially humiliated after the Soviet invasion and forced to move to the periphery with his family. As Vladimír Karfík remarked, "The axis of Viewegh's novel is the escape of the family from great History–of course, a failed one. Even in this escape, the impossibility of tragic clashes is established–whether they lead to futile heroic deeds or surrendering to the pressure of time. Viewegh rules out this tragic position in advance, the distance the family will cover on the run is only 51 kilometers from Prague to Sázava–there is already a clear angle of an ironizing view. He turned irony and exaggeration inside the characters who play in the story rather than to Great History."[43]

Social pressure during normalization is embodied in the book by his superior Šperk, who forces Kvido's father to become (more) politically engaged and "to be seen"–the father then experiences the difficult dilemmas of a gifted professional who wants to stay loyal to at least some of his principles, but must secure the family at the same time. Eventually, he develops paranoia to the

---

literally beating realities of the time are largely concentrated, for example, in her "perestroika road movie" *Rakvičky (Éclairs)* (2018).

[43] Vladimír Karfík, "Báječná léta pod psa," *Literární noviny*, no. 10 (1992): 7.

point that he completely avoids contact outside the family and makes his own coffin in his home workshop.

Viewegh also works with counterpoint in his tragicomic prose. He stated that it is "a kind of a cheerful look back on a cheerless time, a kind of an ironic picture of our recent history."[44] The obligatory figure of the intertwining of "big" and "small" history is then clearly illustrated by the excerpt describing Kvido's experience of the August occupation by Warsaw Pact troops:

> When Kvido's grandfather Josef got up in the kitchen on August 21, 1968, at 4:30 in the kitchen to get to work, he heard a strange thunder that came into the flat through a window from somewhere in the dark sky. He quietly put the kettle on the gas stove, but his precautions were pointless, because the grandmother also could not sleep for a while due to the racket.
> "What is it?" she asked reproachfully from the room.
> "How should I know?" said grandfather sharply. "Maybe the garbagemen."
> He stopped abruptly because he realized he hadn't seen any of the budgies yet. He peered into the room, turned on the light, turned it off, and returned to the kitchen, looked at the closet and the console, pulled the curtain aside–but they were nowhere to be seen.
> "Where are my budgies?" he said, looking at the open window.
> "They're not here."
> "Are you blind?" grandma said. 'Where would they be?"
> "How should I know!" shouted Grandfather angrily as he looked around again. "Then find them for me, Mrs. Smart-ass."
> Unfortunately, he was right: The birds were gone.
> Kvido woke up just before eight. He squinted in surprise at his grandfather, who was supposed to be in the shaft a long time ago, and instead sat in his pyjamas at the table listening to the radio.
> "Our Duckies flew away," grandma said sadly. "I guess something scared them."
> Kvido turned his head to the ceiling and then leaned forward in bed to see the cage. It was empty. [...][45]

---

[44] Cf. Martin Pilař, "Báječná léta pod psa," in *Slovník české literatury:* <Slovník české literatury (slovnikceskeliteratury.cz)> [April 1, 2022], 1994.
[45] Michal Viewegh, *Báječná léta pod psa* (Brno: Petrov, 2002), 32–33.

Mode 2: Imaginative

Pavel Janoušek captured the essence of the imaginative mode in his review of Milan Kozelka's short novel *Život na Kdyssissipy* (*Life on the Once-ssipy*, 2008). According to him, Kozelka, in his narrative, "is very far from just illustrating his memories. He prefers free imagination, literary play, myth to descriptive documenting. He deliberately builds on the tension between the input fact and the amplifying fabrication, exaggeration. He draws his characters into aptly formulated literary situations, which are perhaps a bit real, but more likely a little fictional, or rather made up so as to express the essence of human attitudes and the atmosphere of the evoked moment or place."[46]

The writer and performer Kozelka (1948–2014), who was persecuted and imprisoned for several years during the normalization era, presents in his work the underground milieu. The main characters are the coryphaei of this movement: Ivan Martin Jirous, Egon Bondy, Andrej Stankovič, Vratislav Brabenec, John Bok, and others, while other famous personalities, such as Václav Havel, Jindřich Chalupecký, or Jan Zrzavý, also appear episodically. The goal is not their detailed characteristics, but "only" a sketch of their portrait in a certain situation and a synecdochic highlighting of some of their characteristics or personal qualities. Often, the characters with a real basis are even entirely at the service of the story, or rather the image capturing a certain moment from the underground subculture. The underground is thus (again) considerably mythicized, although a certain grotesque light is thrown on it at the same time; in any case, more general conclusions about life in other communities or society as a whole cannot be made.

Kozelka's book, as well as other works in this mode, is characterized by a more pronounced linguistic stylization and exaggeration, including speech differentiation of characters. With Hrabal-like interest in the people on the periphery, Kozelka highlights well-known and forgotten heroes who lived in a particularly unfavorable social situation for them, with which they refused to (fully) conform. Despite this–or perhaps because of it–these characters are portrayed as self-important, unrestrained, and unrestrainable individuals "transcending" their time: they are sort of legends. This is confirmed in the sections entitled "Lives of the Saints," bearing eloquent subtitles reflecting the authenticity and rawness of these individuals: Lowborn Savage, Quasi-Kerouac, Cellar Adamite, Baron Munchausen, Weirdo, etc. In the manner of the Apocrypha, the non-conformist heroes that Kozelka apparently actually

---

[46] Pavel Janoušek, "Život na Kdysissippi," *Tvar*, no. 12 (2008): 3.

met in the underground communities are hyperbolically presented. The impression of a distinctive hagiography is further enhanced by the incorporation of portraits–black and white icons–by illustrator Andrea Lexová.

In *Life on the Once-ssipy*, we also often observe the connection of the high and the low, as in the excerpt from the short story "Čekání na Vaška (Waiting for Vašek)," where we follow the discussion of the underground protagonists drinking beer, employing different sociolects and registers:

> Frightened out of his wits, Mejla Hlavsa bursts through the door. He stares wide-eyed, his nostrils tremble. "They took Havel!" he announces.
> Time stood still. An empty, boundless silence settled on the room.
> "Well..." Nepraš knocks back his seventh shot of rum.
> "Tempus vulnera sanat," Brikcius downs his fifth beer.
> "Will Václav Havel come?" presses Fromm.
> "Sure, he promised," squawks the parrot in the cage above the faucet. Bondy has a sip of beer.
> "Well" Nepraš knocks back his eighth shot of rum.
> "Terribilis est locus iste," Brikcius downs the sixth beer.
> Stressed out, Hlavsa takes a cigarette from Brabenec, lights it and disappears outside. Stankovič carefully takes a mess kit with a mushroom fry from a plastic bag. "Will you have some?" he asks the others. Fromm and Lopatka taste it.
> "You know, Amík, it's a cunt against the wall. Just true bastards get out behind the Iron Curtain and ordinary people are pissed off. They can just throw up their heels in Bulgaria and on Balaton and hope that in the meantime someone does not steal their Trabant," Brabenec explains the problem.
> "Claustrophilic xenophobes," opines Lopatka.
> "Well..." Nepraš knocks back the ninth shot of rum. Mrs. Jirous closes the window to the street.
> "Ergo bibamus!" Brikcius downs his seventh beer. [...].[47]

However, Kozelka's writing, as Janoušek notes, can have its pitfalls in its considerable implicitness and allusiveness: "it is literature for insiders, the understanding of which is based on the assumption that the reader knows who is hiding behind the names and acts, and is able to decipher the ingenious

---

[47] Milan Kozelka, *Život na Kdyssissippi* (Brno: Host, 2008), 66–67.

tension between inspiration and narration. ... I am afraid it will not take long, and reading this book will be quite inaccessible to readers without extensive endnotes."[48]

Bohuslav Vaněk-Úvalský (born 1970) uses his personal experience with normalization, as well as the rich imagination in his novel *Brambora byla pomeranč mého dětství* (*A Potato Was the Orange of My Childhood*, 2002). In this prose work, published in an extended form in 2021, the author gathers an arsenal of normalization's realities, a substantial part of which he incorporated into his story of "Piolin," a young man with two heads. Although the exaggeration is evident here (in addition, teenagers with semantically charged names such as Masaryk and Hácha appear in the narrative), authenticating factual elements are also very strongly represented.

The character expresses himself, Forrest Gump style, partly in the third-person, partly in an eyewitness first-person. The reader perceives him as a subject and an object at the same time. He has to deal with this handicap, as well as with many other anomalies during a difficult era, and to learn to live:

> The fact that Piolin had two heads was unpleasant for him, but if you want to live, the first prerequisite is to get used to it. Our mother always said: "Get used to the fact that people always get used to things quickly. When they don't get used to something, get out of there because something is wrong." It seems that the primary meaning of life is coded in the phrase "get used to." Only after that comes the word reconciliation.[49]

Piolin's mishaps under Husák's regime end in grandiose (trans)national success: although he dies shortly afterwards, the protagonist eventually becomes president of the "Freely United European Nations."

From a genre-compositional point of view, *A Potato Was the Orange of My Childhood* has the character of free-flowing prose, bringing together a multitude of diverse situations and images. The short chapters follow each other relatively loosely, acting as selected scenes from Piolin's life. The compositional looseness is also confirmed by the fact that several new chapters

---

[48] Janoušek, "Život na Kdysissippi," 3.
[49] Bohuslav Vaněk-Úvalský, *Brambora byla pomeranč mého dětství* (Brno: Petrov, 2002), 36.

have been added to various places for the new edition, without fundamentally disrupting the structure and changing the meaning of the work.

The original elements of the book also include specific dictionary entries–notes that serve as a commentary on the main (narrative) text that the character allegedly wrote down on the realities of the seventies and eighties.[50] In the later, expanded edition of the book, there are a total of 165 such entries. Moreover, in the new edition, the *Youth Typology 1970–1989* is included as a "bonus," containing 15 free-standing items. These explanations are somehow the opposite of Kozelka's implicitness–concise and straightforward, although sometimes perhaps too caricatured, they present to readers the most important items of the space-time of the work. Their documentary character permeates the mystifying, for the (theoretically) absolutely uneducated recipient, they can be misleading, given their straightforwardness and distinctiveness. An unconventional name, an unexpected connection, a striking point, irony, and exaggeration in an effort to entertain are superior to the completeness and exactness but also proportionality, the expectations of which the form of such a "dictionary" raises. As Vaněk-Úvalský states in the afterword to the second edition, the list of key terms is created especially for the youngest generation, who have not personally experienced the Husák regime.[51]

Not only basic socio-political terms such as comrade, moonlighting job, chemical masks, capitalists, the Pioneer organization, State Security, the so-called Baton Act, the German Democratic Republic, and others are explained ironically, but also all sorts of facts such as sucking block, red lemonades, the magazine *The World of Engines*, Pedro, television commercial, Tesil polyester trousers, Elvis Presley, and many more. Important concepts such as normalization or the Communist Party are presented as follows:

Normalization (1970–1989) Husák's invention. It normalized abnormality into normality. Its purpose was to show Moscow that there was no human face left in Czechoslovakia that could be used for socialism.[52]

---

[50] In the first edition, the explanation of individual expressions is made in italics on the margin of the main text; in the second edition, the files of several entries are distributed between the chapters.
[51] Bohuslav Vaněk-Úvalský, *Brambora byla pomeranč mého dětství* (Praha: Krásné nakladatelství, 2021), 343.
[52] Ibid., 237

"**KSČ** was an abbreviation for the Communist government party. Later, when the power left the Communists again, they hid from responsibility by adding the letter M after KSČ. Many people saw through their deception, and so the Communists qualified for the parliament of the free republic. They then disguised their ambitions by saying that they "want to offer assistance." Only the greatest pedants understood that it was more a craving for power."[53]

To a lesser extent, there are also entries like "laugh heartily" or "I do it for children so that they can go to school," humorously commenting on certain behavioral or thought patterns associated with the normalization regime.[54]

The book *A Potato Was the Orange of My Childhood* is one of the prose works that deals with normalization most explicitly and systematically. The author's imagination, using the original concept of the main character, offers a number of possibilities to see the period of the 1970s and 1980s in a new and unconventional way (especially from 1976 to 1984, which is the period of the content in the second edition). However, the opportunity is used only in part: the author does not avoid certain stereotypes and flightiness, at the expense of trying to gain a deeper understanding of the issue, he always prefers an amusing shortcut and rather just recording many–albeit remarkable– phenomena.

Mode 3: Payback, resistance

In many works of prose concerning normalization, there is often also an attempt at some settling scores with Communism, more precisely with the actors of the previous regime and their successors. Due to the essentially retrospective focus of the studied works, it is common for the characters to often contemplate and present the decisive (past) moments of their lives, while negative impressions prevail. Often, the characters realize the depth of the wounds they received from the regime, as well as the impossibility of their

---

[53] Bohuslav Vaněk-Úvalský, *Brambora* (2002), 28–29.
[54] Hyperbolically and in a "political" sense, even seemingly neutral entries are explained, such as walls and small walls: "**Walls and small walls** were a big topic at the time. Communists, who loved order, surrounded their entire governorate, where they experimented with people, with a wall, so that living material would not run here and there. In addition, they drew attention every second to the benefits of living on the right side of the wall. Some individuals did not survive the constant happiness. The Pink Floyd group also sang about the hard life of the builders in 1978." Ibid., 23–24.

(complete) healing. Such retrospection can be quite troubling as it can cause considerable remorse or even resentment towards certain groups. Paradoxically, this can happen after a long time–in some cases, the sense of wrongdoing is stronger than fading memories and commemorative optimism. The sense of wrongdoing is caused by the knowledge that the perpetrators have not yet been punished and the victims have not been compensated in any way. In this mode, a relatively more serious, sometimes even mournful, tone is often employed, emphasizing more clearly the non-literary goals of the given works. More often than in other modes, we also encounter the heroization of the actors (and the corresponding denigration of their opponents).

The prose work in which the above principles are more strongly applied is represented by Petr Placák's set of loosely connected short stories *Škola od svatého Norberta* (*The School of St. Norbert*, 2021). The author (born 1964) has been dealing with the topic of modern Czech history, specifically the period of the Communist regime, for a long time as a historian and has already thematized it in several partially autobiographical books (for example, *Medorek*, 1990; *Fízl*, 2007). In this set, he mainly pursues two goals. First, to recall one's own childhood and youth full of boyhood adventures in Prague's Střešovice, and second, to criticize the education system of (not only) the normalization period. While the first goal corresponds to Mode 1 described here, the second intention modifies it considerably, especially for its intensity: instead of humorous and downplayed elements, the dark sides of socialism, its unpleasant and often fatal consequences are systematically and seriously presented.

The result is a form that approximates an indictment. It is no coincidence that the author's afterword explaining the motivations and clarifying the main message of the book in a non-fiction style is called aggressively and angrily *Tract Contra*. In it, the author openly admits his disillusionment with the contemporary world–embodied in short stories. According to him, the book can be understood "as a polemic with our entire civilization, its setting, way of education, view of the world, society, and man."[55] Settling scores with the Communist regime, or more precisely with what represents it in this context and with those who represented it (Communist teachers, police officers, secret informers, opportunists, etc.), is an integral part of this polemic. In Placák's critique of (post-)normalization education, we thus observe a kind of extension

---

[55] Petr Placák, *Škola od svatého Norberta* (Praha: Torst, 2021), 310–15.

of normalization, or at least some of its attributes–those that have a significant impact up to the present.

The formal education that every citizen in Czechoslovakia had to go through before 1989 is described here as organized institutional evil, which deforms the pupils rather than providing them with a solid foundation for their future lives. The school, "which seemed relatively innocuous among other humanities regulating institutes, was all the more dangerous and caused the most damage to people."[56] The radical nature of the view is related to its universality and breadth: even kindergartens are described as "concentration facilities for preschool children," full of sadistic "supervisors." Placák goes even further, the narrator (identifiable with the author) sharply condemns the situation from the very birth of a person:

> they grabbed him–they rinsed him like a rabbit pulled out of its skin and labelled him with a marker, assigned him a number, made a tick in the records and put him among other similarly affected newborns, which somehow automatically showed that the society, or rather the state, are getting their claws into you–although you were born to a mother and father without anybody else contributing to it, you were also born, or above all, to the father state and the mother republic.[57]

The tone of the narrative corresponds to the overall negative attitude of the main characters. In the words of the narrator, they were of the opinion that "everything that the Communists claimed, that they taught us at school, was inherently bad, even if it was good in itself, and everything that the regime cursed was inherently right, even if it was not so right."[58]

Jan Balabán (1961–2010) expressed himself similarly "without sugar-coating it" against the present and past social and political situation in his prose, as well as in rich journalistic works.[59] With regard to this topic, his second novel *Kudy šel anděl (Where Was the Angel Going?* 2003, second edition 2005), is one of the richest works. In it, the author connected the critique of normalization and its heritage with another of his crucial topics, i.e., the Moravian-Silesian region, especially Ostrava and its inhabitants. According to Balabán, normalization manifested itself in a specific way in the industrial metropolis with a turbulent

---

[56] Ibid., 18.
[57] Ibid., 17–18.
[58] Ibid., 72.
[59] See Jan Balabán, *Povídky; Romány a novely; Publicistika a hry* (Brno: Host, 2010–2012).

history, but, as elsewhere, it left deep traces that lasted until the post-revolutionary period. In *Where Was the Angel Going?*, Ostrava becomes a certain symbol and, at the same time, a metaphor for the whole era, because in it–in Balabán's raw stylization–many of the unfortunate influences of real socialism are manifested.

The main character, Martin Vrána, grew up in the 1970s in a housing estate in Ostrava, which greatly affected him. In addition to the chapters recalling Martin's childhood and youth, the plot develops in a novelized present set in the period of the nineties. Both the young man and the city of hundreds of thousands of inhabitants were once a promising and prosperous system, but now they both stand on the subsoil of siphoned-off funds and find it difficult to find meaning in their continued existence.[60] Martin is not having a happy time right now: he is divorced, he has problems with alcohol, and he finds himself in a life crisis, as is usual for Balabán's characters.

Martin's story, which spans several decades, also has some more general features. Like the other prose we are dealing with here, it captures the generational experience to a large extent. The atmosphere of the era is evoked by a number of specific elements, whether personal in the form of brutal fathers (father-militiaman–Ivan Figura), authoritative teachers ("perverted bachelors of our childhood"), informants (Ivan Figura) and secret informers ("an old narc in a military jacket"), or realities, such as compulsory military service, the still present threat of nuclear war, the displacement of church life on the periphery, and the like.[61] At the same time, the distress of the given space-time affected the characters since childhood ("one of the first vital skills of the children born here was to recognize their entrance, floor and apartment in exactly the same blocks").[62] In addition, Martin becomes an outsider because of his family background–when admitting the fact that he is

---

[60] Milan Fencl, "Balabán není vějička," *Weles*, no. 19 (2004): 113.

[61] The repressive nature of the regime is present mainly in the stories of supporting and episodic characters: for example, Ivan Berezinský, called Figura, who becomes involved in an incident with tragic consequences during the military service, and the victim of his allegation becomes the author of the anti-Communist file. Because Figura eventually commits suicide, he becomes a victim of the Communist regime. Another victim of sanctions is Mrs. Tomská, the mother of Martin's girlfriend, who is forced to work in manual and auxiliary professions after returning from emigration, despite being a doctor. Her colleague Marie Hedvika Sněhotová also could not use her talent for languages because she was too pious for the Communists.

[62] Jan Balabán, *Kudy šel anděl* (Brno: Host, 2005), 31.

evangelical, he was humiliated by his teacher at the age of twelve and was labeled a pious Bible-basher in front of the class.

The key element in Balabán's poetics–a specifically defined space–is described dynamically in the novel: it depends on the period being discussed. In this sense, the Ostrava agglomeration is becoming synonymous with frustration, concern, uprooting, disorder, existential dependence, anger, and hatred. Poor living conditions and a gloomy climate seem almost hopeless; the city can be understood as a kind of isolation ward, as a "materialized image of unrealized paths and escapes."[63] However, there is no improvement even in the post-revolutionary years, when the industrial-devastated city and its inhabitants changed only partially. Skepticism is especially evident when comparing the current situation with circumstances "in those dark seventies, when Ostrava was a very dirty city, so to speak, from the outside as well as from the inside. At that time, white horses in the emblem of a transport company were often not seen at all because of the dirt on the sides of those eternal buses, buses, buses that were used to travel from housing estates to work and school. It used to be cloudy, even when the sun was shining. Today, when already subdued, desulphurized, and dedusted factories barely breathe and fish return to the rivers, the dirt on the backs and underbelly of thoughts and deeds has remained, as in any other city."[64]

It is also possible to incorporate some prose by Petr Šabach (1951-2017) in this mode, a popular author of the Hrabal style and a great inspirer of film scripts. He also partly or entirely set a number of his works in the Communist, i.e., normalization past (see, for example, *Babičky [Grandmas]*, 1998; *Opilé banány [Drunk Bananas]*, 2010, etc.). In the context of the time, he usually developed various boy's escapades anecdotally, or tried more arched family stories covering–albeit fragmentarily–a longer period of time. Similarly based is Šabach's novella *Občanský průkaz (Identity Card*, 2006*)*, which is more radical than the author's other books about the past regime probably because it deals to a significant extent with its most significant repressive components–the police, known as Public Security (VB), and the secret police, State Security Council (StB).

The autobiographical narrator named Petr mainly describes the fights and clashes with these officials, which he and his companions could not avoid from

---

[63] Svatava Urbanová, "Otevřené návraty v prózách Jana Balabána," in *Souřadnice míst*, eds. Svatava Urbanová and Iva Málková (Ostrava: Ostravská univerzita, 2003), 115
[64] Balabán, *Kudy šel anděl*, 137.

the moment they received their ID cards at the age of 15, a common object of interest for the Communist police. As is characteristic of Šabach, he allows himself a number of diversions in a story covering several decades, but the topic of confronting a young man with state power is clearly central. As in other authors' titles, we find a number of funny or tragicomic accounts, often stories within a story, which the characters tell each other on various occasions. One of them is, for example, the memory of how Petr and his friends, as representatives of non-conformist, i.e., even appropriately long-haired youth, took part in the filming of a film scene of the demonstrators' street fight with the police. The joke was that the law enforcement officers were to be played by real members of the Public Security Service, which the young men saw as a unique opportunity to return their oppression by attacking them on the instructions of the director and fighting them without threat. Apart from such truly comic accounts, however, there are quite a few chilling scenes in the book, confirming that the activities of the VB (let alone the StB) were, on the contrary, not light-hearted and that cruelty and even physical attacks were common practice by the police:

> "I live here..." was the only thing Charlie could say. "I live near here...," but no one listened to him, because now they were looking at the hands of the others, and there was a guy in the row in a heavy leather jacket, a relatively older guy, and he said to the cops, "See? Clean...! No, comrades, I didn't throw anything...!" and the young policeman slammed him into those palms with a baton so hard that the man just yelled and put his hands in his armpits, and the policeman waited for a while, all the while just smiling and then shouted: And now show them!" and grabbed his hands at the wrists and pulled them out of his armpits, and then said in a calmer tone and with the gaze of the winner: "They are blue! And when they're blue, you were throwing...!" and the girl who had just begged that she needed to go to the toilet, now sat with a choked expression and resignedly watched the stain on her white trousers, a stain that was slowly growing.[65]

If, in *Občanský průkaz (Identity Card),* Šabach shares with Placák an interest in rebellious young heroes, he also has in common with him (and Balabán) a depiction of normalization as a still unclosed, traumatizing, and still highly radiant stage. It is especially evident in the rather disillusioning conclusion of

---

[65] Petr Šabach, *Občanský průkaz* (Praha: Paseka, 2006), 85–86.

the prose: soon after the fall of Communism, Petr learns who brought all the information to the secret police and that he himself was listed in their files as Agent Cockroach; only the court must decide that he was unjustly registered in these files. The author then confirms the link to real events and his personal story with the final signature: "Petr Šabach, aka Cockroach."

Mode 4: Existential

In some cases, the authors do not have the ambition to downplay the period of normalization or emphasize the negative; rather, they intend to examine it as one of the determinants of a particular life story. Normalization thus functions as a significant external factor in a given prose work, which often in the life of the characters and overlaps and mixes with other factors. The overall situation of a person in unfree conditions is thematized, including their inner experience and perception of "objective" events. In contrast to the usually lighter Modes 1 and 2, in this case, a more sober and, in relation to the main characters, a more serious and holistic view is applied, trying to understand more comprehensively the role of normalization in individual human destinies.

Even in this mode, the motives associated with normalization are not purposeful–in addition to their contribution to the construction of the period atmosphere, they are also important for the dynamics of the story, so the story, simply put, could hardly take place somewhere else. Despite various "self-preserving" strategies, normalization influences the character–either positively or negatively–especially at a young age, when it contributes to shaping their personal identity and integrity.

The prose of this mode includes the rather inconspicuous, but undoubtedly well-crafted work *Příběh v řeči nepřímé* (*A Story in Indirect Speech*, 2016) by the writer and playwright Alena Zemančíková (born 1955). Even in this case, the view of a teenager, an autobiographical narrator who recapitulates her life from the moment she learns of her brother's death, gets significant space. The narration, with its personalization, approximates a confession. The plot is intimate. The intelligent and sensitive heroine is mainly bothered by relationships in her own family (she tries to handle mainly the dominant mother) and soon also by not very successful relationships with men. She loves literature and theater; however, her dream of studying dramaturgy, or studying at all in any humanities faculty, is forbidden to her. Although she does not (yet) want to have anything to do with politics, she cannot avoid strong regime regulations under the given circumstances. She has no choice but to find her own paths, which is difficult and sometimes quite demotivating; on the other hand, sometimes she manages to meet extremely inspiring people on the edge of society, in actuality, real-life teachers for the narrator.

In the narration, which is not entirely linear, retrospective moments alternate with the current narration. Rather than memories of her brother, however, the narrator recalls images of a dominant and very unconventional mother, as she was entrusted to her care after the divorce, while her brother remained with her father. As suggested in the title, the narration can do without one of the traditional stylistic techniques–direct speech, which usually dramatizes the plot and reveals the thinking and interests of the characters, so to speak, in action. In *A Story in Indirect Speech*, however, the external action is backgrounded. Rather than events, the atmosphere of the time is captured, its reflection through thinking, remembering and self-awareness of the protagonist. The young woman constantly searches for the basic coordinates of her life, examines her roots and starting points, and plans her future as far as possible.

Normalization motifs are exposed in different ways: in some passages, they almost completely give way to private ones, in others, on the contrary, they are placed into the background (see the chapter eloquently entitled "Pomsta neschopných–Revenge of the Inept"). In some moments, the unsatisfactory social and family conditions of the main character significantly permeate each other:

> In my mother's opinion at the time, my personality is the work of people who have invested their efforts in me, as if I did not have any talent or will. As if I wasn't good, independent and gifted enough for my twenty years of age, damn it, and as if it wasn't all ruined by Communist Party checks and dismissals, and me and my brother failing to be recommended to study, without which you can't study at a college. As if I were just a failed investment, I turned into a wandering homeless creature, whose qualities were lost in that she couldn't accept the regime in her aunt's flat, which consisted in the rule that I could live there, but I couldn't bring anyone there, which I wasn't even told. I wouldn't take Vlado there at night if we could come together during the day. In fact, it was similar to the situation around, to all that nasty time.[66]

The prosaic experiment of the then debutante Lidmila Kábrtová (born 1971) *Koho vypijou lišky (Whom Foxes Drink Up*, 2013) is also focused on the personal

---

[66] Alena Zemančíková, *Příběh v řeči nepřímé* (Brno: Větrné mlýny, 2015), 122.

level and family relationships. The story of the birth, childhood, and adolescence of a girl named El is presented in brief chapters, each of which has exactly fifty words.[67] Most of the story is precisely dated, taking place between 1970 and 1983. A short epilogue, outlining El's meeting with classmates after many years, is then set in 2011. The sections corresponding to these years are introduced by quoting the titles of *Rudé právo* (later just *Právo*) from the given years: the reminder of domestic and the world affairs illustrates not only the atmosphere of the time but also the way the regime communicated its ideology through the media. Among the seemingly random quotations, a subtle game of meaning is realized. See, for example, excerpts annotated with the year 1972:

> The USSR opens the way to space for us. We must not waste energy. Agitation centers–a permanent source of activity. Set a task for each Communist. Nixon convicted of lying. The young come to the party. The thousandth Soviet film in our cinemas. Increase the effectiveness of economic propaganda and agitation. A million extra pairs of shoes this year. Krkonoše specialties to Moscow. Lenin's path to the further development of our socialist homeland. Billion Action Z. Americans cannot win. Fast and cheap bulk feeding. Human–the main hero of our literature. Fidel Castro warmly welcomed in Prague. Development of Czech nuclear energy until 1990. Socialism is a torch of invincible energy. "Game" made in NATO. Gifts for Soviet women. We have more children.[68]

Brief, concise entries in the personal third-person form then mediate the consciousness of the main character. As Kryštof Špidla notes, it is the third-person form that gives the texts an objectifying character, and creates a raw, cool, to even distant impression.[69] Formally, the texts oscillate between curt stories, sometimes reminiscent of jokes with a punch line, and lyrically tuned reflections reminiscent of poems. The main dramas take place in El's dysfunctional family–quarrels between the mother and the alcoholic father are everyday happenings, as are physical and mental violence. Little El has a somewhat warmer relationship with her kind, believing grandfather, but even he is not able to completely compensate for her parents' distance. Not even a hopeful first love pulls the girl out of gloomy, almost hopeless years–it soon

---

[67] The author used the form from Zdeněk Král's web project called *Příběhy na padesát slov* (*Stories for Fifty Words*) (cf. http://pribehynapadesatslov.cz/).
[68] Lidmila Kábrtová, *Koho vypijou lišky* (Brno: Host, 2013), 27.
[69] Kryštof Špidla, "Normou o normalizaci," *Host*, no. 9 (2013): 73.

ends up with the emigration of her classmate's family. In addition, the grandfather dies shortly afterwards.

Husák's regime also affects El in many ways–both its rules and its absurdities compound El's family problems. Her birth itself is affected by an unspecified political event: if "mom" hadn't been shopping one day, had not got involved in a street protest, and her grandfather had not married her quickly for fear of punishment, El would probably not have been born. In addition, as one of Husák's, so-called, children, she cannot stay away from other normalization phenomena, such as the Pioneers, correspondence with assigned Soviet comrades, all sorts of collective celebrations (especially the liberation anniversary and May Day), ROH Spartakiads, company recreations ROH, so-called Z-events, and the like. There are also other aspects of reality under normalization, such as the lack of consumer goods, listening to the banned broadcasting of foreign radio, forced voting of candidates for the National Front, training in the event of a nuclear strike, and the like. The following excerpt illustrates, among others, the contemporary practices and mood:

> Мuру mup
> "What is мuру mup?" she examines the poster affixed to the railing.
> They will set up a May Day stand here tomorrow.
> "World peace," in Russian,' explains grandpa.
> "They are good men, the Russians."
> "Communist bastards."
> "Russians? When they want peace?"
> "No, Czechs."
> "Why? Because they write in Russian, and people don't understand it?"
> "Because they lie."
> "Lie?"
> "Yeah. But don't say it at school."[70]

Some reviewers see a weakness in a certain stereotypical depiction of normalization motives, which, despite their real historical basis, always threaten to become certain clichés.[71] However, Ondřej Nezbeda aptly remarks

---

[70] Kábrtová, *Koho vypijou lišky*, 117.
[71] See Alena Scheinostová, "O liškách v reálsocialismu," *Tvar*, no. 1 (2014): 23; Špidla, "Normou o normalizaci," 73. Ondřej Nezbeda, "Lišky v domě," *respekt.cz* (2013), Available from: <https://www.databazeknih.cz/recenze/koho-vypijou-lisky-160509> [Acccessed April 1, 2022].

about them that in the given context, "they may not be avoided, and it is their destiny to seem a little annoying forever."[72]

Mode 5: Problematizing

In contemporary prose on normalization, the problematizing mode is significantly minor. Although it cannot be contended in general that works of this type are always more successful as literary works, in relation to the central theme they are usually among the more assertive. Programmatically, they disrupt established ideas and thought patterns in literature and other discourses, whether relating to normalization itself or Communism, (post)socialism, totalitarian regimes and the like. At the same time, they tend to deviate from the ways of literary depiction of normalization described so far, especially in their simpler form. Although even in this mode, a humorous, nostalgic, ironic tone, an attempt at retrospection or even settle accounts can be applied, these aspects do not become dominant. There is a clear distance from normalization attributes in the function of mere (self-serving) scenery and props.

The effort to make uncertain the dichotomous framework of us versus them, which prevails not only in literature but also in a significant part of historiography and journalism, is characteristic. If the modes introduced so far have generally respected the binary "totalist" model, where, on the one hand, there is a Communist regime (or its exponents and collaborators) and on the other hand, the individuals who are controlled by this regime (whether it is its political opponents or "only" those who want to live on their own), in the case of "problematizing" prose, the boundaries tend to be less clearcut. The roles of victims and perpetrators are uncertain, and often overlap for many characters.

Petra Hůlová's (born 1979) *Strážci občanského dobra (Guardians of the Civic Good*, 2010), projecting a specific social arrangement against the background of Czechoslovak history, went beyond the stereotype of the usual thinking about normalization. Although the fictional world formed here is more loosely related to the current world, (quasi)normalization and post-normalization reminiscences are an integral part of it. Hůlová creates an atypical heroine in the form of an intellectually not very gifted narrator who identifies herself with socialism and its Communist establishment. In the first part of the book, describing her adolescence in a socially engineered Czechoslovak "new town," the woman conforms to the state doctrine, then remembers nostalgically the

---

[72] Ibid.

era and regrets the 1989 coup (here called as "counterrevolution").[73] At the same time, in the fictitious Cracow, "the real realities of the lifestyle during normalization in Czechoslovakia are mixed with the image of a completely exhausted and impoverished totalitarian system of the developing state."[74] With regard to politically lax anti-Communist parents and sisters, she undergoes a surprising development and from a class outsider, she becomes a strict teacher after the coup and later the leader of the Communist people's militias.

With a literary flare, Hůlová disrupts the usual scheme of a critical, even negative, view of the pre-revolution system and a rather positive (or at least more favorable) evaluation of the new regime. She expands the opposite pattern, when the main heroine finds for herself and society the current establishment as clearly worse and repeatedly raises the provocative question of whether the overthrow of Communism in Czechoslovakia, and thus in Eastern Europe as a whole, was not a fatal mistake. The reversal of majority values is reflected, among other things, in the negative view of dissidents who are exalted at other times, about whom the narrator expresses her considerable contempt. She calls them "big noses" and always describes them quite scathingly:

> Big noses looked through their fingers at people like my dad, at good people who care about their work and don't poke their noses into other people's things, no matter how honestly they worked. Today they are called the silent majority. The majority of the inhabitants of the Czechoslovak Socialist Republic, thanks to whom it worked here. Vidlička and Šrámek also went to the loo and bought buns in the shop.

---

[73] The originally German term *ostalgia* is sometimes used in this context, directly referring to the longing for certain aspects of life in socialism. See Martin Franc, "Ostalgie v Čechách," in *Kapitoly z dějin české demokracie po roce 1989*, eds. Adéla Gjuričová and Michal Kopeček (Praha: Paseka, 2008), 193–216.

[74] Alena Šidáková Fialová, "V zajetí normalizace," in *V souřadnicích mnohosti. Česká literatura první dekády jednadvacátého století v souvislostech a interpretacích*, ed. Alena Šidáková Fialová (Praha: Academia, 2014), 355-58. "Everything in Cracow was tacky. The houses were wet, the nursery where mum took Milada first had no heating and then no toilet, because the waste was clogged because the pipes were too thin. The swings were often broken, dark stains of water were on buildings, the large tiles in front of the House of Services swayed, and strong boys were able to take them out when there were two of them. But who cares, and it also had a lot of advantages." Petra Hůlová, *Strážci občanského dobra* (Torst: Praha, 2010), 21.

But it would never have occurred to them to comment on such work with appreciation. They took the royal service for granted. Warming up with socialist heating, walking in socialist sweatpants and drinking Communist beer, that's what they liked. And at the same time making counter-revolutionary plans against their poor fellow citizens.[75]

By combining a strong authorial style with an overall conceit that gives space to the mostly marginalized or completely ignored voice of a person who is essentially convinced, even they experience that every day, that "the past was better," *Guardians of the Civic Good* is an extraordinary attempt. In regards to the overall topic, it is also the most speculative prose work (the way out of unfavorable conditions is sought here interestingly in the mobilization of the Vietnamese community), moving on the edge of socio-political satire with historical elements and a mystifying game.[76]

Prose writer and literary scholar Michal Přibáň (born 1966) also portrays normalization in a narratively sophisticated way. He makes his novel *Všechno je jenom dvakrát (Everything Only Happens Twice*, 2016) unusual through a device common to science fiction–time travel. However, this device is only one of the levels of a more complex compositional plan. Not only are three historical and cultural epochs (normalization, the immediately post-revolutionary period, and the period of about fifteen years later) placed in confrontation, but also various individual, psychological times. The meaning is thus spread between the present and the past, and, at the same time, divided into three phases of the narrator's life.

The main narrative role is partly played by the autobiographical character Pavel Klimeš, a former journalist of about forty years, who is still haunted by some unresolved issues from the past. The second narrator is Pavel's father: however, he receives much less space in the diary entries, which he makes during the summer holidays at a corporate holiday cottage in Krkonoše Mountains (a total of 29 entries, the oldest is dated August 18, 1968, the last one July 26, 1977). It is the time of the family Krkonoše recreations to which Pavel Klimeš mainly turns. According to a number of indications, he suspects that something serious happened then, but there is still silence about it, partly

---

[75] Ibid., 65.
[76] See Stehlíková, who also uses the term "apocalyptic parable." Olga Stehlíková, "Všechno v Krakově bylo fórový," in *iLiteratura* (2010). Available from: <https://www.iliteratura.cz/Clanek/26359/hulova-petra-strazci-obcanskeho-dobra> [Accessed April 1, 2022].

because of the lack of witnesses and reliable information. Did his former idol, his father's colleague and family friend cooperate with the state security? And most importantly: Did this man (named Milan Knot) betray his father's other acquaintance during one of the Krkonoše holidays, resulting in his arrest, conviction, and the suffering of his entire family? These are the main questions the main character asks himself.

Pavel Klimeš deals with the issue of collaboration in detail, not only for personal but also for professional reasons. As a former revolutionary student and later a talented young journalist, he writes about these cases in newspapers in the early 1990s. Although he finally leaves the addressed sentence to the journalistic competition, a look into the archives of the StB and the Cibulka lists published at the time clearly confirm at first his belief of the guilt of the acquaintance. Over time, however, his confidence and hostility to his former idol are increasingly eroded by doubts caused by emerging information, which he subsequently obtains from various other sources. He complements his vague memory of the sudden disappearance of the Sudeten German Borovička (aka Borowitschka) and his family, especially his likable daughter, with testimonies of other witnesses and other stakeholders: parents, former classmates (including a post-revolution intelligence worker), former childhood lovers and friends. He also contacts the adult daughter of the arrested, living abroad, and, after years, talks to the accused himself and his wife. However, no one can guarantee the correctness of their version of the story. Although Pavel learns a lot of remarkable partial findings and details, the family friend's secret informing is not directly proven. Most findings are fragmentary, with conflicting statements and opinions often emerging; statements are often based on speculation and unverifiable assumptions, filling gaps in individual knowledge of the case and increasingly leaky memory. Pavel Klimeš realizes that he can hardly get any clear answers and thus judge someone: "When you examine a… a historical matter, you must not look at it from today's point of view. If you do, you will never understand it. You will never understand why people in the 1940s or 1950s acted the way they did. And if your children approach history in this way, they will never understand why you started a strike in November."[77]

Journalist Patrick Zandl (born 1974) also presented a similar, partly tragicomic, and partly nostalgic depiction of normalization in his short story collection *Husákův děda* (*Husák's Grandpa*, 2015). Even in this case, we are dealing with a stylized childhood perspective but often mixed with the life

---

[77] Michal Přibáň, *Všechno je jenom dvakrát* (Brno: Host, 2016), 291.

experiences of an already adult, mature person. Zandl's collection is connected to titles included in Mode 1 mainly by the inclusion of humor and an effort to alleviate the often really funny deformations of the time; in the same way, there is a longing for the former "wonderful" years.

As the name implies, the narrator recalls mainly his childhood, especially the holidays he spent with his unshakable role model, his grandfather. However, the colorful narrative also reconstructs the experiences and impressions of the child, or the experiences of the whole generation growing up in the then Czechoslovakia:

> We children wouldn't mind so much that the secretaries were dying, but the society-wide hysteria involved in it was awful. I remember Brezhnev's death, and I remember just little from the period of my eight years of age. The headmaster of the school told us about the news on the radio and spoke at length in tears that the only guarantee of world peace had died, the only man who held the arms and military appetites of the capitalists in check. For the next few months, Sparks and Pioneers focused on practicing survival in combat conditions. We learned to work with gas masks, to lie on our heels at the epicenter of an atomic explosion, to use plastic bags as protection against radioactive fallout, to run through contaminated areas, to disassemble a submachine gun and much more. When Andropov died, we were told directly that the war was about to come. We cried at school, not because he died, but because we were really scared. In art classes, we drew Pershing missiles falling on the city, and in mathematics we counted word problems such as "When Dašice has 2,000 inhabitants and a bomb kills 500 of them, how many will remain?"[78]

Along with the depiction of the world under normalization, the author also raises more complex questions, either implicitly in the short stories themselves or explicitly in other paratexts of the book. In the preface entitled "Husák's Children" and in the essayistic afterword entitled "On Communist Patterns and Guilt," he directly formulates his main motivations for writing the book–he is convinced that in the case of the previous regime, the victims and perpetrators cannot be reliably distinguished, the need to forgive should be promoted to a greater extent: "This question comes back whenever it comes to Communism. Who was the good one, and who were the bad ones? And most importantly,

---

[78] Patrick Zandl, *Husákův děda* (Praha: Argo, 2015), 65-66.

who were we, our parents, and grandparents, who lived, learned, and worked under Communism?"[79]

In his own story, the author demonstrates the fundamental pitfalls of any (historical, journalistic, sociological, or other) generalization: it always fails to capture the real stories of specific people, their incomparable destinies and complex, but barely discernible motives. Although in a relatively conventional literary form, Zandl suggests in his short stories about the young boy's relationship with the admired grandfather-Communist that a post-Communist and post-normalization reflection must include a nuanced, sensitive debate that respects the unique situation of specific individuals.

Conclusion:
Prevalent tendencies of contemporary Czech prose on normalization

Although the timing and conceptualization of normalization as a historical fact is debatable, there is no doubt that it is a societal phenomenon that is part of the Czech collective memory. So far, it has strongly influenced Czech society. Subsequently created and often reproduced cultural images of normalization include the image formed by literature: prose dealing with this topic is one of the most productive in post-revolution literary works. In these works, normalization usually becomes a specific semantic complex; it is one of the most prominent post-revolution topoi.

Although this tendency is characterized by considerable variability–we have identified five largely distinct, independent modes–several more general tendencies can be observed. Above all, the analyzed works exhibits a considerable autobiographical nature: the main characters are in agreement in the basic socio-demographic indicators (age, gender, education, etc.) with the author, at least to the extent that we as readers are able to recognize them. Narratively, first-person or personal narratives dominate, often stylized as personal memories of the time, but adjusted by time distance, other life experiences, as well as knowledge of subsequent historical developments (especially the awareness of the end of the Communist regime in 1989). The relationship between author and narrator and (main) character often gets blurred, which brings the prose closer to the realm of readers' favorite memoir and biographical literature.

Related to this is the densely determining view of a minor (child or adolescent) character. The authors draw inspiration and information about

---

[79] Ibid., 159.

normalization mainly from autopsy, while the often one-sided, simplistic, but subjectively "authentic" view of a young person is a value of its kind to the creators. At the suprapersonal level, one often aspires to a certain form of generational statement. Private or family life is often exposed as the counterpart to the public existence of man, determined by normalization rules: heroes and heroines, in addition to their academic, professional, or general social assertion (or rather restrictions), often deal with relationships with parents or grandparents, siblings, partners, and the like. The topic of normalization also often goes hand in hand with the traditionally popular constellation of Czech literature of a "small (ordinary) man in the wake of great (unpredictable and ruthless) history."

In a frequently visited topic in the context of popular "retromania," authors seldom avoid a certain oversimplification, whether it is a portrayal of normalization reality as categorically negative, patterned view of social relations, or the conventional use of notorious "props." In addition to the relatively straightforward setting accounts of Communists and Communism (most prominent in Mode 3), there are also other prose works in which the author's position is evident and unambiguous from the beginning. One of the consequences is the mostly transparent distribution of forces, or a clear definition of the characters into positive (standing aside from the Communist regime) and negative (collaborating with the regime). In this respect, with some exceptions, the historiographical tendencies mentioned in the introduction, which reject the black-and-white understanding of normalization in the sense of "enslaved society–repressive regime," do not reflect much in the literature. However, even certain schemes do not have to reduce the artistic value of the work, let alone its attractiveness to the readership: the merit of many texts lies in something else (e.g., in the overall atmosphere, humor, linguistic brilliance or even more pronounced "authenticity" and "personal liability").

The customary subtopics also include confrontation with institutions–given the aforementioned focus on the childhood and young years of the characters, it is primarily the school that represents the bodies of the Communist system. The school is not only one of the typical places of maturing and self-awareness of the characters, it is often one of the most important signposts in their careers, whether they realize it at the moment or not. However, rather than a gateway to knowledge, the (socialist, normalization) school is portrayed as an obstacle to personal and knowledge development; the most important things are mostly learnt elsewhere. The school is also shown as the first official tool of civic segregation, as well as ubiquitous regime propaganda. At the same time, it is an ambiguous element because it combines both nostalgic and often funny memories and many traumatic experiences: the first personal experiences of manipulation and intimidation, repression, political coercion, and/or unification (*Gleichschaltung*) of human individuals.

Finally, prose on normalization is also characterized by a strong connection to the present: the turn of 1989 is often thematized–then and now is compared, not only what has changed is considered, but also where there is more continuity. Obviously, in many cases, the authors do not aim just to literally "use" a topic and entertain the reader, but also to give serious testimony, presenting to the public their own report on the time, which should–in the best scenario–have (or at least potentially could have) an impact on the present. Artistic ambitions are thus often complemented by a (sometimes explicitly acknowledged) "memory" function, i.e., the desire to preserve some experiences evaluated by the authors as historically significant for the future. More than once, it is also a moral message–the authors intend to say what is (was) good and evil, what behavior is worth appreciating and what is worth rejecting. Their attempts to capture normalization are the more successful, the clearer it is that they could not be presented otherwise, that is, within other genres or competing discourses, such as journalism, historiography, memory studies, sociology, and the like.

Bibliography

Assmann, Aleida. *Prostory vzpomínání: podoby a proměny kulturní paměti.* Praha: Univerzita Karlova, Nakladatelství Karolinum, 2018.
Assmann, Jan. *Kultura a paměť: písmo, vzpomínka a politická identita v rozvinutých kulturách starověku.* Praha: Prostor, 2001.
Balabán, Jan. *Kudy šel anděl.* Brno: Host, 2005.
———. *Povídky; Romány a novely; Publicistika a hry.* Brno: Host, 2010–2012.
Bílek, Petr A. and Blanka Činátlová. *Tesilová kavalérie: popkulturní obrazy normalizace.* Příbram: Pistorius & Olšanská, 2010.
Brabec, Jiří. "Druhá původní novinka." *Literární noviny* 10, no. 7 (1999): 16.
Bren, Paulina. *Zelinář a jeho televize: kultura komunismu po pražském jaru 1968.* Praha: Academia, 2013.
Činátl, Kamil, Jan Mervart, and Jaroslav Najbrt, eds. *Podoby československé normalizace: dějiny v diskuzi.* Praha: Ústav pro studium totalitních režimů, 2017.
Činátl, Kamil. *Dějiny a vyprávění: Palackého Dějiny jako zdroj historické obraznosti národa.* Praha: Argo, 2011.
Čornej, Petr. "Věčný problém: Jak psát dějiny." In *O psaní dějin: teoretické a metodologické problémy literární historiografie,* edited by Kateřina Piorecká and Ondřej Sládek, 13–29. Praha: Academia, 2007.

Dousková, Irena. *B. Proudew.* Translated by Melvyn Clarke. Praha: Pálava Publishing, 2016.

——. *Hrdý Budžes.* Praha: Hynek, 1998.

Dvořák, Tomáš and Tomáš Borovský. *Úvod do studia dějepisu.* Brno: Masarykova univerzita, 2014.

Fencl, Milan. "Balabán není vějička." *Weles,* no. 19, (2004): 113.

Franc, Martin. "Ostalgie v Čechách." In *Kapitoly z dějin české demokracie po roce 1989,* Edited by Adéla Gjuričová and Michal Kopeček, 193–216. Praha: Paseka, 2008.

Halbwachs, Maurice. *Kolektivní paměť.* Praha: Sociologické nakladatelství, 2009.

Haman, Aleš. "Poláčkovské téma z jiné perspektivy." *Nové knihy* 39, no. 1 (1999): 4.

Havel, Václav. *Moc bezmocných.* Praha: Lidové noviny, 1990.

Horský, Jan. *Teorie a narace: k noetice historické vědy a teorii kulturního vývoje.* Praha: Argo, 2015.

Hůlová, Petra. *Strážci občanského dobra.* Praha: Torst, 2010.

Jandourek, Jan. "Oněgin byl Rusák, komunisti byli...." *Aktualne.cz.* (2006). Available from: <https://magazin.aktualne.cz/kultura/umeni/onegin-byl-rusak-komunisti-byli/r~i:article:162231/> [Accessed April 1, 2022].

Janoušek, Pavel. "Život na Kdysissippi." *Tvar,* no. 12 (2008): 3.

Jechová, Květa. "Postavení žen v Československu v období normalizace." In *Česká společnost v 70. a 80. letech: sociální a ekonomické aspekty,* edited by Oldřich Tůma and Tomáš Vilímek, 176–246. Praha: Ústav pro soudobé dějiny AV ČR, 2012.

Kábrtová, Lidmila. *Koho vypijou lišky.* Brno: Host, 2013.

Karfík, Vladimír. "Báječná léta pod psa." *Literární noviny,* no. 10 (1992): 7.

Klíčová, Eva. *Lopaty, inženýři, inkousti a ostatní. Transformace hodnot v normalizační pracovní próze.* Brno: Masarykova univerzita, Filozofická fakulta, 2018. Available from: https://is.muni.cz/th/rmjc4/.

Klusák, Pavel. *Gott: československý příběh.* Brno: Host, 2021.

Kolář, Pavel and Michal Pullmann. *Co byla normalizace?: studie o pozdním socialismu.* Praha: Nakladatelství Lidové noviny, 2016.

Kozelka, Milan. *Život na Kdyssissippi.* Brno: Host, 2008.

Kratochvil, Jiří. "Obnovení chaosu v české literatuře." *Literární noviny* 3, no. 47 (1992): 5.

Linhart, Jiří. "Šedá zóna." In *Sociologická encyklopedie,* edited by Zdeněk Nešpor. Praha Sociologický ústav AV ČR, 2018. Available from: <https://encyklopedie.soc.cas.cz/w/%E2%80%9E%C5%A1ed%C3%A1_z%C3%B3na% E2%80%9C> [Accessed April 1, 2022].

Machonin, Pavel. *Česká společnost a sociologické poznání.* Praha: ISV nakladatelství, 2005.

Mencl, Vojtěch. *Křižovatky 20. století: světlo na bílá místa v nejnovějších dějinách.* Praha: Naše vojsko, 1990.

Mervart, Jan. "Rozdílnost pohledů na československou normalizaci." In *Podoby československé normalizace: dějiny v diskuzi*, edited by Kamil Činátl, Jan Mervart, and Jaroslav Najbrt, 40–80. Praha: Ústav pro studium totalitních režimů, 2017.

Nezbeda, Ondřej. "Lišky v domě." *respekt.cz* (2013). Available from: <https://www.databazeknih.cz/recenze/koho-vypijou-lisky-160509> [Accessed April 1, 2022].

Otáhal, Milan. *Normalizace 1969–1989: příspěvek ke stavu bádání*. Praha: Ústav pro soudobé dějiny AV ČR, 2002.

Pilař, Martin. "Báječná léta pod psa." In *Slovník české literatury* (1994): <Slovník české literatury (slovnikceskeliteratury.cz)> [Accessed April 1, 2022].

Placák, Petr. *Škola od svatého Norberta*. Praha: Torst, 2021.

Přibáň, Michal. *Všechno je jenom dvakrát*. Brno: Host, 2016.

Pullmann, Michal. *Konec experimentu: přestavba a pád komunismu v Československu*. Praha: Scriptorium, 2011.

Šabach, Petr. *Občanský průkaz*. Praha: Paseka, 2006.

Scheinostová, Alena. "O liškách v reálsocialismu." *Tvar* 23, no. 1 (2014). Available from: <https://www.databazeknih.cz/recenze/koho-vypijou-lisky-160509> [Accessed April 1, 2022].

Šidáková Fialová, Alena. "V zajetí normalizace." In *V souřadnicích mnohosti. Česká literatura první dekády jednadvacátého století v souvislostech a interpretacích*, edited by Alena Šidáková Fialová, 355–58. Praha: Academia, 2014.

Šidáková Fialová, Alena. *Poučeni z krizového vývoje: poválečná česká společnost v reflexi normalizační prózy*. Praha: Academia, 2014.

Šiklová, Jiřina and Vilém Prečan, eds. *Kočka, která nikdy nespí II: Jiřině Šiklové k narozeninám*, Praha: James H. Ottaway, Jr, 2015.

Špidla, Kryštof. "Normou o normalizaci." *Host*, no. 9 (2013): 73.

Stehlíková, Olga. "Všechno v Krakově bylo fórový." *iLiteratura* (2010). Available from: <https://www.iliteratura.cz/Clanek/26359/hulova-petra-strazci-obcanskeho-dobra> [Accessed April 1, 2022].

Švehla, Marek. *Magor a jeho doba: život Ivana M. Jirouse*. Praha: Torst, 2017.

Tůma, Oldřich and Tomáš Vilímek, eds. *Česká společnost v 70. a 80. letech: sociální a ekonomické aspekty*. Praha: Ústav pro soudobé dějiny AV ČR, 2012.

Urbanová, Svatava. "Otevřené návraty v prózách Jana Balabána." In *Souřadnice míst*, edited by Svatava Urbanová, Iva Málková, 103–16. Ostrava: Ostravská univerzita, 2003.

Vaněk-Úvalský, Bohuslav. *Brambora byla pomeranč mého dětství*. Brno: Petrov, 2001.

———. *Brambora byla pomeranč mého dětství*. Praha: Krásné nakladatelství, 2021.

Vašíček, Zdeněk, Robert Krumphanzl, and Karel Palek, eds. *Jak se dělají filosofie*. Praha: Triáda, 2012.

Verderyová, Katherine. "Co byl socialismus a proč padl?" In *Podoby československé normalizace: dějiny v diskuzi*, edited by Kamil Činátl, Jan

Mervart, and Jaroslav Najbrt, 261–82. Praha: Ústav pro studium totalitních režimů, 2017.
Viewegh, Michal. *Báječná léta pod psa*. Brno: Petrov, 2002.
——. *Bliss Was It in Bohemia*. Translated by David Short. London: Jantar Publishing, 2015.
Zandl, Patrick. *Husákův děda*. Praha: Argo, 2015.
Zemančíková, Alena. *Příběh v řeči nepřímé*. Brno: Větrné mlýny, 2015.

Chapter 6

Against everything: the brothers Topol and the second generation of the underground

Daniel Webster Pratt
McGill University

Abstract

In the 1980s, the two brothers, Jáchym (b. 1962) and Filip Topol (1965–2013), became leaders of a new generation of dissent in Prague. The sons of the director, playwright, and dramaturg Josef Topol of *Divadlo za branou* fame, the two young boys were thrown into the so-called worlds of dissent after their father signed Charter 77. Both Jáchym and Filip followed their father into dissent, becoming major players in the underground of the 1980s. Jáchym wrote poetry, lyrics, and stories, also founding *Revolver Revue*, and his brother fronted the band Psí vojáci, a legendary group in the underground. The two figures remained major players into the 90s, and Jáchym remains one of the most important Czech writers alive.

The brothers Topol represent the second generation of dissent, the generation that grew up when the rules of dissent were already written. They were too young to have a say in major documents such as the Charter, but they were old enough to be jailed for signing it. Both Filip and Jáchym rebelled not only against the Czechoslovak Socialist regime, but also against the previous generation of dissent. They created alternative arts in the form of zines, music shows, and DIY-happenings, less so in the traditional art forms, and they challenged the status quo in both the previous generation's underground and official arts.

The brothers Topol challenge our perceptions of the dissident era because they do not fit neatly into the logic of the previous generation. They never experienced the relative freedom of the Prague Spring, but rather came of age during the fallout of Charter 77. The previous generation were not simply heroes in their mind, but rather a kind of establishment to rebel against. In an interview, Jáchym claimed "there was a difference between us–i.e., those who weren't driven or thrown into the world of the banned but were simply born into it–and those who belonged to that already existing sphere that some of us tentatively described as 'the established underground' or even the 'underground establishment.'" Members of this generation rebelled not only against the regime, but also against the previous generation of the underground as well.

Keywords: Dissent, Filip Topol, Jáchym Topol, Punk Rock, Underground.

* * *

"It sounds ridiculous but it's not," Miloš Forman claimed in a documentary about the Beatles, but "I'm convinced the Beatles are partly responsible for the fall of Communism."[1] Forman is by no means alone in his assessment; Peter Wicke argues that "rock musicians were instrumental in setting in motion the actual course of events which led to the destruction of the Berlin Wall and the disappearance of the GDR."[2] According to Sabrina Petra Ramet, "Václav Havel, former president of Czechoslovakia, even maintains that the revolution *began* in the rock scene."[3] Music, and specifically rock music, seems to hold a special place in the downfall of the Socialist Bloc in Europe, casting musicians into heroic counterforces to the oppressive regimes.

On the other hand, Jolanta Pekacz, the Polish musicologist, provides a more nuanced understanding of Rock'n'Roll, suggesting that rock musicians cannot be lumped into a single monolithic group that opposed a singularly monolithic state; rock musicians opposed, supported, and at times did not care about the regime, so placing the responsibility for the fall of Communism on the back of these musicians seems a bit far-fetched. The "rock 'revolt,'" Pekacz argues, "was not *against* the dominant culture, but *within* it."[4] For Pekacz, rock was not by nature antagonistic to the regime, but worked within the specific historical situation of late Socialism, acting sometimes in tandem with the regime and

---

[1] *The Beatles Revolution*, 2000, directed by Rudy Bednar.
[2] Peter Wicke, "'The Times They Are A-Changin': Rock Music and Political Change in East Germany," *Rockin' the Boat: Mass Music and Mass Movements*, ed. Reebee Garofalo (Cambridge, MA: South End Press, 1992), 81.
[3] Sabrina Petra Ramet, *Rocking the State: Rock Music and Politics in Eastern Europe* (New York: Routledge, 2019), 1. Emphasis in the original.
[4] Jolanta Pekacz, "Did Rock Smash the Wall? The Role of Rock in Political Transition," *Popular Music* 13, no. 1 (January 1994): 48.

sometimes in opposition, but always within the structures of the Socialist society.

Placing rock and roll within the culture begs the question of what happens to rock musicians when that culture fundamentally changes? In tracing underground music at the end of the Communist era in his *Notes from Underground: Rock Music Counterculture in Russia*, Thomas Cushman asks, "What happens to cultural communities whose existence and social significance are fundamentally related to the structural conditions characteristic of a state socialist society when they encounter new forms of social and economic organization characteristic of capitalist society?"[5] Both Cushman and Anne Szemere, in their book on the Hungarian underground, *Up from the Underground*, answer that underground and dissident bands simply fade during the end of Communism, as the specter of Communism itself fades and the new generation of musicians takes over. According to Szemere, "the transition posed the most challenge for those musicians and artists whose identity and politics had been molded by their dissent from the communist state."[6] Both authors claim that without something to oppose, underground and, more specifically, *dissident* groups lose their political importance and thus lose their ability to appeal to their audiences.

In Czechoslovakia, underground music certainly had an extensive influence on the dissident movement. The Plastic People of the Universe became a widely known band, not only in their native land but also across the world, because of their arrest for organized disturbance of the peace, the following "Trial of the Plastics," and their connection to Charter 77, the first major dissident challenge to the Communist government. Their story largely follows the narratives set out above, where they were connected to the dissident movement, and they largely faded after the fall of Communism, only to reemerge in 1997 on nostalgia tours like so many aging rockers.

Psí vojáci (The Dog Warriors), however, the rock group founded by Filip Topol, initially using texts from his older brother Jáchym, defied the expectation that dissident and underground bands would fade away. Instead of becoming less popular after the end of state socialism, Psí vojáci actually became more popular after 1989, with increasing audiences, live broadcasts of their concerts on national television, and a 1994 film *Žiletky* (Razors) that was

---

[5] Thomas Cushman, *Notes from Underground: Rock Music Counterculture in Russia* (Albany: SUNY Press, 1995), xv.

[6] Anna Szemere, *Up from the Underground: The Culture of Rock Music in Post-Socialist Hungary* (University Park: Pennsylvania State University Press, 2001), 13.

inspired by the Psí vojáci song of the same name, starring Filip himself.[7] That same year, Psí vojáci released a companion album to Jáchym's novel *Sestra* (*Sister*, translated by Alex Zucker as *City, Sister, Silver*), one of the most important post-socialist novels and a foundational text in Czech postmodernism. Both brothers became national stars in music and literature after the end of Communism, but remained connected to the Prague underground from which they emerged in the 1980s. In comparison to other bands, such as The Plastic People of the Universe, Psí vojáci have lasted, despite their deeper commitment to dissent and the underground. The same is true for Jáchym, who remains one of the most important authors living in the Czech Republic to this day.

The success of Psí vojáci and Jáchym Topol challenge the reigning narratives of the underground in the late socialist period, as advocated by both those who see music as contributing to the fall of socialism and those who saw underground figures fading away. Although Psí vojáci was certainly a dissident band, they were not a part of the more intellectual dissident movement, despite their lyrics directed at the regime and their familial (and personal) connections to Havel himself. They would have no hand in creating the revolution, since their audience was limited to the Prague underground, and neither Filip nor Jáchym would play a major role in the government after the revolution. Secondly, their success defies the narrative of fading away, showing that something in Psí vojáci's lyrics and music remained important even after the revolution. Both issues emerge out of the emphasis on the first generation of the underground and dissent. However, there was a large generational shift between the 60s generation and the so-called second generation of dissent, i.e., those who grew up after the relative freedom of the Prague Spring.

When thinking of Czech dissident and underground culture, most scholarship has focused on the standard set of figures: Václav Havel, Ivan Klíma, Jaroslav Seifert, The Plastics, Ivan Martin Jirous, and Egon Bondy. This group, along with the great filmmakers of the Czech New Wave, all born between roughly 1930 and 1950, still constitute the basis of most discussions of Czech culture under Socialism. To a certain degree, their innovations, cultural value, and international appeal justify their position. What has received a great deal less scholarly attention, however, is the generation that came next, that had never known the relative freedom of the "Prague Spring" and grew up in

---

[7] For more on Psí Vojáci in the post-socialist era, see Tomáš Jirsa, "Charting Post-Underground Nostalgia: Anachronistic Practices of the Post-Velvet Revolution Rock Scene," *Iluminace* 29, no 3 (2017): 65–86.

the fallout of Charter 77, just as the brothers Topol did. The brothers Topol, along with Vít Kremlička, Petr Placák, Anna Wágnerová, Jiří Hášek (JH Krchovský), Viktor Karlík, and others, form the so-called second generation of dissent, and they have become leading voices in contemporary Czech letters, music, and the plastic arts.

The shadow of the 60s generation is not the only reason for the lack of attention paid to the second generation of dissent, especially in the West: the second generation does not fit into the emancipatory narratives about dissent more broadly. They did not have the chance to take part in the relative freedom of the 1960s, nor did they have the opportunity to put their own stamp on the dissident or underground community writ large because both communities were already dominated by the previous generation. Many of the members of the second generation came from dissident families, which ensured that they would not be able to obtain the same level of education due to the reprisals on their families. They did not experience the same success following the fall of the Czechoslovak Socialist Republic, since none of them were invited to become a part of Havel's government, nor did they have the same cultural cachet as the members of the 60s generation. Unlike that previous generation, the brothers Topol eschewed any utopian impulses in their music and literature, privileging artistic expression that was against everything, verging on the nihilistic. The accusation from the government organs about the nihilism of the underground in the 1970s may not have applied to the 60s generation, but in carving out a space between the 60s generation and the official culture, the brothers Topol took on the mantle of nihilism, with songs about suicide and the loss of libido and with a novel about the general loss of meaning both before and after the Velvet Revolution.

I am using the brothers Topol to examine this generation, since they became leaders in journalism, literature, as well as rock music in the 1980s and 1990s, and their writings on the second generation contain powerful descriptions of the Prague underground. Jáchym's apartment was often used as an exhibition space, where concerts, recitations, and artistic happenings took place, and he had his own bands as well. However, the brothers Topol are not totally emblematic of the underground. They came from a staunchly dissident family with a strong literary pedigree. Josef Topol, their father, is considered one of the greatest playwrights of the second half of the twentieth century, and their maternal grandfather was *Devětsíl* author and interwar member of parliament Karel Schulz. Many members of this second generation had links to the previous generation of dissent or the underground, however, Jáchym and Filip probably had the best connections of any, making them elites in the underground world. Although they had greater connections than others, the story of the brothers still illuminates the generational differences in both the underground and dissent, and it is this difference that I want to emphasize.

Generations of the Underground

The Underground, following the most important scholar of the scene, Martin Pilař, can be divided into three main periods: the 1950s, the 1970s, and the 1980s, the last being the least discussed in the scholarship.[8] Egon Bondy, Bohumil Hrabal, Karel Marysko, and Skupina 42 became the foundation of the earliest underground movements in the 1950s, and they remained virtually untouchable throughout the next forty years. In the 1960s, there was an explosion of culture that could be legally obtained, from film and music to the literature and poetry of previously banned artists, making the underground less useful and powerful. Because writers such as Hrabal, Jiří Kolář, and future Nobel Laureate Jaroslav Seifert were able to publish, the underground structures weakened considerably during this time. Many members of the underground saw the 1960s as the lowest point because they lost their social cachet because of what could be published across various media.[9] Yet at the same time, the 1960s marked one of the high points of Czech culture in the last century, with the appearance of works by Milan Kundera, Vaclav Havel, Josef Škvorecký, and many others that have come to represent the pinnacle of Czech literature, not to mention great films of Miloš Forman, Věra Chytilová, Jiří Menzel, Jan Němec, and others. The era was marked by a general hope in the potential for government reform, optimism, and the development of official literature.

After the Warsaw Pact Invasion of 1968 and the resulting change in censorship practices, the underground became the locus of a utopian individualism. In their analysis of Egon Bondy, whose *Invalidní sourozenci* (*Invalid Siblings*) became one of the manifestos of the era, Jana Bartůňková and Alena Zachová compare Bondy and the Czech underground to Kurt Vonnegut and the corresponding Western one, claiming "Vonnegut created obvious fiction, whereas Bondy hid the history of 1970s Czech dissent in a utopian story... while the basis of the underground of the west was protest resulting in nihilism, the basis of the essential part of our dissent in the underground was a

---

[8] See Martin Pilař, *Underground, aneb Kapitoly o českém literarním undergroundu*. 2nd ed. (Praha: Host, 2002), 14.

[9] See Ibid., chapter 3: "Peripetie a 'krize' českého undergroundu v 60. letech."

positive program of creating higher ethical criteria, stressing the right of the individual, but still connecting it with responsibility."[10] Bartůňková and Zachová find a utopian sense in the act of individuality of the Czech underground in the 1970s, despite the regime's repression.

The rhetoric of the underground was not directly aimed at being against Communism, but, however, preached non-conformity, often coupled with the ideal of being *a*political, and being against "the establishment" and not the government. In his famous "Report on the Third Czech Musical Revival," Jirous complained of other rock bands that compromised with the establishment:

> Why did these musicians do it? I think it was because they lacked, and they are still lacking, the awareness of what art is, what function it has in the world, and what responsibilities should have those who were awarded with the gift of creativity. Anyone who is not absolutely clear about that in his own mind can easily get off the track. The Plastic People maintained their integrity not because they were good musicians. Yet during the most difficult period, when they were lacking equipment, had nothing to fall back on and no public prospects, one thing was clear to them: **It is better to not play at all than to play music that does not flow from one's own convictions. It is better not to play at all than to play what the establishment demands.** And even this statement appears too mild. It is not better, it is absolutely essential. This stand must be taken right at the beginning. For as soon as the first compromise is made, whether it is accompanied by hypocritical excuses or it springs from an honest belief that it doesn't really matter, everything is lost. As soon as the devil (who today speaks through the mouth of the establishment) lays down the first condition: cut your hair, just a little, and you'll be able to play–you must say no. As soon as the devil (who today speaks through the mouth of the establishment) says– change your name and you'll be able to continue playing what you've been playing–you must say no, we will not play at all.[11]

---

[10] "Ještě jednou Invalidní sourozenci," *Iniciály* nos. 23/24 (1991): 45.
[11] Ivan Martin Jirous, "Report on the Third Czech Musical Festival," in *Views from the Inside. Czech Underground Literature and Culture (1948-1989): Manifestos – Testimonies – Documents*, ed. Martin Machovec (Prague: Karolinum Press, 2018), 17. Emphasis in the original.

I wanted to use this rather long quotation in its entirety because of its vehement commitment to an idea of an independent art world, and also because it demonstrates the connection of the underground in Czechoslovakia to underground music the world over, with its general rejection of "the establishment" and its espoused artistic purity, disregarding to which political party the "establishment" belongs. The emphasis here is on choice, on being able to choose your own way, even if that way is not to play.

Jirous wrote this essay after the first arrests of members of the underground in 1974, anticipating the so-called "Trial of the Plastics" in 1976, which eventually became the motivation for Charter 77. In the second half of the 1970s, the government did begin to crack down on the underground because it was simply getting too big: the Plastics had one of their shows outside of České Budějovice canceled and many in the audience arrested in 1974, and in 1976 Jirous and the saxophonist Vratislav Brabenec from the Plastics as well as Pavel Zajíček of DG 307, a related and also popular band, and the minister/folk-singer Svatopluk Karásek were arrested and charged with anti-social behavior and disturbing the peace. Later the story changed a bit to become the legendary trial of the Plastics, and it provoked a reaction in the underground, building up a dissident community within it.

The distinction between the intellectual leaders behind Charter 77 and the underground remains an important point for the 60s generation. As Martin Machovec claims, "Unlike the later Charter 77 community, the underground community was essentially a group of close friends, and friends of friends, who were attracted to each other partly by the desire to 'live differently,' in their case as a non-conformist collective, in defiance of the 'real socialism' of the 'normalization' regime."[12] The dissident community was largely a more international, intellectual group of writers and thinkers, whereas the underground was bound by a more non-conformist ethos. Even if Charter 77 was tied to the Plastic People of the Universe, the reverse was not true. As Machovec points out, four members of the group never signed the Charter.[13]

The division between the underground and dissidence did remain to some degree, as people could choose not to sign Charter 77 and remain in the underground, but the stakes were changing. The act of rejecting the establishment began to involve accepting the terms of Charter 77. Instead of

---

[12] Martin Machovec, *Writing Underground: Reflections on Samizdat Literature in Totalitarian Czechoslovakia* (Prague: Karolinum Press, 2020), 45.
[13] Ibid., 46.

relying on personal choice, as Jirous had insisted in his manifesto, there was a push to conform to the terms of the merging forces of dissent and the underground. What I want to point to here most clearly is that for the generation that came of age before the 1968 invasion, the potential to be apolitical, to be part of an underground which, was mostly ignored by a system concentrating more on pursuing those who directly opposed it, still existed. To the next generation, however, this choice was lost.

Psí vojáci against everything

Neither of the brothers, Topol, remembers the Invasion of the Warsaw Pact, but they certainly felt the results. Their father was pushed out of his position as director of *Divadlo za branou* during the first years of Normalization, and he spent much of the remainder of the Socialist period as a laborer. The two brothers were forced out of Prague schools and into a school on the Southeast outskirts of the city in Radotín, where they shared classrooms with many of the children of other people on the edge of society, including Jan Machaček, the co-founder of the journal *Respekt* and lead singer of the underground band Garage, Betina Landovská, daughter of actor and dissident Pavel Landovský, and Veronika Němcová, daughter of the philosopher and dissident Jiří Němec, and many others.[14]

For the second generation of the underground, becoming a part of the underground was less of a choice. As Jáchym claims, "there was a difference between us–i.e., those who weren't driven or thrown into the world of the banned but were simply born into it–and those who belonged to that already existing sphere that some of us tentatively described as 'the established underground' or even the 'underground establishment.'"[15] In this rich quotation, two aspects of the second underground generation are evident: first, the previous generation had become enshrined as yet another establishment to protest against. Instead of thinking of the underground as a happy family, intergenerational strife existed. The second point is that the Topol generation was born into the underground, not a part of its creation, not forced into it, but always already within it. Not only is there no agency involved, but there is not even any movement, but rather, through merely existing, one ends up in the

---

[14] For more on Radotín's role, see Trever Hagen, *Living in The Merry Ghetto: The Music and Politics of the Czech Underground* (Oxford: Oxford University Press, 2019), 128-30.

[15] Jáchym Topol, "The Story of *Revolver Revue*," in *Views from the Inside: Czech Underground Literature and Culture (1948-1989)*, ed. Martin Machovec (Prague: Karolinum Press, 2018), 81-82.

underground. The only agency available was to distance oneself from that previous generation of the underground. For someone who is always already in the underground, the only way to move is more underground. We see this drive in the poetry of Jáchym written in the 1980s and in Filip Topol's lyrics, which are significantly more nihilistic than those of the Plastics.

Filip Topol's band Psí vojáci was one of the most successful bands of the second underground generation. They played a kind of melodic punk rock, centered around Filip at the piano, which he played with such ferocity he often left blood on the keyboard after shows (at least legendarily). Jáchym initially contributed lyrics to the band, and he even sang occasionally, before forming his own band Národní třída in 1981 with Krchovský, Vít Kremlička, and Viktor Karlík, with whom he would eventually establish *Revolver Revue*. Filip's band played its first show at Havel's cottage, opening for The Plastics themselves. Their second show was the 1979 Prague Jazz Days, after which Filip was interrogated for the first time. He was only 14, so his mother had to come and vouch for his identity since he had not been issued any personal identification documents.

Revolver Revue was the main mouthpiece of the second generation, their version of *Vokno* that played a similar role for the previous one. One of the major differences between the two, however, was that *Revolver Revue* contained more translations, including of rather high-level theoretical texts, such as Susan Sontag, whereas *Vokno* focused more on the underground scene in Czechoslovakia. I see this as further evidence of the combining of the underground and dissent in the second generation. Between *Revolver Revue* and Psí vojáci, the Topol Brothers became the central hub for this second generation. At concerts of Psí vojáci, prints from several artists would be displayed, and before the concerts, others would read poetry. The group of young friends would meet at Jáchym's apartment or at one of the several clubs and bars where Filip's band played (Na Chmelnici for example).

Both Jáchym's and Filip's lyrics were, at times, outright nihilistic. One of Psí vojáci's most famous songs, one that would become the name of a film in the 90s, was *Žiletky* or razorblades, and it is explicitly about a failed suicide attempt. Jáchym wrote a similar song for his group called Stop that contains the lyrics: "*teď ti krev cáká z úst / a cáká z žil / párkrát se tu votočíš / a jdeš do kytek / jak podřezanej dobytek / Já tu stojím jako vůl / Jako němej v plotě kůl / zas vražděnej touhle bídou / demonstrační suicídou.*"[16] (Blood is splashing out of

---

[16] Národní třída, *Je třeba si zvykat*, title 9, Black Point Music, 1999.

your mouth, and splashing from your veins, you turn a few times and go to the flowers, like cattle with your throat slit. I stand here like an ox, like a dumb stake in a fence, once again murdered by this misery, by a demonstration suicide). Disaffection and suicidal thoughts run throughout the songs of the Second Generation Underground, offering little hope for the future, repeating the "No Future" mantra of punk rock. Filip himself comments on his angst-ridden music that he "wanted to make music so dark, even the Commies would slit their own throats."[17]

Writing on the Plastics has consistently rejected any claims of nihilism in their work, instead focusing on the apoliticality of their lyrics. Havel describes the Plastics as merely young musicians who "had no political past, or even any well-defined political positions. They were simply young people who wanted to live in their own way, to make music they liked, to sing what they wanted to sing, to live in harmony with themselves, and to express themselves in a truthful way."[18] Although this naïve reading of the Plastics is somewhat problematic, there was at least some room for maneuvering between the official establishment discourse and the dissidents. Havel's rationale for this reading was anything but naïve. As Jonathan Bolton points out, Havel needed groups like the Plastics to justify his philosophical discussion of dissent. He needed a "blank slate," people without a "political past" to make his argument about injustice in Czechoslovakia.[19] For the state to crack down on dissidents would make sense, but for them to do so against apolitical musicians who simply want to make some people happy is quite another. Havel marshaled the myth of the "blank slate" underground to unite the disparate groups of the dissident and underground community against the Communist government. The underground became "a common denominator, that they could take a stand for."[20]

Although there is a problem in making the underground of the 60s generation into such a blank state, there was some room to do so. There was a utopian bent

---

[17] Matthew Healey, "Filip Topol, a Rock Musician of the Czech Revolution, Dies at 48," *The New York Times*, June 25, 2013, https://www.nytimes.com/2013/06/26/arts/music/filip-topol-rock-musician-of-czech-revolution-dies-at-48.html (accessed January 27, 2024).

[18] Václav Havel, *Disturbing the Peace: A Conversation with Karel Hvížďala* (New York: Vintage, 1991), 128.

[19] See Jonathan Bolton, *Worlds of Dissent: Charter 77, The Plastic People of the Universe, and Czech Culture Under Communism* (Cambridge: Harvard University Press, 2014), 131-43.

[20] František Stárek, quoted in Bolton, *World of Dissent*, 141.

to the 60s generation that we can see in both the contemporary analysis and later descriptions of the group. For example, in Ivan Martin Jirous's famous essay "Report on the Third Czech Musical Revival," he claims:

> The aim of the underground in the West is the destruction of the establishment. The aim of the underground here in Bohemia is the creation of a second culture; a culture that will not be dependent on official channels of communication, social recognition, and the hierarchy of values laid down by the establishment; a culture which cannot have the destruction of the establishment as its aim because in doing so, it would drive itself into the establishment's embrace; a culture which helps those who wish to join it to rid themselves of the skepticism which says that nothing can be done and shows them that much can be done when those who make the culture desire little for themselves and much for others.[21]

The two utopian elements in this argument are in the ability to exist outside of the establishment, to be able to create in a way that ignores the world as it is and find something "true," and that this culture will then relieve people of their nihilistic outlooks, convincing them that there is a possibility for another way.

This outlook dovetails with the famous greengrocer from Václav Havel's essay "The Power of the Powerless." In that essay, Havel describes a greengrocer who is faced with the dilemma of whether to put up a sign with a Communist slogan in his window. He carries no socialist conviction, but only puts up the sign because "it has been that way for years, because everyone does it, and because that is the way it has to be done."[22] But, the greengrocer can decide not to put up that sign, and in doing so, he "has shattered the world of appearances, the fundamental pillar of the system."[23] He can break through the lies of the system and get closer to the truth. The greengrocer can either put up his sign and effectively support the regime and admit to his obedience, or he can decide to live in the truth. This moment of decision, and self-knowledge, is at the heart of both Havel's understanding of politics and at the 60's generation underground's claim to be able to create a second culture independent of the establishment. There is access in both to a world that is *pre*-political, where we

---

[21] Jirous, "Report," 35–36.
[22] Václav Havel, "The Power of the Powerless," trans. Paul Wilson, *East European Politics and Societies* 32 (2018): 359.
[23] Ibid., 368.

can discover a truth that is unencumbered by the ideological structures around us. Regardless of the actual truth of the Plastics' and Havel's lived experience, this is the rhetoric used around that generation.

However, the brothers Topol experienced the world in a way that was changed after the trial of the Plastics and Charter 77. For them, the pre-political moment, if it had ever existed, had disappeared. The second generation underground admitted to always already being political, to the idea that being in the underground actually meant being a dissident, and they rejected the space between dissidence and the establishment. For them, nihilistic music, and thus the idea of suicide, made sense as the only escape. Neither the system nor the 60s generation of the underground or dissident offered any way out.

The situation ultimately had an effect on how the second generation of the underground succeeded after the end of Socialism in Czechoslovakia. Whereas many of the previous generations of dissent were able to enter into government positions, academic jobs, or other prestigious positions, the second generation was more suspicious of the new government, as was Jirous and some of the other members of the older generation of the underground. The change in government just shifted power from one establishment to the next in the perception of the second generation. Both Topols initially stayed within their underground community, and they continued to be supported by it. Jáchym's *Sestra* certainly comes out of his underground mentality, as does Filip's post-Communist albums.

One song written by Filip in 1991 called "*Chce se mi spát*" (I Want to Sleep), demonstrates this connection:

> Once one woman told me,
> That I look like James Dean,
> But it's evident
> That I drink too much.
> What to say to that,
> I would like to sleep.
> She was beautiful and smelled good,
> Smoked expensive cigarettes and always laughed
> She had flames in her eyes
> It was a great love
> But what to do, I want to sleep.
> I don't want to look like James Dean
> I don't want to smoke
> I don't want to laugh

I don't want to swallow the flames
It won't work anyway
I just want to sleep
Because when I come home in the morning, I sit and turn on the TV
Outside pretty girls go by
A new day starts
Yeah, well, what to do
I just want to sleep.[24]

Here, Filip rejects the most basic form of vitality: the libido. Even with the hope of a new day, something that carries quite another meaning in 1991, all he yearns for is sleep and escape from the world. This is hardly representative of an emancipatory narrative about the fall of Communism.

Suicide had long been understood as a political act in the Communist world, from Sergei Esenin to Jan Palach, and the repeated references to suicide in the lyrics of Psí vojáci can be read in a similar vein. And indeed, sickness was another reference to the alternative universe, as can be seen in this quote from the famous article "*Nová vlna se starým obsahem*" (A New Wave in an Old Package) from 1983, in which the writer, under a pseudonym but certainly a part of the governmental organs, criticized exactly this type of music:

> Monotonous, repetitive melodies (if one can call such high-decibel sound that at all) accompanies texts whose authors could be considered inmates of psychiatric wards rather than people who call themselves artists. Unfortunately, the thing is more complicated and more important. Texts, which, for example, repeat "sophisticated" words "*kat'a, pat'a hat'a*" (Pražský výběr) [Prague Choice] or scream for five minutes, "*Bejby, bejby dej mi kadilak*" [baby, baby, give me a Cadillac] or "*hipi hipi šejk*" [Hippie, Hippie Shake] or vulgar texts 'she has a dirty back, she doesn't drink doesn't salt things, doesn't smoke, but she likes it" or a song with the name, "Get Out of Here, You Bastard" or "Our Master Is King, He Has the Name Heroin" look like the production of a diseased mind, and are in reality and expression of nihilism and

---

[24]From Psí vojáci, *Leitmotiv*, title 3, Globus International, 1991, compact disc.

cynicism, a deep lack of culture, and ideological attitudes which are alien to socialist society.[25]

Instead of being accepted as a critique the article became something of a mantra for the next generation of the underground.

Filip took almost every example of what is "alien" to the socialist society and made it a part of his music, but I think there is more to the use of suicide in his music. Suicide is not just a rejection of a certain governmental system, it is a rejection of life itself. Filip is protesting not only against the regime as establishment, but also against the previous generation of the underground as establishment, against all that he was "born into" in the words of his older brother. The only possibility to reject what one is born into is to negate that birth, to end one's life. Disaffection and suicidal thoughts are throughout the songs, offering little hope for the future, repeating the "No Future" mantra of punk rock that the authorities found so threatening.

Coming out of a time when Communism seemed an eternal given, something which would never change, this disaffection is understandable. But with all the excitement of those heady days in the early nineties, it seems strange that such music would still be so popular... and yet it was. In an interview in 1992, Filip wondered about this: "We were a dark underground group with a dark past and a group of snobs went to see us. Thirty-five-year-old smokers and blatherers bothered us and sometimes slapped us on the back, that it was good. Then came a change–a younger public came to our concerts, which reacted to our songs and sang with us."[26] I find this quote, particularly telling because Filip mocks the distanced relationship of the older members of the underground and looks to the more immediate one he has with the younger generation. When Filip made this statement in 1992, someone who was 35 would have been born in the 1950s, would have a better memory of the events in 1968, and could have been a part of the underground movement of the 70s, when bands like DG 307 and the Plastics were at their peak. An eighteen-year-old, on the contrary, would have been born in 1974, after the Warsaw Pact Invasion, with very little awareness of the early underground, and would be a major part of the post-socialist society, in a way unimaginable even to Topol's generation.

---

[25] Published originally in the weekly *Tribuna*, no. 12, 1983 under the pseudonym Jan Krýzl.
[26] Milan Ležák, "Připadám si jako ementál (tvrdí o sobě Filip Topol)," *Melodie* 30, no. 10 (1992): 12.

What I will want to propose here is that it is precisely the unironic disaffection, the absolute against everything, or the punk slogan of "No Future," in Topol's songs that allowed him to remain popular both in the underground of the eighties and in the first decade following the revolution. During the underground period, disaffection was read as dissidence, it was a non-acceptance of the status quo, but it was an emotional release, the pedal-to-the-metal version of the dissident attitude. Filip was not against the establishment; he was against everything. The choice was not between the government and the underground because the underground had become yet another establishment. His lyrics were not political, but neither could they be apolitical, rather they were against the very idea of the political and the apolitical: Psí vojáci took the idea of dissent to another level and dissented against life itself.

In one of his songs from the mid-eighties, *Už je to let* (It has been years), this idea is made explicit. The song describes two people seeing each other after many years, in a typically nostalgic moment. The lyrics are filled with melancholy at not seeing each other, with the chorus, "*Víc kouříš víc piješ víc žvaníš míň jíš.*" (You smoke more, you drink more, you babble more, you eat less).[27] Otherwise, it seems as though the other interlocutor has had some degree of success, he now has a beautiful wife, a decent job, and plays in a decent band. All this seems to be going well, but the final line undermines it all, "*tak proč ses proboha podřezal?*" (Then why in God´s name did you slit your throat?).[28] The question is left unanswered not because it is impossible to answer, but rather because it is so easy to understand. Life just may not be worth living, no matter how many individual successes a person may have, and no matter what regime is ruling the country.

Sister and temporality

Filip's brother Jáchym developed a similar attitude of general nihilism, but his work showed the lack of differentiation between the era before and after the Velvet Revolution for his generation of the underground. Topol burst onto the Czech literary scene with his 1994 novel *Sestra*, a picaresque tale about a young man named Potok in the "years 1, 2, 3, etc. after the explosion of time."[29] Although he was well known in the Prague underground, *Sestra* became the

---

[27] Psí vojáci, *Nechoď sama do tmy: Tvorba z let 1983–1986*, title 9, Black Point, 1995.
[28] Ibid.
[29] Jáchym Topol, *Sister, City, Silver*, trans. Alex Zucker (North Haven, CT: Catbird Press, 2000), 50.

novel of a generation and made Topol a national figure. It is a deeply anti-narrative tale that rejects a number of constructions of temporality, from the emancipatory narrative around the end of Communism, the Marxist narrative of dialectical-materialist progress, and the narrative that Communist Czechoslovakia's dissidents were the saviors of an independent Czech Republic.

The novel begins with East Germans traveling through Prague on their way to West Germany via Hungary and Austria in September of 1989 and then moves through those first few transitional years of the "Wild East." Potok, like the author himself, comes out of the Prague Underground, called the 'Sewers' in the lingo of the novel. He engages in what is initially petty banditry and then develops into more serious criminality. In order to escape punishment for his crimes, both from rival gangs and from the authorities, he travels across Czechoslovakia to the Eastern border with Ukraine, all while searching for his "Sister," a metaphor for meaning in the new world, whom he may or may not have killed earlier in the novel. The novel ends without any real conclusion, and it is unclear what meaning is to be found in the world after the explosion of time.

The novel eschews a traditional narrative, not only through its inconclusive ending, but even on the linguistic level. In the period after the collapse of Communism, the narrator Potok realizes "Czech had exploded along with time."[30] Topol writes with a mixture of underground slang, old Slavic, foreign languages, high and low registers, and neologisms, relying on tropes from North American indigenous history, ancient Czech culture, Christianity, paganism, and gangster lingo. One of the minor characters Jícha, a thinly veiled version of Jáchym himself, describes his act of writing a novel in the story in what I see as a metatextual statement on the novel itself: "I wrote something different. And what I wrote, O hunters and chieftains, was a book, I wrote it in nothing but my own words, I was in a trap, so I didn't give a damn if that book was hygienic… what came out of me, sisters and girlfriends, was blather, babel, and Babylon, what it was, dear good she-demons and cuddly soothsayers, was a sort of lesser pornography with a humanist spin, and Pragocentric to boot, what it was, kind of potential she-reader and nosy Nelly, was cheap trade, on the trashy side, but in my own slave tongue… so I'd no longer be a slave.. but it was so powerful I coulda not even been… I hacked my tongue, and stroked it, and gave it right back, my tongue was alive!"[31] Even in this short quote, the

---

[30] Ibid., 41.
[31] Ibid., 175.

layering of temporalities is evident, with the forms of different registers of Czech, use of ancient titles like "hunters and chieftains" and "demons and prophetesses" alongside more colloquial phrases and words such as nosy Nelly (*zvědavka*). Topol plays with the word tongue (*jazyk*) in both the figurative sense of language and the physical part of the body. At times, the language of the text obfuscates the reality of an event, deliberately vague as to whether it is a metaphor, a dream, or real life.

The mixed language of the novel gives the reader an uneasy sense of temporality. The pagan elements give the novel a mythic feel, but the city slang contradicts this sensibility, making the novel feel more like a work of *noir*. The language puts the novel into several timelines at once, simultaneously old and new, or as Gertraude Zand calls it, a "*staronový svět*."[32] These timelines also put the novel into several genres simultaneously, as it shifts from epic tale to fantasy, from adventure novel to essayism. The novel is an intertextual work with shifting genres, from high to low, from Robert Musil and Bohumil Hrabal to Jack London and Karel May. There are little songs in the novel, bits of poetry, parodies of the national anthem, and essayistic sections, all of which defy easy classification. In many ways, the novel participates in much older styles, such as Menippean satire and the picaresque novel. It reveals the way that a traditional narrative has become a more expected part of literature, and Topol does not give us the resolution we might expect to any of the narrative genres he employs.

In particular, Topol resists the traditional emancipatory narratives around the end of Communism. There was a widespread belief, at least in the West, that the end of Communism would be accepted as a watershed moment in Central Europe. In an interview with Piotr Czarniecki promoting her book *The Taste of Ashes*, the intellectual historian Marci Shore discussed her interest in the rise of illiberalism in Central and Eastern Europe after the fall of Communism: "One of the first, most naïve questions I wanted to understand was: Why was there no 'happily ever after'? From the point of view of an American teenager, nineteen eighty-nine was a fairy tale: for all of my life and my parents' lives, there was an Evil Empire where people were thrown into prison, sometimes beaten and tortured, at the very least condemned to live in greyness and sadness, forbidden from leaving–and then suddenly one day it

---

[32] Gertraude Zandová, "'Výbuch času' 1989: Jáchym Topol a staronový svět jeho románu *Sestra*," in *Česká literatura na konci tisíciletí. Příspěvky z 2. kongresu světové literárněvědné bohemistiky* (Praha: Ústav pro českou literaturu Akademie věd České republiky, 2001), 793-800.

was over. I thought that coming to Eastern Europe would be like arriving at a non-stop party, that everybody would be celebrating his or her liberation."[33] Topol's text not only counters the expectation of a fairy tale ending, he avoids the moment of revolution altogether.

The absence of any representation of the revolution itself underscores the lack of any real change between the two periods. I disagree with Peter Zusi, who, following Terry Eagleton, claims that Topol ignores the revolution because "Topol adheres to a venerable tradition of regarding revolutionary action as inherently unrepresentable."[34] Instead, Topol insists on the continuity between the Communist era and the early capitalist one. In the book, the power structures are largely the same before and after the fall of Communism, where the top businessmen are former apparatchiks, and former state security agents now work for a private agency that the government subcontracts to, making them even less accountable. Jícha (the thinly veiled version of Jáchym) describes his position after 1989: "maybe I ceased to be a slave, but instead I became a servant."[35] Topol even dissolves the distinction between the aims of the dissidents and the committed Communists. Potok claims that for his generation under Communism, "The present, which our families felt was a world built on falsehood, and the period prior to the invasion, which they clung to, were both the same gobbledygook to us."[36] Here, Topol equates the reform Communists and dissidents who remembered the Prague Spring with the normalization Communists of the 1970s and 80s, showing a disdain for both camps even after 1989.

Ultimately, Topol's novel offers little other than a larger critique of narrative constructions of time. Each character in the novel searches for some kind of meaning, some kind of aim for a new narrative. One character hopes for a new messiah, another for retribution from the Communist past (the stone-age in the novel), a third for simple improvement in life, a fourth for a return to the Sewers, and a fifth for glory in the cultural sphere. But instead of finding any

---

[33] Piotr Czarniecki, "The Lingering of the Past: A conversation with Marci Shore, professor of intellectual history and author of *Taste of Ashes*," *New Eastern Europe*, December 10, 2013, https://neweasterneurope.eu/2013/12/10/the-lingering-of-the-past/. Accessed January 27, 2024.
[34] Peter Zusi, "History's Loose Ends: Imagining the Velvet Revolution," in *The Inhabited Ruins of Central Europe*, ed. Dariusz Gafijczuk and Derek Sayer (London: Palgrave Macmillan, 2013), 237.
[35] Topol, *Sister*, 169.
[36] Ibid., 17.

consensus, each one fails to create a meaningful understanding of time. Topol revels in his existential bleakness and gives sometimes puerile description of sex and violence, but the destructive impulse of the novel remains.

The impossibility of meaning in Topol's work emerges from the horrors of the Second World War. Potok takes a dream trip to Auschwitz, where he walks on a sea of bones and talks with a skeleton about the shared responsibility for the Shoah. There, Potok says "No time bomb exploded, brothers, an some of the acting an dancing I'd done was the dance of the dead, of a man without time, an that was a mistake, an arrogant mistake. Time died in the land of ashes, it hit me. Because one tribe had tried to kill off another an it almost worked and the wheel of the world of human tribes had broken."[37] The moral cataclysm of the Shoah destroyed any narrative whatsoever for Topol, and he has no fantasies about any real change. Topol resists any indication of the world progressing, preferring to destroy any narratives he comes across.

Conclusion

Returning to the question Cushman asks about the fate of rock musicians "whose existence and social significance are fundamentally related to the structural conditions characteristic of a state socialist society when they encounter new forms of social and economic organization characteristic of capitalist society?" My answer here is that the phrasing of the question undermines our ability to accurately understand the situation. The Topol brothers' existence and social significance are not fundamentally related to the structural conditions characteristic of a state socialist society, they were created by those structural conditions. Being born into the structural condition does not allow for a pre-political moment. This makes the rebellion in Psí vojáci's music and in Jáchym's novel against *any* structural conditions which create one's existential and social significance, making their art transferrable to any generation that wants to rebel against the structural conditions of the society. The generation coming of age in the early nineties understood their situation in a similar fashion, as they were born into the transitional period, which explains their attitude towards Psí vojáci's music and Jáchym's novel.

The anti-everything sentiment is certainly not unique to Topol's band, as it was a sentiment shared by many American bands in the early nineties as well (Nirvana being the prime example). Disaffection sold well in the nineteen-nineties. However, in 1997, Filip almost died due to his heavy alcoholism, and

---

[37] Ibid., 123.

he had to have half of his pancreas removed. After he quit drinking, his style and outlook shifted: there came a modest optimism, by no means a rosy view of the world, but a modest optimism, nonetheless, as is shown in his novella *Karla Klenotníka cesta na Korsiku*. This coincided with the decline in popularity of his band, and although they continued playing, with a few breaks, until his death, they no longer could fill the house as they had in the earlier part of the nineties. Filip's decline in health in the mid-nineties also marked a shift in the view of dissent as *ostalgie*, or nostalgia for socialism, emerged in Central and Eastern Europe. Old singers that had been aligned with Communism, such as Karel Gott who signed the anti-Charter against Charter 77, reemerged in 1996 (he won the "Český slavík" (Czech Nightingale), the annual award for the best singer in the country, twice in a row in 1996-97, and then every year from 1999-2017). The economy improved and the widespread discontent with the world began to disappear, or at least went into a new underground, marking what may become the next generation of the underground.

Bibliography

Bartůňková, Jana and Alena Zachová. "Ještě jednou Invalidní sourozenci." *Iniciály*, nos. 23/24 (1991): 45.

Bednar, Rudy (director). *The Beatles Revolution*, 2000: ABC.

Bolton, Jonathan. *Worlds of Dissent: Charter 77, The Plastic People of the Universe, and Czech Culture Under Communism*. Cambridge: Harvard University Press, 2014.

Cushman, Thomas. *Notes from Underground: Rock Music Counterculture in Russia*. Albany: SUNY Press, 1995.

Czarniecki, Piotr. "The Lingering of the Past: A conversation with Marci Shore, professor of intellectual history and author of *Taste of Ashes*." *New Eastern Europe*, December 10, 2013, https://neweasterneurope.eu/2013/12/10/the-lingering-of-the-past/ Accessed January 27, 2024.

Hagen, Trevor. *Living in The Merry Ghetto: The Music and Politics of the Czech Underground*. Oxford: Oxford University Press, 2019.

Havel, Václav. *Disturbing the Peace: A Conversation with Karel Hvížďala*. New York: Vintage, 1991.

——. "The Power of the Powerless." Translated by Paul Wilson. *East European Politics and Societies* 32 (2018): 353-408.

Healey, Matthew. "Filip Topol, a Rock Musician of the Czech Revolution, Dies at 48." *The New York Times*, June 25, 2013, https://www.nytimes.com/2013/06/26/arts/music/filip-topol-rock-musician-of-czech-revolution-dies-at-48.html Accessed January 27, 2024.

Jirous, Ivan Martin. "Report on the Third Czech Musical Festival." In *Views from the Inside. Czech Underground Literature and Culture (1948-1989)*:

Manifestos – Testimonies – Documents, edited by Martin Machovec, 7–36. Prague: Karolinum Press, 2018.

Jirsa, Tomáš. "Charting Post-Underground Nostalgia: Anachronistic Practices of the Post-Velvet Revolution Rock Scene." *Iluminace* 29, no. 3 (2017): 65–86.

Krýzl, Jan. "Nová vlna se starým obsahem." *Tribuna*, March 23, 1983, 1–5. Reprinted in https://www.ceskatelevize.cz/specialy/bigbit/vyhledavani/no vá%20vlna/clanky/188-nova-vlna-se-starym-obsahem/ Accessed January, 27, 2024.

Ležák, Milan. "Připadám si jako ementál (tvrdí o sobě Filip Topol)." *Melodie* 30, no. 10 (1992): 11–13.

Machovec, Martin, ed. *Views from the Inside. Czech Underground Literature and Culture (1948-1989): Manifestos – Testimonies – Documents*. Prague: Karolinum Press, 2018.

——. *Writing Underground: Reflections on Samizdat Literature in Totalitarian Czechoslovakia*. Prague: Karolinum Press, 2020.

Národní třída (Jáchym Topol, Vít Kremlička, J. H. Krchovský, Viktor Karlík, Václav Stádník, Tomáš Schilla, Vít Brukner). *Je třeba si zvykat*. Black Point Music, 1999, Compact Disc.

Pekacz, Jolanta. "Did Rock Smash the Wall? The Role of Rock in Political Transition." *Popular Music* 13, no. 1 (January 1994): 41–49.

Pilař, Martin. *Underground, aneb Kapitoly o českém literarním undergroundu*. 2nd ed. Praha: Host, 2002.

Psí vojáci. *Leitmotiv*, Globus International, 1991, Compact Disc.

——. *Nechoď sama do tmy: Tvorba z let 1983–1986*. Black Point, 1995, Compact Disc.

Ramet, Sabrina Petra. *Rocking the State: Rock Music and Politics in Eastern Europe*. New York: Routledge, 2019.

Szemere, Anna. *Up from the Underground: The Culture of Rock Music in Post-Socialist Hungary*. University Park: Pennsylvania State University Press, 2001.

Topol, Jáchym. *Sister, City, Silver*. Translated by Alex Zucker. North Haven, CT: Catbird Press, 2000.

——. "The Story of *Revolver Revue*." In *Views from the Inside: Czech Underground Literature and Culture (1948-1989)*, edited by Martin Machovec, 79–91. Prague: Karolinum Press, 2018.

Wicke, Peter. "'The Times They Are A-Changin': Rock Music and Political Change in East Germany." In *Rockin' the Boat: Mass Music and Mass Movements*, edited by Reebee Garofalo, 81–107. Cambridge, MA: South End Press, 1992.

Zandová, Gertraude. "'Výbuch času' 1989: Jáchym Topol a staronový svět jeho románu *Sestra*." In *Česká literatura na konci tisíciletí. Příspěvky z 2. kongresu světové literárněvědné bohemistiky*, 793–800. Praha: Ústav pro českou literaturu Akademie věd České republiky, 2001.

Zusi, Peter. "History's Loose Ends: Imagining the Velvet Revolution." In *The Inhabited Ruins of Central Europe*, edited by Dariusz Gafijczuk and Derek Sayer, 227–45. London: Palgrave Macmillan, 2013.

Chapter 7
Eda Kriseová: Writing human ecology. Serving poetic justice to truth and love

Hana Waisserová
University of Nebraska

Abstract

Eda Kriseová is a prominent female writer emerging from the Czech literary dissent, who worked closely with Václav Havel. The relationship between people and their environment is central to her work, as her texts showcase the interconnectedness of society, individuals, and the environment and reveal how biopolitics and totalitarian control disrupt personal and national histories. Her texts revisit the consequences of human actions on society and the natural world and vice versa. Kriseová adds spirituality to this equation. Furthermore, her work exemplifies a multifaceted and profound exploration of the almost metaphysical and timeless use of *truth and love* as a storytelling trope and repelling tool of totalitarianism rooted in the Czech national mythology. This chapter argues, however, that many dissident intellectuals have embraced and imbued their own vernacular meanings of truth and love, and their interpretations might not always align with contemporary understandings of truth. The chapter provides context for the evolution of Eda Kriseová's writing, and it focuses on her post-1990 published texts: *Kočičí životy* (*Cats' Lives*, 1997), *Čísi svět* (*Someone's World*, 2004), *Duši, tělo opatruj* (*Care for Your Soul and Body*, 2014), *Mezi pannou a babou* (*Between a Maiden and an Old Woman*, 2018), *Talking Mountain* (*Mluvící hora*, 2021). It suggests that green and feminist literary studies converge, offer new frameworks for literary interpretations, and serve poetic justice to women's literature.[1]

Keywords: human ecology, Václav Havel, truth and love, dissent, ecocriticism, biopolitics, spirituality, poetic justice.

---

[1] An early version of this chapter was presented at the panel "New Research on Czech Literature" at the AATSEEL conference in 2021.

* * *

Introduction:
Green cultural studies on biopolitics:
examining the human-nature connection

It's night, and I'm sitting on the shore of the ocean, as if I want to have my conscience washed away by salt water, to take off my skin, to be nobody and from nowhere, to start and end nowhere. Finally, I manage to become one wave that rises confidently, settles in pebbles and empty shells, and then humbly retreats until it disappears. It's just water, just water.[2]

Eda Kriseová stands out as one of the very few prominent female writers emerging from the Czech literary dissent, traditionally dominated by male writers like Václav Havel, Ivan Klíma, Josef Škvorecký, Milan Kundera, or Ludvík Vaculík. Though she was an active dissident writer and wrote texts *repelling totalitarianism*,[3] Kriseová's work transcends the national and speaks to universal themes. Her voice gains new resonance in the era of decolonization of the literary canon and amid growing ecological and global concerns. Her texts can be read in a multitude of ways: they correct the distorted and not fully understood notions of Central European womanhood, its potential for self-definition and free expression, and her writing serves justice to the gendered "impasse of dissent."[4] Kriseová, a prominent journalist silenced at the peak of her career in the spring of 1969, found her voice again in literature. Her social journalism instilled a deep empathy for marginalized individuals, and her investigative skills allowed her to delve into their diverse realities.

This chapter focuses on Kriseová's literary contribution, especially in her post-1990 freelance writing. Unlike many writers who depict dissent through

---

[2] Eda Kriseová, *Mluvící hora* (Praha: Práh, 2020), 37–38.
[3] Brenda A. Flanagan and Hana Waisserová, *Women's Artistic Dissent: Repelling Totalitarianism in Pre-1989 Czechoslovakia* (Lanham, MD: Lexington Books, 2023).
[4] The term "Impasse of Dissent" is used by Jonathan Bolton as the name of the first chapter in his *Worlds of Dissent: Charter 77, the Plastic People of the Universe, and Czech Culture under Communism* (Cambridge: Harvard University Press, 2012). The title of my chapter follows up on it and suggests that perhaps gender and gendering dissent represent the major *Impasse of Dissent* and is a very conflated and contested topic.

testimonial and collective narratives, Kriseová has focused on portrayals of individuality and the *power of the powerless* as well as new notions of *living in truth*, deeply embedded in the Czech cultural context. She highlights broader cultural, social, and historical issues while spotlighting unique human beings with their own fates, memories, roots, fears, beliefs, and desires. In the past, this approach dismantled the simplistic, unproblematic portrayal of individuals often found in socialist narratives. Furthermore, in today's world, her work explores the diverse connections between humans and nature, challenging the distorted polarizing narratives of the former era of unfreedom. While ecological humanism and totalitarianism might have seemed incompatible under totalitarianism, her novels demonstrate otherwise.

Concretely, this chapter examines her vernacular use of the social ecology lenses as she examines the human-nature connection against biopolitics, as those stand out as the main themes in her writing, and it discovers her investment in using *truth and love* tropes. In her texts, those concepts of *truth and love* become aligned with the gradual growth of the writer's interest in human and social ecology. This chapter focuses on her two novels, *Cats' Lives* (*Kočičí životy*, 1997 and republished in 2023) and *Between Maiden and Old Woman* (*Mezi pannou a babou*, published in 2018, but drafted in the late 1970s), and her three recent texts, collections of short stories and reflective philosophical essays, *Someone's World* (*Čísi svět*, 2004), *Care for Your Soul and Body* (*Duši, tělo opatruj*, 2014) and *Talking Mountain* (*Mluvící hora*, 2020).[5]

Cats' Lives focuses on multigenerational stories of an ethnic Czech family in Ruthenia, while *Between Maiden and Old Woman* is set in Central Bohemia. Both novels present protagonists who examine and become entangled with intimate and (un)known histories of their ancestors, amid nationalist tensions, social conventions and expectations appended to their gender roles. Both novels outline the protagonists' struggles, successes, tragedies, and even suicides that cast a shadow on the families against colorful sociocultural and historical contexts. Yet, both novels are set in nature, in lands, in landscapes; they share smells, shadows, changing seasons, and physical sensations. Both novels also explore topics of bans, aspirations and frustrations, and sexuality, as well as escape to nature (long walks, alternative life in the country) and real and meaningful work.

---

[5] All translations of titles and from Eda Kriseová's texts included in this chapter are translated by Hana Waisserová unless otherwise noted.

Growing concern for humanistic and ecological themes is visible throughout Eda Kriseová's writing. However, it culminates in her latest texts, such as *Someone's World* (2004), *Care for Your Soul and Body* (2014) and *Talking Mountain* (2020). All three later books are collections of short stories merged with philosophical essays, travel essays, and unorthodox memoirs presenting a clear author's voice. All texts promote humble humanity, explore and study unfortunate fates, offer rich personal observations and reflections, and highlight the need to care for a better world that is spiritual and respectful towards the vulnerable and nature alike.

In other words, this chapter examines Eda Kriseová's vernacular use of social ecology, which examines the interconnectedness of society, individuals, and the environment. Her work focuses on how these elements interact and influence each other and what are the consequences of human actions on the natural world and vice versa. Additionally, she employs social ecology to exemplify and comprehend the impacts of human activities on the environment in explicit or implicit ways, either woven into the narrative or through the characters' experiences. She explores power dynamics, especially in her later travel-inspired works, as she comments, for example, on unequal access to resources, and the role of sociopolitical and economic systems in shaping environmental issues. In *Someone's World*, she wrote: "Men mostly overlook feminism and ecology as something unnecessary and utterly useless. They rape nature, women, and everyone who is weaker."[6]

Further, she shares her experience with utopian communities, seeking to live in harmony with nature. She uses scientific evidence and statistics, as well as poetic language, to expose the impacts of human-caused harm to the environment. Eda Kriseová shares her planetary warnings, such as in *Someone's World*:

> Environmentalists estimate that our artificial speed destroys about 15,000 animal species per year, and about 50 animal species die out every day. We move all over the globe, and we have lost our sense of distance, of changing seasons, but above all, we no longer have a relationship with one piece of land. We lose our sensitivity, everything is too much, and it follows one another too quickly.[7]

---

[6] Eda Kriseová, *Čísi svět* (Praha: Prostor, 2004), 68.
[7] Ibid, 109.

These later meditative and philosophical texts, such as *Someone's World* and *Talking Mountain*, raise questions about humanity's relationship with nature. She treats plants, locations, nature, or cities as witnesses. By examining these themes, her use of social ecology lenses encourages her readers to assess the relationship with the environment critically, rethink the potential consequences of human actions elsewhere, and encourages one to explore possibilities for creating a more sustainable and just future, yet in connection to the burning global issues or from learning lessons from the turbulent Czech and Central European history of the twentieth century alike. Her narratives blend fiction with local and transnational histories and reflect on the turbulent twentieth century, when people were displaced, fates altered, and suffering, isolation, and oppression became pervasive. Yet, nature remains constant and has a calming presence. Environment and landscapes, man-made monuments, architecture, and even cities become witnesses, offering solace and inviting reflections of both survival and death under oppressive regimes.

However, her narratives go beyond rewriting history and understanding global warming or unveiling. In her early texts, she is inspired by the mentally disabled, later by the relocated ethnic Czechs to Ruthenia, the victims of Communist or Nazi persecution, or remembering families of executed enemies of the state. She seeks understanding for disillusioned individuals, and she humanizes those overlooked by official narratives. Individuality and making ecological and spiritual connections stand at the center of her works. Her texts, while reflecting on her own experiences, transcended personal narratives or communal memories; they invoke compassion and encourage understanding, such as with the current war in Ukraine.

Her novel *Cats' Lives*, set in Ruthenia, was republished in 2023, as the text has sparked public interest in neglected stories of Ukraine and interest in the looming Russian question. Kriseová has been invited to many readings, debates, and interviews. She shared: "Putin, paradoxically, founded the Ukrainian nation and showed it to the whole world. I really admire the Ukrainian nation especially when I imagine what they have already tried. Maybe that's why they're so good, because they have courage and endurance already in their genes. I think our sympathy for the Ukrainians is so great because we experienced it too."[8]

---

[8] See this program on Czech TV: "Kočičí životy volyňských Čechů aktualizovalo současné dění v Evropě." <https://ct24.ceskateleveze.cz/clanek/kultura/kocici-zivoty-volynskych-cechu-aktualizovalo-soucasne-deni-v-evrope-7590>.

Readers are fascinated by how she narrates the repeated suffering, the sense of loss of transnationality, pressures of Soviet ideology and Russian nationalism, which causes inhumane suffering as ideology is elevated above humanity, leaving people bitter, sad, alienated, and disconnected:

> Our people, well, we do not say that anymore, he smiled. No people are ours anymore. Before the war, under Poland, ours were the Poles, Ukrainians, Russians, Jews, Czechs, and strangers were those who came from outside. Soviets were never our people.[9]

By presenting diverse fates and human struggles, she embarked on a literary quest for human dignity, often undermined by totalitarian ideologies. This topic is relevant even during the thirty years of transitioning to democracy and opening to the world, as Czech society still struggles with reconciliation with the past.

However, not retelling the past, but the relationship between people and their environment is central to Kriseová's work. Her texts showcase the timeless interdependence of individuals, collectives, and institutions. They reveal how biopolitics disrupted personal and familial histories yet did not fully determine them. Throughout her literary work, we see how individuals, narratives, memories, events, and the natural environment are intricately linked. This approach challenges traditional interpretations rooted in historical memory and ideological biases. It allows for fresh perspectives through environmental criticism, highlighting the role of individual memory and perceptions against flora and fauna as silent witnesses. These elements provide readers with a deeper understanding of the settings and their impact on transgenerational narratives. The ecological/land-related and social issues challenge the notion of biopower, highlighting the land's role as a link to the past, shaping personalities, and offering protection, sustenance, and being a silent witness. The social ecology approach allows her to explore themes of complicity, interdependence, historical myths connected to Central European culture, and the importance of literature in individual and community histories. This approach transcends local and global polarization, offering examples of *glocal* (meaning global and local) sustainability.

---

[9] Eda Kriseová, *Kočičí životy* (Praha: Hynek, 1997), 171.

In the Czech literary canon, the question remains: who tells whose story?

When I sometimes walk through the forest, I feel that inviolable confidence in myself, knowing that my life is perfectly connected to the life of plants and that it cooperates with them to create eternity. For me and the plants it is about survival in accordance with the law of nature. Life demands me to live it, it needs my bones, muscles, and blood to manifest itself. This deep feeling calms me down, but at the same time it upsets me so much that I can't sleep. So I sit on my chair, look into space and meditate. But the universe is ultimately more exciting, unknown, infinite, terrifying.[10]

In the Czech and Central European context, the question remains: is it nature and missing and demolished places and monuments that tell the story? Or is it human beings? And what about elsewhere? Kriseová's work offers a compelling answer, demonstrating how both the environment and nature and humans shape narratives, leaving their mark on each other across generations, as "Life demands me to live it, it needs my bones, muscles and blood to manifest itself."[11]

In this context and in a clear, unassuming voice, Kriseová shares her unwavering quest for *truth and love* in the face of personal experience, observation, and accumulated wisdom as if the truth is in nature. As she witnesses the world's growing need for solidarity and informed concern amidst countless tragedies and crises, her pursuit of *truth* intensifies. This maturing quest manifests itself in her later texts, offering fresh perspectives, rhythms, and imagery and concerns nature.

With profound empathy and rich, imaginative prose, Kriseová narrates diverse aspects of the human condition. She tackles complex family histories, expressing empathy for those displaced, exiled, and brutalized, for forbidden love, vanishing plant life, abandoned homes, and forgotten legacies. She expands her dissent-driven exploration of truth and love into multifaceted quests: historical truth, forbidden truths, truth as the antithesis of hate, the truth of creation, spiritual truth, the truth of aging, truth as beauty, philosophical inquiry, collective versus individual truth, the truth of civilizations, myths, and legends, pragmatic truths, and the truth of our own feelings, perceptions, and thoughts, even the truth that lies within natural laws.

---

[10] Kriseová, *Mluvící hora*, 17.
[11] Ibid.

This multifaceted exploration of *truth and love* is compelling and free from dictates, ideologies, or moralizing pronouncements. Kriseová's inventive and interpretive approach offers a wealth of humane and insightful meanings and texts seeking to reinvent poetics that transcend the limitations of politics, history, memory, and culture.

"Every day lived as a decent day was my act of defiance against the regime,"[12] explained Eda Kriseová her philosophy of the dissident's *life in truth*. Her experience with dissent, personal courage, and acquired wisdom fueled these profound insights, as she aligned with truth-seeking and writing, finding in the latter an outlet to express her personal ethics, and her inclination towards, and support for, dissenting viewpoints. Her experiences under oppression honed her commitment to living authentically. The motto of her life can be read as her refusal *to live a lie*. Kriseová's practice of *life in truth* and her becoming a writer converge, as her writing provides space to express her personal views or uncover the truth as she sees it.

Her work exemplifies a profound exploration of *truth and love*, interwoven with concerns for social justice, historical omissions, ecology, and spirituality. *Love* emerges as a powerful aspect of *truth* in her writings. However, the notion of *living in truth* promoted somewhat ambiguous and complex interpretations of *truth*, which many dissidents embraced and imbued with their own vernacular meanings. These interpretations might not always align with contemporary understandings of *truth*, particularly regarding gender equality.

Beyond being a writer, Kriseová is an activist, public intellectual, and engaged citizen dedicated to rebuilding and strengthening civil society and integrating refugees, especially vulnerable women.[13] A pro-European advocate, she has always been deeply connected to nature, human spirituality, and the healing power of both. Her writing offers valuable insights for both the first and third worlds alike:

> I close my eyes and listen to the ocean, which is the same as it was three years ago, when the wise men chanted the vedas they knew by heart.

---

[12] Quoted in Marcela Linková and Naďa Straková, *Bytová revolta: Jak ženy dělaly disent* (Praha: Academia, 2017), 144.

[13] Most recently, she has been a member of the organization *Grandmas without Borders*, which is involved in helping migrants, pro-migrant advocacy, and direct help to Ukrainian women refugees. The organization is very vocal and targets politicians to seek dialogue. For more on her activism, see "Introduction" in Flanagan and Waisserová, *Women's Artistic Dissent*.

When they tried to teach people how to get rid of their ego, how to dissolve it in cosmic space, in divinity. How to be detached from things, possessions, power, body and get rid of suffering. How to be happy. And now it seems that individuality swells, asserts itself and fights with everyone else. The more and more people do not fit, the more they were not satisfied with the collective family, common religion, sects, castes. The ego may grow the faster the personality has been suppressed by religion, caste systems and colonizers.[14]

Kriseová's personal observations and narratives, shaped by her early social journalism experience, dissident bravery, and commitment to truth, intertwine with her global and ecological concerns. Her sensitivity to mechanisms of control and her deep empathy for humanity shines through in her writing, which is also known for its humor and celebration of life, even in its flawed and imperfect forms. Many of Kriseová's texts explore themes of belonging, rootedness, and place within the context of social ecology and humanism. Her work fosters empathy for all, particularly women, transcending traditional feminist narratives. She exemplifies a unique strain of endemic vernacular feminism, distinct from Western platforms until 1989, yet connected to the traditions of bold Central European women writers and activists and their collectives, as well as diverse artistic and spiritual traditions from Europe and beyond.

Thus, experiencing a complex twentieth century in Central Europe, Kriseová's search for *life in truth* has matured into a deeply humane and worldly concern that becomes especially meaningful amid the global security and global warming crises. However, her voice is more nuanced, experienced, deeply empathetic, and surprising. If empathy has been a bit of a downplayed trait of women's literature, Kriseová's case has proven strongly that it should not be so. She features empathy as not simply inborn but can-be-acquired and taught by living in certain circumstances, such as in the turbulent twentieth century and life in dissent. In a very positive sense, Kriseová's writing and her instances for empathy and, truth and love highlight awareness of underlying planetary connections and associations with cultures like the Central European one, often dismissed as gray Soviet buffer zone, Holocaust horror space, but also perceived as dissident bohemian space (such as in works by Ivan Klíma, Milan Kundera or Philip Roth), a space producing wise fools (best known in works of Bohumil Hrabal or Jaroslav Hašek), or Kafkaesque absurdity

---

[14] Kriseová, *Mluvící hora*, 36–37.

(Franz Kafka and Václav Havel). However, though all cultural and literary themes do have some degree of self-defined empathy and awareness, all are seen as unreliable measurements, allowing for checking for conscious and unconscious biases for the truth and love. She seems to confirm the latest finding on the need for empathy to cure global maladies: "If we are to move in the direction of a more empathic society and a more compassionate world, it is clear that working to enhance our native capacities to empathize is critical to strengthening individual, community, national, and international bonds."[15]

This chapter argues that variations of *truth and love* lie at the core of Eda Kriseová's creative writing and her investment in social and human ecology, and community advancement. Kriseová's texts are deeply humane, complex and inspirational as they promote finding selves against complex historical and cultural backgrounds while reinforcing women's voices, and women's powers, along with themes of social ecology, and humanist awareness.

From social journalist to social ecology writer

Eda Kriseová had a career as a celebrated social journalist in *Listy* until this most prominent progressive magazine was banned.[16] Her last officially published article featured Jan Zajíc's funeral and was on the title page of *Listy* in March 1969.[17] Jan Zajíc burnt himself on Wenceslas Square a month after Palach on February 25th, 1969, as an act of revolt against events signaling the new direction of Czechoslovakia after the Russian invasion.

Her reporting style showed much empathy with the uncompromising young mind. Her text celebrates dignified humanity and seeks justice for self-sacrifice that was meant to shake citizens out of their complacency with the impacts of the Russian invasion and the change of the social and moral climate that emerged after the crushing of the Prague Spring reform movement. It

---

[15] Helen Riess, "The Science of Empathy," *Journal of Patient Experience* 4, no. 2 (2017): 74–77.

[16] *Listy* was a Czechoslovak cultural and political weekly of the Union of Czechoslovak Writers. In 1968, it was published under the name *Literární listy* (February 22, 1968–August 15, 1968). This magazine was published from 1927 until May 1969, and again from 1990 until 2020. Circulation in the period 1968 to 1969 reached 300,000 copies per edition.

[17] Jan Zajíc was a high school student who immolated himself following Jan Palach. The article on Zajíc was: Eda Kriseová and Marta Marková, "Zandete si dvacet kroků," *Literární listy*, no. 12 (March 1969), title page.

highlights how these ultimate acts of courage become impactful and meaningful to society and to the nation–and can be interpreted as acts of *truth and love*. It conveys the tragedy, but it also reminds the dissenting community of their responsibility to keep Palach and Zajíc's legacies alive and not to give in. Finally, it conveyed that there is pride, dignity, and even love in such desperate acts and that patriotism and courage to protest and bear the ultimate cost must be cherished and not forgotten.

Her article narrates not only the act of the personal desperation of a student who set himself on fire, but it also narrates the family and communal reactions to deeply ingrained cultural and individual need for expressing oneself in the quest for truth. An independent Czechoslovak nation was formed with T. G. Masaryk's motto, "Truth Shall Prevail," referring to Jan Hus's "Truth Prevails." Adopted as the national motto, it appears on the presidential standard of the Czech Republic and is designated by the Czech Constitution as a national symbol. But how does the mythology of nation-making by believing "that the truth shall prevail" or the centuries-long belief that it is worth dying for truth feature in Eda Kriseová's writing? Well, it is at its core as she shares the beliefs. Her writing shows a deep interest in truth and love unmuddled by the historical and cultural circumstances of totalitarianism.

She comes from a pro-European and avantgarde family: her parents were architect Jindřich Krise and sculptress Zdenka Schwarzerová-Kriseová, who experienced a short period of Czechoslovak democracy and studied in Berlin and Paris but also experienced Nazism and Communism. Nurtured by her upbringing in a family bearing totalitarian misfortunes, Eda Kriseová becomes invested in creating an authentic and intimate intellectual relationship with the historical *truth and love*, including traditional European transnationality.

Later, she embraces the Havelian motto: *Truth and love shall prevail over lies and hatred*. The same motto has been welcomed worldwide as a universal spiritual and humanistic incentive, even a cliché. Eventually, she became one of the promoters of this Havelian motto, the so-called "*pravdoláskař* (truth-lover),"[18] who believed that *truth and love* should be the most effective tools to foster civil and social change, which was needed in the society devastated by

---

[18] *Pravdoláskař* is a compound word formed from *pravda* + *láska*. The term was derived from the words of Václav Havel during or shortly after the Velvet Revolution *pravda a láska musí zvítězit nad lží a nenávistí* (Truth and love must prevail over lies and hatred). It is viewed positively by some, while it has been mocked as naive by the opposition.

totalitarianism. Like many others, Eda Kriseová developed her own meanings of these distinct notions of truth and love.

The motto on powers of *truth and love* became notoriously known from Havel's texts, speeches, cultural meditations, and his reflections on the times of normalization.[19] Havel's iconic essay, *The Power of the Powerless* (1978), was built upon Havel's mentor, Jan Patočka's concept of *the solidarity of the shaken*,[20] whose seminars Eda Kriseová attended as well. Both essays explicated empowering notions of the meanings of truth [and love] and were widely understood, shared, and observed by the dissenting community. Havel's essay prominently features *living in a lie*, as living in a state of self-deception, living with a split personality, in which individuals sacrifice their own needs, expressions, desires, and their authentic notions of truth and love to the ideology, which imposes an artificial system on all spheres of lives. Thus, *living in truth* stands as a direct opposite and contradiction of *living a lie*.

Havel wrote: "Individuals can be alienated from themselves only because there is something in them to alienate. The terrain of this violation is their authentic existence. *Living the truth* is thus woven directly into the texture of *living a lie*."[21] In other words, Havel encourages one to seek authentic expression in order to reduce manipulative ideology or technocracy, its performative rituals, its simplified and omnipresent narratives, which were crushing the arts' and writing's free expression and invited conformity. Thus, *living in truth* turned personal and became unorganized, authentic, spontaneous, inventive, original, controversial, and persecuted.

In her early dissident era, Eda Kriseová wrote many texts inspired by forgotten patients in a mental institution, where she volunteered.[22] She wrote about their true authenticity, their zest for life, and their right to happiness. She was inspired and committed to sharing the truth, as she was heavily invested in observing dignity among patients in the mental asylum. For example, she

---

[19] Normalization refers to the era from 1968 until 1989, after the Warsaw Pact invasion of Czechoslovakia in August 1968. It was a period that signaled the end of reforms and freedoms and conformity to Soviet Communist norms.

[20] Martin Palouš and Ivan Chvatík, *The Solidarity of the Shaken: Jan Patočka's Philosophical Legacy in the Modern World* (Washington, DC: Academica Press, 2019).

[21] Václav Havel, "Power of the Powerless," trans. Paul Wilson, in Václav Havel, *The Power of the Powerless* (London: Vintage, 2018), 143-44.

[22] For many years, Eda Kriseová volunteered in a mental institution in Želiv, which inspired her early texts like *The Cavalry of a Coachmen, The Sun Dial,* and *The Bat's Clavicle and Other Stories.*

wrote a fascinating short story, "How Many Resurrections," about female sexuality in which free, unrestricted sexuality mirrors liberation and freedom.[23] As Foucault in *The History of Sexuality* suggests, many regimes have appropriated rights to free sexuality to impose control. If the grasp of the *normalizing* power over sexuality and the body is compromised, it can have fatal consequences.[24] In this short story, institutional care is a metaphor for the normalization regime's control of all aspects of one's life. Eda Kriseová features an old, short, fat, and forgotten Mrs. Koubková, who used to be a nymphomaniac, but now she is doped, immobile, and pitiful. She is in a hospital room that serves as a last resort; she is among those awaiting their death. She has no future, no family, and no hope. A social worker remembers her as "the old whore,"[25] who would run and make out with any man she could find and how she hated chasing after her, as she had to find her and bring her back. Now, she is expected to die soon.

Suddenly, however, the old woman miraculously improves, as she stashes her drugs away instead of taking them–she refuses to be controlled, she refuses *to live a lie*. She starts making indecent proposals again and is caught performing *in flagranti delicto*. Again, she is caught, doped, and locked up. Then, unexpectedly, this mental institution patient repeats her trick, and she flees. She keeps walking in slippers for a few days and sleeps in haystacks to save the little money she has. She is over seventy now. She reaches a town, gets a room in a cheap hotel, and starts offering herself: "She charged only ten crowns, as she was a decent woman."[26] However, the institution hears about where she is, and the staff comes to get her again. They lock her up in the secure psychiatric ward again and dope her with pills. She becomes apathetic. Soon, her health deteriorates, and she dies. The social worker, who lives a rather monotonous and unhappy life, feels exhausted and suddenly imagines Mrs. Koubková "twiddling her thumbs, her fat eyes blinking lasciviously as if saying, 'All of you are long dead, only me, I was alive.'"[27]

This text uses humor, juxtaposes normal and abnormal lives, narrates Mrs. Koubková, the forgotten and the overlooked old woman, with dignity, and it pays tribute to her taste for life, as she exercises *her power of the powerless*, her

---

[23] Eda Kriseová, "How Many Resurrections," trans. Káča Poláčková-Henley, *Prairie Schooner* (Winter 1992), 17-18.
[24] Michel Foucault, *The History of Sexuality* (New York: Vintage Books, 1984).
[25] Kriseová, "How Many Resurrections," 17-18.
[26] Ibid.
[27] Ibid.

active refusal to be "doped" and "controlled." The story frames personal freedom as a source of hope and vitality. It shows that happiness exists in a life that some might see as lost or even decadent, in contrast to the conventional life that is dull. Everyone can live with dignity, it argues, and have some happiness. The story does not mock the rebellious Mrs. Koubková, but it treats her with respect and honesty, offering vivid descriptions of her state, looks, and the hospital, and cheers for her resilience and *resurrection*.

It is an example of a text which reads well and uses smart, subversive strategies. Similar texts and narratives exist or appear in oral histories focusing on women. Narratives told in women's voices correct the distorted and not fully understood notions of womanhood. The strategy of celebrating life, even if seemingly pitiful and less than ordinary, is powerful.

Eda Kriseová's writing on patients in mental institutions lasted for about ten years; when she paradoxically found mental institutions freer and more liberal than the controlled life under normalization.[28] During this period, she belonged to Havel's dissident writing circle[29] or *intellectual ghetto* as she would call it.[30] Others would call it *parallel polis* (Václav Benda) or *second culture* (Ivan Martin Jirous), which all refer to a parallel society to the normalized society, even if this position has shown itself as impractical, utopian, and even counterproductive as isolation may prevent creating and growing sustainable communities, and transgress political borders.[31] Eda Kriseová lived in a ghetto, but she believed in cultivating communities and spaces without boxing them or separating them, without compromising her freedom. Such openness and empathetic interest in others lie at the heart of her social humanistic approach.

---

[28] For more on Eda Kriseová's dissident writing featuring mental institutions, or on Havel's notion of "society as straitjacket," see Waisserová, *Women's Artistic Dissent*, 156-61. See also, Hana Waisserová, "Eda Kriseová and Her Prophecy of the Velvet Revolution: 'The Gates Opened' (1984)," *Kosmas. Czechoslovak and Central European Journal*, n.s., 2, no. 2 (2019): 59-76.

[29] Both contributed to the samizdat magazine *Obsah*, and Havel's *Expedice* published Eda Kriseová's texts.

[30] See, for example, Edith Kurzweil, "An interview with Eda Kriseová," *Partisan Review* 70, no. 1, (2003): 89; or Flanagan and Waisserová, *Women's Artistic Dissent*, Chapter 1.

[31] See Václav Benda, et al. "Parallel Polis, or an Independent Society in Central and Eastern Europe: An Inquiry," *Social Research* (1988): 211-46; Ivan Martin Jirous, "Report on the Third Czech Musical Revival," trans. Paul Wilson and Ivan Hartel, in *Views from the Inside: Czech Underground Literature and Culture, 1948-1989*, ed. Martin Machovec (Praha: Karolinum, 2018), 34.

Nevertheless, her writing was shaped by her experience and indirectly promoted authenticity while reflecting on the views common among those in the intellectual ghetto. Kriseová and Havel belonged to the same writers' circle, and both writers became trusted friends. And their friendship and mutual respect lasted beyond dissent. During the Velvet Revolution, Kriseová was a member of the coordinating committee as well as the spokesperson for Václav Havel at the Civic Forum (*Občanské forum*).[32] Václav Havel invited her to serve in his first free Czechoslovak government. Havel appointed her in charge of the *Office of Pardons and Paroles*, which, in practical terms, meant to seek justice and truth in many cases of historical injustice, as a way of rebuilding the pathways for truth and love to be entered in the political and societal culture or distorted legal system. Her job was dealing with the multitude of complaints addressed to Václav Havel and seeking justice for the crimes and injustice that the Communist regime had caused to Czechoslovak people during the past forty years. She mentioned that her experience as a journalist and writer was essential for this particular job:

> In the Castle, I was using everything I've learned from my life. I really could work with my fatalistic philosophy and intuition, and sensitivity as a writer. There were so many people who needed to be heard and share the stories of the injustice. Finally, they were hoping that someone would listen to them. The three of us in my office answered piles of letters and requests.[33]

Writing these historical pains overlap with Eda Kriseová's post-1989 experience at Havel's first government. Havel also encouraged Eda Kriseová to write his biography, which he authorized.[34] In *Someone's World,* she commented on the

---

[32] The Civic Forum (*Občanské fórum*, OF) was a sponateneous civic platform in Czechoslovakia, established during the Velvet Revolution in 1989. It never became a political party; it was a platform spearheading the transition to independent Czechoslovakia.

[33] In a personal interview in 2017. Eda Kriseová's experience from her work in the first Havel government has also been covered in *Osudy*, Czech Radio, in an interview with Jill Beverly in 1991, and oral memory projects, such as *Paměť národa*. This experience is also discussed in her lecture "From Illusion to Reality," delivered for the William Phillips Lecture Series, The New School for Social Research on November 4, 2014 at The New School. It was published under the same title in 2015.

[34] Eda Kriseová. *Václav Havel: The Authorized Biography*, trans. Caleb Crain (New York: St. Martin's Press, 1993).

immense historical neglect of truth and justice, she confronted in her position from 1990 to 1992:

> In those days, there were ten thousand complaints and requests for redress. Seven thousand letters of complaint per month plus personal visits. People finally wanted some kind of justice after forty or rather fifty years of the reign of terror... I didn't know how much misfortune had swelled in this country.[35]

She left the Castle with the Velvet Divorce.[36] Since 1993, she has been a freelance writer. Eda Kriseová has evolved into an important and widely recognized author, promoting the notions of identity connected to truth and love, which became the spontaneously embraced and widely popular key concepts of rebuilding civil society.

Living and writing truth and love

After being fully banned as a journalist and from any form of publishing, Eda Kriseová gradually reinvented herself as a writer. Creative writing offered her a safe space in which she could speak her voice, where she could be true to herself, and where she could feel detached from the so-called *life in a lie* that was taking place in the world around her. Eventually, she had three written manuscripts by the time the first one was published in *samizdat*. It took several years before her former colleague from *Listy*, Ludvík Vaculík, asked her to provide her manuscripts for the underground *Edice Petlice* (Padlock Edition) press. Later *Edice Expedice* (Edition Expedition), and other unofficial editing venues or exile publishing houses followed, and her texts were smuggled out and back to her native country.[37] Translations were published in the Netherlands, Germany, Switzerland, and the United States.

---

[35] Kriseová, *Čísi svět*, 41.
[36] Velvet Divorce meant the peaceful split of Czechoslovakia into two countries: the Czech Republic and Slovakia.
[37] In the *samizdat* Petlice Press (1972–1990), Eda Kriseová published twelve texts: *Křížová cesta kočárového kočího* (no. 91, 1977), *Sluneční hodiny* (no. 119, 1978), *Perchta z Rožmberka aneb Bílá Paní* (no. 125, 1978), *Pompejanka* (no. 144, 1979), *Klíční kůstka netopýra* (no. 167, 1979), *Ryby raky* (no. 248, 1983, and no. 311, 1985), *Prázdniny Bosonožkou* (no. 287, 1984), *Sedm lásek* (no. 310, 1985), *Bratři* (no. 312, 1985), *Arboretum* (no. 352, 1986), *Terezka a Majda na horách* (no. 367, 1987), *Co se stalo...* (no. 375, 1987). Re-editions of Eda Kriseová's texts were published in other underground publishers such as Krameriova Expedice (1978–1990; organized by Vladimír Pistorius), and in Expedice

To comprehend Eda Kriseová's use of *truth and love* in her writing, one needs to revisit the communal understanding of the dissenting community, which shared an interest in pro-democracy efforts and human rights advocacy. Being part of this unofficial culture, Eda Kriseová's life and work illustrate how an individual can neutralize ideological pressures via everyday activities, writing, and creating healthy alternative communities, and by cultivating friendships with writers of the so-called *Kvartál*, at gatherings of authors of the *Petlice* publishing house between 1981 and 1989.

Kvartál meetings replaced the public readings and allowed banned writers to connect and discuss their works, exchange ideas, and support each other. Such networking events encouraged writers to share their writing, get feedback and criticism, support each other in mental and material ways, express solidarity, help with childcare, typing, cooking, and much more.[38] Sometimes, these gatherings coincided with group meetings of the authors of an underground literary and cultural review *Obsah*, an underground magazine to which both Kriseová and Havel belonged. It became a prominent cultural platform,[39] although Václav Havel, imprisoned for four-and-half years, could not participate for long. Václav Havel, however, quickly emerged as one of the leading oppositional figures and was internationally visible since the 1960s as a successful playwright, mirroring the absurd political life. Eda Kriseová liked to go to see his plays in the 1960s. Eventually, he stands at the very heart of the

---

(1975–1990; organized by V. Havel). She is also represented in a number of *samizdat* anthologies, such as *Hodina naděje. Almanach české literatury 1968–1978* (1978); *Hlasy nad rukopisem Českého snáře* (1981); *Danny je náš* (for Josef Škvorecký, 1984); *Světlá lhůta* (for Jiří Gruša, 1988), *Hodina naděje. Almanach české literatury 1968-1978* (In German, Luzern, 1978; in Czech, Toronto, 1980); *The Writing on the Wall* (Princeton, 1983), *Mein Lesebuch* (Frankfurt am Main, 1983), *Verfemte Dichter* (Köln am Rhein, 1983), *Doba páření* (Toronto, 1986), *Generace 34-45* (München, 1986). After 1989, her texts are included, for example, in *Aus zwanzig Jahren Finsternis* (Wien, 1991), and *Good-Bye, Samizdat* (Evanston, 1992).

[38] *Kvartál* was a gathering of Czech, Moravian, and Slovak writers who published with Petlice, and it took place in various locations. *Obsah* was a monthly underground cultural review, published in 1981 to 1989.

[39] It existed from 1981 until 1989, with about fifty or hundred copies per issue. Among its contributors were Petr Kabeš, Jan Trefulka, Milan Uhde, Ivan Klíma, Ludvík Vaculík, Alexandr Kliment, Karel Pecka, Miroslav Červenka, Eva Kantůrková, Sergej Machonin, Lenka Procházková, and Věra Jirousová. It was initiated by the circle of writers around Petlice. It contained poetry, short stories, essays, feuilletons, translations, and various articles on history, music, and politics.

"cultures of dissent,"[40] which shared humanistic, artistic, cultural, political, and environmental concerns. However, Havel's understanding of the dissenting agenda was gradually and eventually co-created with his dissident peers, including Eda Kriseová.

In 1983, Princeton's Karz-Cohl Publishing published *The Writing on the Wall: An Anthology of Contemporary Czech Literature*, featuring eighteen authors (including only two women) who had published in a *samizdat* Padlock Edition run by Ludvík Vaculík.[41] In its foreword, an exiled critic, Antonín Liehm, praises dissent Czech literature: "In its 150 years of modern existence, Czech literature has never known such a flowering of talent… as in these very days of its persecution."[42] This volume, he added, offers "first-class authors, treated as second-class citizens," who created the "second" or "parallel" literature of Czechoslovakia, "which is far superior to the products of the establishment's publishing houses."[43] Eda Kriseová is introduced as one of "the foremost young journalists of the second half of the 1960s," whom the normalization "regime drove […] away from journalism and literally forced her–most fortunately, as it turned out–to become an author of fiction."[44]

This volume brought attention to the cause of *samizdat* literature. Book reviews praised the collection for its literary qualities, and a few reviews appreciated and spotlighted a story by Eda Kriseová:

> This anthology is devoid of pathos, sermonizing, passions of the wounded. Instead, the kind, wise humor of those who have witnessed brutalization and normalization prevails. This is also the case of "A Knight of the Cross" by Eda Kriseová, a touching story of a pathetically

---

[40] See Bolton, *Worlds of Dissent*.
[41] *Samizdat* stands for the illegal publishing by underground publishing houses. The published works included works of literature, Czech or in translation, magazines, newsletters, information bulletins, and Charter 77 documents, which were typed out on typewriters, usually with about eight carbon copies on onionskin paper were circulated in a trusted network. To learn more about Czech *samizdat* writing, see Martin Machovec, *Writing Underground. Reflections on Illegal Texts in Communist Czechoslovakia* (Praha: Karolinum Books, 2019).
[42] Antonín Liehm, "Foreword," in *The Writing on the Wall: An Anthology of Contemporary Czech Literature* (Princeton: Karz-Cohl, 1983), x.
[43] Ibid., xiii.
[44] Ibid., xiv.

honest farmer who successfully defies brutal authorities by feigning ultrapatriotic insanity. This is the best chapter in the book."[45]

Fully banned at home, she greatly appreciated the Western support and exile publications. She shared that she was allowed to travel to the United States on an invitation in 1988, and described what she felt when, during a 1988 visit to Harvard, the library computer showed that it contained her underground manuscripts on file. "I burst into tears," she told us. "I felt like a victorious Robinson Crusoe whose message in a bottle had washed up on shore."[46]

However, until 1989, the general Czechoslovak readership was unaware of her writing since she enjoyed no promotion, recognition, or public readings, though some remembered her journalism. She earned some recognition from being published in translations or in foreign anthologies.[47]

Truth and love applied: from "Havel's truth" to Kriseová's truth and love

The notions of *living in truth*, is famously explained in Havel's iconic essay "The Power of the Powerless":

> Living within the truth, as humanity's revolt against an enforced position, is, on the contrary, an attempt to regain control over one's own sense of responsibility![48]

---

[45] Otto Ulc, *Slavic Review* 43, no. 3 (1984): 528–29.
[46] She shared this story at a 1992 conference *What was gained with the passing of Communism?*, organized by *Partisan Review*. In Nick Owchar, "What Was Lost: Dissident Artists After Soviet Communism," *Agni* 36 (1992): 256–69, https://www.jstor.org/stable/23009518.
[47] Anthologies and English language publications include *The Writing on the Wall: An Anthology of Contemporary Czech Literature; Good-Bye, Samizdat*, and others. The translated texts include: "How Many Resurrections," trans. Káča Poláčková-Henley, *Prairie Schooner*, (Winter 1992), 17–18; "Morning in Church," trans. Milan Pomichalek and Anna Mozga, in *Good-Bye, Samizdat*, ed. Marketa Goetz-Stankiewicz (Evanston, IL: Northwestern University Press, 1992), 88–94; "A Whirl of Witches," *Partisan Review* 66 (1999), 611-24; "The Hackney Coachman's Funeral," trans. Dagmar Herrmann, *Prairie Schooner* 66, no. 4 (1992): 56–72. Other anthologies include German ones: *Mein Lesebuch* (Frankfurt am Main, 1983), *Verfemte Dichter* (Köln am Rhein, 1983), *Doba páření* (Toronto, 1986), *Generace 34-45* (München, 1986), *Aus zwanzig Jahren Finsternis* (Wien, 1991).
[48] Václav Havel, "Power of the Powerless," in *Open Letters* (New York: Vintage Books, 1992), 153.

This text suggests regaining our own responsibility by integrating being true to self with love as a moral act when love becomes the greatest strength of the powerless. It promoted a new civic and political culture centered around vague notions of *truth and love*. These terms help to set a baseline for a humane political life (which is not dehumanized and technocratic); they help to refresh the stale and empty language of the previous era. *Truth and love* became new imaginative metaphors, which were embraced widely. The concepts invited many new broadly understood meanings, encouraged new ideas, interpretations, and practices, and had a new life in diverse contexts. They were meant as a stepping-stone to a new public culture, a practical recipe, and an invitation for everyone to employ personal responsibility. Though *truth and love* became the famous international legacy of Václav Havel, one understands that these concepts are conditioned by social contexts and environments and invite a multitude of interpretations to become meaningful. Many dissidents based their opposition to the regime on *rejecting living a lie* and dismantling false morality. Many others agreed with Havel as they disapproved of the loss of individual responsibility. In his 1984 essay "Politics and Conscience," Havel highlights the need for respecting ethical and spiritual values that guide one and help to refuse technocratic power; if those are accepted as common values, they help create a civic culture and provide shared purpose and give meaning to civic communities.[49]

Havel and Kriseová both also warned against impersonal, dehumanized, and abstract ideological compliance that would go against one's consciousness. They warned against global crises caused by the degradation of human politics, leading to creating global conflicts much beyond Europe. Much of these beliefs were shared within the dissenting community, reflected in their understanding of living in truth, which was spontaneously practiced. Additionally, the Czech dissident community embraced a deep interest in observing human dignity and human rights. Respect for humanity and interest in ecology and nature became topics respected and cultivated by many dissent intellectuals, especially women, who believed in the powers of culture, arts, activism, social work, and ecology.

A fresh impulse to comprehend the meanings of *truth* as adopted and understood by Václav Havel is offered by Kieran Williams in his "Truth" (2022).[50] He explains the context and understanding of Havel's Truth in its

---

[49] In Havel, "Politics and Conscience," *Open Letters*, 249–71.
[50] A chapter that focuses on Havel's truth in David S. Danaher and Kieran Williams, eds., *Václav Havel's Meanings: His Key Words and Their Legacy* (Prague: Karolinum, 2022).

"avouching and veracity," leaning on truth as a tool of practical living, and as understood and promoted within Central European intellectual tradition that influenced Havel's conceptual notions. His living philosophy and practices are shaped by local cultural history and notions of "authentic" Czech identity. Williams wrote:

> Havel's willingness to go to prison several times rather than leave the country or renounce his dissident activity is itself an illustration of the first and most fundamental of his understandings of truth, as a personal avouching: "Putting it very simply and succinctly, truth for me is information but at the same time is something more. Of course, it is information which, like all other kinds of information, is clearly shown or confirmed or verified or is simply convincing in the context of a certain system of coordinates or paradigms, but at the same time it is information for which a human being avouches their entire existence, their reputation, their honor, their name. [...] [*Tomáš*] Masaryk's stance [on the forged *Královédvorský* and *Zelenohorský* manuscripts] shows that really standing for truth means not looking at whether or not it benefits a person, whether they are esteemed or cursed by the public, whether their struggle ends in success or in derision and finally in oblivion."[51]

Kieran Williams' analysis highlights what truth may be in Havel's cultural and historical understanding, as well as what truth may not represent for Havel. Williams suggests revisiting possible archeological/philosophical and genealogical origins of Havel's grasp of truth, which has existential and identity-seeking contours.

Searches for evidence of *truth* in Eda Kriseová's literary work, also overlap and connect with the meanings of the historical truth or national truth. Eda Kriseová does not shy away from formulating her understanding of *truth and love* when thinking of Czechs, their culture, their notions of a nation, and religion, which is similar to Havel's quest for truth! In *Someone's World*, she thinks about the truth in the connection to the nature of the Czech nation. She writes:

---

[51] Václav Havel, "Acceptance of an Honorary Degree from the University of Michigan," in *Václav Havel's Meanings: His Key Words and Their Legacy*, ed. David Danaher and Kieran Williams (Prague: Karolinum, 2022).

The Czechs later rebelled against both the emperor and the Pope and invented the first communism in Europe. They always gravitated towards communism, towards social justice and leveling. They didn't like it when someone overstepped or stepped out of line. If they didn't execute him, they at least expelled him. They didn't like either or, they didn't like the tragic contradiction between love and hate, they didn't like to look into the abyss, they didn't see the heights... They wanted everything small and ours, including literature and art. They live in a kind of merciful but terrifying fog in which anything, even a miracle, can happen. And above all, one doesn't believe anyone who means what one says.[52]

In this regard, Kriseová, like many other writers and intellectuals, feels the need to discuss the nationhood, which is defined by its culture, by its memory, and shows in the nation's nature.[53] According to Jiří Přibáň in *In Quest of History: On Czech Statehood and Identity* (2019), Czechs are not a political nation but a cultural one. The culture has been preoccupied with the Central European story and the role of culture traditionally since the times of the National Revival, and especially for Masaryk and the creation of the Czech nation, the culture demonstrated the need to be spelled, and defined. It was elevated into a realm bearing universal ideals of humanity. The imagination of a spiritually and morally awakened independent nation became a topic among dissent writers. Their writing focused on the search for true identity, a search for the historical truth.[54]

Kriseová is also a product of this culture that looks back, to use Jacques Rupnik's metaphoric title *Central Europe as a Bird with Eyes at the Back of its Head*,[55] which refers to the fact that Czech past and presence alike is preoccupied with looking back, and not living now or looking forward. However, while many works of Eda Kriseová look back, her texts are also very much set in the present or look outward and forward, seeking poetic justice for local memory or global future alike.

---

[52] Kriseová, *Čísi svět*, 88–89.
[53] For a discussion of the nation among the dissidents, see, for example, Jan Patočka, Petr Fidelius, and Ivan Chvatík, *Češi* (Praha: Oikoymenh, 2006).
[54] Jiří Přibáň and Karel Hvížďala, *In Quest of History: On Czech Statehood and Identity* (Prague: Karolinum Press, 2019).
[55] See Jacques Rupnik, *Střední Evropa je jako pták s očima vzadu* (Praha: Novela bohemica, 2018).

Kriseová does not join the battles or quests to rediscover the cultural mythologies, nor does she address major historical silences as her primary goal. Instead, she focuses on the connectivity, the storytelling of individual stories, set in particular locations, in nature, as places are created and (de)populated by people, overgrown by plants, trees, and rivers. She focuses on her protagonists and the course of life and nature accompanying their fate. The complex twentieth-century reality, as well as Czech nationalist, philosophical, political, and other modern nation's needs, are not her primary concern.

For example, *Talking Mountain* offers a glimpse of such worldly conversations, touching on human solidarity, but also limits, naiveté, anger, arrogance, or humility:

> We became quiet. We, the white ones, were ashamed of our pettiness. We would love to be as carefree. None dared to challenge the shepherd's good faith and all arguments seemed weak and ineffective. We have to believe that we can save the world.[56]

This interaction certainly targets many current globally concerned mindsets, yet it also points at Western arrogance and skepticism as it does not offer much mindful sustainability. As she opts to highlight the need to connect humans to nature, she describes those who seek and promote rooted existence that may generate some good faith and hope. This conversation among the nagging, yet caring individuals, who are prone to skepticism continues, showing an educated understanding of the ecology and the need to preserve the planet:

> We agree that plants in their simple forms occupied the land as the first ones, and that they cover all hearts' surface from the Polar plains to the equator rainforests. No other species can sustain itself in such extreme cold and extreme heat. They are bigger and stronger than animals and they live longer. But animals and us people depend on them. But they can't survive systematic plundering, which we do, even though we could perish without it.[57]

Though this passage introduces general belief about the importance of plants, it serves as an introduction setting the tone of the story. After such a teaser, she tends to fill her texts with detailed observations of a receptive ornithologist or

---

[56] Kriseová, *Mluvící hora*, 15.
[57] Ibid.

a botanist who, with impressive detail, retells the old known *truth* recited by nations, we shall value the nature's domain, we warn to protect, observe and respect it. As if in communication with Native American wisdom: "All things are connected. Whatever befalls the earth befalls the children of the earth."[58]

For Eda Kriseová, her interests in nature and spirituality have been her lifelong true companions, and in *Care for Your Soul and Body,* she shares that she learned to meditate naturally in her childhood:

> In my childhood, I entered emptiness or fullness, depending on how we perceive it, involuntarily… It was natural, and it always came when I was alone; it never happened in someone's presence. It grabbed me like a gentle, light breeze; I couldn't summon it; I didn't even want to get out of it… My senses turned off by themselves. I only realized that it was meditation back then, a stronger being when I started practicing yoga.[59]

This spiritual ability became her resistance. It helped her to manage fears, frustrations and hatred, and deal with pressures. It also helped her to connect with others, to feel connected with humans and nature alike, to generate empathy–to live in *truth and love. Love* in the spiritual sense. She shares that when she meditates, she also envisions scenes from her childhood, nature, the countryside, and places. In a certain way, while meditation worked as her resistance strategy against surreal normalization, it also became a powerful tool in her perceptive writing, it helped her to deal with complex realities and chronic back pain, to concentrate and stay focused on writing amid stressful oppressed lives. Many fellow dissidents faced existential gloom, alcoholism, the open hedonism of their partners, lack of resources, various shortages, lack of privacy, possible distrust of the community, paranoia, lack of recognition, no meaningful jobs, as well as ostracization. However, dissident writers and their families drew strengths from their solidarity and integrity, observing human dignity, helping each other and the vulnerable ones, and providing help to the needy and forgotten. For many, it was natural that later, they could help refugees or socially marginalized people like those whom they used to help during times of political persecution. These encounters also help to remember

---

[58] Chief Seattle in Kent Nerburn, *The Wisdom of the Native Americans* (New York: MJF Books, 2009), 3.
[59] Eda Kriseová, *Duši, tělo, opatruj* (Praha: Práh, 2014), 169.

and not to forget. Eda Kriseová shared her belief that by helping refugees and people in need, people and society help themselves.[60]

Writing social ecology and filling in historical silences

> I listen to the sea and wind. Here is greenery, quiet, and peace. Under my feet lie bones, no one knows how many people, and no one ever will search for who the dead were. There are countries where people do not even believe in their graves. And would one find a nation in Europe that would not have to be ashamed?[61]

In the short story "Alma" from *Talking Mountain*, Eda Kriseová recounts an impactful visit to Latvia, a region labeled the "bloodlands"[62] by Timothy Snyder due to the mass killings of Jews and collaboration with the Nazis during World War II. Inspired by the tragic story of her schoolmate whose family perished in the gulag, Kriseová's narrator proposes that the landscape itself acts as a silent witness, forever intertwined with the human stories it holds. Deserted houses stand as silent testaments, echoing the narratives of the desperate, the displaced, the purged, and the victims of the Holocaust. Kriseová's evocative prose paints vivid snapshots, transporting the reader on a poignant journey. Her words are charged with emotion, igniting empathy and prompting reflection on memory and the weight of history. This powerful emotional resonance can be attributed to her artistic sensibility, her deep empathy for those who suffered.

Throughout her life, Kriseová has cultivated a spiritual resilience that helped her endure hardship and instilled a deep respect for spiritual wisdom and the enduring power of past experiences. While she observes unsettling spiritual markers, she seeks peace for those who suffer, as if nature and time offers solace and *truth*.[63] This complex understanding of life becomes the tapestry of everyday existence, as exemplified by individuals like Alma.

Prior to 1990, the painful historical experiences of those punished by the regime were shrouded in silence. Revealing these truths would have been

---

[60] In a personal interview with Hana Waisserová in June 2023.
[61] Kriseová, *Mluvící hora*, 123.
[62] See Timothy Snyder, *Bloodlands: Europe between Hitler and Stalin* (New York: Basic Books, 2012).
[63] The impact of the yoga and meditation experience on Eda Kriseová's life and writing is a subject of *Duši, tělo opatruj*, however, it is also much mentioned in *Čísi svět*.

impossible in official media or literature, if at all. However, inspired by intellectual dissent, many writers and historians emerged, dedicated to uncovering the truth and filling the historical gaps. They felt compelled to do justice to the stories of those who endured restrictions, bans, humiliations, and curtailments of freedom, often subjected to both psychological and physical abuse. This act of solidarity was crucial, and these narratives remain essential tools in the pursuit of reconciliation.

Beyond respecting human dignity and searching for truth, Eda Kriseová and her fellow writers from intellectual ghetto promoted respecting human rights as well as civic responsibilities and decency–guided by one's consciousness and its notions of *truth*. One of her protagonists in *Between Maiden and Old Woman*, declares: "When you feel your soul, you can't do anything bad, she is watching over you. Maybe it is the feeling of your own wholeness, which can't be disturbed, or it is the unity of all with everything, with a stone, a tree, a cloud, the whole universe."[64] This is an early text published only in 2018. It documents the author's early and prevailing interest in plants and nature as silent witnesses receptive to human fates.

Spirituality of truth and love

Less well-known is the fact that Central European literary culture, invested in humanistic spirituality, was not confined to any single church.[65] Figures like Eda Kriseová and Václav Havel sought personal truth and questioned their relationship with religion. While respecting figures like the Pope and the Dalai Lama as representatives of important religious traditions within Central Europe, they avoided aligning themselves with either Catholic or Protestant traditions.

> Václav Havel balances proclivities to Christian and equivalent values and symbols with an inclination toward non-Christian religious cultures. Buddhism plays a special place among them. In his New Year's

---

[64] Eda Kriseová, *Mezi pannou a babou* (Praha: Práh, 2018), 31.

[65] In this regard, their spirituality is a complex issue. However, Kriseová and Havel both respected and promoted the Dalai Lama and his message. Kriseová helped to arrange the last Dalai Lama's visit for Havel before he passed away.

speech from 1990, Havel announced to his people a plan to bring the Pope–and the Tibetan Dalai Lama–to Czechoslovakia for a visit.[66]

The Dalai Lama became a close friend of Havel's and co-founded the annual FORUM 2000 convention,[67] which continues to serve as a think tank for global leaders. He visited Havel and Prague on numerous occasions, including a final farewell visit to the ailing president shortly before he passed away. Eda Kriseová, among others, facilitated this last meeting. While Martin C. Putna, who mapped Havel's spiritual journey, has not pinpointed the exact reason for their special bond, however, it is well-known that Havel, Kriseová, and their circle shared a deep respect and interest in Eastern philosophies, Platonism, the occult, Tibetan human rights, and spiritual resistance.

After 1990, Kriseová remained active in the Czech yoga community and frequently traveled to India. She was involved in Krishnamurti's schools and various Indian spiritual projects. These interests were nurtured in the *Kampademie*,[68] a group that studied Socratic and Platonian philosophy, mythologies, religions, rituals, and human spiritual history and experience. Their sessions explored diverse traditions, including holotropic breathing,[69]

---

[66] In Martin C. Putna, *Václav Havel, Duchovní portrét* (Praha: Knihovna Václava Havla, 2011), 289. This extract is translated by Hana Waisserová.

[67] The Forum 2000 Foundation pursues the legacy of Václav Havel by supporting the values of democracy and respect for human rights, assisting the development of civil society, and encouraging religious, cultural, and ethnic tolerance. See <https://www.forum2000.cz/en/homepage>.

[68] *Kampademie* ("Academy at Kampa") was an intellectual fellowship, sometimes labeled as the renewed platonic academy at Kampa or a philosophical association whose members included Ivan M. Havel and leading Catholic intellectuals Zdeněk Neubauer, Radim Palouš, Martin Palouš, Daniel Kroupa, Pavel Bratinka, Tomáš Halík, and others. *Kampademie* in the time of Havel's imprisonment inspired correspondence-dialogue whose world-famous output was Havel's *Letters to Olga*. For more on *Kampademie*, see *Dějiny Kampademie* (Praha: Knihovna Václava Havla, 2010).

[69] Holotropic breathing is a method developed in the mid-1970s by the Czech psychiatrist and psychotherapist Stanislav and Christina Grof. It emerged from their research of human consciousness, especially its extraordinary states, induced, for example, by the ingestion of psychotropic substances such as LSD. The Grofs tried to find an alternative, yet effective method without using substances. This breathing therapeutic strategy opened the possibility of inducing other states of consciousness by means of intensive breathing or, conversely, holding the breath. It was inspired by shamanic practices, indigenous healing ceremonies, hypnosis, and other psychotherapeutic and spiritual

hypnosis, Taoism, shamanism, and major Catholic and Eastern philosophies. They even sought spiritual truth in various texts, such as the *Tibetan Book of the Dead*.

Eda Kriseová's writing, and her spiritual sensitivity and empathy have been cultivated by her lifelong practice of yoga and meditation, and her deeply spiritual and intimately religious interests. What is truly remarkable in her writing is the refined sensitivity and empathy with which she approaches female minds and bodies, which in male writing have been traditionally patronized or framed as aesthetic objects or objects of sexual desire. In her writing, all is connected: bodies come alive, they have their own will, they reflect, they are present, and they are in a complex relationship with a soul. In *Care for Your Soul and Body*, her philosophizing memoir, she focuses on this intricate relationship. In this text, however, she is not concerned about bodies being the witnesses of her time, having the physical presence, or seeking poetic justice for *bodies she knew*, but again, she engages in Platonian dialogue. She frames her text with this motto:

> The history of philosophy argues about what is more important: soul or body? I can only describe my experience with both. I am not a philosopher, and I do not think so well in abstract terms. When I was listening to my body for the first time, I heard honking lonely trains, bubbling tropical marshes, clicking muddy steps, squeaking baby birds, sound sea waves mixing with the swishing wind in a lonely spruce tree and with the whirling ancient mill. The heart beats, without paying him my attention, and under closed eyelids, falling leaves fizz. My organs and their voices are created by nature. It took her millions of years to put together the man. If the body is as old, then the soul, which is housed in the body, must be even older.[70]

This introduction is revealing. Eda Kriseová's approach to the female/human body is poetic, universal, and generous as it pays tribute to nature. It considers humans to be living particles of the universe in its timeless existence. Despite everything, humans and their histories do coexist together, surrounded by nature, by stars, by other living organisms, and by memories, sounds, or spiritual energies. This is the core of her dissent experience that lies in her

---

practices. See Richard Tarnas and Sean Kelly, eds., *Psyche Unbound: Essays in Honor of Stanislav Grof* (San Jose, CA: Multidisciplinary Association for Psychedelic Studies, 2022).
[70] Kriseová, *Duši, tělo opatruj*, 7.

human ecology approach. Finally, this theme of a Platonian dialogue between reason and emotion, or between body and soul becomes a bold topic threading Eda Kriseová's work.[71] Such a timeless and universal dispute becomes the theme of overarching ideological implications and testimonial literature reporting injustices.

Finally, she becomes invested in world spiritual traditions, world matters, such as legacies of colonialism, as well as planetary truth. In *Talking Mountain*, she opens up and thinks more about the white privilege as such, and rethinks connections between spirituality and ecology:

> White men, who are here because they believe that only plants can still save the world, envy the cowherd's unshakeable faith in survival. The people who live in the valley, have no doubt at all that the world is born of the trinity of gods Siva, Vishnu and Krishna, and the supreme power is Brahma, and he will continue to improve the world. Why else would we be here? The world is indestructible because it is a reflection of God, constantly being created and destroyed.[72]

In the end, humans still have a choice to face their fate with humble dignity, and a reconciliation process can happen, such as in her short story "Morning in Church." It is set in the center of Prague, the place of her childhood, to which she feels spiritually connected. The story offers rich meditation on how the church's architecture feels as there is a "mossy smell of the holy water that emanates from the front."[73] Her protagonist positions herself so she can soak up the peace of the place:

> I am sitting in my pew in the Egyptian posture, spine erect, calves at a right angle to the floor; I close my eyes and withdraw my senses the way a turtle withdraws its head and climbed into its shell. And then I open myself upward toward the Gothic vault and the sky vaulting above it; I open to all sides, straighten up and change into a pillar, its top burning with a cold flame. I am here and not here.[74]

---

[71] See Waisserová, *Women Artistic Dissent*, 182–83.
[72] Kriseová, *Mluvící Hora*, 14–15.
[73] Kriseová, "Morning in Church," 89.
[74] Ibid., 89.

She is suddenly confronted by a devil-like man loudly chanting his prayer, which turns into a lament, then a curse. The loudly lamenting man calls her a hypocrite and stupid, who does not pray loudly to reveal her true herself. Suddenly, her premonition and deep empathy awakens, and she tries to help and heal the unfortunate man:

> I don't know how long it has been since I last prayed in words, but now I need them. I am casting a spell on the pain sitting next to me motionless like the blind, the deaf, and the dead, like a shell from which the life has slipped and is now running through the lanes of the Old Town, hands above the head; I see him, running against the sun, on the run from the pain, and it is calmly and silently sitting her. I get up, slip out of the pew, and move backward so that it can't attack me, I move toward the door. Then I walk where he may have run, pulled by a strange force.[75]

This story offers a caring and healing power that is generated by the place, by experience, by intuition, by empathy, and by some special women's attributes.

Interdependence and biopolitics: examining the history and human-nature connection

Though Kriseová's novels, novellas, or short stories vary in setting, spanning historical eras and locations from the Czech Republic to foreign lands, her characters consistently grapple with dilemmas relatable to ordinary lives amidst diverse historical contexts marked by totalitarianism and political oppression. Notably, her work *Cats' Lives* exemplifies this, experiencing renewed popularity and new editions during the War on Ukraine, despite being written in 1989, prior to the Velvet Revolution. Set in Ruthenia and Czechoslovakia, the narrative traverses the periods of Russian, Soviet, Nazi, and Communist rule, encompassing the cleansing and displacement that followed World War II. The women at the heart of the story embody the weight of Central European trauma during the tumultuous twentieth century, echoing the experiences of many who lost families, homes, loved ones, and faced political persecution. These transnational female protagonists, enduring profound loss, are forced to make difficult choices: remaining, relocating, or seeking exile, often witnessing the dispersal of their families. The novel offers even a comparative sigh: "This is a small world… Yes, this is the difference

---

[75] Ibid., 94.

between Europe and America, that in America, people will never understand the horror of being forced out of one's home."[76]

The theme of forced departures, expulsions, and the bittersweet nostalgia for home and lost loved ones permeates Kriseová's writing. Through it, she explores the search for historical truth, as she explores circumstances and context for the decisions to stay or emigrate. Her protagonists narrate their life choices, regrets, and dreams that irrevocably altered their destinies as they grapple with the complex meaning of *life in a lie* in their specific circumstances. Her protagonist in *Cats' Lives* shares the pain of *living in a lie*: "You cannot imagine being born somewhere, where they would lie to you from the beginning of your life, and no news would reach you."[77]

Eda Kriseová also narrates the non-materiality of people who lost everything but who mourned, not for material things, but for their dead, for the loss of their roots and ancestors, similar to the trauma of the Holocaust of those who survived deportations, purges and ethnic cleansing, and even feel guilty about surviving: "She doesn't mind leaving behind her house and all furnishings, but she minds that she left living people behind, and she thinks it is not fair to leave the dead behind there too. As if a man had all life a duty to live near his ancestors, and not to be distanced too much."[78]

Humans and nature: spiritual essence and interconnectedness

Kriseová's concern for nature and its coexistence with humans culminates in her most recent work *Talking Mountain*. It contains eight short stories that could also be read as philosophical essays. The first story, "The Hill of the Madmen" (*Kopec bláznů*), honors the founder of a biodiversity project set in Kerala, visited by the narrator. The narrative pays tribute to the founder, an ethnic German Wolfgang, who dedicates his life to saving as many species of jungle plants, as possible. While his fight to save nature and diverse species, as well as his political battles with the Indian government, are important aspects of his story, the truly fascinating and humbling narrative lies in his witness to the plants' survival and their ability to experience emotions and consciousness. He believed that plants and humans could communicate. He once recalled a man who threatened to kill a flower the next day, and sadly, the flower indeed died. This experience solidified his belief. He emphasized the need for patience

---

[76] Kriseová, *Kočičí životy*, 268.
[77] Ibid., 266.
[78] Ibid., 198.

and understanding when interacting with plants, as their perception of time differs greatly from ours. Eda Kriseová presents a truly fascinating and humbling narrative: "A man needs to find time and patience for plants, as their time is different from our time."[79] The story often blurs the lines between humans and the natural world, treating the plants, the jungle, and even the birds as if they possessed human-like qualities. The story mentions an anecdote that *Homo sapiens* evolve into subspecies of *Homo digitalis* and lose their connection with nature. While we humans create conflict and destruction through our ever-evolving laws, nature operates under its own, often mysterious, set of rules. The writer meditates:

> Sometimes when I walk through the forest, I have this impenetrable faith in self, that my life connects to the life of the plants, and that together we can reach eternity. Life asks me to be lived, needs my bones, muscles, blood, to show me itself. This deep feeling calms me, but also excites me so much that I can't sleep.[80]

In these many instances and ecological mediations, Kriseová touches on the meaning of life and our mortality, and that nature teaches us patience, kindness, as embraced by various spiritual traditions, such as Taoism or Buddhism. She also contemplates seeds, and their inventive ways of survival, and that there are as many seeds as stars in the sky. These nature observations teach humility, compromise, and respect to other living organisms, and encourage the reader not to lose the ability to communicate, and all living organisms are existentially interconnected: "Perhaps, he has already turned into a plant, and his legs grew in the ground…"[81] and "Gardeners can save our world, our planet."[82]

Kriseová wields nature as a potent metaphorical tool, offering lessons in survival through evocative imagery. Take, for instance, her description of a banyan tree's expansive growth, where new branches sprout from the mother tree, eventually transforming into trunks themselves. This symbolizes the mother's eventual replacement by her children, her form consumed by their growth. Yet, Kriseová's focus extends beyond the natural world, encompassing the lives of man-made objects as well. She posits that creators imbue their

---

[79] Kriseová, *Mluvící hora*, 27.
[80] Ibid., 17.
[81] Ibid., 29.
[82] Ibid., 31.

creations with meaning, weaving them into the fabric of place, culture, and history. Furthermore, Kriseová delves into comparative thought, questioning the stark contrast between European and Japanese attitudes toward space. Why, she asks, do Europeans fear emptiness and austerity, cluttering their homes with old furniture, while the Japanese embrace minimalism? This comparative lens invites reflection on cultural norms and their underlying values. Finally, Kriseová equates natural beauty with a form of truth, suggesting an intrinsic connection between aesthetics and authenticity.

Kriseová imbues plants with a spiritual essence worthy of observation and respect. She rejects the notion of human domination over nature and fellow beings. Throughout her writings, she weaves together numerous mini-stories, meticulously highlighting the interconnectedness of plants and people, emphasizing their mutual dependence and reflective relationship: "Some plants bloom in need and destitution, and out of lack of love, so they say. Even the trees bloom most and bear fruit shortly before they die, as if from their last powers."[83]

The quotation suggests a stark difference between humans and plants; both are sensitive to their environment. While plants lack power over humans, Kriseová reminds us not to be solely human-centered and power-driven. Plants and the environment matter deeply, reflecting how we treat them. Their condition reveals their state. Plants are the foundation of sentient existence, embodying the essence of sustainable life. They transform carbon dioxide into life-sustaining carbohydrates and oxygen. Kriseová's work advocates for human-nature connections built on mutual love and respect. When humans leave, nature reclaims its space. Witnessing abandoned houses overtaken by greenery, we see the opening for multigenerational life, vibrant colors, and the diverse presence of a reactive nature. This silent witness covers the scars of the past, the bad, the painful, the bloodlands, with new life.

While her early novels explore the Czech lands and Central Europe, later works concern both the homeland and world locations. Kriseová juxtaposes Czechs with their international legacies, exemplified, for example, by journeys and forgotten and rediscovered legacies of architects Sammer and Raymond, who left their homeland to create world-renowned works in India and Japan, yet faced repression and erasure in their own country. She weaves together personal stories of individuals from diverse backgrounds–India, Switzerland, Germany, Indonesia, the Netherlands, Canada, Britain, Zambia, Kenya, Russia,

---

[83] Kriseová, *Mezi pannou a babou*, 7.

Latvia–highlighting how cultural histories and personal beliefs shape lives and perspectives. Nature acts as a silent yet omnipresent witness to these local and world journeys. Kriseová intertwines individual and national narratives, examining historical myths and family histories to uncover personal truths. This scope could be seen as a Central European exploration balancing traditional transnationalism with twentieth-century nationalism. Yet, her voice remains distinctly worldly, non-judgmental, and humble. While challenging memory, ideological myths, and the unfortunate course of twentieth-century Central European history, her texts offer detours and comparisons, seeking deeper metaphysical meaning beyond local concerns.

Serving poetic justice to truth and love of Czech women's lives and writing

In this regard, I would argue that literary criticism would benefit from employing better frameworks and approaches to better understanding Czech women's literature. As suggested by Martha Nussbaum's *Poetic Justice* concept (1995), we need literary imagination to understand humane conditions from various points of view, and studying literature can have significant pragmatic uses. She argues that literature should be read as an important source of civic education, as literary imagination mediates constant and meaningful focus on individual feelings and individual emotions, as it helps to raise modern social awareness and provides society with knowledge of the overlooked people (or undesirable archetypes, banned families, histories, individual fates, such as in Kriseová's fiction).

Poetic Justice may be used as a reading recipe that provides justice to those who are hardly known in mainstream society for various ideological, historical, or social reasons and restrictions, including problematic gender norms. *Poetic Justice* suggests that it is beneficial to identify with fictional characters, to broaden the concerns for "the disadvantaged, to encourage imaginary inclusion to be built into the structure of the literary experience,"[84] even though one must be aware of many ideological catches and traps of ideological approaches to literature, which Central Europe has experienced and has embedded in its arts and culture. However, Nussbaum's argument is a bit broader, and it encourages the cultivation of perspectives and considerations for various aspects of storytelling conventions while it invites new efforts to rehabilitate genres. Certainly, it can serve as a helpful framework for the interpretation of emphatic Kriseová's work, especially beyond the literary

---

[84] Martha C. Nussbaum, *Poetic Justice: The Literary Imagination and Public Life* (Boston: Beacon Press, 2007), xvi.

puzzles, stereotypes, and known mythologies of dissent, which is an unclear and slippery label anyway, and beyond the known literary conventions. Furthermore, we shall not dismiss those complex activities of dissent, including writing that included women and needs gendered interpretations.[85] In this regard, Eda Kriseová's texts do serve poetic justice to the *truth of women's experience*. Her texts examine impact of the everyday life on women, on culture, and offer a nuanced understanding of the diverse cultural negotiations in the context of Central European contested histories and historical realities.

According to Jan Matonoha, Czech dissident literature lacks authentic feminist voices, with the exceptions of Eda Kriseová and Eva Kantůrková.[86] Matonoha argues that although Czech literature has had a long and bold tradition of Czech women's literature that can be considered feminist, however, feminism and women's rights were not discussed within the dissident community. As a result, the previous Czech literary tradition of women's voices was disrupted, and it took time to rebuild it again. He argues that in the majority of the texts, women become objects rather than subjects, and arts and literature contain many contradictory gendered images, insensitive messages, silences, accounts, plots, and problematic, ironic, and cynical epistemologies. Thus, the gendered accounts of (post)dissent writing by women need to be investigated, promoted, and explored.

By searching for human dignity among the overlooked, such as chronic mental hospital patients, minorities, and suicidal individuals, Eda Kriseová allows them to enter society, gain a voice, and become visible. She depicts a reality far different from the dissent stifled by the restrictive normalization period, current waves of prejudice and hatred, or even the pervasive machismo of some Czech male writers in contemporary Czech culture and fiction. Her unwavering human solidarity and refined social ecology challenge prevailing trends. She refuses to succumb to any form of oppression or exclusion. She recharges her energy with her travels and returns as she discovers places and people, their stories, visits temples, swims in the rivers, oceans and immerses herself in nature, which seems to have helped her discover a renewed purpose and energy for writing. She is concerned with plants, nature, self-connection,

---

[85] Bolton, *Worlds of Dissent*, or Robert Brier, "Gendering dissent," *Eurozine*, September 2, 2019, https://www.eurozine.com/gendering-dissent/.

[86] Jan Matonoha, "Dispositives of Silence: Gender, Feminism and Czech literature between 1948 and 1989," in *The Politics of Gender Culture under State Socialism* (New York: Routledge, 2014), 174-99.

and spirituality as well as global concerns, currently with the War on Ukraine and immense human suffering caused by the Russian invasion. Her work explores the universal interconnectedness between land and people. Clarissa Pinkola Estes, in her book *Women Who Run with the Wolves*, writes, "We are all filled with a longing for the wild. There are few culturally sanctioned antidotes for this yearning. We were taught to feel shame for such a desire."[87] Eda Kriseová reinvents her interest in human ecology in a similar manner. Her texts honor women and their archetypal human relations to nature. They serve as a healthy incentive to explore Eda Kriseová's quest for freedom, *life in truth*, as reflected in her scope of human and social ecology as it is gradually bulking up in her works.

Conclusion

Rooted in her dissident experience, Kriseová's work seeks to liberate the past, decolonize stories, rewrite history, and make connections. Her texts revisit the past and reflect on the present, reintroducing multinational identities and promoting multiformity and fluidity. They advocate for understanding human diversity in all its forms–ethnicity, sexuality, ecology, spirituality–and encourage solidarity with global humanity. Her texts invite readers to explore new meanings of womanhood, transnationality, intersectionality, and otherness. They delve into the processes of accepting, rejecting, and reversing the social, economic, and psychological effects of totalitarianism. This system systematically distorted human relationships, traditions, culture, and connections to land and nature. Kriseová challenges *life in a lie* promoted by totalitarian regimes and seeks to decipher new forms of *living authentically* in a complex world. Kriseová's writing, as well as her personal journey of rediscovering the truth, becomes a call to action. She encourages her nation, once locked behind the Iron Curtain, to open up to the world, embrace diverse ethnic histories, and acknowledge otherness, including mental disabilities. She narrates missing gendered histories and connects to global concerns about ecology and social injustice. Her writing displays a nuanced yet clear woman's voice and serves poetic justice (Martha Nussbaum) to *truth and love* by sharing authentic notions of women's experience. Her contribution to literature is significant, challenging traditional socialist realism and male-dominated narratives. She delves into new meanings of *truth and love* beyond the ideological constraints of the twentieth century, uncovering truths hidden in

---

[87] Clarissa P. Estes, *Women Who Run with the Wolves: Myths and Stories of the Wild Woman Archetype* (New York: Ballantine Books, 2003), 1.

the forgotten fates of Holocaust and Communist survivors or distant people and places.

Bibliography

Benda, Václav, et al. "Parallel Polis, or An Independent Society in Central and Eastern Europe: An inquiry." *Social Research* (1988): 211–46.

Bolton, Jonathan. *Worlds of Dissent: Charter 77, the Plastic People of the Universe, and Czech Culture Under Communism*. Cambridge: Harvard University Press, 2014.

Brier, Robert. "Gendering dissent: Human rights, gender history and the road to 1989." *Eurozine*, September 2, 2019, https://www.eurozine.com/gendering-dissent/.

Danaher, David S., and Kieran Williams, eds. *Václav Havel's Meanings: His Key Words and Their Legacy*. Prague: Karolinum, 2022.

Dějiny Kampademie. Praha: Knihovna Václava Havla, 2010.

Estes, Clarissa P. *Women Who Run with the Wolves: Myths and Stories of the Wild Woman Archetype*. New York: Ballantine Books, 2003.

Flanagan, Brenda A. and Hana Waisserová. *Women's Artistic Dissent: Womanhood and Oppression in Pre-1989 Central Europe*. Lanham, MD: Lexington Books, 2023.

Foucault, Michel. *The History of Sexuality*. New York: Vintage Books, 1984.

Goetz-Stankiewicz, Marketa, ed. *Good-Bye, Samizdat: Twenty Years of Czechoslovak Underground Writing*. Evanston, IL: Northwestern University Press, 1992.

Havel, Václav. *The Power of the Powerless*. Translated by Paul R. Wilson. London: Vintage, 2018.

——. *Open Letters. Selected Writings 1965–1990*. Selected and edited by Paul Wilson. New York: Vintage Books, 1992.

——. "Acceptance of an Honorary Degree from the University of Michigan." In *Václav Havel's Meanings: His Key Words and Their Legacy*, edited by David Danaher and Kieran Williams. Praha: Karolinum, 2022.

Jirous, Ivan Martin: "Report on the Third Czech Musical Revival." Translated by Paul Wilson and Ivan Hartel. In *Views from the Inside: Czech Underground Literature and Culture (1948–1989)*, edited by Martin Machovec, 7–36. Praha: Karolinum, 2018.

Kurzweil, Edith. "An interview with Eda Kriseová." *Partisan Review* 70, no. 1 (2003): 89.

Kriseová, Eda. "A Knight of the Cross." Translated by Suzanne Rappaport. In *The Writing on the Wall: An Anthology of Contemporary Czech Literature*, edited by Antonín Liehm and Peter Kussi, 134–51. Princeton: Karz-Cohl Pub., 1983.

——. *Čísi svět*. Praha: Prostor, 2004.

——. *Duši, tělo opatruj*. Praha: Práh, 2014.

———. "From Illusion to Reality. A public lecture at New School, New York. November 4, 2014." *The William Phillips Series.* New York: The New School for Social Research, 2015.

———. "How Many Resurrections." Translated by Káča Poláčková-Henley. *Prairie Schooner* (Winter 1992): 17–18.

———. *Kočičí životy*. Praha: Hynek, 1997.

———. *Mezi pannou a babou*. Praha: Práh, 2018.

———. "Morning in Church." Translated by Milan Pomichalek and Anna Mozga. In *Good-Bye, Samizdat: Twenty Years of Czechoslovak Underground Writing*, edited by Marketa Goetz-Stankiewicz, 88–94. Evanston, IL: Northwestern University Press, 1992.

———. *Mluvící hora*. Praha: Práh, 2020.

———. *Václav Havel: The Authorized Biography*. Translated by Caleb Crain. New York: St. Martin's Press, 1993.

Kriseová, Eda and Marta Marková. "Zandete si dvacet kroků." *Literární listy*, no. 12 (March 1969), title page.

Liehm, Antonín and Peter Kussi, eds. *Writing on the Wall: An Anthology of Contemporary Czech Literature*. Princeton: Karz-Cohl Pub., 1983.

Linková, Marcela, and Naďa Straková. *Bytová revolta: Jak ženy dělaly disent*. Praha: Academia, 2017.

Machovec, Martin. *Writing Underground. Reflections on Illegal Texts in Communist Czechoslovakia*. Praha: Karolinum Books, 2019.

Matonoha, Jan. "Dispositives of Silence: Gender, Feminism and Czech Literature between 1948 and 1989." In *The Politics of Gender Culture under State Socialism*, edited by Hana Havelková and Libora Oates-Indruchová, 174–99. New York: Routledge, 2014.

Nerburn, Kent. *The Wisdom of the Native Americans*. New York: MJF Books, 2009.

Nussbaum, Martha C. *Poetic Justice: The Literary Imagination and Public Life*. Boston: Beacon Press, 2007.

Owchar, Nick. "What Was Lost: Dissident Artists After Soviet Communism." *Agni* 36 (1992): 256–69. https://www.jstor.org/stable/23009518.

Palouš, Martin, and Ivan Chvatík. *The Solidarity of the Shaken: Jan Patočka's Philosophical Legacy in the Modern World*. Washington, DC: Academica Press, 2019.

Patočka, Jan, Petr Fidelius, and Ivan Chvatík. *Češi*. Praha: Oikoymenh, 2006.

Putna, Martin C. *Václav Havel, Duchovní portrét v rámu české kultury 20. století*. Praha: Knihovna Václava Havla, 2011.

Přibáň, Jiří, and Karel Hvížďala. *In Quest of History: On Czech Statehood and Identity*. Prague: Karolinum Press, 2019.

Riess, Helen. "The Science of Empathy." *Journal of Patient Experience* 4, no. 2 (2017): 74–77. https://journals.sagepub.com/doi/10.1177/2374373517699267.

Rupnik, Jacques. *Střední Evropa je jako pták s očima vzadu: O české minulosti a přítomnosti*. Praha: Novela Bohemica, 2018.

Snyder, Timothy. *Bloodlands: Europe between Hitler and Stalin.* New York: Basic Books, 2012.

Tarnas, Richard and Sean Kelly, eds. *Psyche Unbound: Essays in Honor of Stanislav Grof.* San Jose, CA: Multidisciplinary Association for Psychedelic Studies, 2022.

Waisserová, Hana. "Eda Kriseová and Her Prophecy of the Velvet Revolution: 'The Gates Opened' (1984)." *Kosmas. Czechoslovak and Central European Journal.* n.s. 2, no. 2 (2019): 59–76.

About the contributors

Andrew M. Drozd is an Associate Professor of Russian at the University of Alabama, where he has taught for 30 years. He is the author of *Chernyshevskii's What Is to Be Done?: A Reevaluation* (Northwestern UP, 2001), co-editor of *Reading Darwin in Imperial Russia* (Lexington Books, 2023), and co-editor of *Revisiting Russian Radicals* (Lexington Books, 2024). In recent years, much of his research focus has been on Czech-Russian literary interrelations, and he has been working on a monograph with the working title of *The Russian Echo of František Ladislav Čelakovský*. For several years he was the manager of the SEELangs discussion list and currently maintains the Czech Studies discussion list (Czech@listserv.ua.edu) and the Russian Radicals discussion list (Chernyshevsky@listserv.ua.edu).

Karen von Kunes has been in charge of Czech studies at Yale University for years. Prior to Yale, she taught at Harvard University, the University of Texas, Tufts University, and Boston College. Dr. von Kunes is the author and co-author of a number of books and publications in the fields of literature, language, film, and culture. In 2019, she published *Milan Kundera's Fiction: A Critical Approach to Existential Betrayals*. With the late Oxford scholar, James Naughton, she co-authored Routledge's *Czech: An Essential Grammar*. Another manuscript, *Milan Kundera Known and Unknown,* is currently in print, and her interdisciplinary monograph on Milos Forman is scheduled to be published in 2026. Dr. von Kunes was a Contributing Editor to Plamen Press, and has been contributing to *Literary Encyclopedia*, a reviewer for *Slavic Review*, the *Czech Science Foundation, Comparative Literature Studies*, and *Slavic and East European Journal*, and for years she was a weekly contributor to *The Prague Post*. She also published an award-winning novel on diaspora, *Among the Sinners*, and her innovative manuscript on the structure of Czech is due for submission in 2024.

Mary Orsak is a Rhodes Scholar and DPhil student at the University of Oxford in the Faculty of Medieval and Modern Languages, focusing on issues of gender in Czech, Slovak, Polish, and Russian modern and contemporary literature.

Jan Matonoha works at the Institute of Czech Literature of the Czech Academy of Sciences. In 2008, he received his Ph.D. from Charles University, Prague, and his M.Phil. from the University of Glasgow, UK. In the years 2012-2014, he received a Newton Fellowship from the British Academy (University of Sheffield, the UK). He has taken part in several grant projects from both the Czech Republic and the EU, and he has participated in a number of conferences both abroad (Cambridge, Nottingham, Manchester, Sheffield, Dublin, Boston, San Francisco, Toronto, Brussels, Zurich, Vienna, Hamburg, Leipzig, Warsaw, Budapest, Tallinn) as well as in the Czech Republic (Prague, Brno, Olomouc, etc.). He has published several articles (both in Czech and English), two books (*Writing Outside of Logocentrism. Discourse, Gender, Text*, 2009; *Beyond / For (De)Constructivism. Overview of Critical Concepts of Literary and Cultural Theory*, 2017, both in Czech by Academia Publishing, Prague), and participated in several others, including *The Politics of Gender Culture under State Socialism. Expropriated Voice*, edited by Hana Havelková and Libora Oates-Indruchová (Routledge, 2014). One book (in Czech) entitled *Parallel Anatomy. Injurious Attachments, Discursive Emergence of Silence and Gender in Czech Literature in the Period of 1948-1989* is to be completed in early 2024 (most likely issued by Academia Publishing). He has delivered several courses in both Czech and English for domestic as well as US and Erasmus exchange students at Charles University, Prague and in Brno. His research interests are the theory of literature, twentieth-century Czech and Central European literature, feminism and gender studies in literature, and non-human animal studies in literature.

Jonathan Lahey Dronsfield wrote his chapter whilst a Dobrovský Research Fellow at the Institute of Philosophy of the Czech Academy of Sciences in Prague. Dronsfield is currently researching philosophies of dissent. Recent publications on dissent include "The Language of Inner Freedom for Dissent: Müller and Liiceanu Before and After the Revolution," in Wohl & Pacurar (eds.), *Language of the Revolution: The Discourse of Anti-Communist Insurgencies in the "Eastern Block" Countries* (Palgrave MacMillan, 2023), "Dissent Non-dissenting: 'Resistance through Culture,'" *Journal of Educational Philosophy and Theory*, 55(5) 2023, "The Rhetoric of Inner Freedom," *Journal of Romanian Studies* 4(2) 2022, and "Dissonant dissent: Du Bois and the Terrible Beauty of Rap Music," *Humanities Bulletin* 5(1) 2022.

Marek Lollok studied Czech language and literature at Masaryk University in Brno, currently works at the Department of Czech Language and Literature of the Pedagogical Faculty of Masaryk University, and also cooperates with the Institute for Czech Literature of the Academy of Sciences of the Czech Republic. He specializes in stylistics, contemporary Czech prose and drama, and literary and theater criticism. He published the monograph *Critique in motion: Literary criticism and meta-criticism of the 1990s* (Masaryk University 2019); he is also the co-author of the anthology *Czech Surrealist Drama* (Academia 2023; co-editors T. Kubart and J. Šotkovská).

Daniel W. Pratt is an assistant professor of Slavic culture in the Department of Languages, Literatures, and Cultures at McGill University. He works on Central and Eastern European culture, specifically Czech, Polish, Russian, Hungarian, and Austrian. He did his undergraduate education at Princeton University, spent two years in the Czech Republic, and then completed his Ph.D. at the University of Chicago. He is a comparativist, broadly interested in the intersection of literature, history, and philosophy. He has written on the meaning of history in Central Europe, Socialist World Literature, and the philosophical connections of Gilles Deleuze and Witold Gombrowicz, amongst other topics. He is currently finishing his book manuscript *Against Narrative: Non-Narrative Temporalities in Central Europe*, while working on a second book on Bruno Jasieński, socialist world literature, and the pursuit of internationalism.

Hana Waisserová is an associate professor of practice of Czech and Central European Studies and an affiliate of the Harris Center for Judaic Studies at the University of Nebraska-Lincoln. She earned a Ph.D. in Anglophone transnational literature from Palacký University, Olomouc, and a Gender Graduate Certificate from Texas A&M University. She has co-authored the book, *Women's Artistic Dissent. Repelling Totalitarianism in Pre-1989 Czechoslovakia* (Lexington Books, 2023). She has published articles concerning South Asian and Central European women's transnational literature, women's totalitarian experiences, women dissidents and their activism, medieval Czech literature, and Czech-American culture in Nebraska with *Litteraria Pragensia, Kosmas: Czechoslovak and Central European Journal, Czech Language News, Literature, Media and Cultural Studies, American and British Studies Annual, Great Plains Quarterly, Fema.*

Index

A

Adorno, Theodor W., 38, 55
Althusser, Louis, 40, 41
amor fati, 20, 22
Andropov, Yuri, 140
Anti-Charter, 106, 167
Arendt, Hannah, 55
Aristotle, 92
Assmann, Jan, 109, 110
Aurelius, Marcus, 6
Austerlitz, Battle of, 23

B

Balabán, Jan, 128, 129, 130, 131
Bartůňková, Jana, 152, 153
Bass, Eduard, 5
Bataille, Georges, 54, 89
Baudelaire, Charles, 52
Beatles, 148
beautiful, the, 85, 93
Beauvoir, Simone de, 45
Benda, Václav, 49, 182
Bendová, Kamila, 47
Beneš, Edvard, 5
Benjamin, Walter, 55
Berlin Wall, 148
Binar, Ivan, 46
biopolitics, 169, 170, 171, 174, 198
Blok, Alexander, 52
Bok, John, 122
Bolton, Jonathan, 157, 170
Bondy, Egon, 122, 123, 150, 152
Borodino, Battle of, 23
Boučková, Tereza, 42

Brabenec, Vratislav, 122, 123, 154
Bratinka, Pavel, 195
Brezhnev, Leonid, 140
Brikcius, Eugen, 123
Broch, Hermann, 38, 80, 88
Brodsky, Joseph, 16, 17, 44
Brown, Wendy, 39, 40, 49, 54, 67
Buddhism, 194, 200
Bunin, Ivan, 17
Butler, Judith, 39, 40, 49, 67

C

Camus, Albert, 80, 92
Čapek, Josef, 5
Čapek, Karel, viii, 1, 2, 3, 4, 5, 6, 7, 8, 9, 10, 11, 12
Castro, Fidel, 134
Černý, Václav, 46
Chalupecký, Jindřich, 122
Chamberlain, Neville, 4
Charter 77, 106, 147, 149, 151, 154, 157, 159, 167, 186
Chekhov, Anton, 16
Christian, R. F., 23
Chytilová, Věra, 152
Civic Forum, 183
Cixous, Hélène, 39
Communism, vii, viii, ix, xi, 8, 27, 41, 48, 49, 52, 57, 59, 74, 77, 84, 90, 92, 93, 94, 104, 105, 111, 112, 115, 116, 118, 126, 127, 128, 129, 130, 131, 132, 134, 135, 136, 137, 138, 140, 141, 142, 148, 149, 150, 153, 157, 158, 160, 161, 163, 164,

165, 167, 173, 179, 180, 183, 187, 198, 205
Communist Party, 87, 88, 106, 110, 111, 112, 114, 119, 125, 126, 133, 134
Čornej, Petr, 107
Čulík, Jan, viii
Cushman, Thomas, 149, 166
Czarniecki, Piotr, 164

D

Dalai Lama, 194, 195
Dean, James, 159
Deleuze, Gilles, 85
Derrida, Jacques, 76, 95
Descartes, René, 13
Devětsíl, 151
DG 307, 154, 161
Diderot, Denis, 16, 17, 34, 60, 81
Dienstbier, Jiří, 46
dissent, x, xi, xii, 45, 46, 47, 48, 49, 50, 70, 73, 74, 75, 77, 94, 97, 99, 113, 147, 148, 149, 150, 151, 152, 154, 155, 156, 157, 159, 162, 167, 169, 170, 175, 176, 177, 180, 182, 183, 186, 188, 189, 190, 192, 194, 196, 203, 204
Dostoevsky, Fyodor, 15, 16, 17, 30, 34
Dousková, Irena, 117, 118, 119, 120
Dubenka. *See* Gifford, April
Durkheim, Emil, 109
Dworkin, Andrea, 54

E

Eagleton, Terry, 165
Esenin, Sergei, 52, 160

Estes, Clarissa Pinkola, 204
eternal return, 15, 18, 19, 20, 21, 22, 25, 28, 29, 79, 81
existentialism, 20, 26, 80
Expedice, 182, 184

F

feminism, 37, 38, 39, 41, 42, 44, 46, 47, 49, 50, 53, 54, 55, 56, 57, 60, 63, 64, 65, 66, 67, 169, 172, 177, 203
Forman, Miloš, 148, 152
Foucault, Michel, 38, 41, 181
freedom, x, xi, 9, 27, 62, 66, 73, 74, 75, 77, 82, 87, 89, 95, 97, 98, 114, 147, 150, 151, 180, 181, 182, 194, 204

G

Galenus, Claudius, 6
Garage, 155
gender, 37, 38, 39, 40, 41, 42, 44, 46, 48, 49, 50, 52, 54, 55, 57, 61, 63, 64, 66, 67, 141, 170, 171, 176, 202, 203, 204
Genet, Jean, 54
Gifford, April (Dubenka), 91
Goethe, Johann Wolfgang von, 34, 52
Gogol, Nikolai, 17
Gott, Karel, ix, 106, 167
Gramsci, Antonio, 52
Grof, Christina, 195
Grof, Stanislav, 195
Gruša, Jiří, 46, 48, 185
Guattari, Félix, 85

Index

H

Haas, Hugo, 12
Hácha, Emil, 124
Hagan, John, 24
Halík, Tomáš, 195
Hašek, Jaroslav, 177
Havel, Ivan M., 195
Havel, Václav, viii, xi, xii, 1, 10, 11, 42, 44, 45, 46, 48, 91, 112, 115, 122, 123, 148, 150, 151, 152, 156, 157, 158, 159, 169, 170, 178, 179, 180, 182, 183, 185, 186, 187, 188, 189, 194, 195
Havelková, Hana, 40, 49
Havlíček, Karel, 47
Heczková, Libuše, 44
Hegel, Georg Wilhelm Friedrich, 89, 92
Heidegger, Martin, 19, 94
Heim, Michael, ix, 4
Hejdánek, Ladislav, 46
Hippocratic Oath, 1, 5, 8
Hitler, Adolf, 2, 4, 21
Hlavsa, Milan, 123
Holocaust, 9, 45, 166, 177, 193, 199, 205
Holub, Miroslav, 89
Horkheimer, Max, 38
Hrabal, Bohumil, x, xi, 42, 45, 52, 73, 74, 76, 77, 78, 79, 82, 83, 84, 85, 86, 89, 90, 91, 92, 93, 94, 95, 97, 98, 99, 122, 130, 152, 164, 177
Hrzánová, Bára, 119
Hůlová, Petra, 136, 137
Hus, Jan, 179
Husák, Gustáv, ix, 57, 106, 107, 116, 124, 125, 135, 139, 140

I

inner freedom, 73, 74, 75, 77, 87, 93, 94, 98
Irigaray, Luce, 39, 45, 57
Iron Curtain, 123, 204
irony, 52, 73, 74, 82, 87, 120, 125

J

Janáček, Leoš, 5
Janoušek, Pavel, 122, 123
Jesus Christ, 20
Jirous, Ivan Martin, 122, 150, 153, 154, 155, 158, 159, 182
Jirousová, Věra, 48, 185
Joyce, James, 30, 31

K

Kábrtová, Lidmila, 133
Kadár, Ján, 8, 10
Kafka, Franz, 53, 178
Kant, Immanuel, 73, 76, 82, 83, 84, 92, 93, 94
Kantůrková, Eva, 42, 46, 47, 48, 49, 185, 203
Karásek, Svatopluk, 154
Karfík, Vladimír, 120
Karlík, Viktor, 151, 156
Kaufmann, Walter, 19, 20
Kierkegaard, Søren, 95
Klein, Melanie, 57
Klíma, Ivan, 42, 48, 150, 170, 177, 185
Klíma, Ladislav, 82, 84, 85
Kliment, Alexandr, 42, 185
Klímová, Ruth, 47
Klos, Elmar, 8, 10
Kohout, Pavel, 42, 48, 52

Kolář, Jiří, 152
Kozelka, Milan, 122, 123, 125
Krchovský, JH, 151, 156
Kremlička, Vít, 151, 156
Krise, Jindřich, 179
Kriseová, Eda, xii, 42, 46, 47, 48, 169, 170, 171, 172, 173, 174, 175, 176, 177, 178, 179, 180, 181, 182, 183, 184, 185, 186, 187, 188, 189, 190, 191, 192, 193, 194, 195, 196, 197, 198, 199, 200, 201, 202, 203, 204
Kristeva, Julia, 39, 57, 60
Křížková, Kamila Ruth, 47
Kroupa, Daniel, 195
Kundera, Ludvík, 59
Kundera, Milan, vii, viii, ix, x, xi, 1, 10, 11, 13, 15, 16, 17, 18, 19, 20, 21, 22, 25, 27, 28, 30, 31, 32, 33, 34, 37, 38, 39, 40, 41, 42, 44, 48, 50, 51, 52, 53, 55, 57, 59, 60, 61, 63, 64, 65, 66, 67, 73, 74, 75, 76, 78, 79, 80, 81, 82, 84, 85, 87, 88, 89, 95, 96, 97, 98, 99, 152, 170, 177
Kvartál, 185

L

Laclos, Pierre Choderlos de, 34
Landovská, Betina, 155
Landovský, Pavel, 155
Lenin, Vladimir, 134
Lermontov, Mikhail, 52
Lexová, Andrea, 123
Liehm, Antonín, 186
living in truth, 171, 176, 180, 187, 188
London, Jack, 164
Lopatka, Jan, 123

Loukotková, Jarmila, 49
ludibrionism, 82, 84
Lustig, Arnošt, 42, 45

M

Machaček, Jan, 155
Machonin, Pavel, 113
Machonin, Sergej, 46, 185
MacKinnon, Catharine, 54
Macura, Vladimír, 52
Majerová, Marie, 49
Mandelstam, Osip, 17
Marvanová, Anna, 47
Marxism, viii, 39, 40, 52, 163
Marysko, Karel, 152
Masaryk, Tomáš Garrigue, 1, 5, 10, 124, 179, 189, 190
Matonoha, Jan, 203
May, Karel, 164
Mayakovsky, Vladimir, 52
Menzel, Jiří, 84, 152
metaphysics, 73, 74, 76, 82, 90, 94, 97, 98
misogyny, x, 37, 38, 51, 53, 59, 65, 66, 67
Moliere, 60
Munich Agreement, 4
Musil, Robert, 38, 80, 164

N

Národní třida, 156
Nazi, vii, viii, 1, 2, 4, 8, 9, 30, 45, 56, 65, 173, 179, 193, 198
Němcová, Dana, 47
Němcová, Veronika, 155
Němec, Jan, 152
Němec, Jiří, 155
Nepraš, Karel, 123

Neubauer, Zdeněk, 195
Nezbeda, Ondřej, 135
Nietzsche, Friedrich, ix, 15, 18, 19, 20, 21, 22, 25, 26, 29, 73, 76, 79, 80, 81, 82, 92, 95
Nirvana, 166
Nixon, Richard, 134
Normalization, xi, 50, 91, 103, 105, 106, 107, 110, 111, 112, 114, 115, 116, 117, 119, 120, 122, 124, 125, 126, 127, 128, 130, 131, 132, 133, 135, 136, 137, 138, 139, 140, 141, 142, 143, 154, 155, 165, 180, 181, 182, 186, 192, 203
Novák, Arne, 7
Novák, Jan, 48
November 1989. *See* Velvet Revolution
November Revolution. *See* Velvet Revolution
Nussbaum, Martha, 202

O

O'Brien, John, x, 30, 32, 37, 38, 39, 42, 44, 50, 54, 56, 63, 66, 67
Orten, Jiří, 52
Orwell, George, 11
ostalgie, 167
Otáhal, Milan, 112
Otčenášek, Jan, 49

P

Palach, Jan, 160, 178, 179
Palouš, Martin, 195
parallel polis, 49, 50, 182
Parmenides, ix, 18, 19, 21, 22, 28
Pasternak, Boris, 17
Patočka, Jan, 46, 180

Pechar, Jiří, 46
Pekacz, Jolanta, 148
Pekárková, Iva, 42
Pelán, Jiří, 85
Pelc, Jan, 48
Penčeva, Anželina, 42, 50, 51, 58, 67
Peroutka, Ferdinand, 5
Petlice (Padlock), 47, 184, 185, 186
Pilař, Martin, 52, 152
Pistorius, Vladimír, 184
Pithart, Petr, 47
Pithartová, Drahomíra, 47
Placák, Petr, 127, 128, 131, 151
Plato, 92, 195, 197
play, 73, 74, 77, 78, 81, 82, 87, 122
Poláček, Karel, 5, 118
polyphony, x, 5, 87
Pope, 194, 195
Popovičová, Iva, 50
Popper, K. R., 107
power of the powerless, 158, 171, 180, 181, 187
pragmatism, 5, 76
Prague Spring, xi, 77, 89, 91, 105, 111, 147, 150, 165, 178
Presley, Elvis, 125
Přibáň, Michal, 138, 190
Psí vojáci, 147, 149, 150, 155, 156, 160, 162, 166
Pujmanová, Marie, 49
Pushkin, Alexander, 52
Putna, Martin C., 195

R

Rabelais, François, 81
Ramet, Sabrina Petra, 148
Rashomon Effect, 1, 5
Revolver Revue, 147, 155, 156

Richardson, Samuel, 34
Rilke, Rainer Maria, 52, 53
Rimbaud, Arthur, 52
Robespierre, Maximilien, 21
Rorty, Richard, 73, 76, 94, 95, 96
Roth, Philip, 177
Rotrekl, Zdeněk, 46
Rousseau, Jean-Jacques, 34
Ruddick, Sara, 57
Rupnik, Jacques, 190

S

Šabach, Petr, 130, 131, 132
Šabatová, Anna, 47
Sabina, Karel, 52
Salivarová, Zdena, 44
samizdat, 45, 46, 47, 91, 92, 116, 182, 184, 186
Sartre, Jean-Paul, 80, 92
Sayer, Derek, vii
Schelling, Friedrich Wilhelm Joseph, 92
Schiller, Friedrich, 92
Schmiedt, Jiří, 119
Schopenhauer, Arthur, 92
Schulz, Karel, 151
Schwarzerová-Kriseová, Zdenka, 179
Seifert, Jaroslav, 150, 152
selective attention, 7, 8
Shakespeare, William, 60
Shaw, George Bernard, 2, 12
Shore, Marci, 164
Sidon, Karol, 46
Šiklová, Jiřina, 41, 49, 113
Šimečka, Milan, 112
Šimečková, Eva, 47
Šimsa, Jan, 47
Skupina 42, 152

Škvorecký, Josef, xi, 42, 48, 52, 60, 90, 91, 152, 170
Snyder, Timothy, 193
social ecology, 171, 172, 173, 174, 177, 178, 193, 203
Socialist Realism, 52, 90, 204
Socrates, 195
Sontag, Susan, 156
Soviet, 30, 95, 110, 120, 134, 135, 174, 177, 180, 198
Speransky, Mikhail, 23
Špidla, Kryštof, 134
Stalin, Josef, 30, 82
Stankovič, Andrej, 46, 122, 123
StB (State Security Council), 130, 131, 139
Stendhal, 28
Sterne, Laurence, 34, 81
Stýblová, Valja, 49
sublime, the, 93
suicide, x, 15, 17, 29, 30, 31, 32, 33, 45, 129, 151, 156, 159, 160, 161
Šustrová, Petruška, 47
Szemere, Anne, 149

T

Taoism, 196, 200
Tatarka, Dominik, 46
The Plastic People of the Universe, 149, 150, 153, 154, 156, 157, 159, 161
Thirlwell, Adam, 85
Tolstoy, Leo, ix, x, 15, 17, 18, 19, 22, 23, 24, 25, 26, 29, 30, 31, 32, 33, 34
Tominová, Zdena, 47
Topol, Filip, xi, 147, 149, 150, 151, 155, 156, 157, 159, 160, 161, 162, 166, 167

Index

Topol, Jáchym, xi, 147, 149, 150, 151, 155, 156, 159, 162, 163, 164, 165, 166
Topol, Josef, 147, 151, 155
totalitarianism, viii, xi, 6, 55, 73, 74, 75, 85, 87, 88, 89, 91, 94, 97, 98, 111, 112, 136, 137, 169, 170, 171, 174, 179, 180, 198, 204
Trakl, Georg, 52
trauma, vii, viii, x, xi, xii, 117, 143, 198, 199
Trefulka, Jan, 46, 185

U

Übermensch, 20, 29
underground, the, xi, 122, 123, 147, 148, 149, 150, 151, 152, 153, 154, 155, 156, 157, 158, 159, 161, 162, 163, 167, 184, 185, 186, 187

V

Vaculík, Ludvík, 42, 46, 48, 91, 170, 184, 185, 186
Vaněk-Úvalský, Bohuslav, 124, 125, 126
Vašíček, Zdeněk, 108
Vašinka, Radim, 46
VB (Public Security), 130, 131
Velvet Divorce, 184
Velvet Revolution, ix, xi, xii, 91, 112, 115, 116, 137, 139, 141, 151, 162, 165, 179, 183, 198

Viewegh, Michal, 120, 121
Vokno, 156
Volková, Bronislava, 42, 50, 51, 58
Vonnegut, Kurt, 11, 152
Vostrá, Alena, 44

W

Wágnerová, Anna, 151
Wallace, R. Jay, 1, 7
Warsaw Pact, 15, 59, 105, 110, 111, 121, 152, 155, 161, 180
Wasiolek, Edward, 22, 24
Wicke, Peter, 148
Wilde, Oscar, 52
Williams, Kieran, 188, 189
Williams, Linda, 54
Wittig, Monique, 39
WWI, vii, 2
WWII, 8, 10, 48, 53, 55, 104, 166, 193, 198

Z

Zachová, Alena, 152, 153
Zajíc, Jan, 178, 179
Zajíček, Pavel, 154
Zand, Gertraude, 164
Zandl, Patrick, 139, 140, 141
Zemančíková, Alena, 132
Zrzavý, Jan, 122
Zusi, Peter, 165